GIANT DAYS

VOLUME SIX

BOOM! BOX

BOOM! BOX™

GIANT DAYS Volume Six, October 2017. Published by BOOM! Box, a division of Boom Entertainment, Inc. Giant Days is ™ & © 2017 John Allison. Originally published in single magazine form as GIANT DAYS No. 21-24. ™ & © 2016, 2017 John Allison. All rights reserved. BOOM! Box™ and the BOOM! Box logo are trademarks of Boom Entertainment, Inc., registered in various countries and categories. All characters, events, and institutions depicted herein are fictional. Any similarity between any of the names, characters, persons, events, and/or institutions in this publication to actual names, characters, and persons, whether living or dead, events, and/or institutions is unintended and purely coincidental. BOOM! Box does not read or accept unsolicited submissions of ideas, stories, or artwork.

BOOM! Studios, 5670 Wilshire Boulevard, Suite 450, Los Angeles, CA 90036-5679. Printed in China. First Printing.

ISBN: 978-1-68415-028-1, eISBN: 978-1-61398-705-6

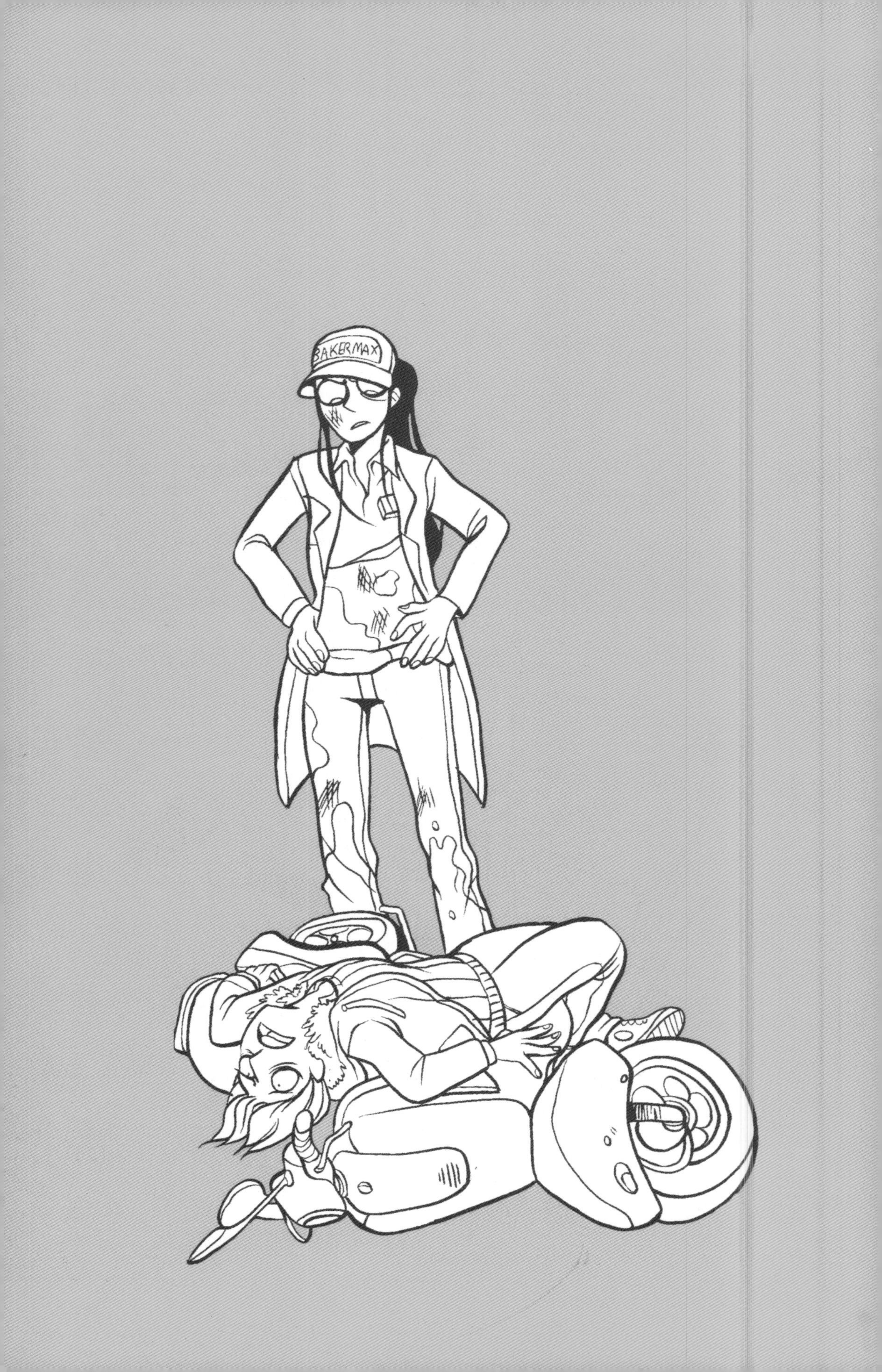
BAKERMAX

GIANT DAYS

CREATED & WRITTEN BY
JOHN ALLISON

ILLUSTRATED BY
MAX SARIN

INKS BY
LIZ FLEMING

COLORS BY
WHITNEY COGAR

LETTERS BY
JIM CAMPBELL

COVER BY
LISSA TREIMAN

DESIGNER
MICHELLE ANKLEY

EDITORS
SHANNON WATTERS & JASMINE AMIRI

CHAPTER TWENTY ONE

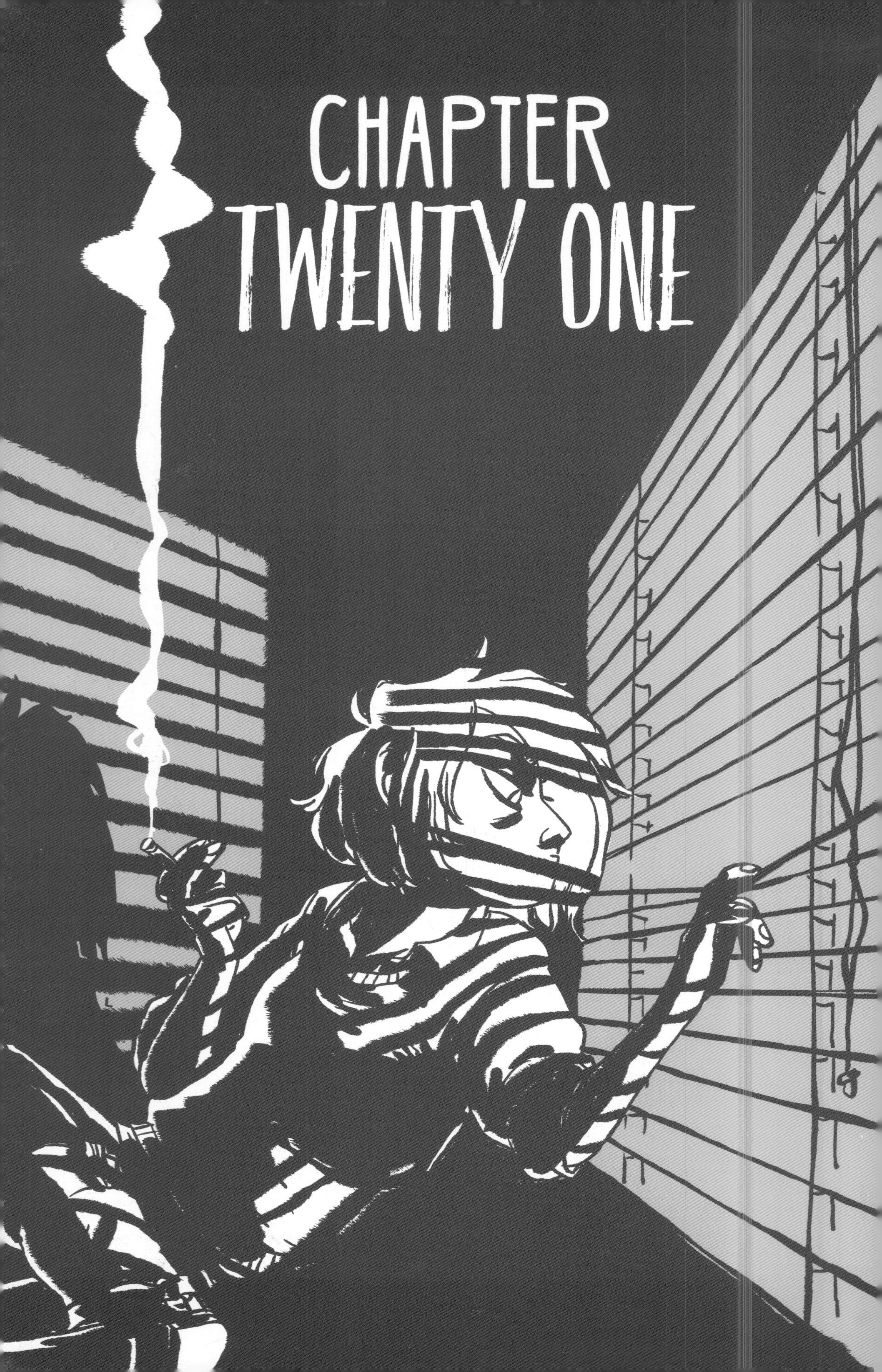

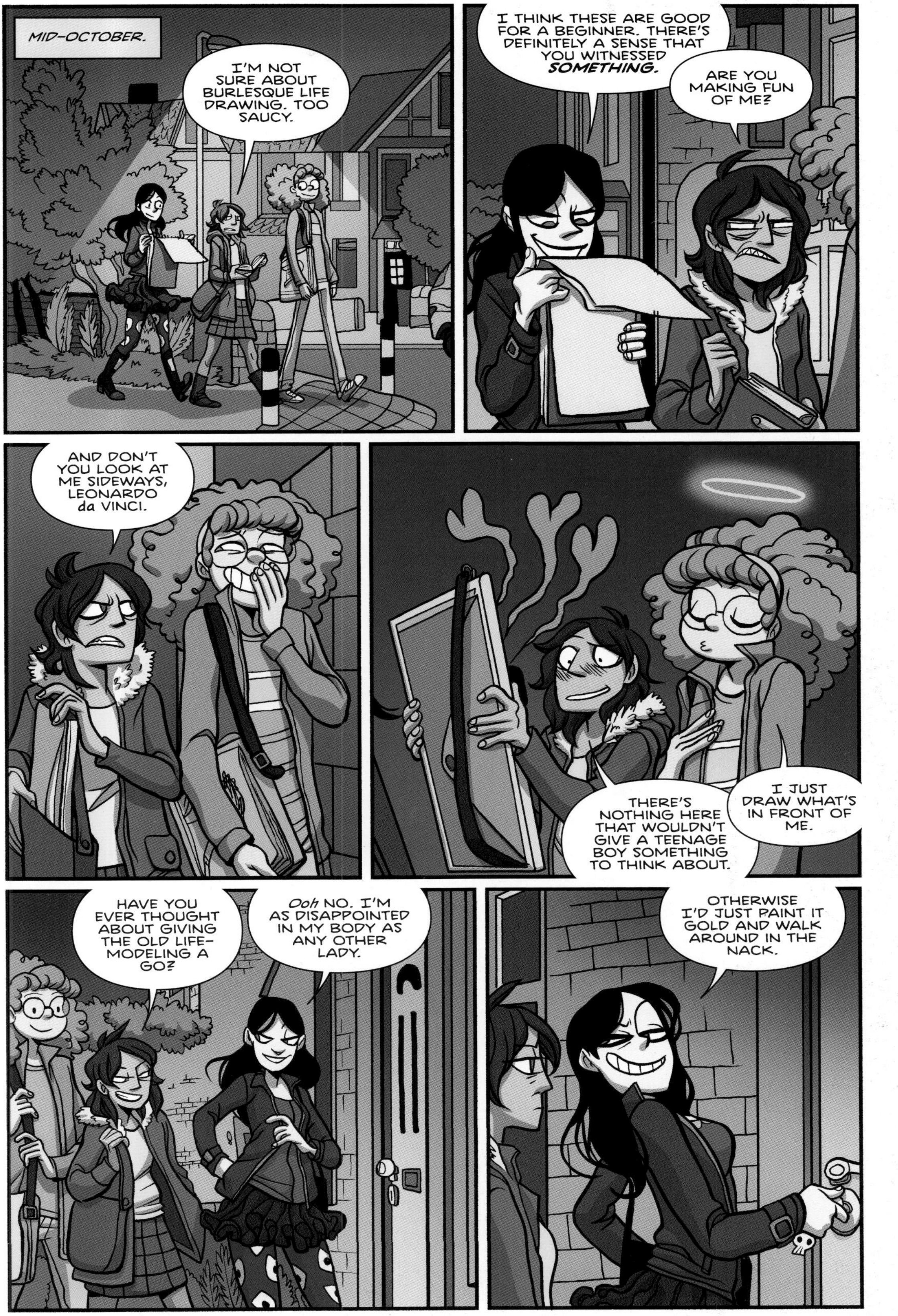
MID-OCTOBER.
I'M NOT SURE ABOUT BURLESQUE LIFE DRAWING. TOO SAUCY.
I THINK THESE ARE GOOD FOR A BEGINNER. THERE'S DEFINITELY A SENSE THAT YOU WITNESSED SOMETHING.
ARE YOU MAKING FUN OF ME?
AND DON'T YOU LOOK AT ME SIDEWAYS, LEONARDO da VINCI.
THERE'S NOTHING HERE THAT WOULDN'T GIVE A TEENAGE BOY SOMETHING TO THINK ABOUT.
I JUST DRAW WHAT'S IN FRONT OF ME.
HAVE YOU EVER THOUGHT ABOUT GIVING THE OLD LIFE-MODELING A GO?
Ooh NO. I'M AS DISAPPOINTED IN MY BODY AS ANY OTHER LADY.
OTHERWISE I'D JUST PAINT IT GOLD AND WALK AROUND IN THE NACK.

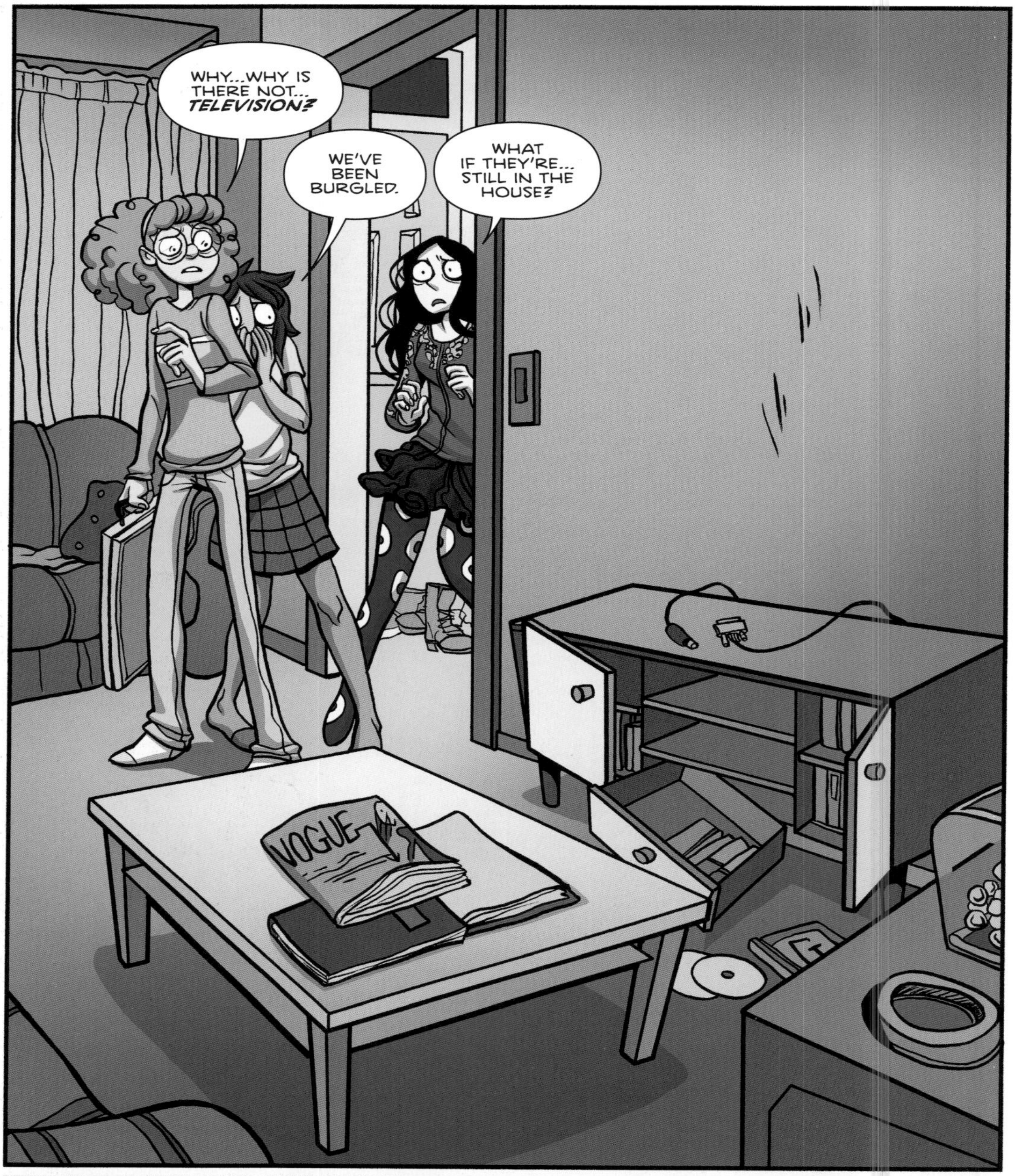
WHY...WHY IS THERE NOT... TELEVISION?
WE'VE BEEN BURGLED.
WHAT IF THEY'RE... STILL IN THE HOUSE?
VOGUE

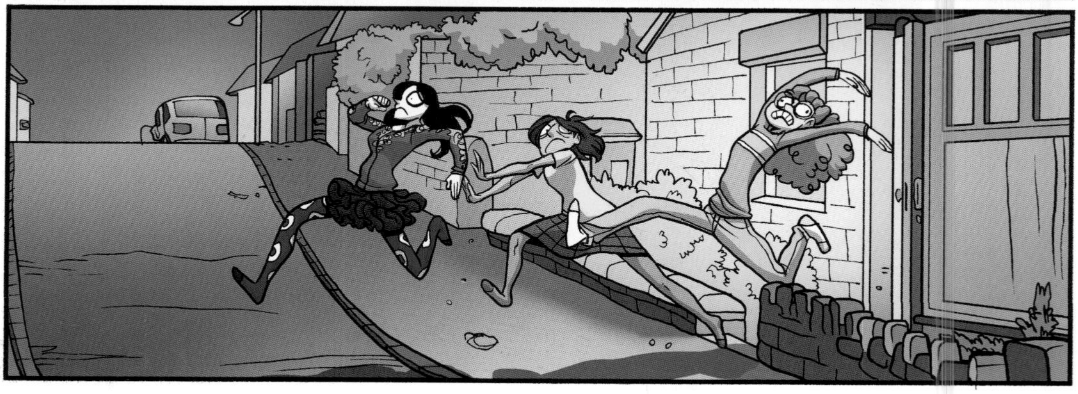

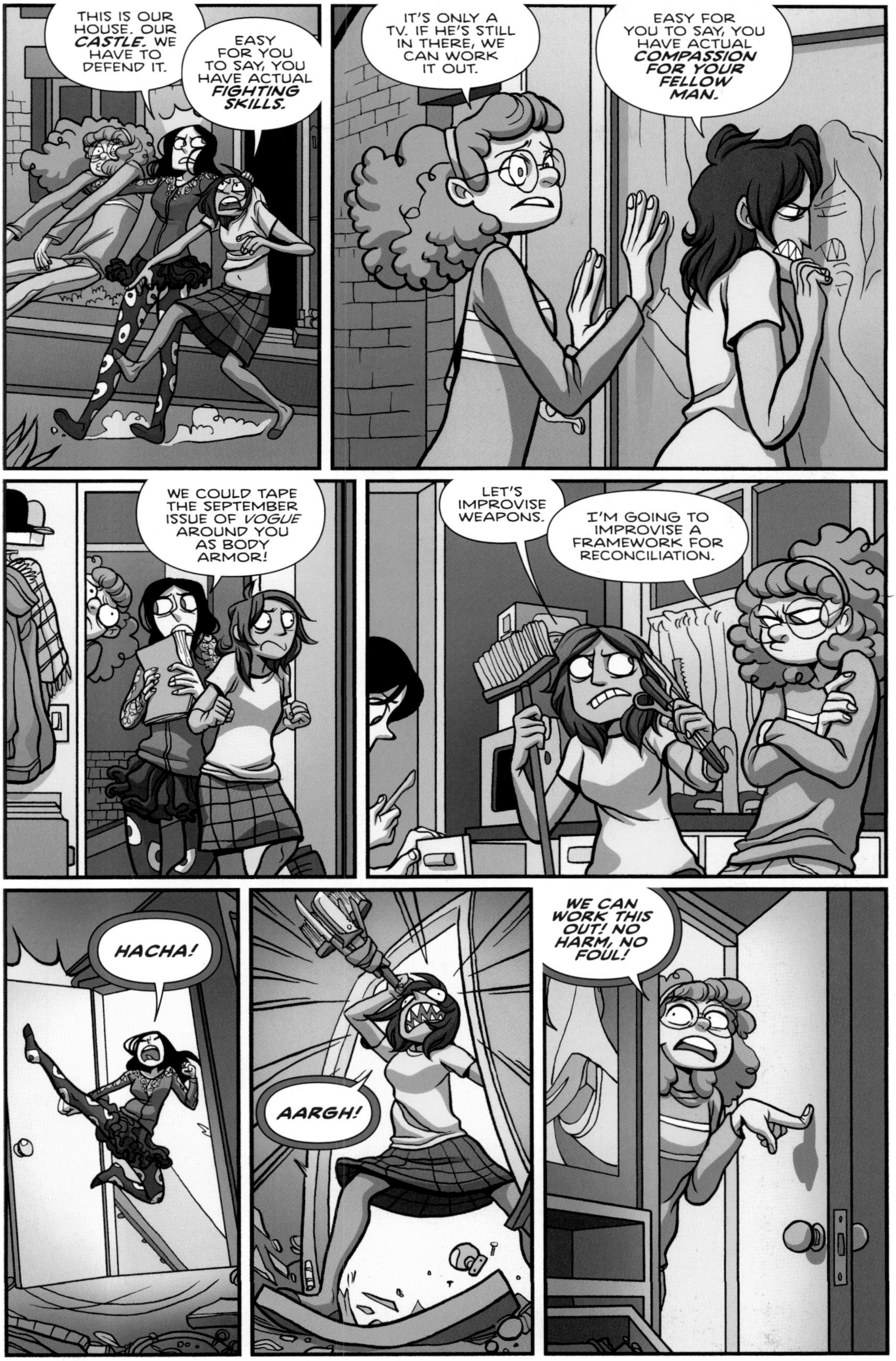
THIS IS OUR HOUSE. OUR CASTLE. WE HAVE TO DEFEND IT.
EASY FOR YOU TO SAY, YOU HAVE ACTUAL FIGHTING SKILLS.
IT'S ONLY A TV. IF HE'S STILL IN THERE, WE CAN WORK IT OUT.
EASY FOR YOU TO SAY, YOU HAVE ACTUAL COMPASSION FOR YOUR FELLOW MAN.
WE COULD TAPE THE SEPTEMBER ISSUE OF VOGUE AROUND YOU AS BODY ARMOR!
LET'S IMPROVISE WEAPONS.
I'M GOING TO IMPROVISE A FRAMEWORK FOR RECONCILIATION.
HACHA!
AARGH!
WE CAN WORK THIS OUT! NO HARM, NO FOUL!

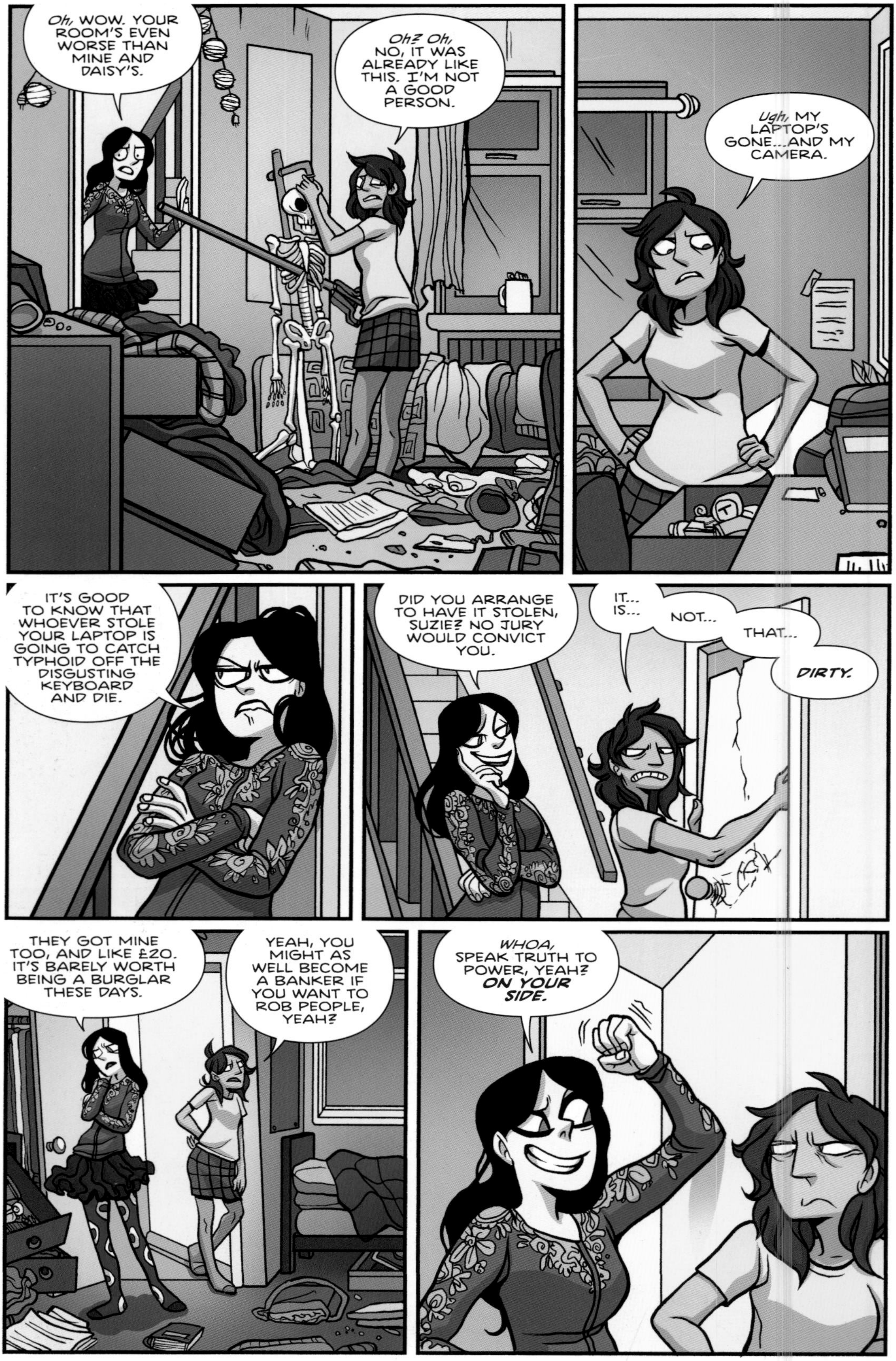
Oh, WOW. YOUR ROOM'S EVEN WORSE THAN MINE AND DAISY'S.
Oh? Oh, NO, IT WAS ALREADY LIKE THIS. I'M NOT A GOOD PERSON.
Ugh, MY LAPTOP'S GONE... AND MY CAMERA.
IT'S GOOD TO KNOW THAT WHOEVER STOLE YOUR LAPTOP IS GOING TO CATCH TYPHOID OFF THE DISGUSTING KEYBOARD AND DIE.
DID YOU ARRANGE TO HAVE IT STOLEN, SUZIE? NO JURY WOULD CONVICT YOU.
IT... IS...
NOT...
THAT...
DIRTY.
THEY GOT MINE TOO, AND LIKE £20. IT'S BARELY WORTH BEING A BURGLAR THESE DAYS.
YEAH, YOU MIGHT AS WELL BECOME A BANKER IF YOU WANT TO ROB PEOPLE, YEAH?
WHOA, SPEAK TRUTH TO POWER, YEAH? ***ON YOUR SIDE.***

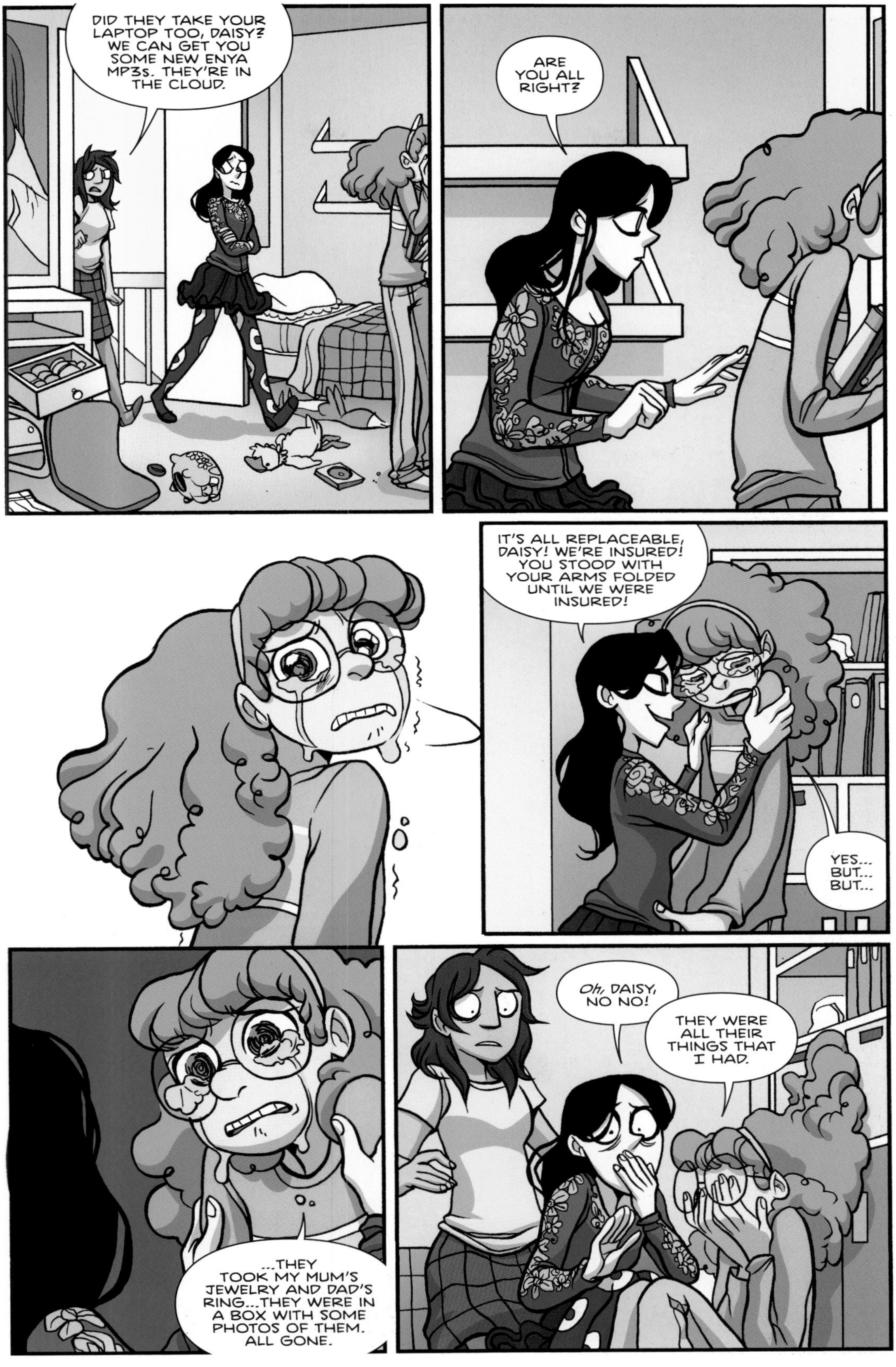
DID THEY TAKE YOUR LAPTOP TOO, DAISY? WE CAN GET YOU SOME NEW ENYA MP3s. THEY'RE IN THE CLOUD.
ARE YOU ALL RIGHT?
IT'S ALL REPLACEABLE, DAISY! WE'RE INSURED! YOU STOOD WITH YOUR ARMS FOLDED UNTIL WE WERE INSURED!
YES... BUT... BUT...
...THEY TOOK MY MUM'S JEWELRY AND DAD'S RING...THEY WERE IN A BOX WITH SOME PHOTOS OF THEM. ALL GONE.
Oh, DAISY, NO NO!
THEY WERE ALL THEIR THINGS THAT I HAD.

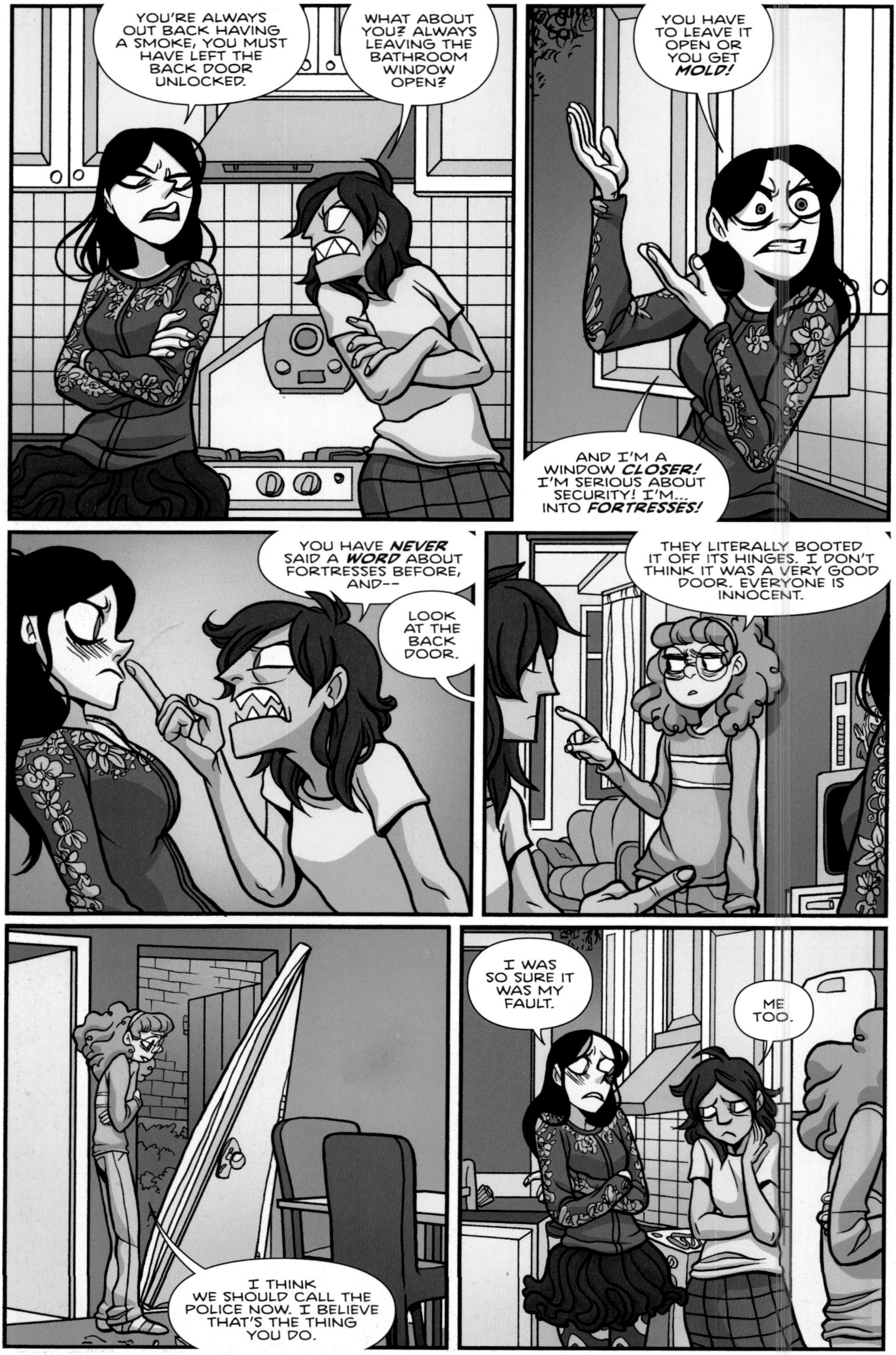
YOU'RE ALWAYS OUT BACK HAVING A SMOKE, YOU MUST HAVE LEFT THE BACK DOOR UNLOCKED.
WHAT ABOUT YOU? ALWAYS LEAVING THE BATHROOM WINDOW OPEN?
YOU HAVE TO LEAVE IT OPEN OR YOU GET MOLD!
AND I'M A WINDOW CLOSER! I'M SERIOUS ABOUT SECURITY! I'M... INTO FORTRESSES!
YOU HAVE NEVER SAID A WORD ABOUT FORTRESSES BEFORE, AND--
LOOK AT THE BACK DOOR.
THEY LITERALLY BOOTED IT OFF ITS HINGES. I DON'T THINK IT WAS A VERY GOOD DOOR. EVERYONE IS INNOCENT.
I THINK WE SHOULD CALL THE POLICE NOW. I BELIEVE THAT'S THE THING YOU DO.
I WAS SO SURE IT WAS MY FAULT.
ME TOO.

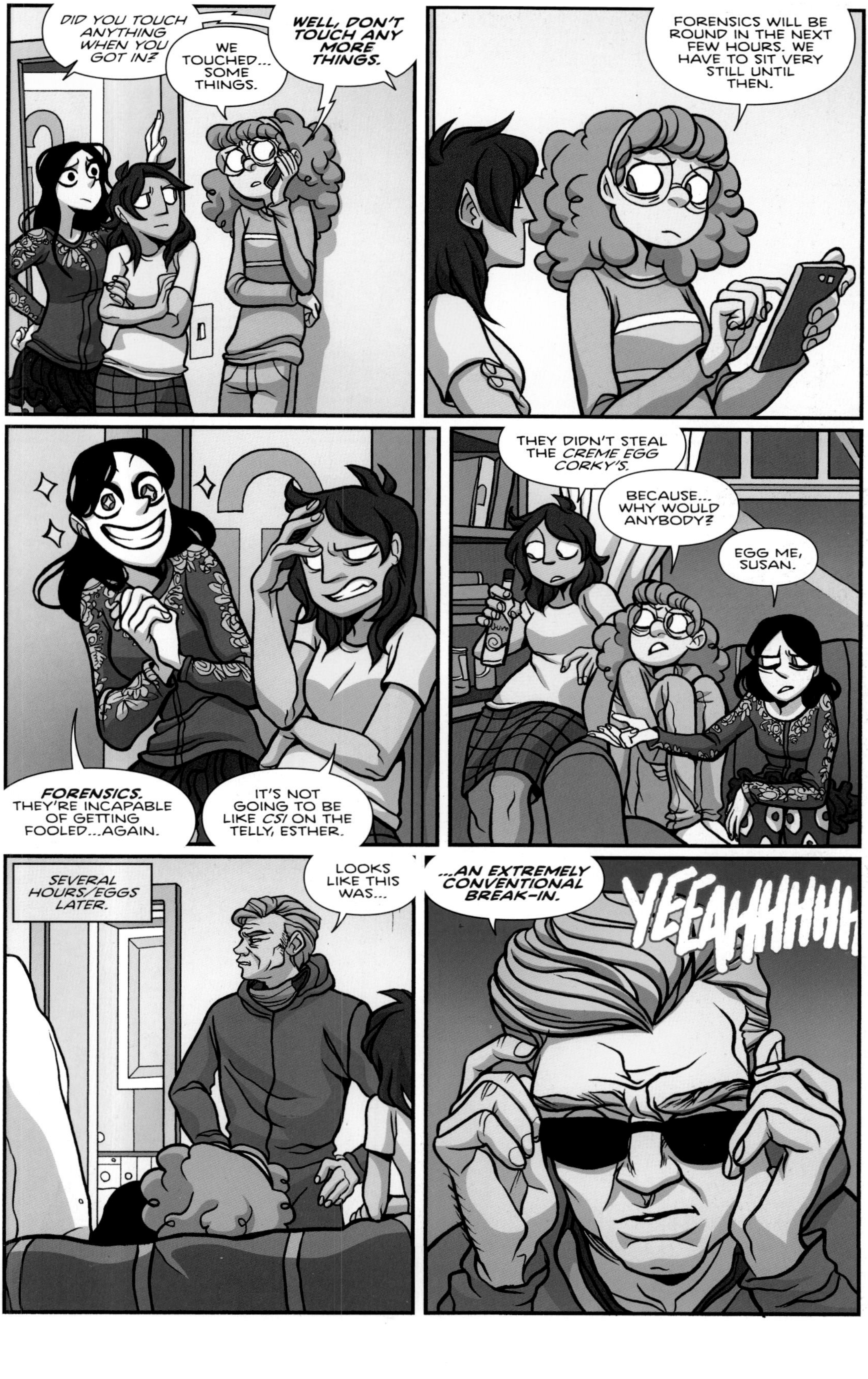

DID YOU TOUCH ANYTHING WHEN YOU GOT IN?
WE TOUCHED... SOME THINGS.
WELL, DON'T TOUCH ANY MORE THINGS.
FORENSICS WILL BE ROUND IN THE NEXT FEW HOURS. WE HAVE TO SIT VERY STILL UNTIL THEN.
FORENSICS. THEY'RE INCAPABLE OF GETTING FOOLED...AGAIN.
IT'S NOT GOING TO BE LIKE CSI ON THE TELLY, ESTHER.
THEY DIDN'T STEAL THE CREME EGG CORKY'S.
BECAUSE... WHY WOULD ANYBODY?
EGG ME, SUSAN.
SEVERAL HOURS/EGGS LATER.
LOOKS LIKE THIS WAS...
...AN EXTREMELY CONVENTIONAL BREAK-IN.
YEEAHHHHHH

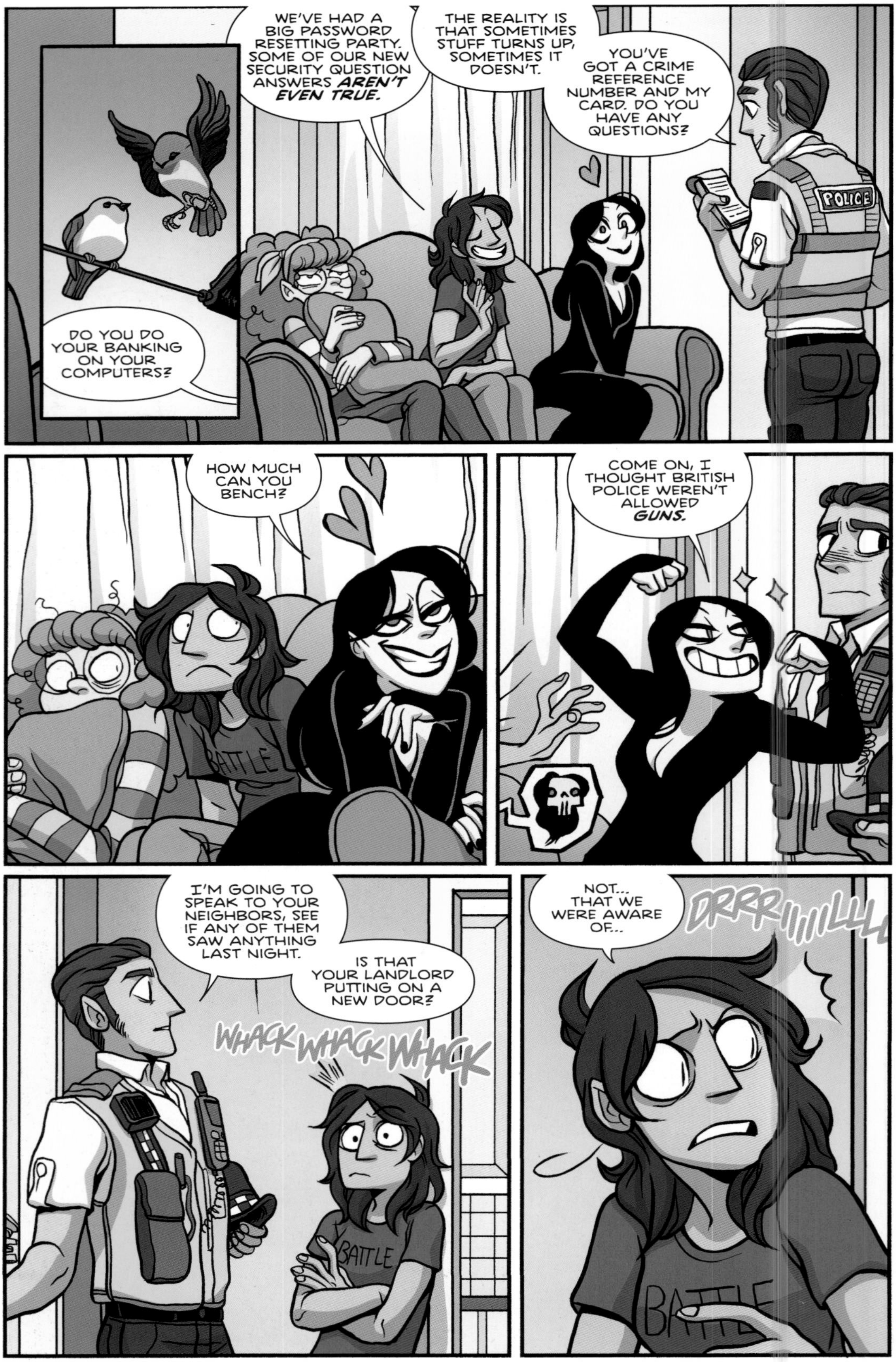

DO YOU DO YOUR BANKING ON YOUR COMPUTERS?
WE'VE HAD A BIG PASSWORD RESETTING PARTY. SOME OF OUR NEW SECURITY QUESTION ANSWERS *AREN'T EVEN TRUE.*
THE REALITY IS THAT SOMETIMES STUFF TURNS UP, SOMETIMES IT DOESN'T.
YOU'VE GOT A CRIME REFERENCE NUMBER AND MY CARD. DO YOU HAVE ANY QUESTIONS?
POLICE
HOW MUCH CAN YOU BENCH?
BATTLE
COME ON, I THOUGHT BRITISH POLICE WEREN'T ALLOWED *GUNS.*
I'M GOING TO SPEAK TO YOUR NEIGHBORS, SEE IF ANY OF THEM SAW ANYTHING LAST NIGHT.
IS THAT YOUR LANDLORD PUTTING ON A NEW DOOR?
WHACK WHACK WHACK
BATTLE
NOT... THAT WE WERE AWARE OF...
DRRRIIIIILLLL
BATTLE

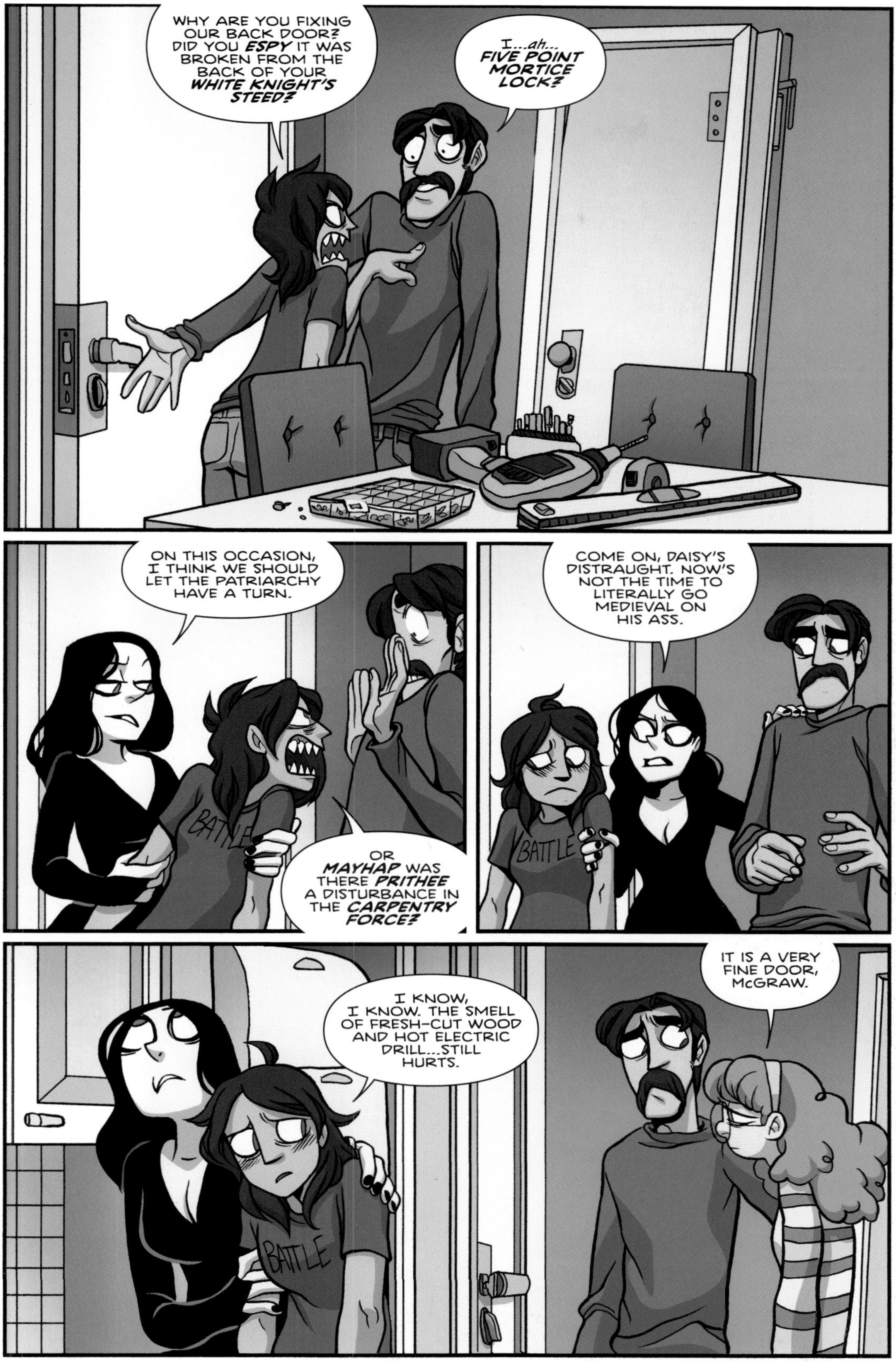
WHY ARE YOU FIXING OUR BACK DOOR? DID YOU ESPY IT WAS BROKEN FROM THE BACK OF YOUR WHITE KNIGHT'S STEED?
I...ah... FIVE POINT MORTICE LOCK?
ON THIS OCCASION, I THINK WE SHOULD LET THE PATRIARCHY HAVE A TURN.
BATTLE
OR MAYHAP WAS THERE PRITHEE A DISTURBANCE IN THE CARPENTRY FORCE?
COME ON, DAISY'S DISTRAUGHT. NOW'S NOT THE TIME TO LITERALLY GO MEDIEVAL ON HIS ASS.
BATTLE
I KNOW, I KNOW. THE SMELL OF FRESH-CUT WOOD AND HOT ELECTRIC DRILL...STILL HURTS.
BATTLE
IT IS A VERY FINE DOOR, McGRAW.

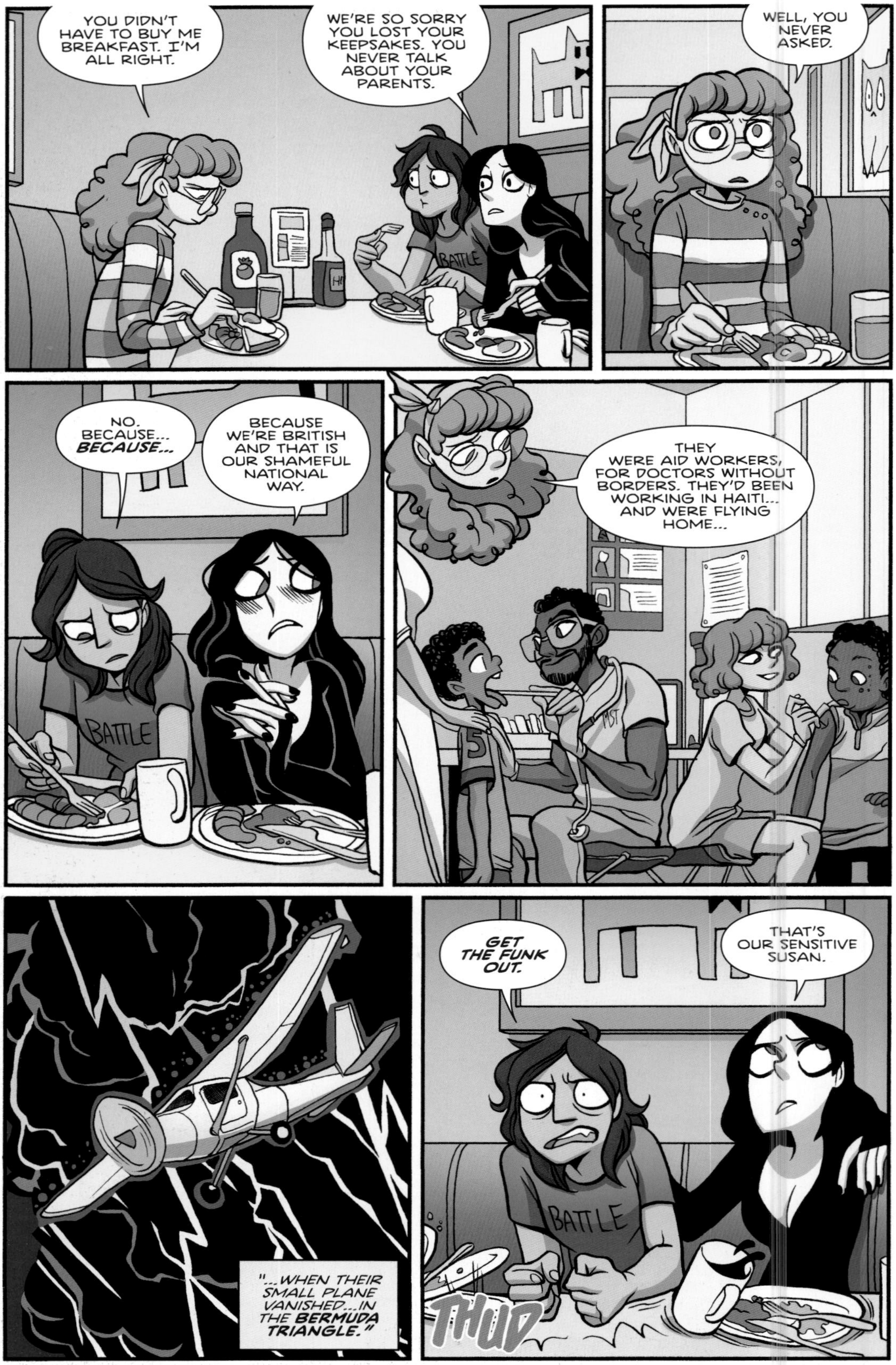
YOU DIDN'T HAVE TO BUY ME BREAKFAST. I'M ALL RIGHT.
WE'RE SO SORRY YOU LOST YOUR KEEPSAKES. YOU NEVER TALK ABOUT YOUR PARENTS.
WELL, YOU NEVER ASKED.
NO. BECAUSE... BECAUSE...
BECAUSE WE'RE BRITISH AND THAT IS OUR SHAMEFUL NATIONAL WAY.
THEY WERE AID WORKERS, FOR DOCTORS WITHOUT BORDERS. THEY'D BEEN WORKING IN HAITI... AND WERE FLYING HOME...
"...WHEN THEIR SMALL PLANE VANISHED...IN THE BERMUDA TRIANGLE."
GET THE FUNK OUT.
THAT'S OUR SENSITIVE SUSAN.
THUD

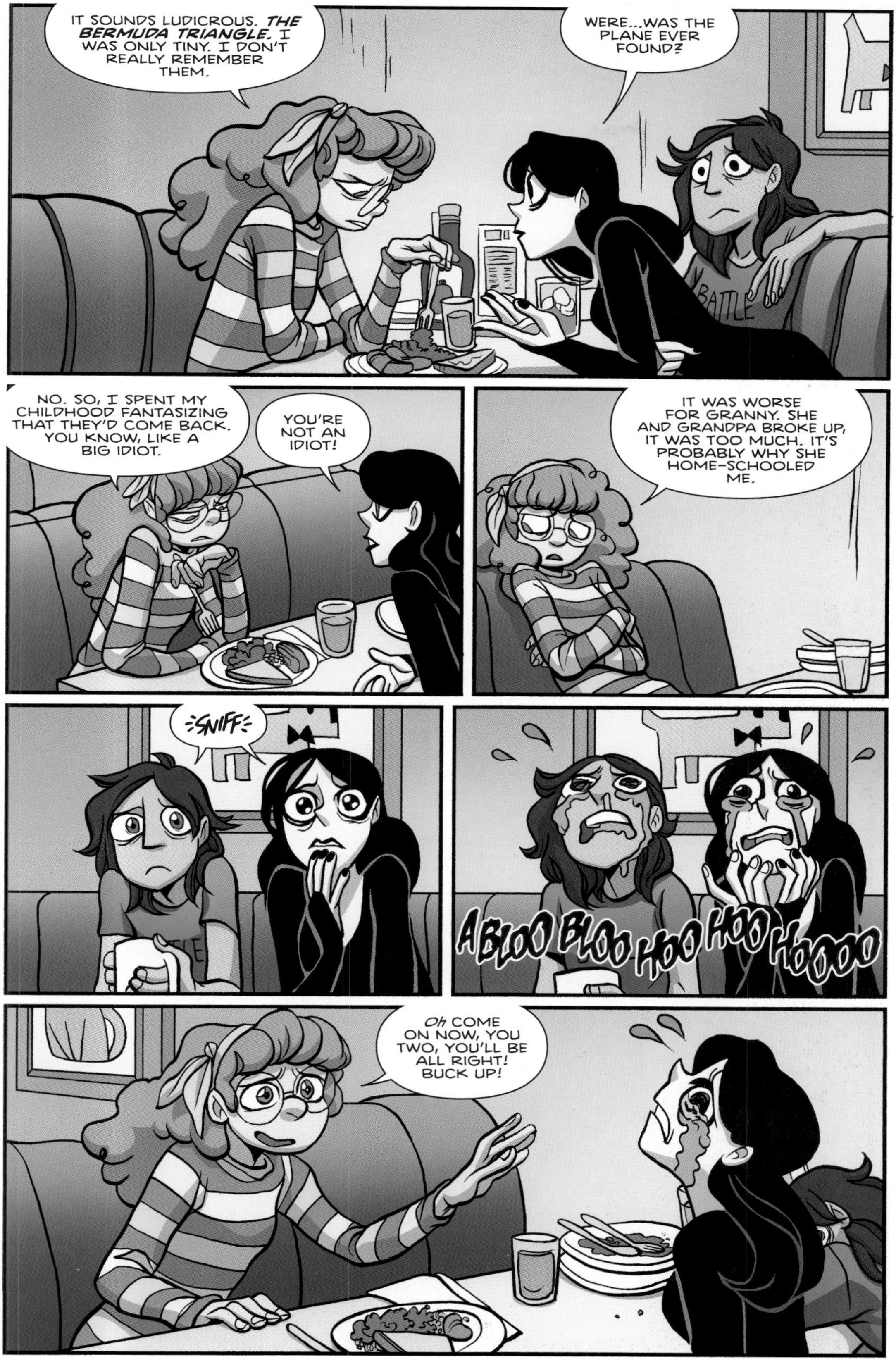
IT SOUNDS LUDICROUS. *THE BERMUDA TRIANGLE.* I WAS ONLY TINY. I DON'T REALLY REMEMBER THEM.
WERE...WAS THE PLANE EVER FOUND?
NO. SO, I SPENT MY CHILDHOOD FANTASIZING THAT THEY'D COME BACK. YOU KNOW, LIKE A BIG IDIOT.
YOU'RE NOT AN IDIOT!
IT WAS WORSE FOR GRANNY. SHE AND GRANDPA BROKE UP, IT WAS TOO MUCH. IT'S PROBABLY WHY SHE HOME-SCHOOLED ME.
SNIFF
ABLOO BLOO HOO HOO HOOOO
Oh COME ON NOW, YOU TWO, YOU'LL BE ALL RIGHT! BUCK UP!

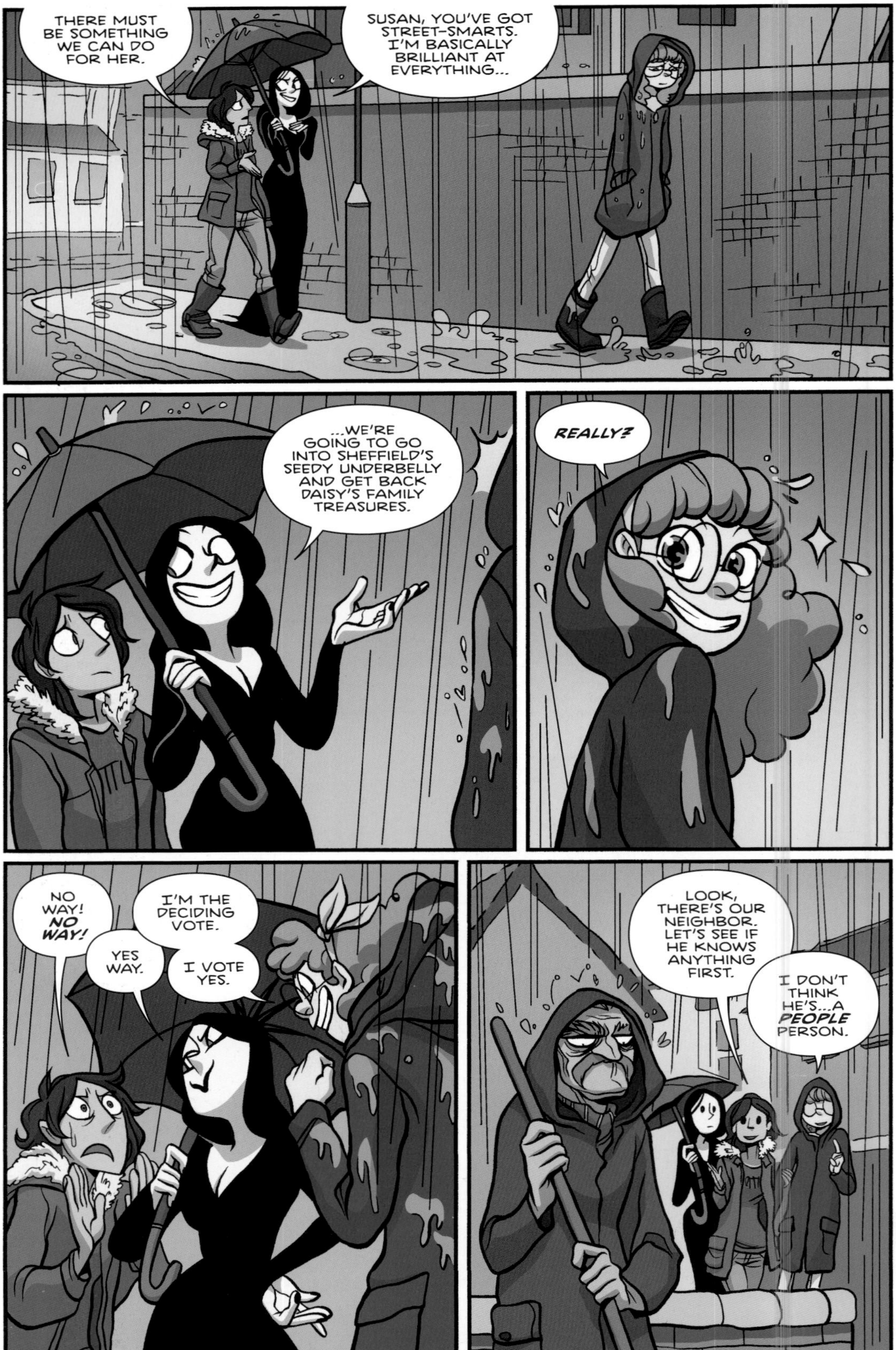
THERE MUST BE SOMETHING WE CAN DO FOR HER.
SUSAN, YOU'VE GOT STREET-SMARTS. I'M BASICALLY BRILLIANT AT EVERYTHING...
...WE'RE GOING TO GO INTO SHEFFIELD'S SEEDY UNDERBELLY AND GET BACK DAISY'S FAMILY TREASURES.
REALLY?
NO WAY! NO WAY!
YES WAY.
I'M THE DECIDING VOTE.
I VOTE YES.
LOOK, THERE'S OUR NEIGHBOR. LET'S SEE IF HE KNOWS ANYTHING FIRST.
I DON'T THINK HE'S...A PEOPLE PERSON.

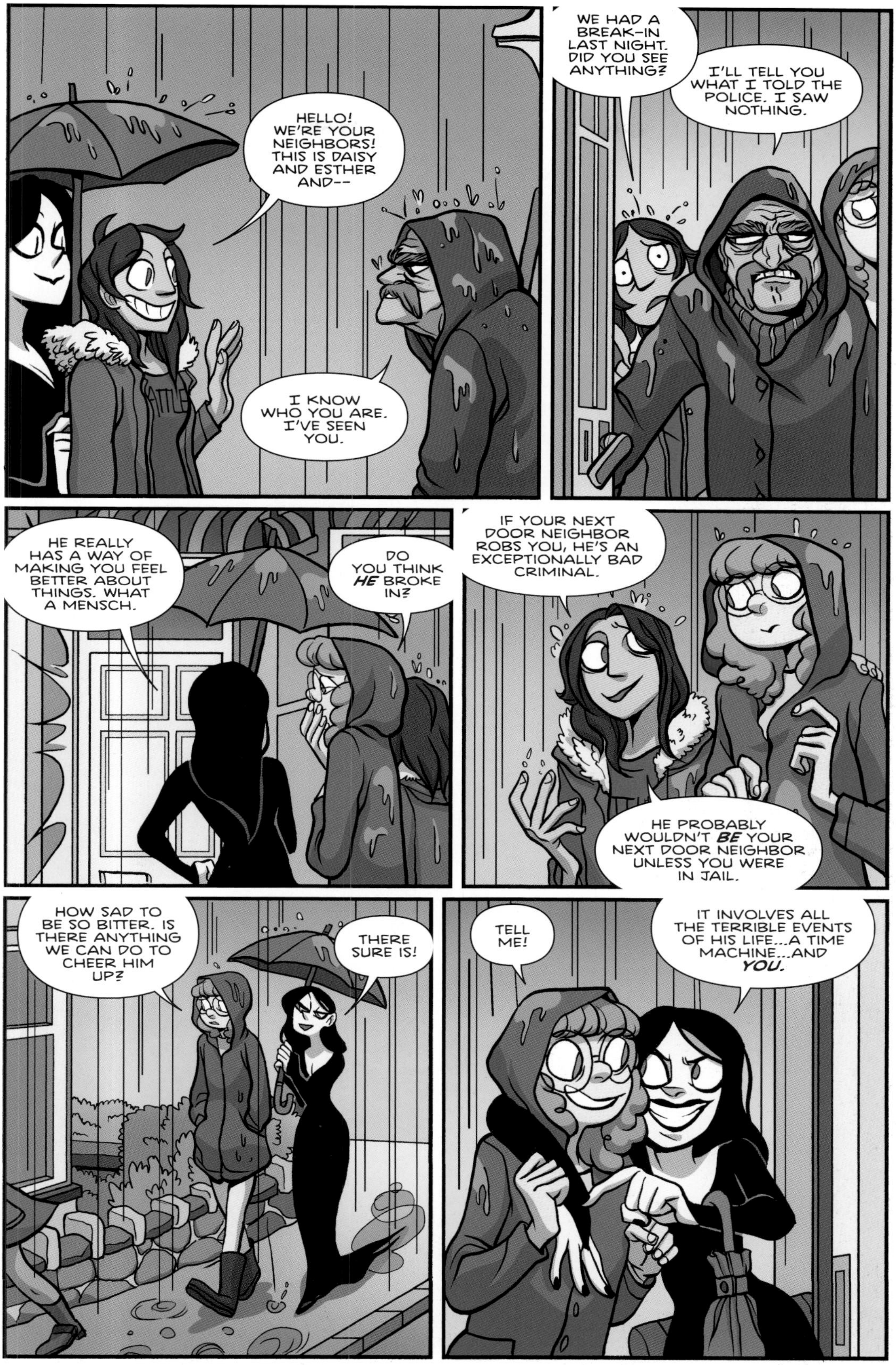
HELLO! WE'RE YOUR NEIGHBORS! THIS IS DAISY AND ESTHER AND--
I KNOW WHO YOU ARE. I'VE SEEN YOU.
WE HAD A BREAK-IN LAST NIGHT. DID YOU SEE ANYTHING?
I'LL TELL YOU WHAT I TOLD THE POLICE. I SAW NOTHING.
HE REALLY HAS A WAY OF MAKING YOU FEEL BETTER ABOUT THINGS. WHAT A MENSCH.
DO YOU THINK ***HE*** BROKE IN?
IF YOUR NEXT DOOR NEIGHBOR ROBS YOU, HE'S AN EXCEPTIONALLY BAD CRIMINAL.
HE PROBABLY WOULDN'T ***BE*** YOUR NEXT DOOR NEIGHBOR UNLESS YOU WERE IN JAIL.
HOW SAD TO BE SO BITTER. IS THERE ANYTHING WE CAN DO TO CHEER HIM UP?
THERE SURE IS!
TELL ME!
IT INVOLVES ALL THE TERRIBLE EVENTS OF HIS LIFE...A TIME MACHINE...AND ***YOU.***

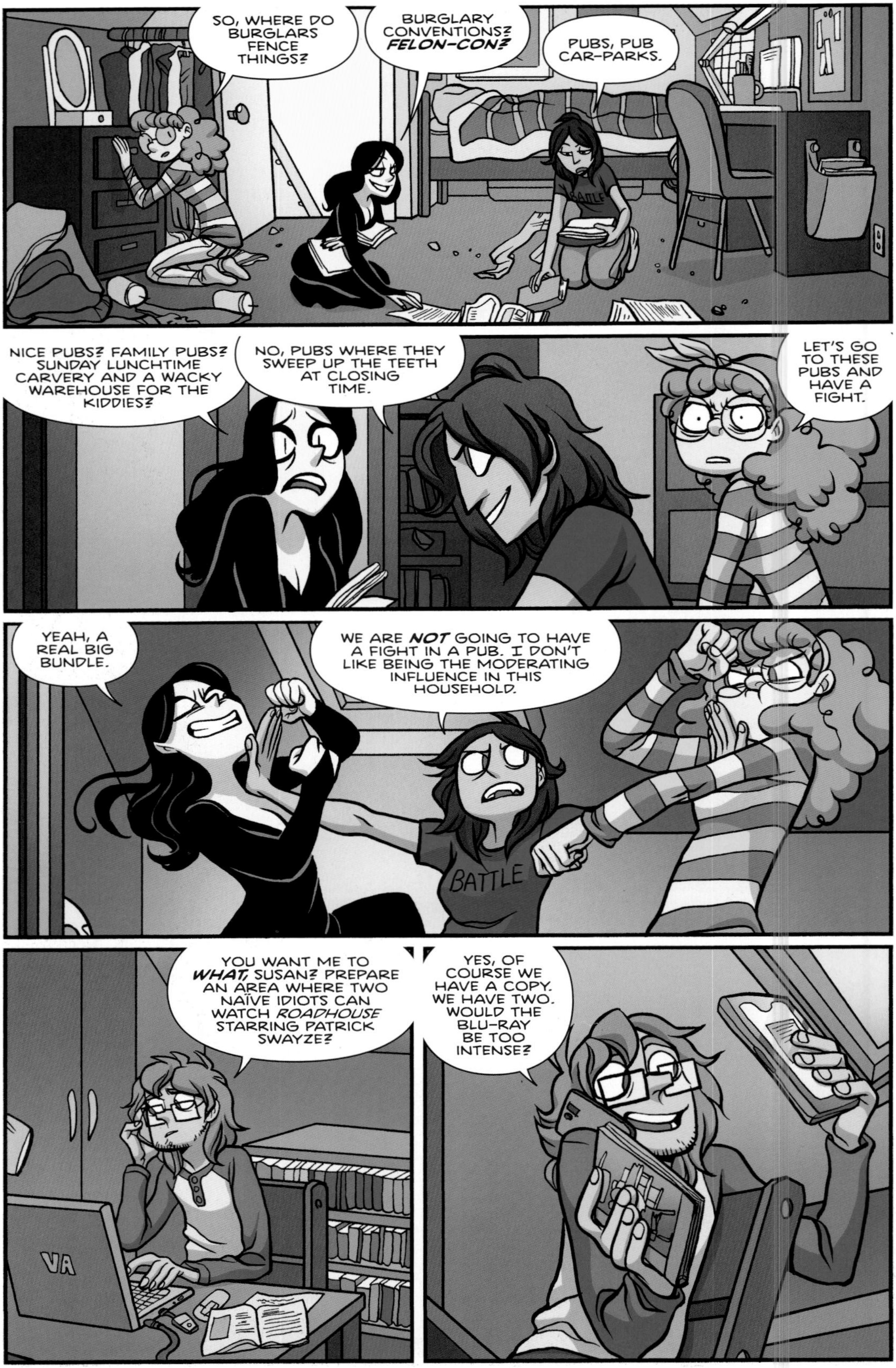
SO, WHERE DO BURGLARS FENCE THINGS?
BURGLARY CONVENTIONS? FELON-CON?
PUBS, PUB CAR-PARKS.
NICE PUBS? FAMILY PUBS? SUNDAY LUNCHTIME CARVERY AND A WACKY WAREHOUSE FOR THE KIDDIES?
NO, PUBS WHERE THEY SWEEP UP THE TEETH AT CLOSING TIME.
LET'S GO TO THESE PUBS AND HAVE A FIGHT.
YEAH, A REAL BIG BUNDLE.
WE ARE NOT GOING TO HAVE A FIGHT IN A PUB. I DON'T LIKE BEING THE MODERATING INFLUENCE IN THIS HOUSEHOLD.
BATTLE
YOU WANT ME TO WHAT, SUSAN? PREPARE AN AREA WHERE TWO NAÏVE IDIOTS CAN WATCH ROADHOUSE STARRING PATRICK SWAYZE?
VA
YES, OF COURSE WE HAVE A COPY. WE HAVE TWO. WOULD THE BLU-RAY BE TOO INTENSE?

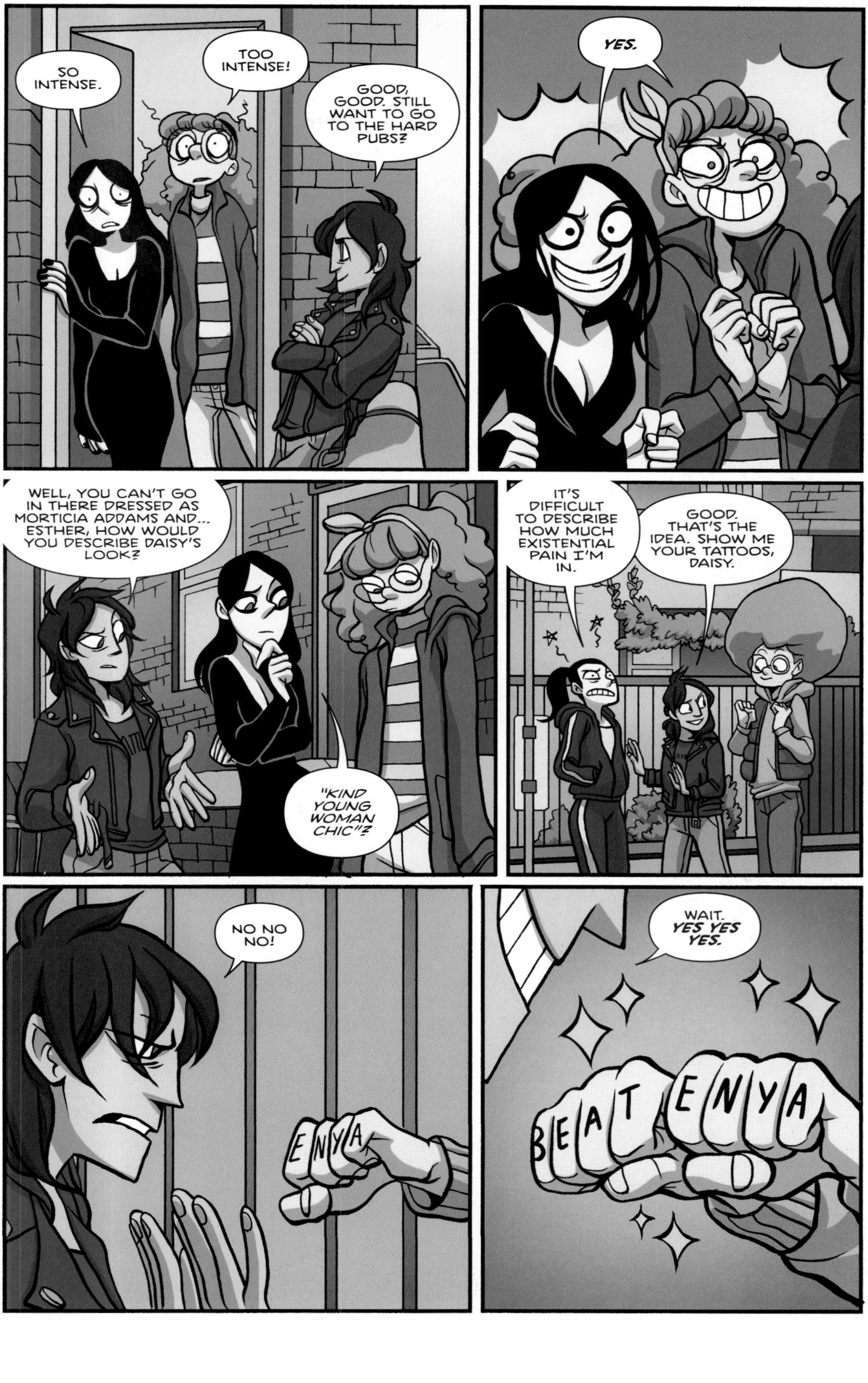

SO INTENSE.
TOO INTENSE!
GOOD, GOOD. STILL WANT TO GO TO THE HARD PUBS?
YES.
WELL, YOU CAN'T GO IN THERE DRESSED AS MORTICIA ADDAMS AND... ESTHER, HOW WOULD YOU DESCRIBE DAISY'S LOOK?
"KIND YOUNG WOMAN CHIC"?
IT'S DIFFICULT TO DESCRIBE HOW MUCH EXISTENTIAL PAIN I'M IN.
GOOD. THAT'S THE IDEA. SHOW ME YOUR TATTOOS, DAISY.
NO NO NO!
ENYA
WAIT. YES YES YES.
BEAT ENYA

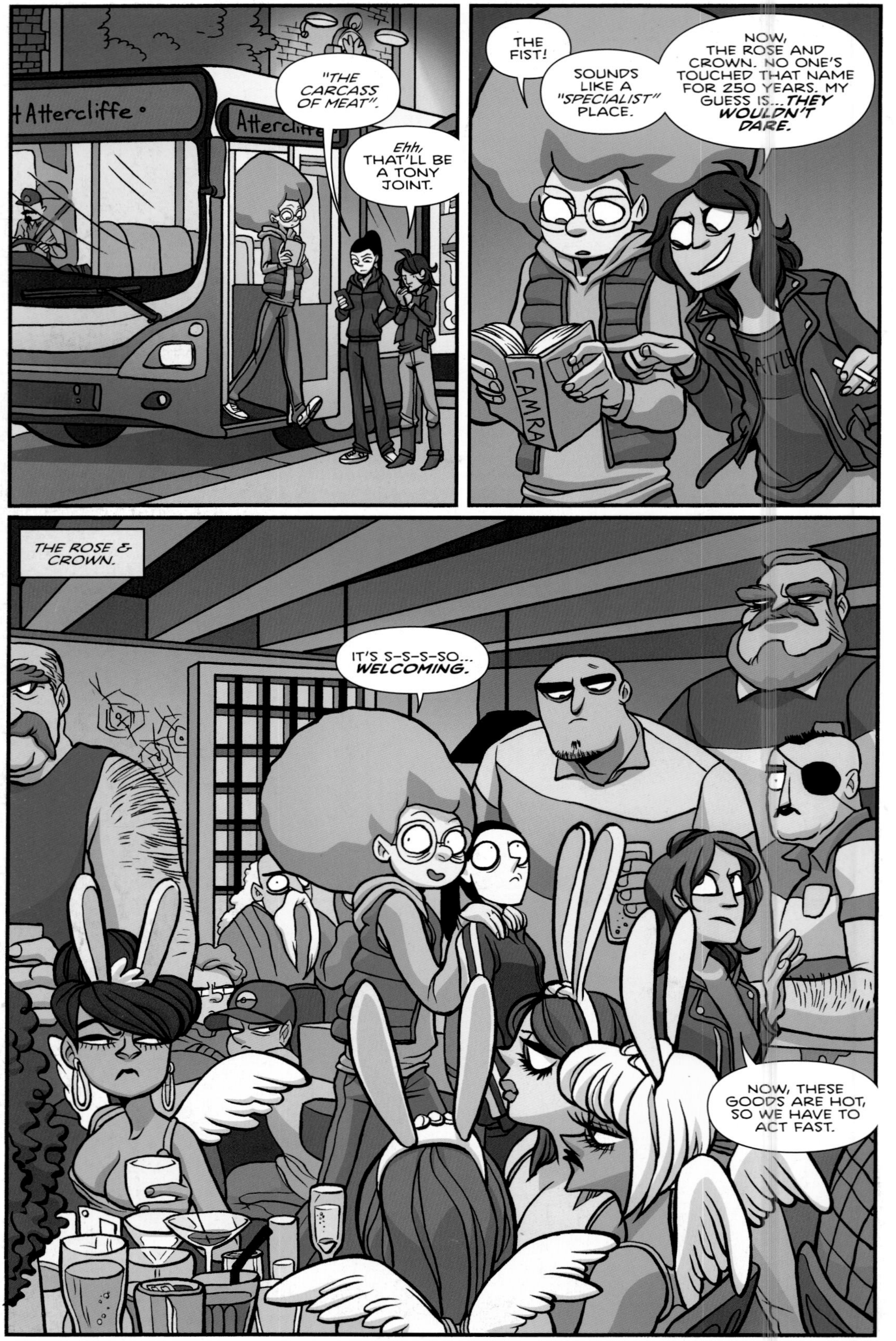

Attercliffe
Attercliffe
"THE CARCASS OF MEAT".
Ehh, THAT'LL BE A TONY JOINT.
THE FIST!
SOUNDS LIKE A "SPECIALIST" PLACE.
NOW, THE ROSE AND CROWN. NO ONE'S TOUCHED THAT NAME FOR 250 YEARS. MY GUESS IS... THEY WOULDN'T DARE.
CAMRA
BATTLE
THE ROSE & CROWN.
IT'S S-S-S-SO... WELCOMING.
NOW, THESE GOODS ARE HOT, SO WE HAVE TO ACT FAST.

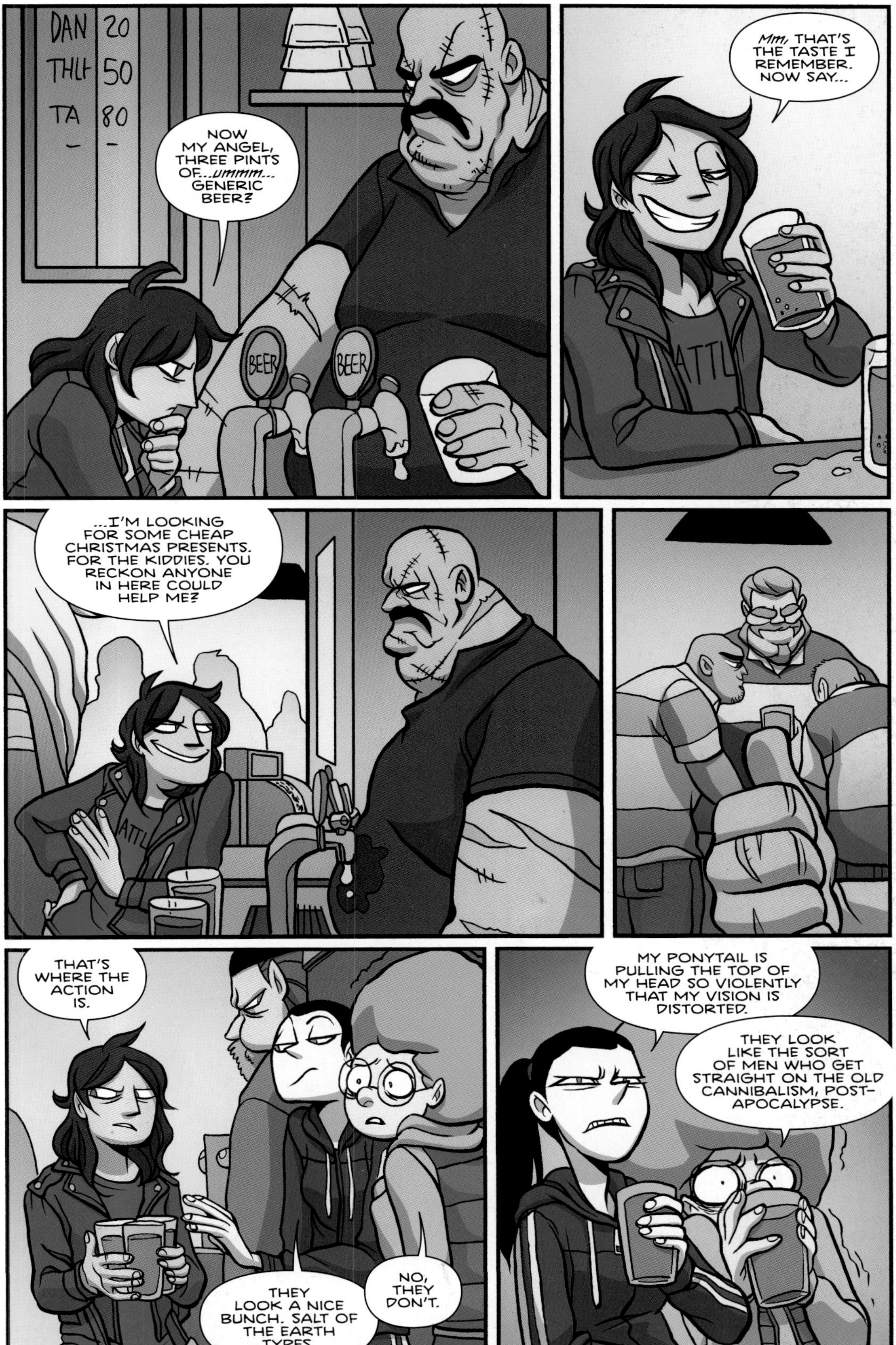
DAN 20
THLH 50
TA 80
NOW MY ANGEL, THREE PINTS OF...ummm... GENERIC BEER?
BEER
BEER
Mm, THAT'S THE TASTE I REMEMBER. NOW SAY...
...I'M LOOKING FOR SOME CHEAP CHRISTMAS PRESENTS. FOR THE KIDDIES. YOU RECKON ANYONE IN HERE COULD HELP ME?
THAT'S WHERE THE ACTION IS.
THEY LOOK A NICE BUNCH. SALT OF THE EARTH TYPES.
NO, THEY DON'T.
MY PONYTAIL IS PULLING THE TOP OF MY HEAD SO VIOLENTLY THAT MY VISION IS DISTORTED.
THEY LOOK LIKE THE SORT OF MEN WHO GET STRAIGHT ON THE OLD CANNIBALISM, POST-APOCALYPSE.

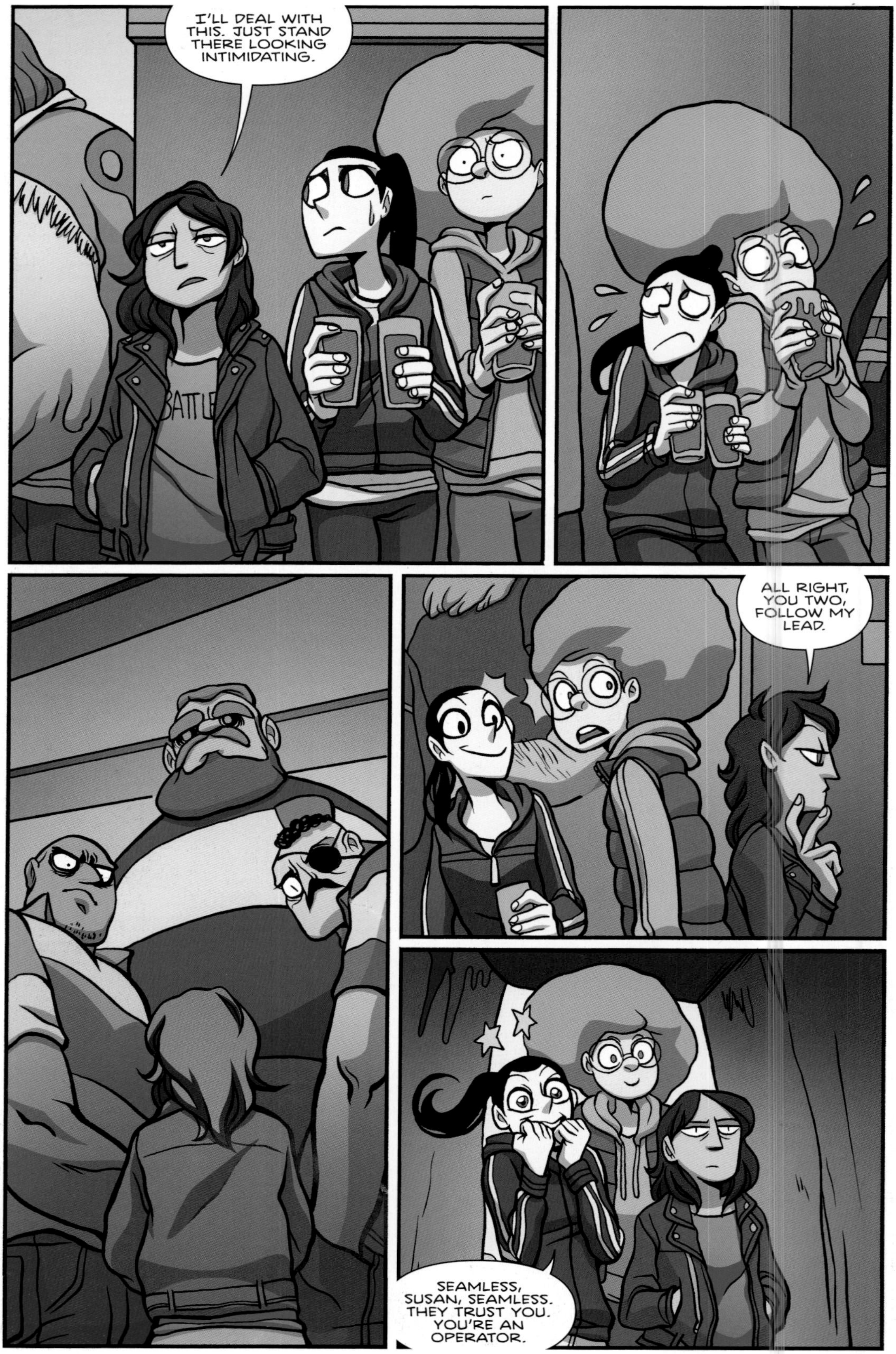
I'LL DEAL WITH THIS. JUST STAND THERE LOOKING INTIMIDATING.
BATTLE
ALL RIGHT, YOU TWO, FOLLOW MY LEAD.
SEAMLESS, SUSAN, SEAMLESS. THEY TRUST YOU. YOU'RE AN OPERATOR.

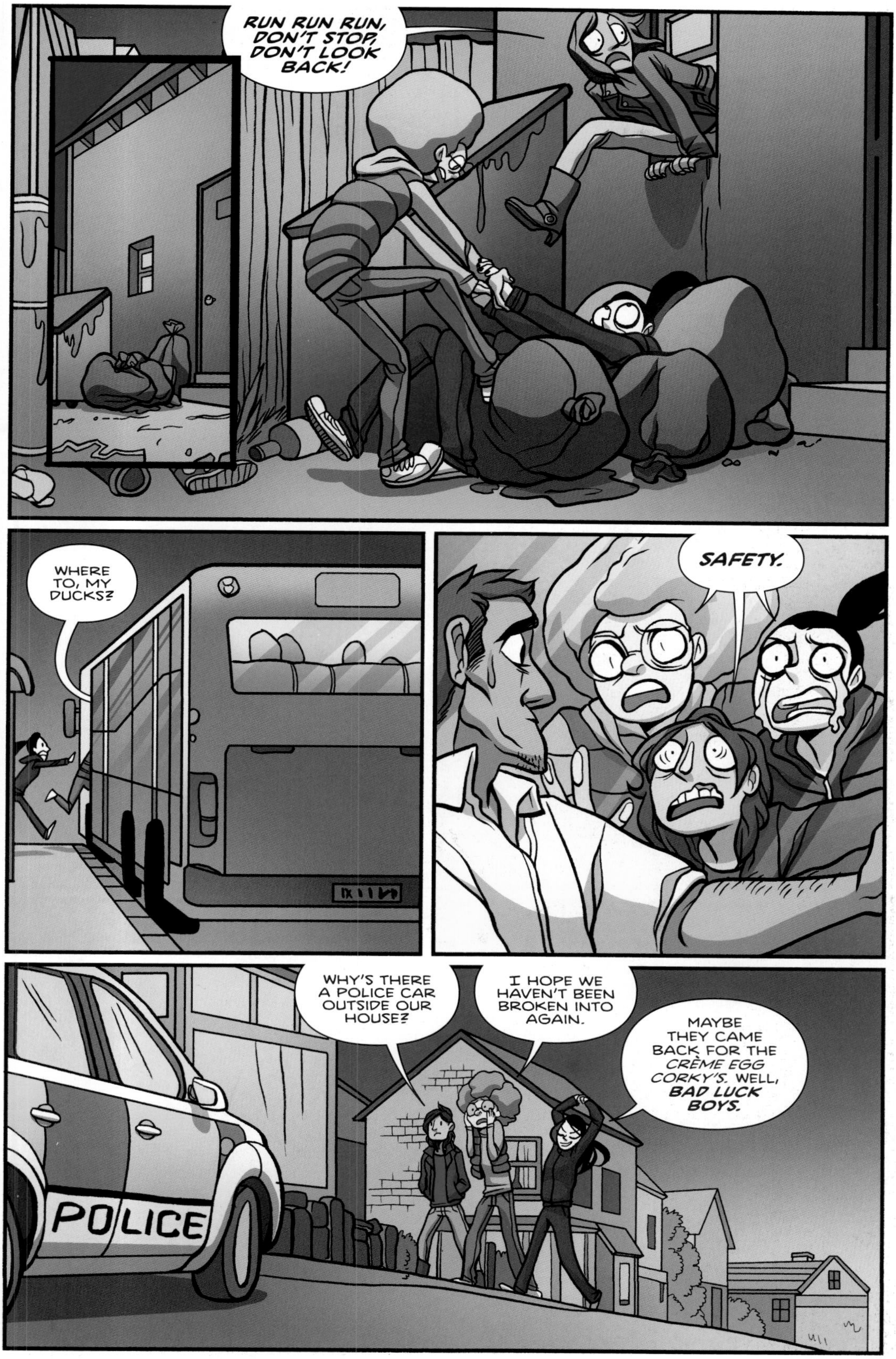
RUN RUN RUN, DON'T STOP, DON'T LOOK BACK!
WHERE TO, MY DUCKS?
SAFETY.
WHY'S THERE A POLICE CAR OUTSIDE OUR HOUSE?
I HOPE WE HAVEN'T BEEN BROKEN INTO AGAIN.
MAYBE THEY CAME BACK FOR THE *CRÈME EGG CORKY'S*. WELL, ***BAD LUCK BOYS.***
POLICE

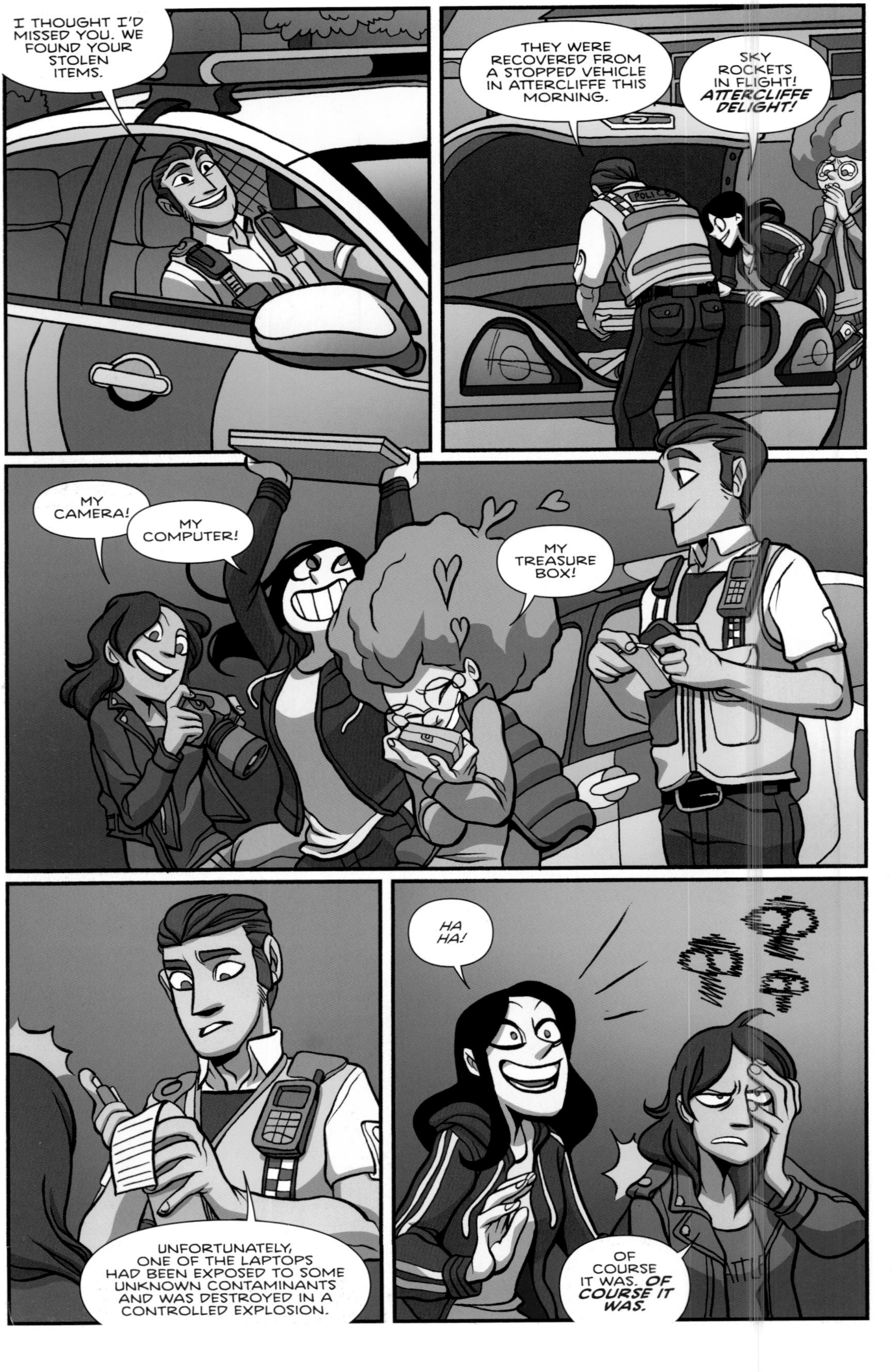
I THOUGHT I'D MISSED YOU. WE FOUND YOUR STOLEN ITEMS.
THEY WERE RECOVERED FROM A STOPPED VEHICLE IN ATTERCLIFFE THIS MORNING.
SKY ROCKETS IN FLIGHT! *ATTERCLIFFE DELIGHT!*
MY CAMERA!
MY COMPUTER!
MY TREASURE BOX!
UNFORTUNATELY, ONE OF THE LAPTOPS HAD BEEN EXPOSED TO SOME UNKNOWN CONTAMINANTS AND WAS DESTROYED IN A CONTROLLED EXPLOSION.
HA HA!
OF COURSE IT WAS. ***OF COURSE IT WAS.***

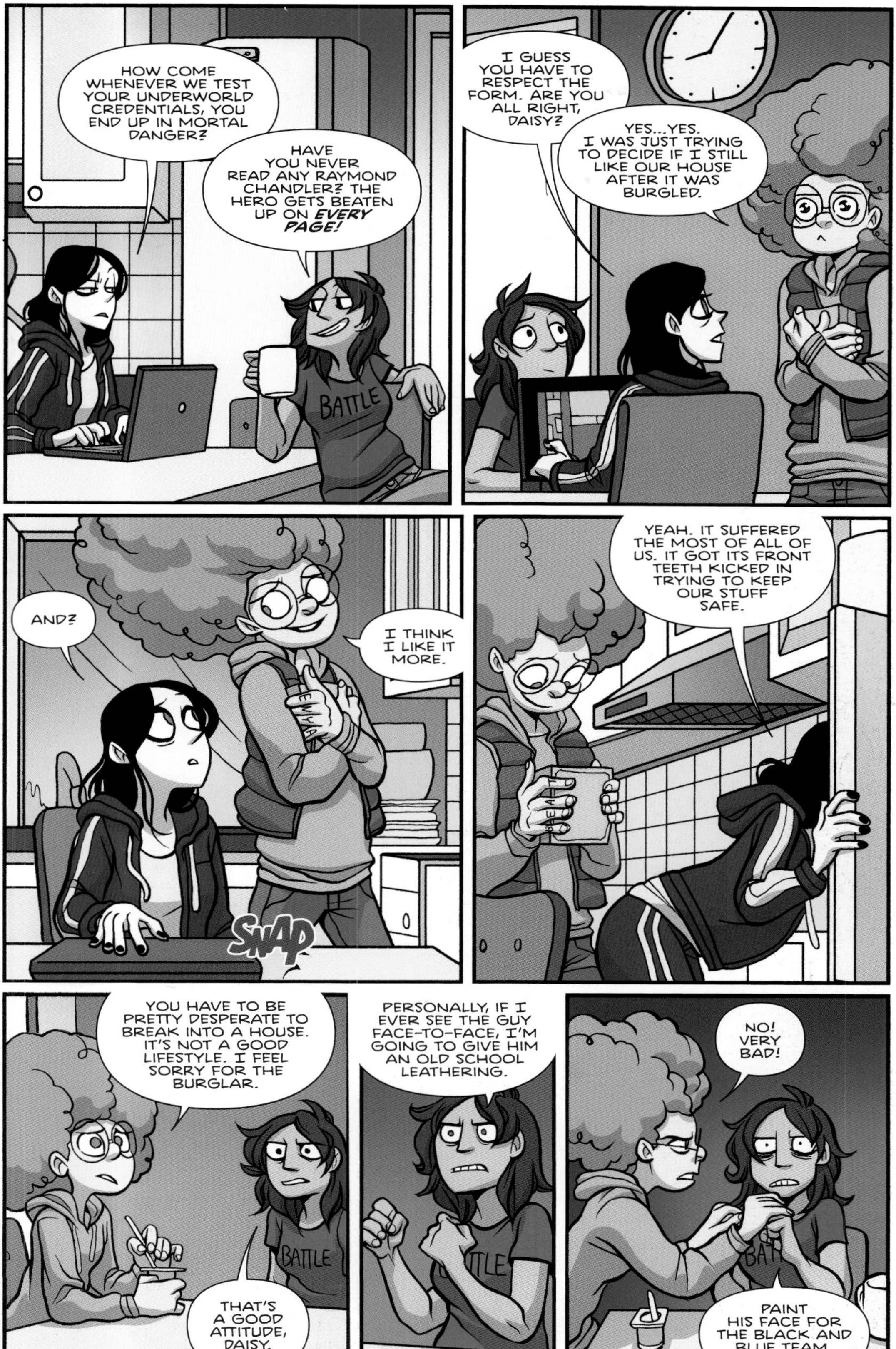
HOW COME WHENEVER WE TEST YOUR UNDERWORLD CREDENTIALS, YOU END UP IN MORTAL DANGER?
HAVE YOU NEVER READ ANY RAYMOND CHANDLER? THE HERO GETS BEATEN UP ON *EVERY PAGE!*
BATTLE
I GUESS YOU HAVE TO RESPECT THE FORM. ARE YOU ALL RIGHT, DAISY?
YES...YES. I WAS JUST TRYING TO DECIDE IF I STILL LIKE OUR HOUSE AFTER IT WAS BURGLED.
AND?
I THINK I LIKE IT MORE.
SNAP
YEAH. IT SUFFERED THE MOST OF ALL OF US. IT GOT ITS FRONT TEETH KICKED IN TRYING TO KEEP OUR STUFF SAFE.
YOU HAVE TO BE PRETTY DESPERATE TO BREAK INTO A HOUSE. IT'S NOT A GOOD LIFESTYLE. I FEEL SORRY FOR THE BURGLAR.
BATTLE
THAT'S A GOOD ATTITUDE, DAISY.
PERSONALLY, IF I EVER SEE THE GUY FACE-TO-FACE, I'M GOING TO GIVE HIM AN OLD SCHOOL LEATHERING.
NO! VERY BAD!
PAINT HIS FACE FOR THE BLACK AND BLUE TEAM.

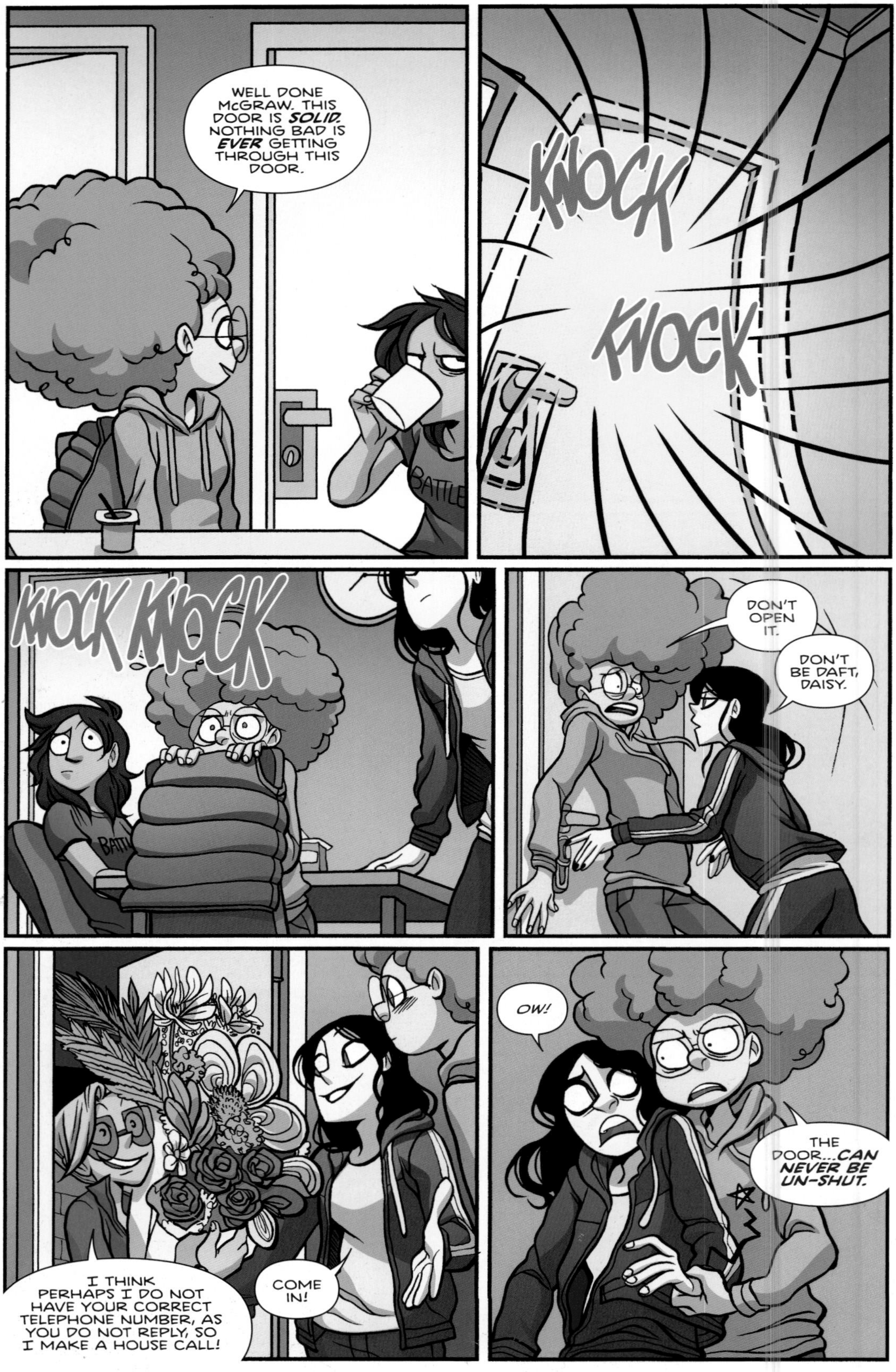
WELL DONE McGRAW. THIS DOOR IS SOLID. NOTHING BAD IS EVER GETTING THROUGH THIS DOOR.
BATTLE
KNOCK
KNOCK
KNOCK KNOCK
BATTL
DON'T OPEN IT.
DON'T BE DAFT, DAISY.
I THINK PERHAPS I DO NOT HAVE YOUR CORRECT TELEPHONE NUMBER, AS YOU DO NOT REPLY, SO I MAKE A HOUSE CALL!
COME IN!
OW!
THE DOOR...CAN NEVER BE UN-SHUT.

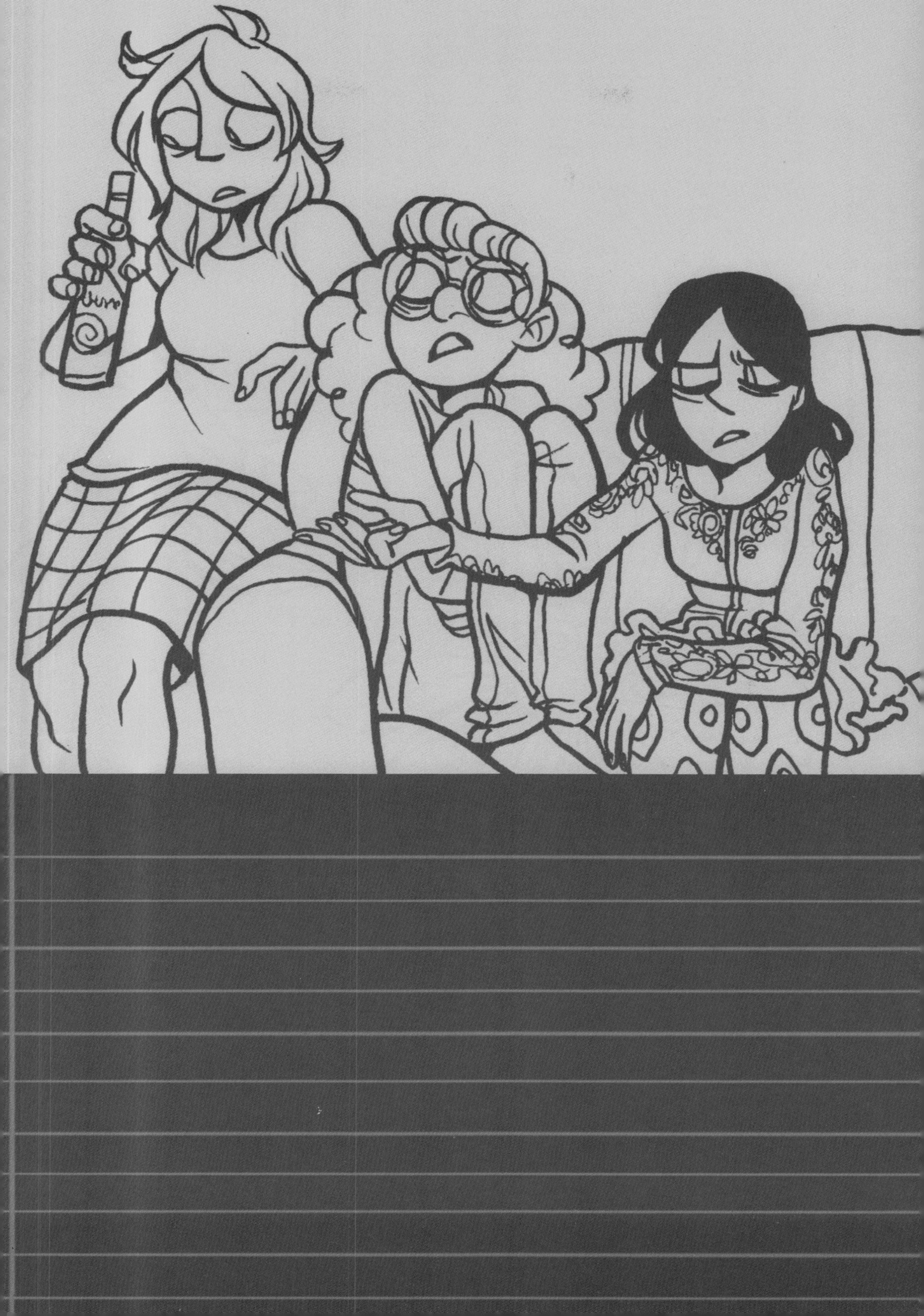

CHAPTER TWENTY TWO

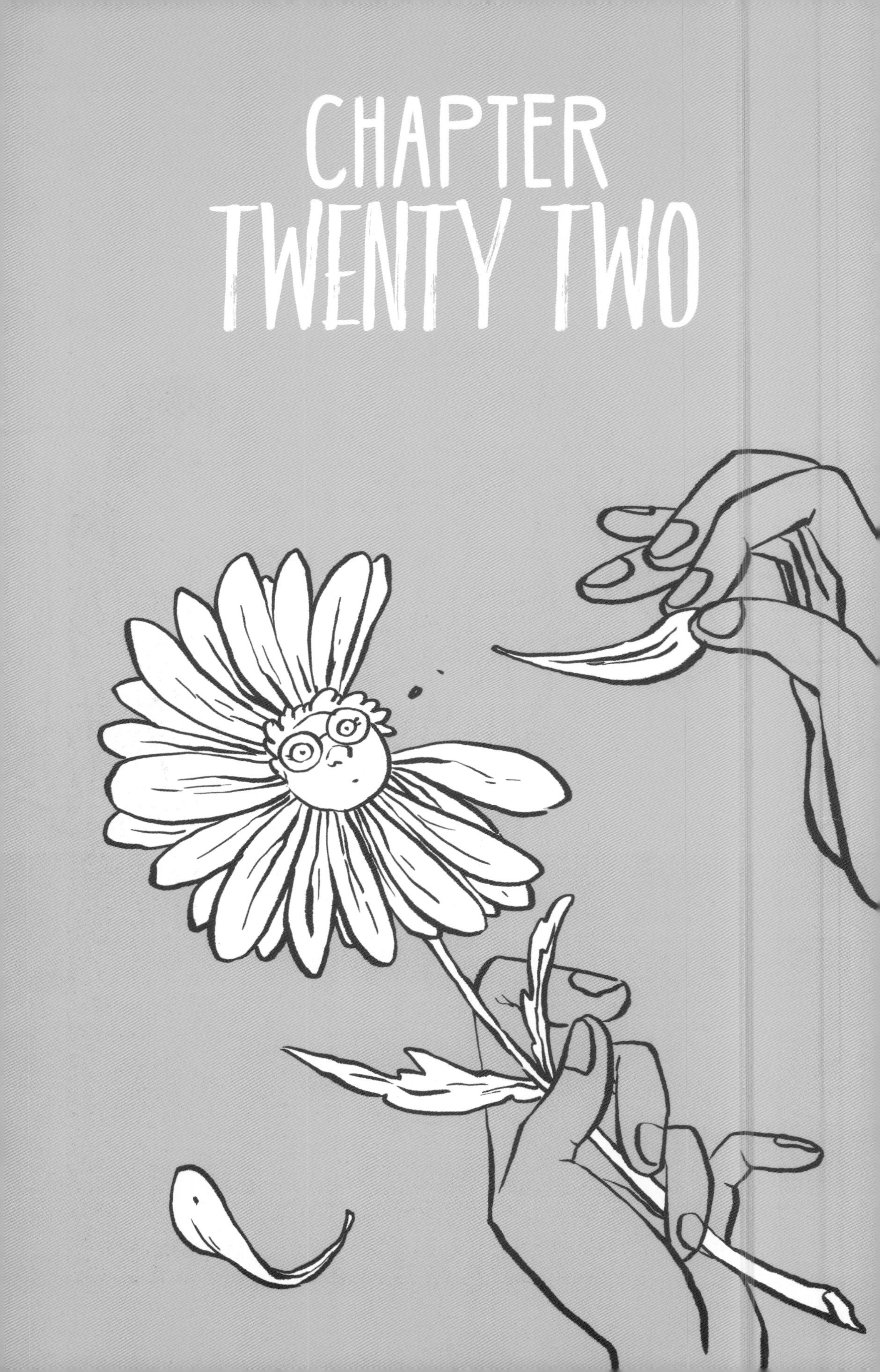

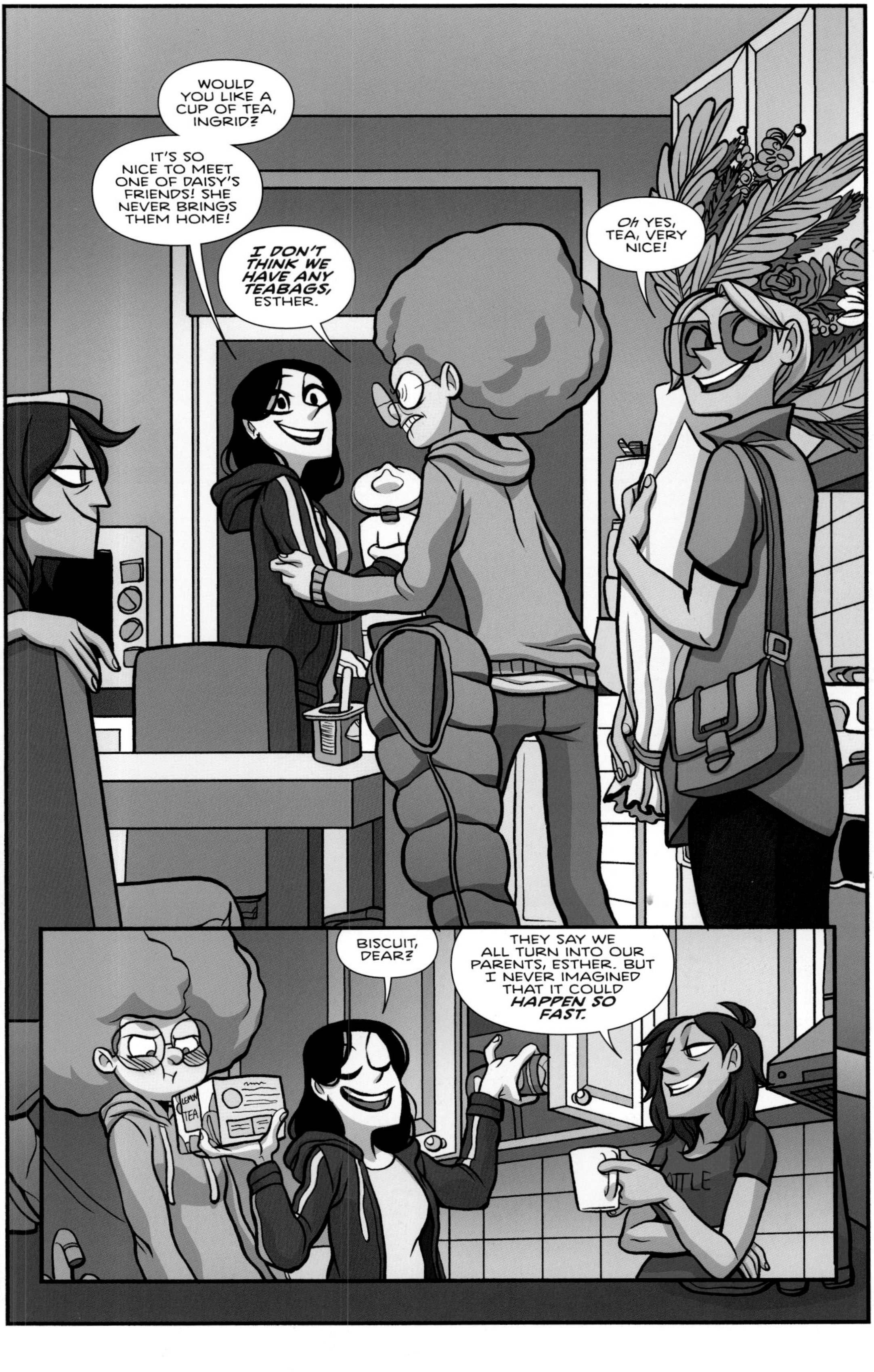
WOULD YOU LIKE A CUP OF TEA, INGRID?
IT'S SO NICE TO MEET ONE OF DAISY'S FRIENDS! SHE NEVER BRINGS THEM HOME!
I DON'T THINK WE HAVE ANY TEABAGS, ESTHER.
Oh YES, TEA, VERY NICE!
BISCUIT, DEAR?
THEY SAY WE ALL TURN INTO OUR PARENTS, ESTHER. BUT I NEVER IMAGINED THAT IT COULD *HAPPEN SO FAST.*
LEMON TEA

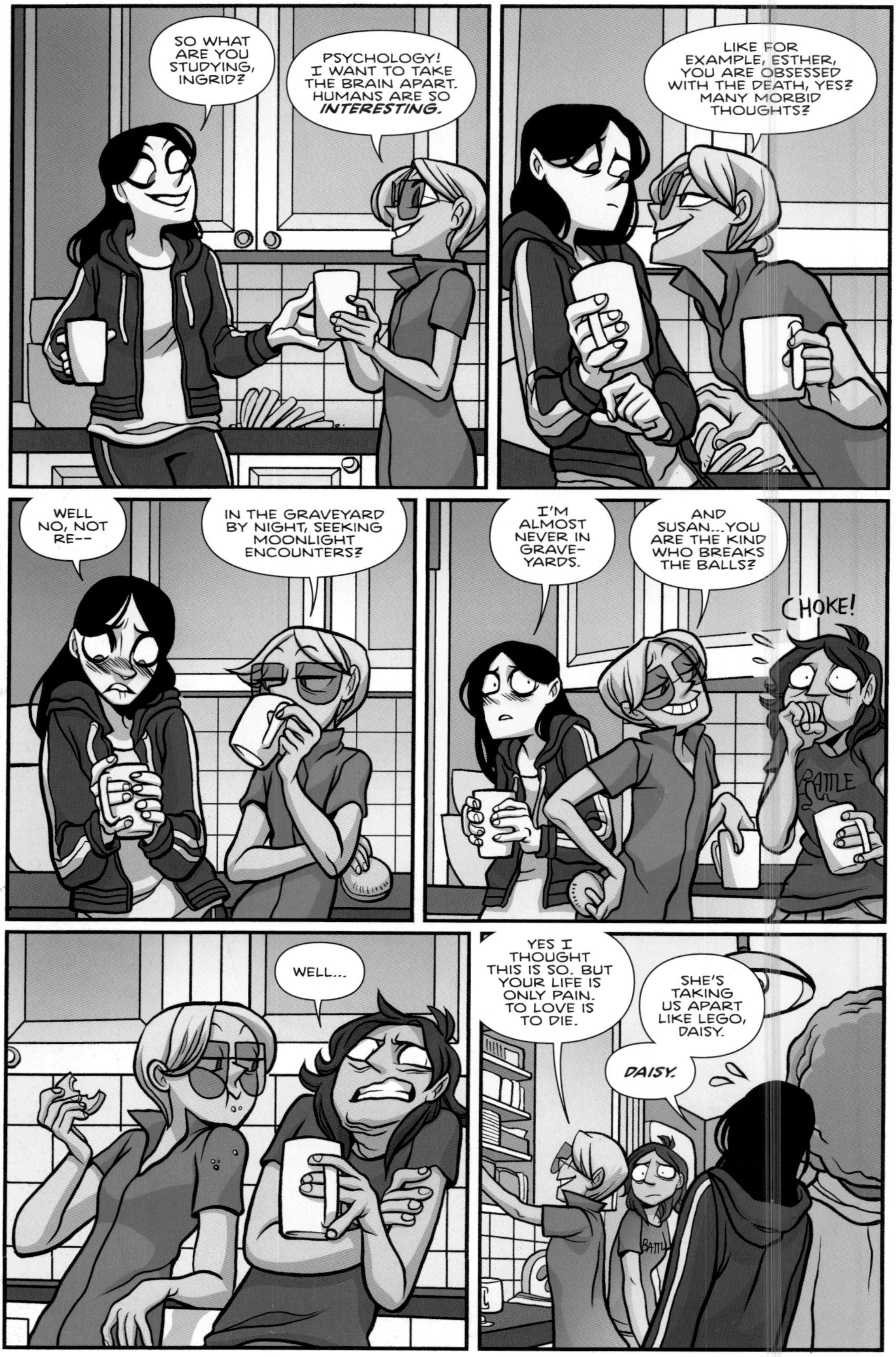
SO WHAT ARE YOU STUDYING, INGRID?
PSYCHOLOGY! I WANT TO TAKE THE BRAIN APART. HUMANS ARE SO INTERESTING.
LIKE FOR EXAMPLE, ESTHER, YOU ARE OBSESSED WITH THE DEATH, YES? MANY MORBID THOUGHTS?
WELL NO, NOT RE--
IN THE GRAVEYARD BY NIGHT, SEEKING MOONLIGHT ENCOUNTERS?
I'M ALMOST NEVER IN GRAVE-YARDS.
AND SUSAN...YOU ARE THE KIND WHO BREAKS THE BALLS?
CHOKE!
RATTLE
WELL...
YES I THOUGHT THIS IS SO. BUT YOUR LIFE IS ONLY PAIN. TO LOVE IS TO DIE.
SHE'S TAKING US APART LIKE LEGO, DAISY.
DAISY.

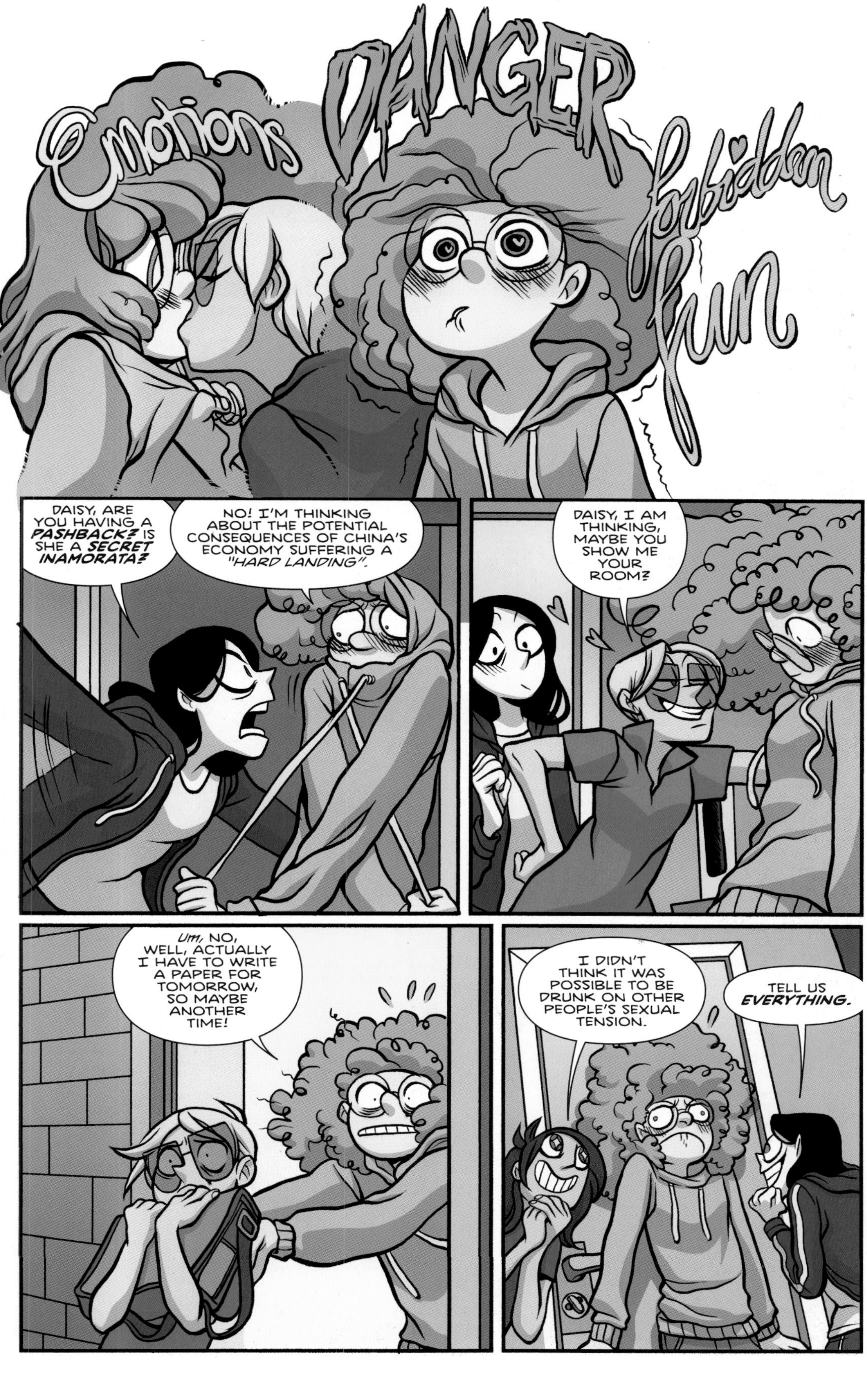

Emotions
DANGER
forbidden fun
DAISY, ARE YOU HAVING A PASHBACK? IS SHE A SECRET INAMORATA?
NO! I'M THINKING ABOUT THE POTENTIAL CONSEQUENCES OF CHINA'S ECONOMY SUFFERING A "HARD LANDING".
DAISY, I AM THINKING, MAYBE YOU SHOW ME YOUR ROOM?
UM, NO, WELL, ACTUALLY I HAVE TO WRITE A PAPER FOR TOMORROW, SO MAYBE ANOTHER TIME!
I DIDN'T THINK IT WAS POSSIBLE TO BE DRUNK ON OTHER PEOPLE'S SEXUAL TENSION.
TELL US EVERYTHING.

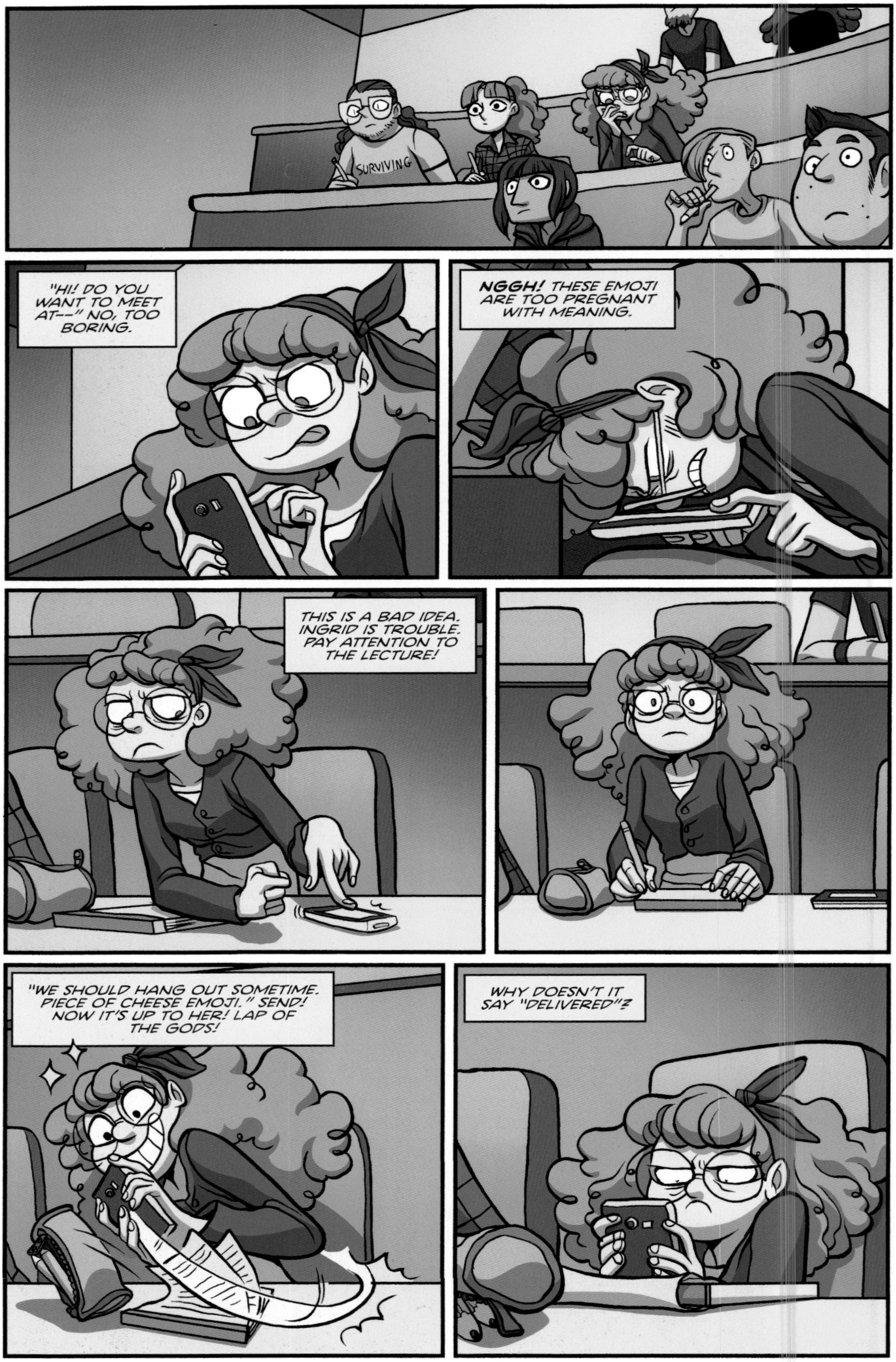
SURVIVING
"HI! DO YOU WANT TO MEET AT--" NO, TOO BORING.
NGGH! THESE EMOJI ARE TOO PREGNANT WITH MEANING.
THIS IS A BAD IDEA. INGRID IS TROUBLE. PAY ATTENTION TO THE LECTURE!
"WE SHOULD HANG OUT SOMETIME. PIECE OF CHEESE EMOJI." SEND! NOW IT'S UP TO HER! LAP OF THE GODS!
WHY DOESN'T IT SAY "DELIVERED"?

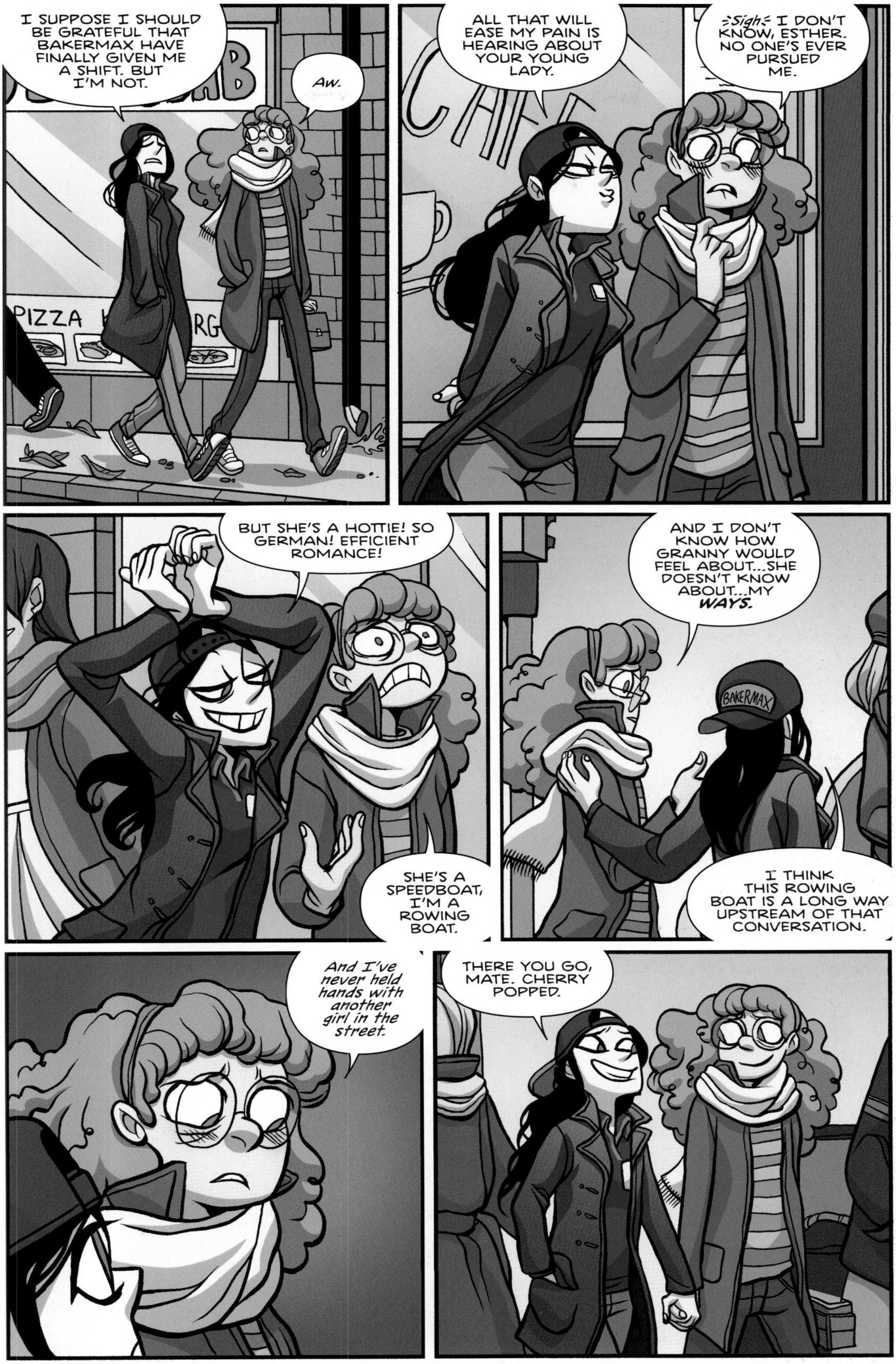

I SUPPOSE I SHOULD BE GRATEFUL THAT BAKERMAX HAVE FINALLY GIVEN ME A SHIFT. BUT I'M NOT.
Aw.
PIZZA
ALL THAT WILL EASE MY PAIN IS HEARING ABOUT YOUR YOUNG LADY.
-Sigh- I DON'T KNOW, ESTHER. NO ONE'S EVER PURSUED ME.
BUT SHE'S A HOTTIE! SO GERMAN! EFFICIENT ROMANCE!
SHE'S A SPEEDBOAT, I'M A ROWING BOAT.
AND I DON'T KNOW HOW GRANNY WOULD FEEL ABOUT...SHE DOESN'T KNOW ABOUT...MY ***WAYS.***
BAKERMAX
I THINK THIS ROWING BOAT IS A LONG WAY UPSTREAM OF THAT CONVERSATION.
And I've never held hands with another girl in the street.
THERE YOU GO, MATE. CHERRY POPPED.

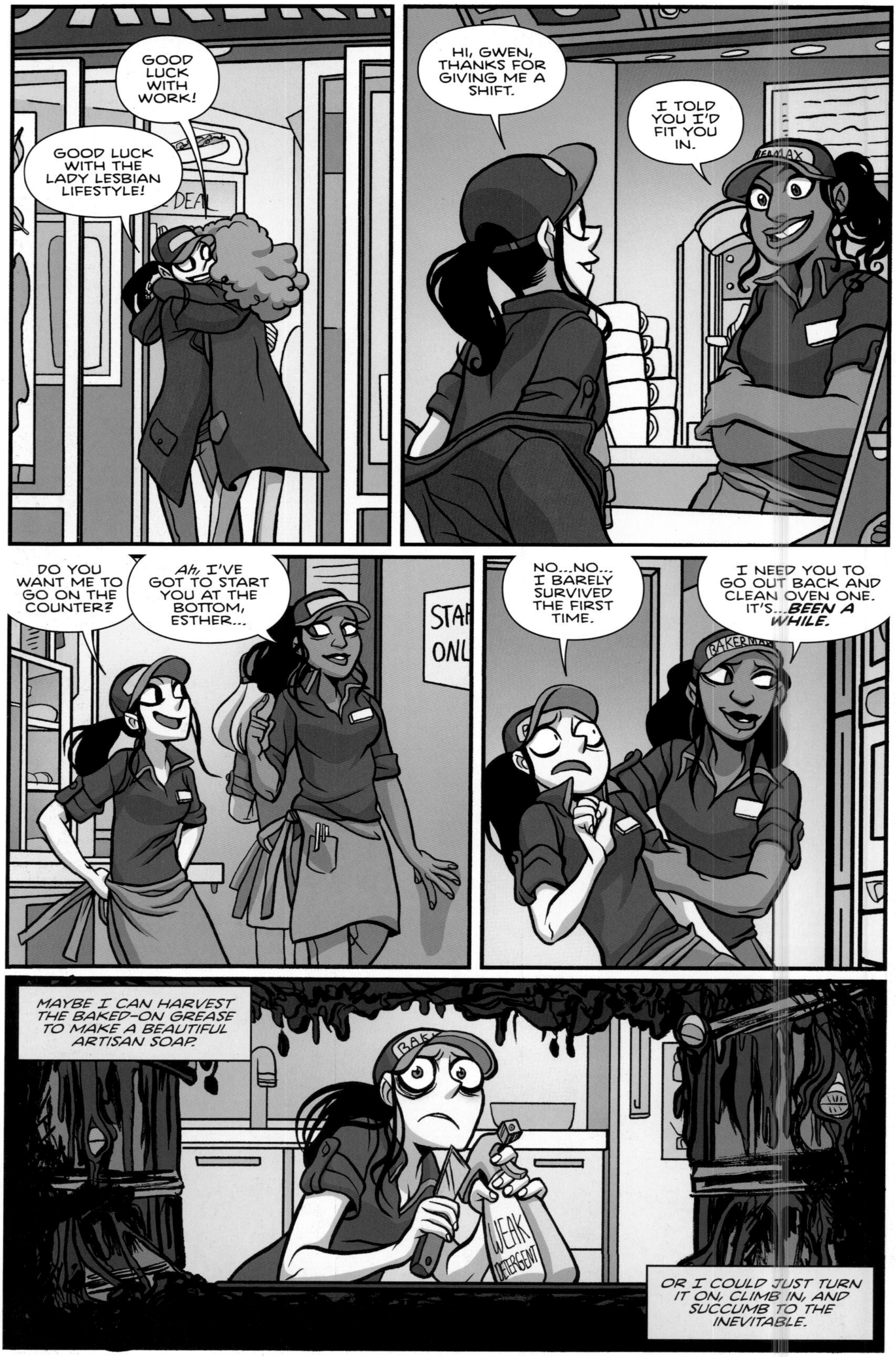
GOOD LUCK WITH WORK!
GOOD LUCK WITH THE LADY LESBIAN LIFESTYLE!
HI, GWEN, THANKS FOR GIVING ME A SHIFT.
I TOLD YOU I'D FIT YOU IN.
DO YOU WANT ME TO GO ON THE COUNTER?
Ah, I'VE GOT TO START YOU AT THE BOTTOM, ESTHER...
NO...NO... I BARELY SURVIVED THE FIRST TIME.
I NEED YOU TO GO OUT BACK AND CLEAN OVEN ONE. IT'S...***BEEN A WHILE.***
MAYBE I CAN HARVEST THE BAKED-ON GREASE TO MAKE A BEAUTIFUL ARTISAN SOAP.
WEAK DETERGENT
OR I COULD JUST TURN IT ON, CLIMB IN, AND SUCCUMB TO THE INEVITABLE.

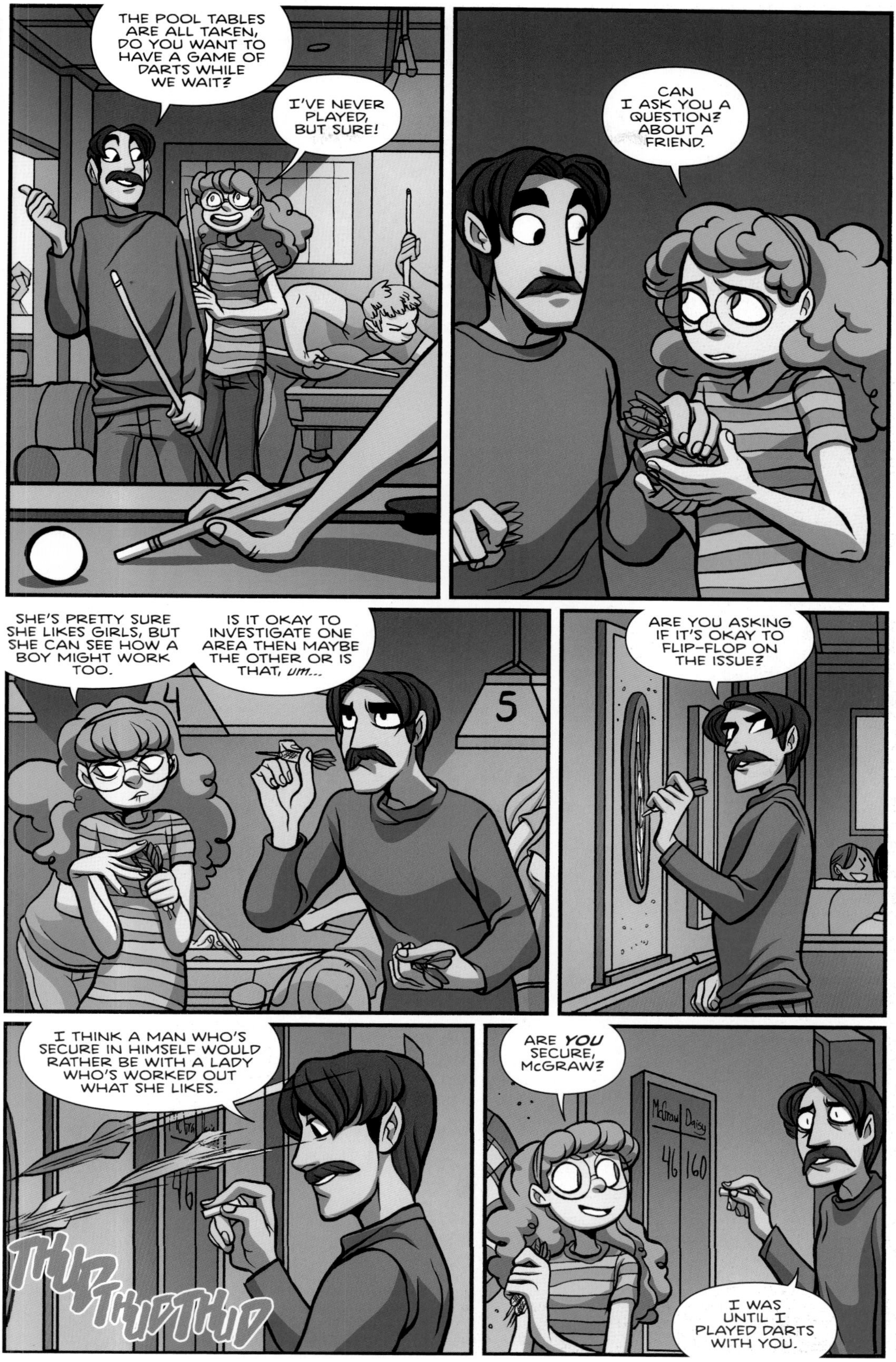
THE POOL TABLES ARE ALL TAKEN, DO YOU WANT TO HAVE A GAME OF DARTS WHILE WE WAIT?
I'VE NEVER PLAYED, BUT SURE!
CAN I ASK YOU A QUESTION? ABOUT A FRIEND.
SHE'S PRETTY SURE SHE LIKES GIRLS, BUT SHE CAN SEE HOW A BOY MIGHT WORK TOO.
IS IT OKAY TO INVESTIGATE ONE AREA THEN MAYBE THE OTHER OR IS THAT, *UM...*
5
ARE YOU ASKING IF IT'S OKAY TO FLIP-FLOP ON THE ISSUE?
I THINK A MAN WHO'S SECURE IN HIMSELF WOULD RATHER BE WITH A LADY WHO'S WORKED OUT WHAT SHE LIKES.
THUD THUD THUD
ARE ***YOU*** SECURE, McGRAW?
McGraw Daisy
46 160
I WAS UNTIL I PLAYED DARTS WITH YOU.

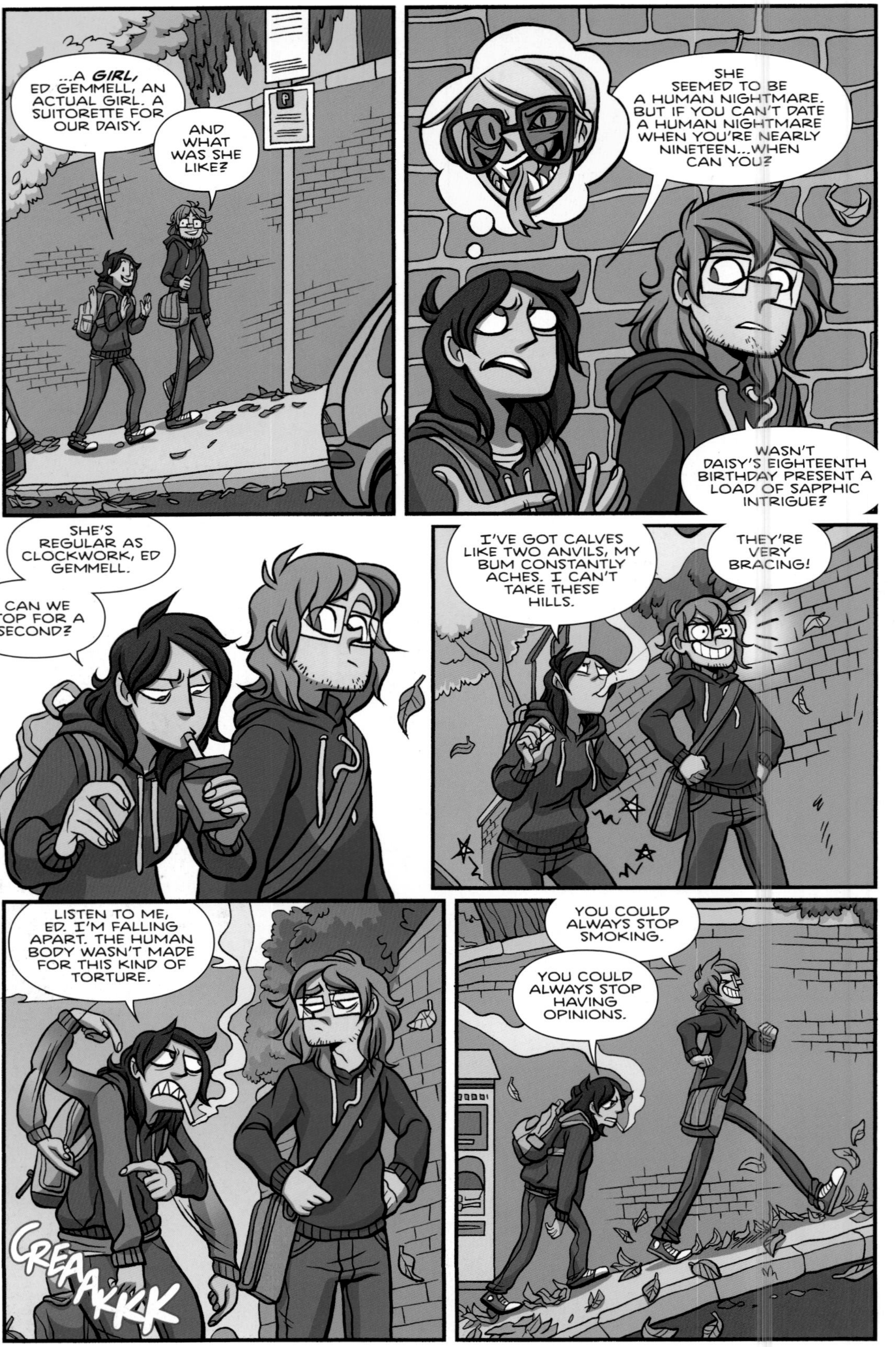
...A GIRL, ED GEMMELL, AN ACTUAL GIRL. A SUITORETTE FOR OUR DAISY.
AND WHAT WAS SHE LIKE?
SHE SEEMED TO BE A HUMAN NIGHTMARE. BUT IF YOU CAN'T DATE A HUMAN NIGHTMARE WHEN YOU'RE NEARLY NINETEEN...WHEN CAN YOU?
WASN'T DAISY'S EIGHTEENTH BIRTHDAY PRESENT A LOAD OF SAPPHIC INTRIGUE?
SHE'S REGULAR AS CLOCKWORK, ED GEMMELL.
CAN WE STOP FOR A SECOND?
I'VE GOT CALVES LIKE TWO ANVILS, MY BUM CONSTANTLY ACHES. I CAN'T TAKE THESE HILLS.
THEY'RE VERY BRACING!
LISTEN TO ME, ED. I'M FALLING APART. THE HUMAN BODY WASN'T MADE FOR THIS KIND OF TORTURE.
CREAAKKK
YOU COULD ALWAYS STOP SMOKING.
YOU COULD ALWAYS STOP HAVING OPINIONS.

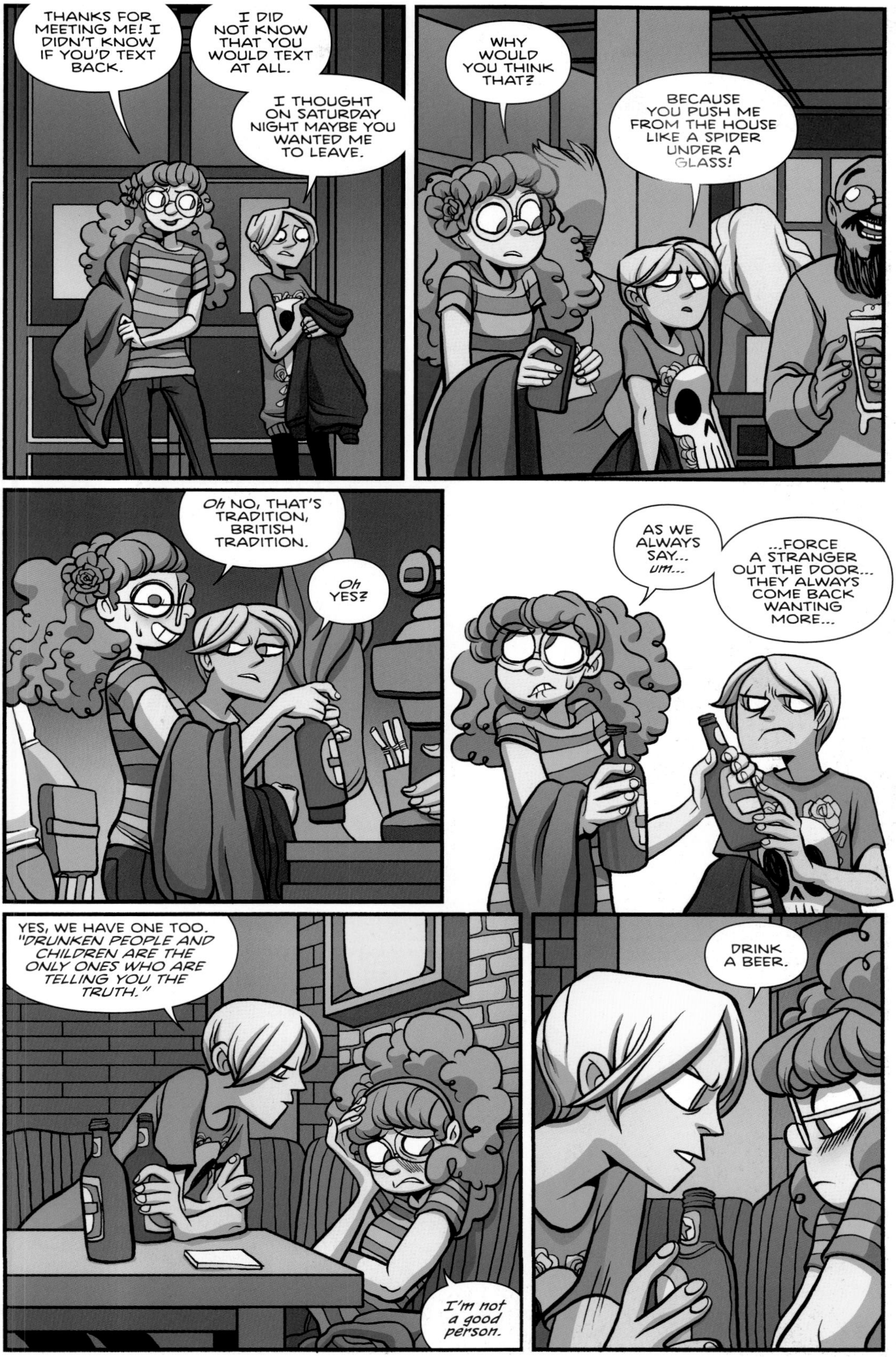
THANKS FOR MEETING ME! I DIDN'T KNOW IF YOU'D TEXT BACK.
I DID NOT KNOW THAT YOU WOULD TEXT AT ALL.
I THOUGHT ON SATURDAY NIGHT MAYBE YOU WANTED ME TO LEAVE.
WHY WOULD YOU THINK THAT?
BECAUSE YOU PUSH ME FROM THE HOUSE LIKE A SPIDER UNDER A GLASS!
Oh NO, THAT'S TRADITION, BRITISH TRADITION.
Oh YES?
AS WE ALWAYS SAY... *um...*
...FORCE A STRANGER OUT THE DOOR... THEY ALWAYS COME BACK WANTING MORE...
YES, WE HAVE ONE TOO. *"DRUNKEN PEOPLE AND CHILDREN ARE THE ONLY ONES WHO ARE TELLING YOU THE TRUTH."*
I'm not a good person.
DRINK A BEER.

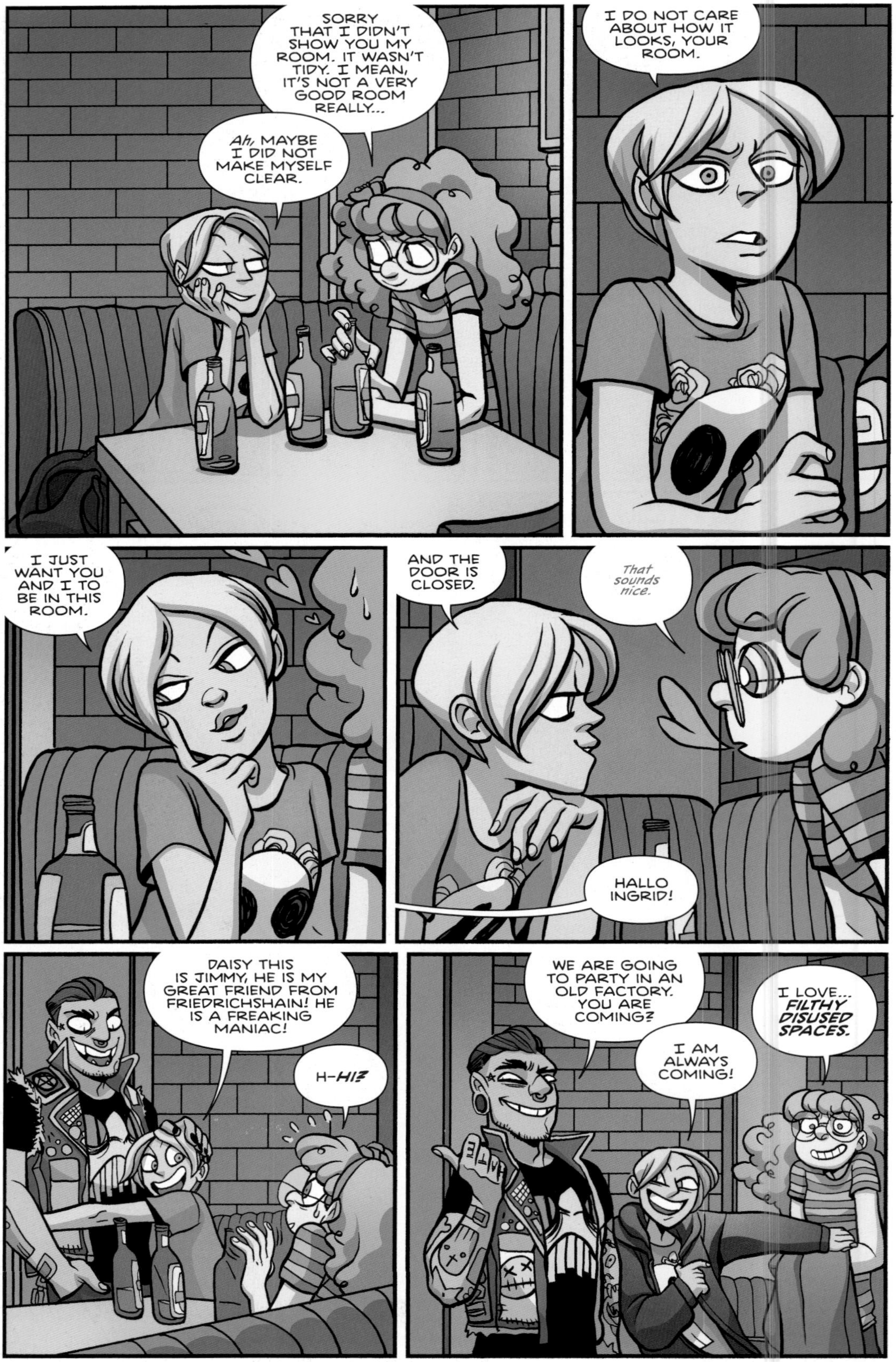
SORRY THAT I DIDN'T SHOW YOU MY ROOM. IT WASN'T TIDY. I MEAN, IT'S NOT A VERY GOOD ROOM REALLY...
Ah, MAYBE I DID NOT MAKE MYSELF CLEAR.
I DO NOT CARE ABOUT HOW IT LOOKS, YOUR ROOM.
I JUST WANT YOU AND I TO BE IN THIS ROOM.
AND THE DOOR IS CLOSED.
That sounds nice.
HALLO INGRID!
DAISY THIS IS JIMMY, HE IS MY GREAT FRIEND FROM FRIEDRICHSHAIN! HE IS A FREAKING MANIAC!
H-*HI?*
WE ARE GOING TO PARTY IN AN OLD FACTORY. YOU ARE COMING?
I AM ALWAYS COMING!
I LOVE... ***FILTHY DISUSED SPACES.***

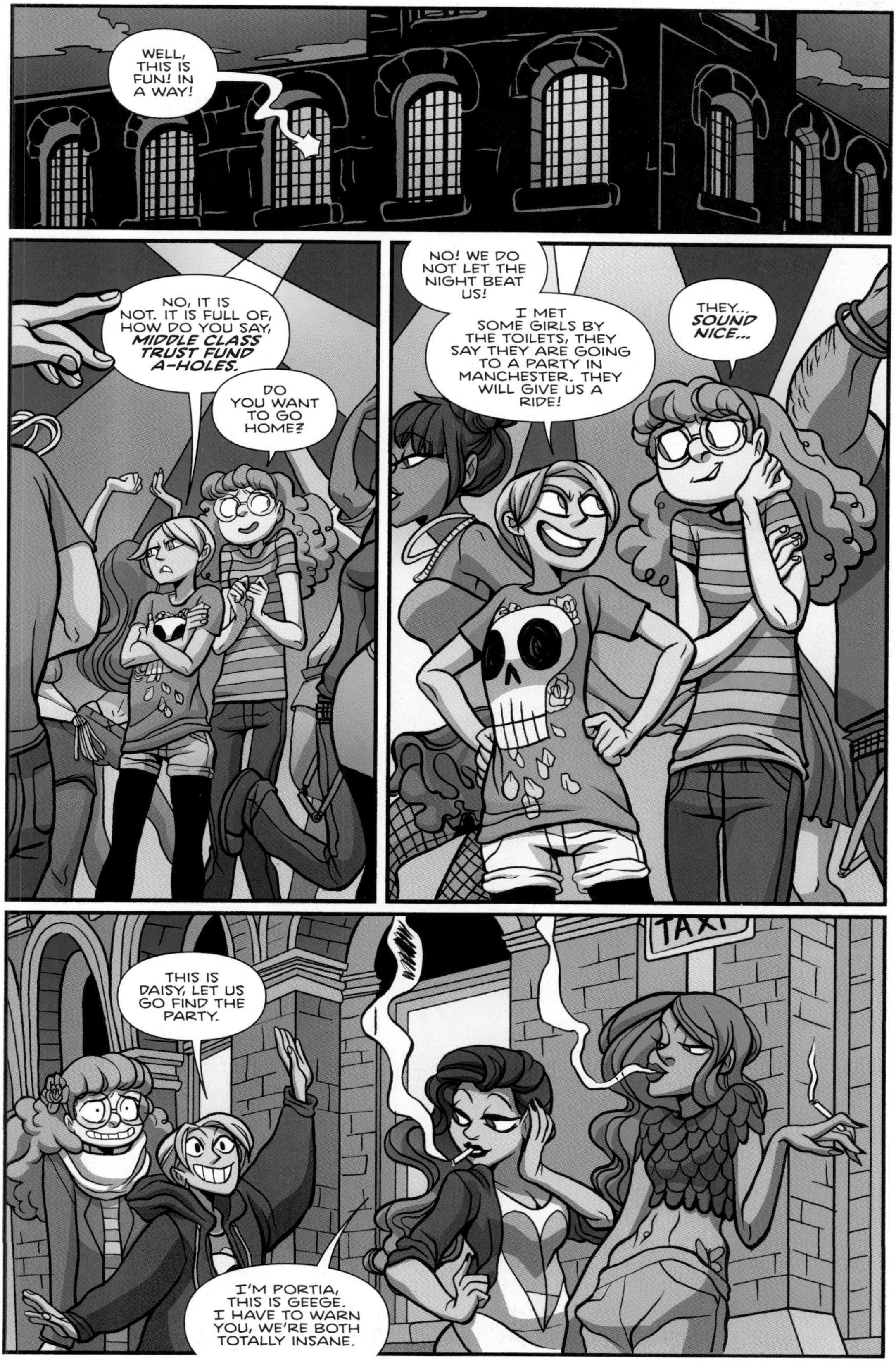
WELL, THIS IS FUN! IN A WAY!
NO, IT IS NOT. IT IS FULL OF, HOW DO YOU SAY, *MIDDLE CLASS TRUST FUND A-HOLES.*
DO YOU WANT TO GO HOME?
NO! WE DO NOT LET THE NIGHT BEAT US!
I MET SOME GIRLS BY THE TOILETS, THEY SAY THEY ARE GOING TO A PARTY IN MANCHESTER. THEY WILL GIVE US A RIDE!
THEY... *SOUND NICE...*
TAXI
THIS IS DAISY, LET US GO FIND THE PARTY.
I'M PORTIA, THIS IS GEEGE. I HAVE TO WARN YOU, WE'RE BOTH TOTALLY INSANE.

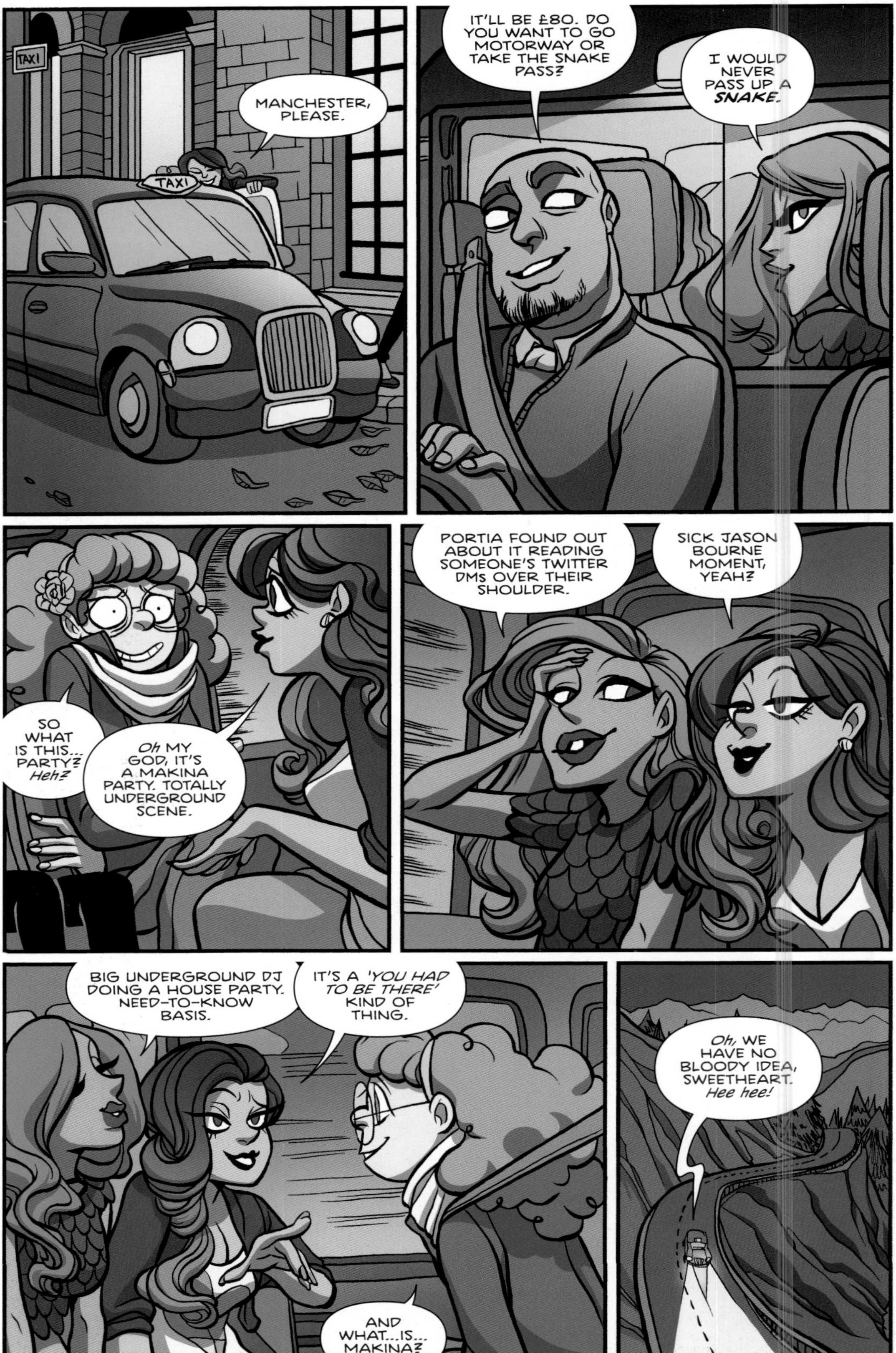
TAXI
TAXI
MANCHESTER, PLEASE.
IT'LL BE £80. DO YOU WANT TO GO MOTORWAY OR TAKE THE SNAKE PASS?
I WOULD NEVER PASS UP A *SNAKE*.
SO WHAT IS THIS... PARTY? *Heh?*
Oh MY GOD, IT'S A MAKINA PARTY. TOTALLY UNDERGROUND SCENE.
PORTIA FOUND OUT ABOUT IT READING SOMEONE'S TWITTER DMs OVER THEIR SHOULDER.
SICK JASON BOURNE MOMENT, YEAH?
BIG UNDERGROUND DJ DOING A HOUSE PARTY. NEED-TO-KNOW BASIS.
IT'S A *'YOU HAD TO BE THERE'* KIND OF THING.
AND WHAT...IS... MAKINA?
Oh, WE HAVE NO BLOODY IDEA, SWEETHEART. *Hee hee!*

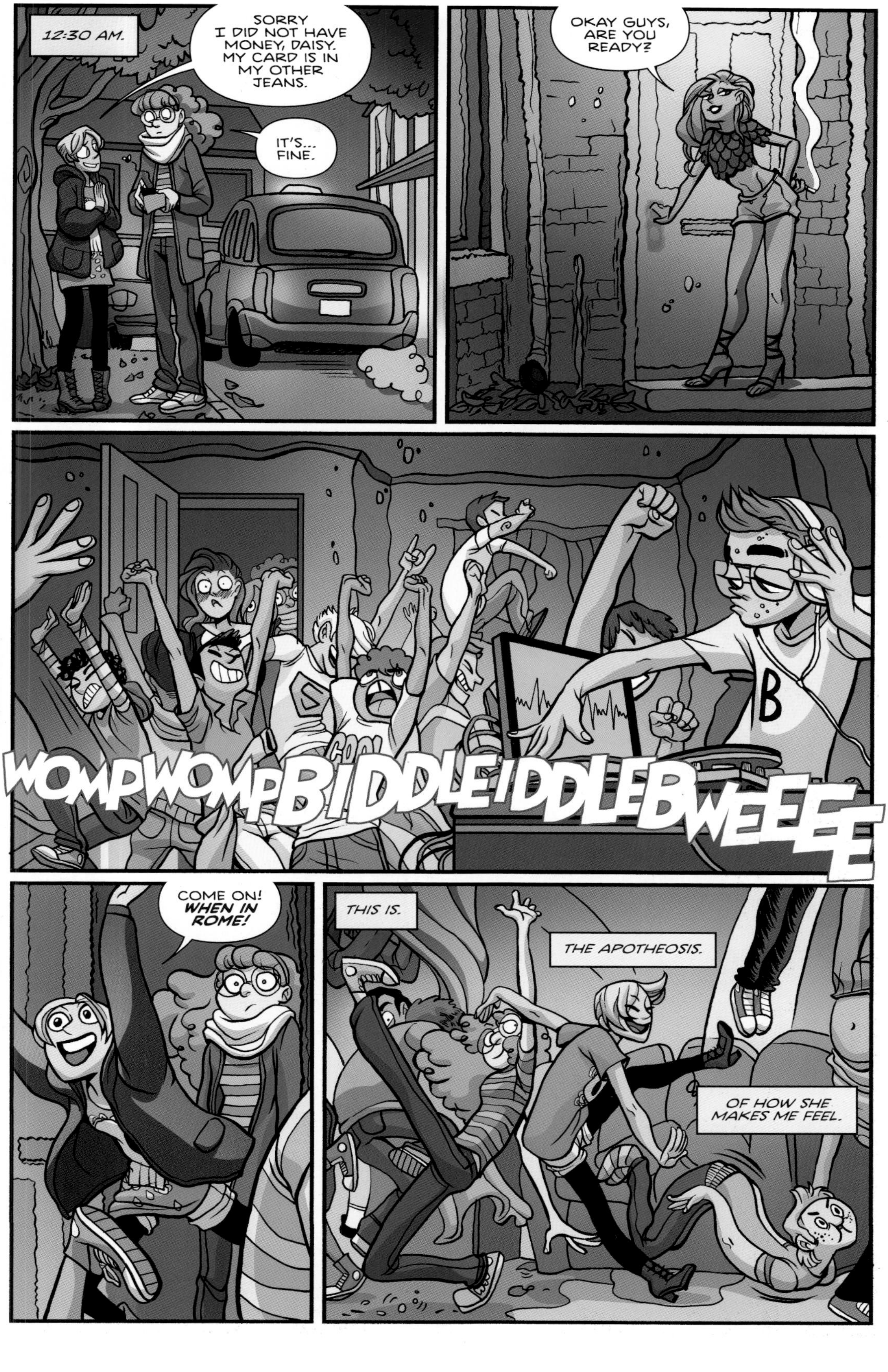
12:30 AM.
SORRY I DID NOT HAVE MONEY, DAISY. MY CARD IS IN MY OTHER JEANS.
IT'S... FINE.
OKAY GUYS, ARE YOU READY?
WOMPWOMPBIDDLEIDDLEBWEEEEE
COME ON! WHEN IN ROME!
THIS IS.
THE APOTHEOSIS.
OF HOW SHE MAKES ME FEEL.

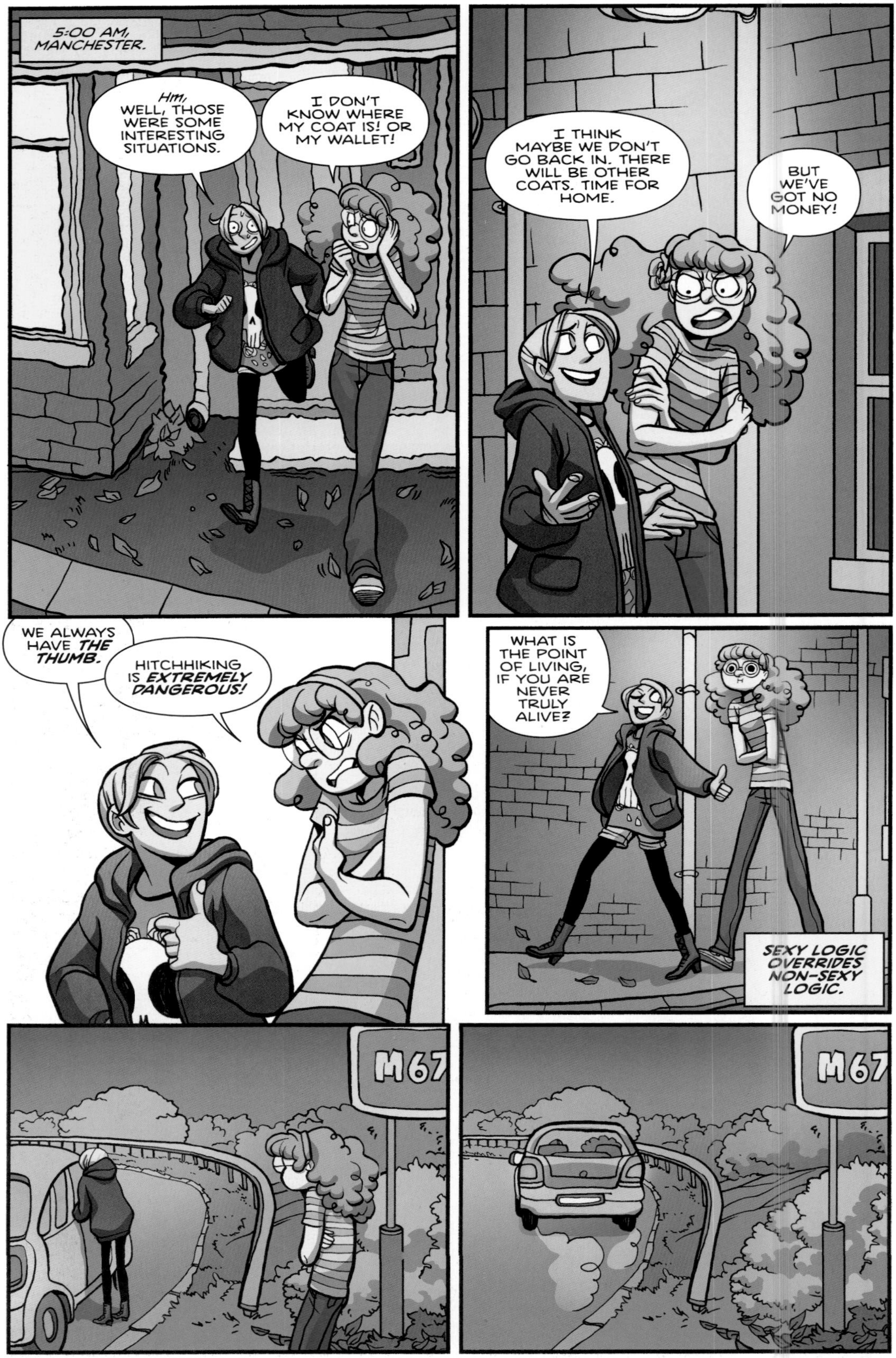
5:00 AM, MANCHESTER.
Hm, WELL, THOSE WERE SOME INTERESTING SITUATIONS.
I DON'T KNOW WHERE MY COAT IS! OR MY WALLET!
I THINK MAYBE WE DON'T GO BACK IN. THERE WILL BE OTHER COATS. TIME FOR HOME.
BUT WE'VE GOT NO MONEY!
WE ALWAYS HAVE ***THE THUMB.***
HITCHHIKING IS ***EXTREMELY DANGEROUS!***
WHAT IS THE POINT OF LIVING, IF YOU ARE NEVER TRULY ALIVE?
SEXY LOGIC OVERRIDES NON-SEXY LOGIC.
M67
M67

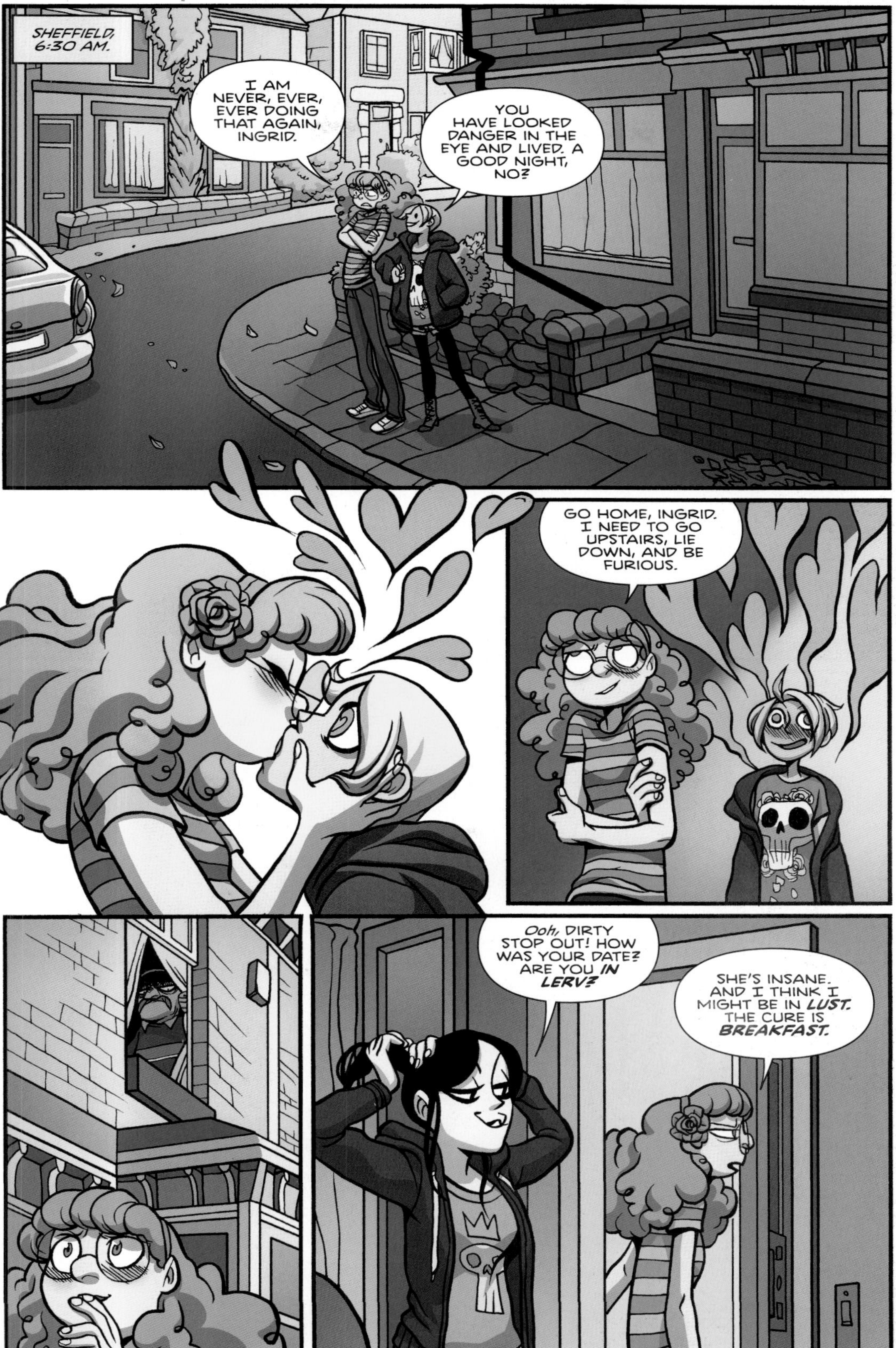
SHEFFIELD, 6:30 AM.
I AM NEVER, EVER, EVER DOING THAT AGAIN, INGRID.
YOU HAVE LOOKED DANGER IN THE EYE AND LIVED. A GOOD NIGHT, NO?
GO HOME, INGRID. I NEED TO GO UPSTAIRS, LIE DOWN, AND BE FURIOUS.
Ooh, DIRTY STOP OUT! HOW WAS YOUR DATE? ARE YOU ***IN LERV?***
SHE'S INSANE. AND I THINK I MIGHT BE IN ***LUST.*** THE CURE IS ***BREAKFAST.***

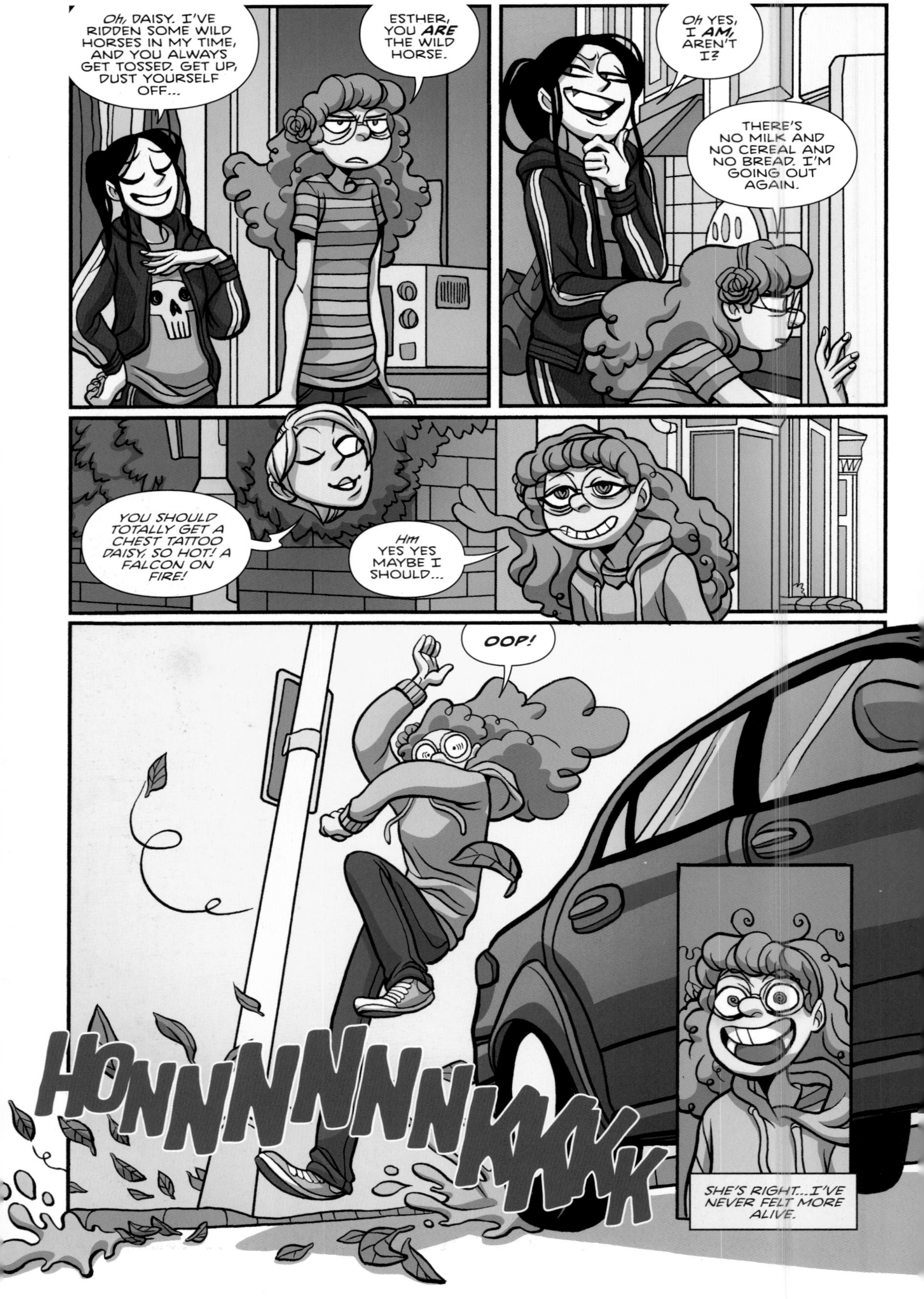
Oh, DAISY. I'VE RIDDEN SOME WILD HORSES IN MY TIME, AND YOU ALWAYS GET TOSSED. GET UP, DUST YOURSELF OFF...
ESTHER, YOU ARE THE WILD HORSE.
Oh YES, I AM, AREN'T I?
THERE'S NO MILK AND NO CEREAL AND NO BREAD. I'M GOING OUT AGAIN.
YOU SHOULD TOTALLY GET A CHEST TATTOO DAISY, SO HOT! A FALCON ON FIRE!
Hm YES YES MAYBE I SHOULD...
OOP!
HONNNNNNNKKKKK
SHE'S RIGHT...I'VE NEVER FELT MORE ALIVE.

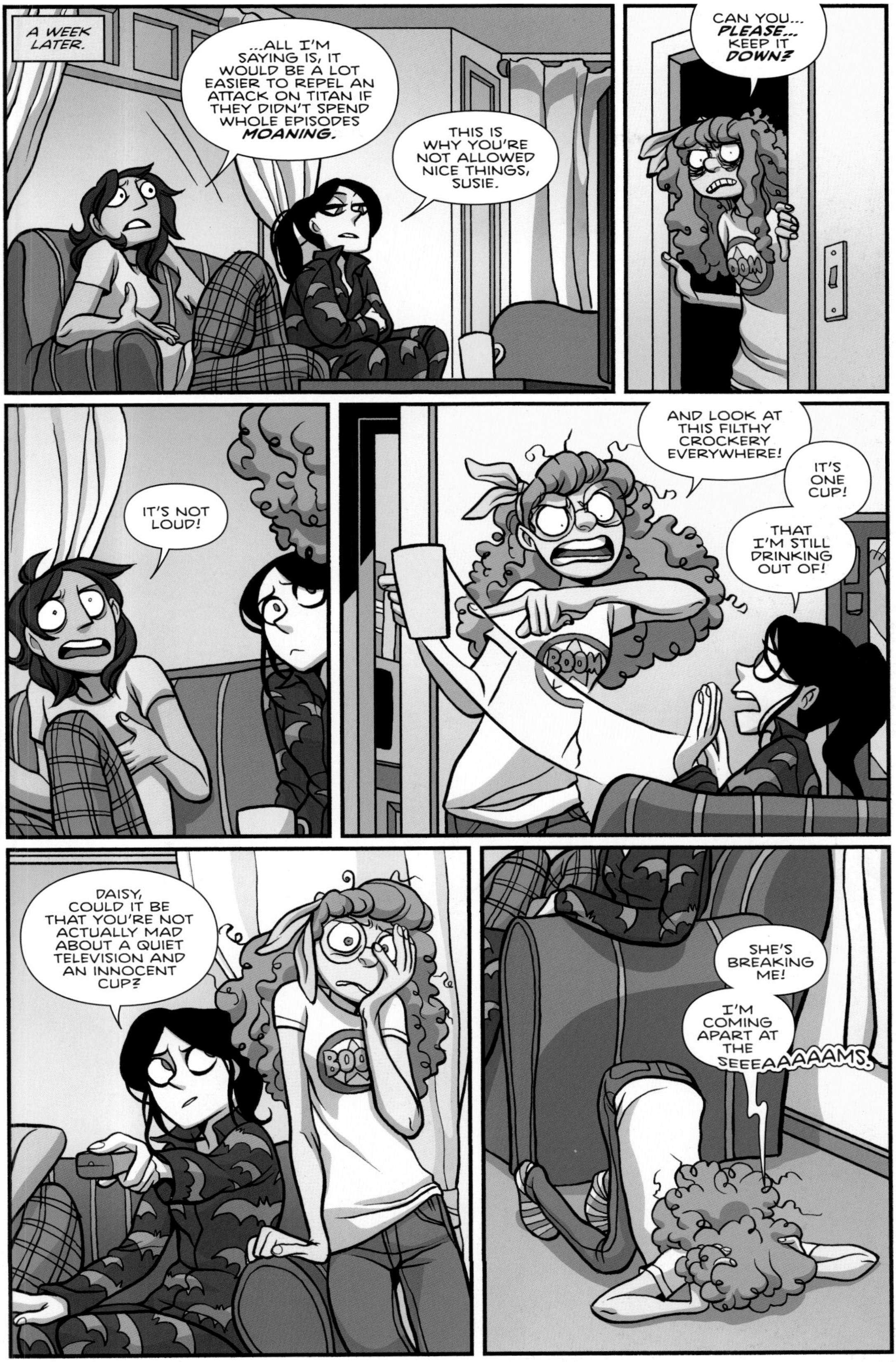
A WEEK LATER.
...ALL I'M SAYING IS, IT WOULD BE A LOT EASIER TO REPEL AN ATTACK ON TITAN IF THEY DIDN'T SPEND WHOLE EPISODES MOANING.
THIS IS WHY YOU'RE NOT ALLOWED NICE THINGS, SUSIE.
CAN YOU... PLEASE... KEEP IT DOWN?
IT'S NOT LOUD!
AND LOOK AT THIS FILTHY CROCKERY EVERYWHERE!
IT'S ONE CUP!
THAT I'M STILL DRINKING OUT OF!
DAISY, COULD IT BE THAT YOU'RE NOT ACTUALLY MAD ABOUT A QUIET TELEVISION AND AN INNOCENT CUP?
SHE'S BREAKING ME!
I'M COMING APART AT THE SEEEAAAAAMS.

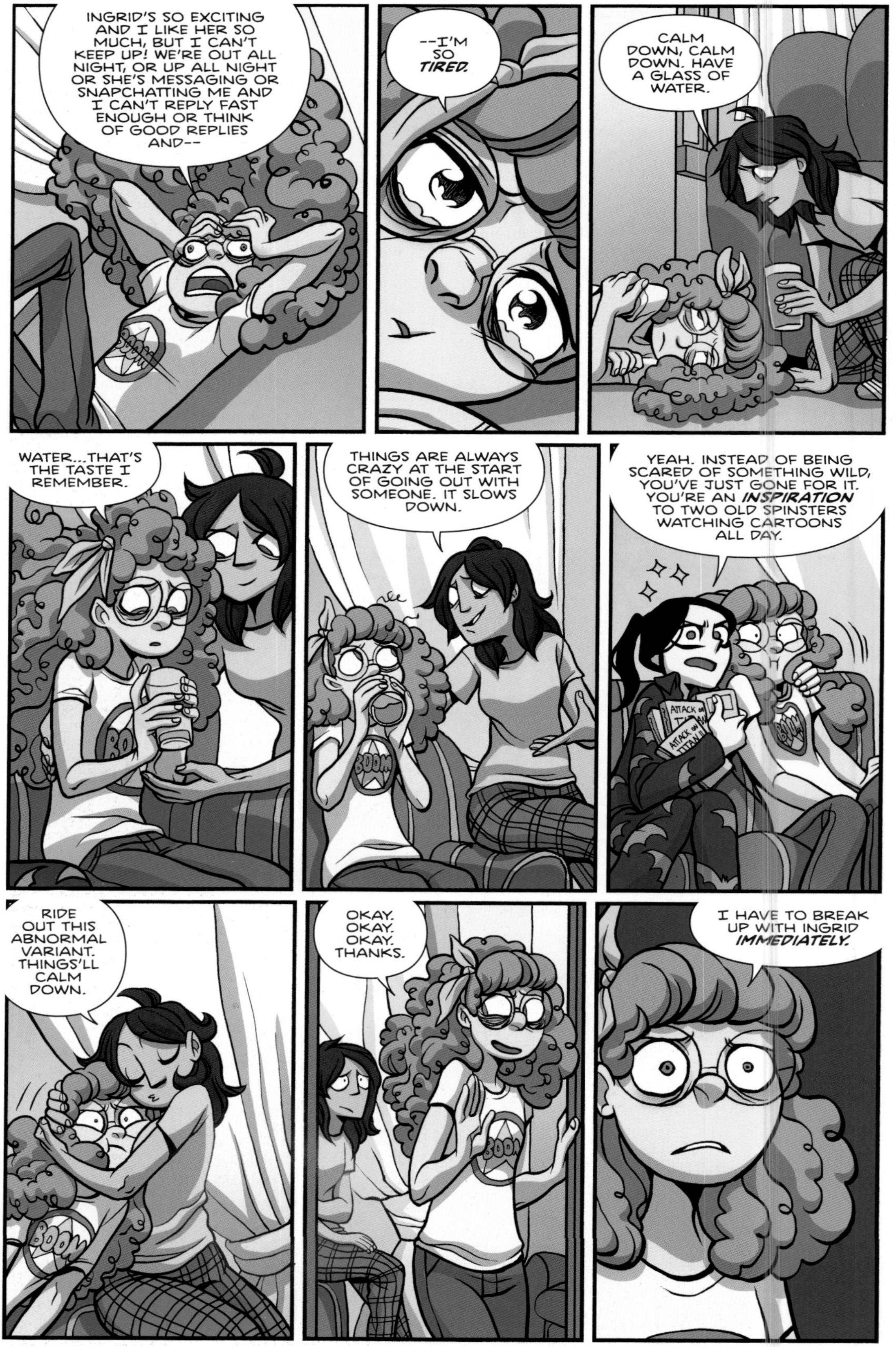
INGRID'S SO EXCITING AND I LIKE HER SO MUCH, BUT I CAN'T KEEP UP! WE'RE OUT ALL NIGHT, OR UP ALL NIGHT OR SHE'S MESSAGING OR SNAPCHATTING ME AND I CAN'T REPLY FAST ENOUGH OR THINK OF GOOD REPLIES AND--
--I'M SO *TIRED.*
CALM DOWN, CALM DOWN. HAVE A GLASS OF WATER.
WATER...THAT'S THE TASTE I REMEMBER.
THINGS ARE ALWAYS CRAZY AT THE START OF GOING OUT WITH SOMEONE. IT SLOWS DOWN.
YEAH. INSTEAD OF BEING SCARED OF SOMETHING WILD, YOU'VE JUST GONE FOR IT. YOU'RE AN *INSPIRATION* TO TWO OLD SPINSTERS WATCHING CARTOONS ALL DAY.
RIDE OUT THIS ABNORMAL VARIANT. THINGS'LL CALM DOWN.
OKAY. OKAY. OKAY. THANKS.
I HAVE TO BREAK UP WITH INGRID *IMMEDIATELY.*

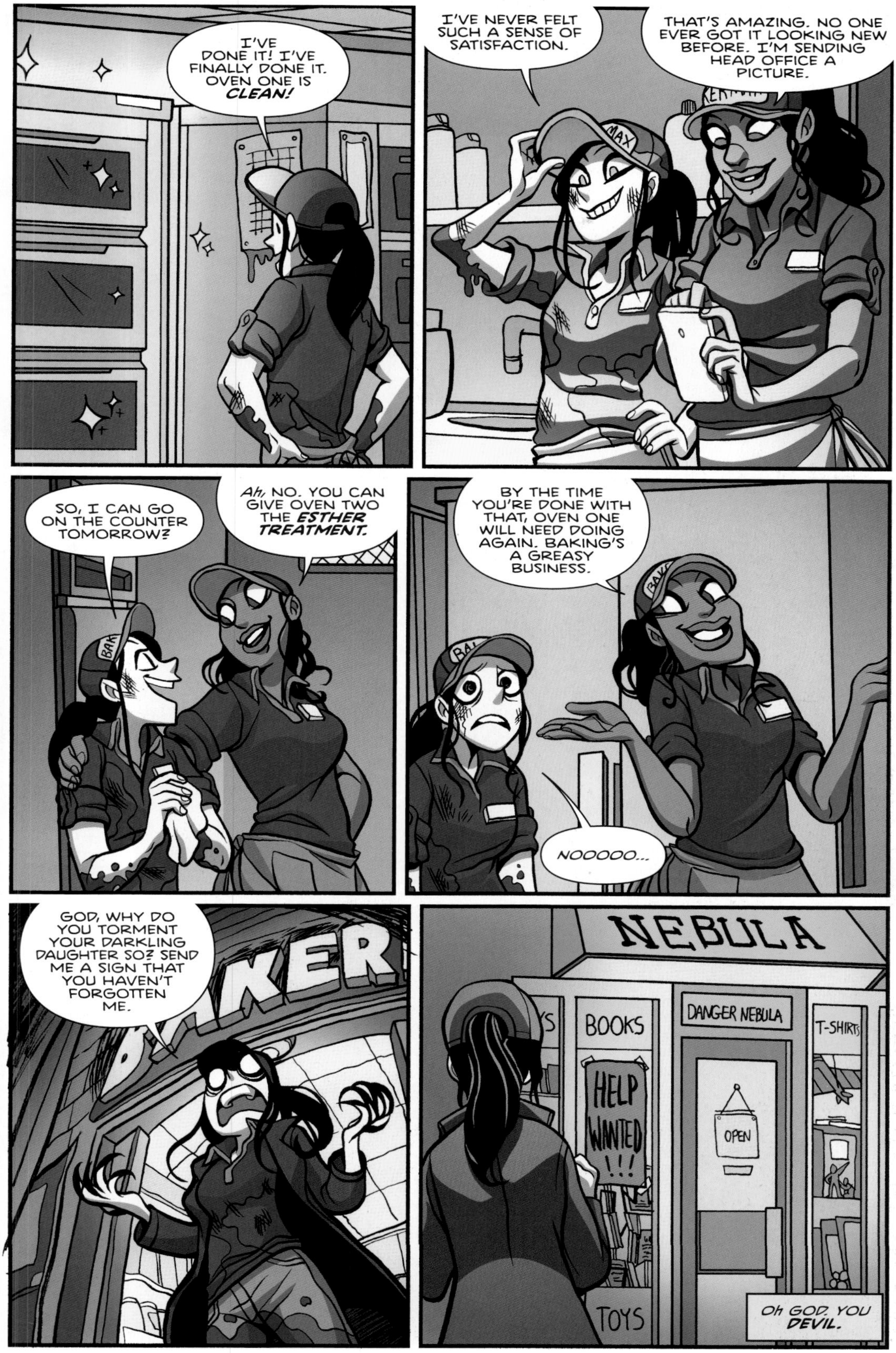
I'VE DONE IT! I'VE FINALLY DONE IT. OVEN ONE IS *CLEAN!*
I'VE NEVER FELT SUCH A SENSE OF SATISFACTION.
THAT'S AMAZING. NO ONE EVER GOT IT LOOKING NEW BEFORE. I'M SENDING HEAD OFFICE A PICTURE.
MAX
SO, I CAN GO ON THE COUNTER TOMORROW?
Ah, NO. YOU CAN GIVE OVEN TWO THE ***ESTHER TREATMENT.***
BY THE TIME YOU'RE DONE WITH THAT, OVEN ONE WILL NEED DOING AGAIN. BAKING'S A GREASY BUSINESS.
NOOOOO...
GOD, WHY DO YOU TORMENT YOUR DARKLING DAUGHTER SO? SEND ME A SIGN THAT YOU HAVEN'T FORGOTTEN ME.
NEBULA
BOOKS
DANGER NEBULA
T-SHIRTS
HELP WANTED !!!
OPEN
TOYS
Oh GOD. YOU ***DEVIL.***

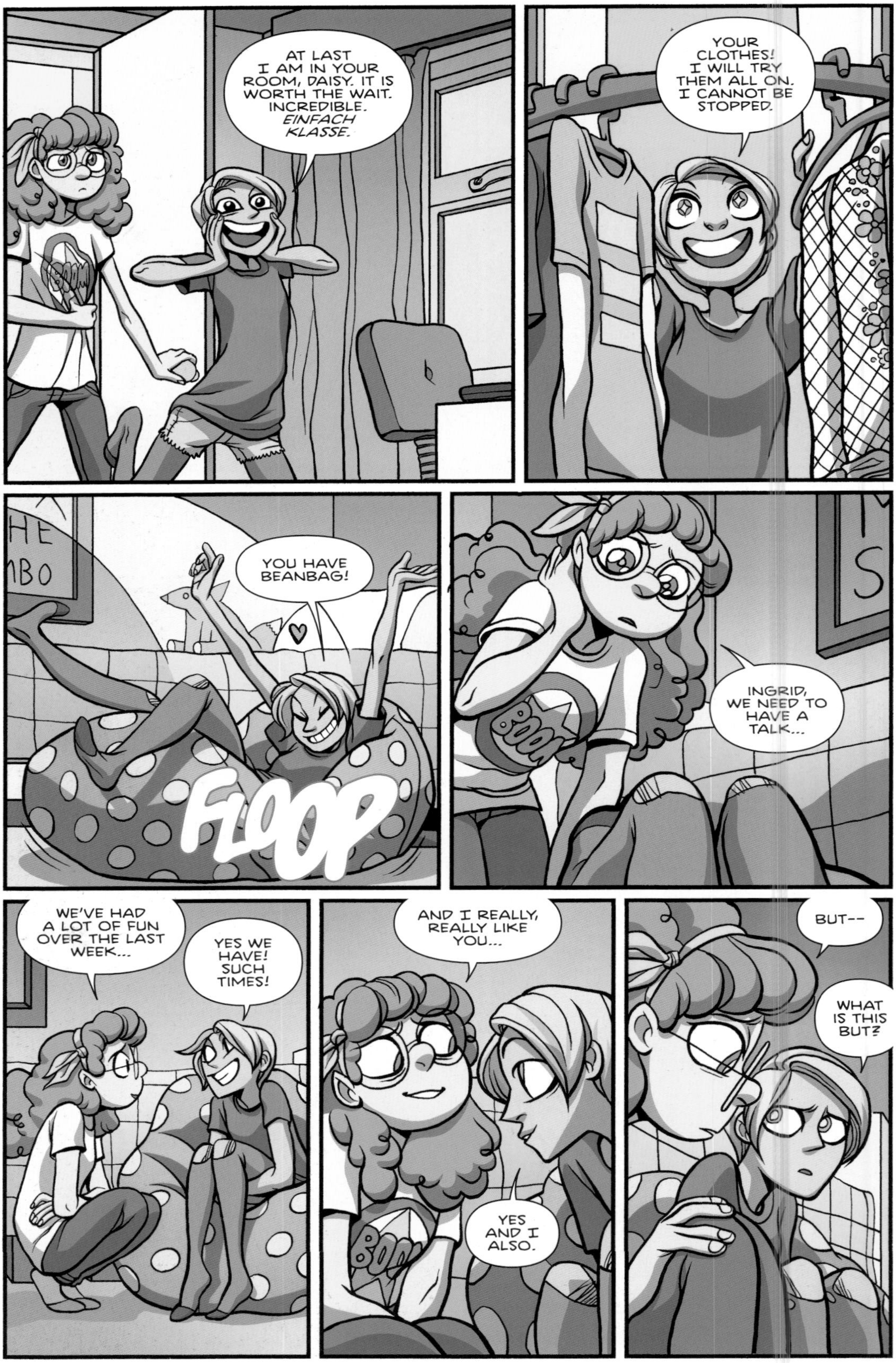
AT LAST I AM IN YOUR ROOM, DAISY. IT IS WORTH THE WAIT. INCREDIBLE. *EINFACH KLASSE.*
YOUR CLOTHES! I WILL TRY THEM ALL ON. I CANNOT BE STOPPED.
YOU HAVE BEANBAG!
FLOOP
INGRID, WE NEED TO HAVE A TALK...
WE'VE HAD A LOT OF FUN OVER THE LAST WEEK...
YES WE HAVE! SUCH TIMES!
AND I REALLY, REALLY LIKE YOU...
YES AND I ALSO.
BUT--
WHAT IS THIS BUT?

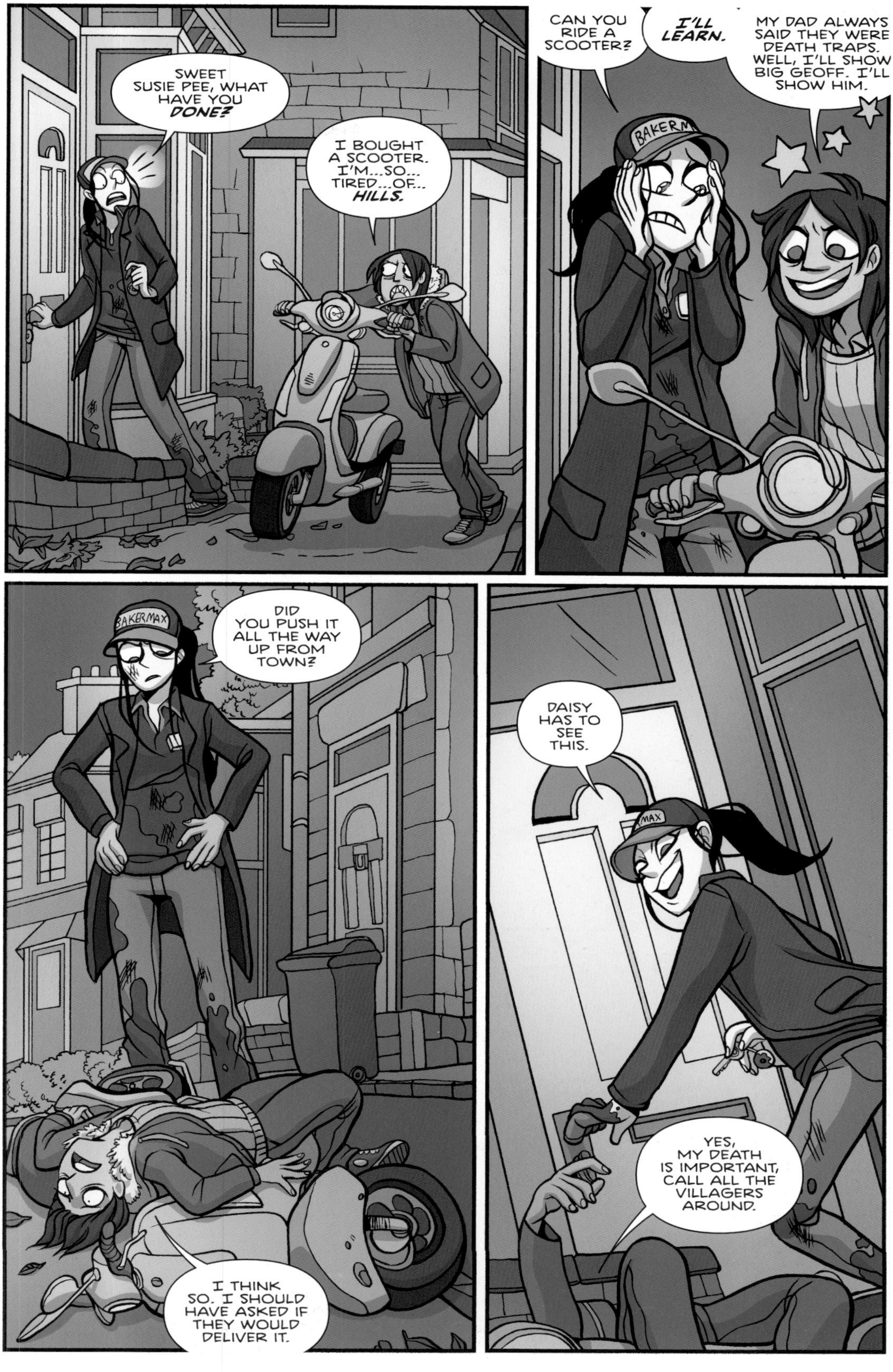
SWEET SUSIE PEE, WHAT HAVE YOU DONE?
I BOUGHT A SCOOTER. I'M... SO... TIRED... OF... HILLS.
CAN YOU RIDE A SCOOTER?
I'LL LEARN.
MY DAD ALWAYS SAID THEY WERE DEATH TRAPS. WELL, I'LL SHOW BIG GEOFF. I'LL SHOW HIM.
BAKERMAX
DID YOU PUSH IT ALL THE WAY UP FROM TOWN?
I THINK SO. I SHOULD HAVE ASKED IF THEY WOULD DELIVER IT.
DAISY HAS TO SEE THIS.
YES, MY DEATH IS IMPORTANT, CALL ALL THE VILLAGERS AROUND.

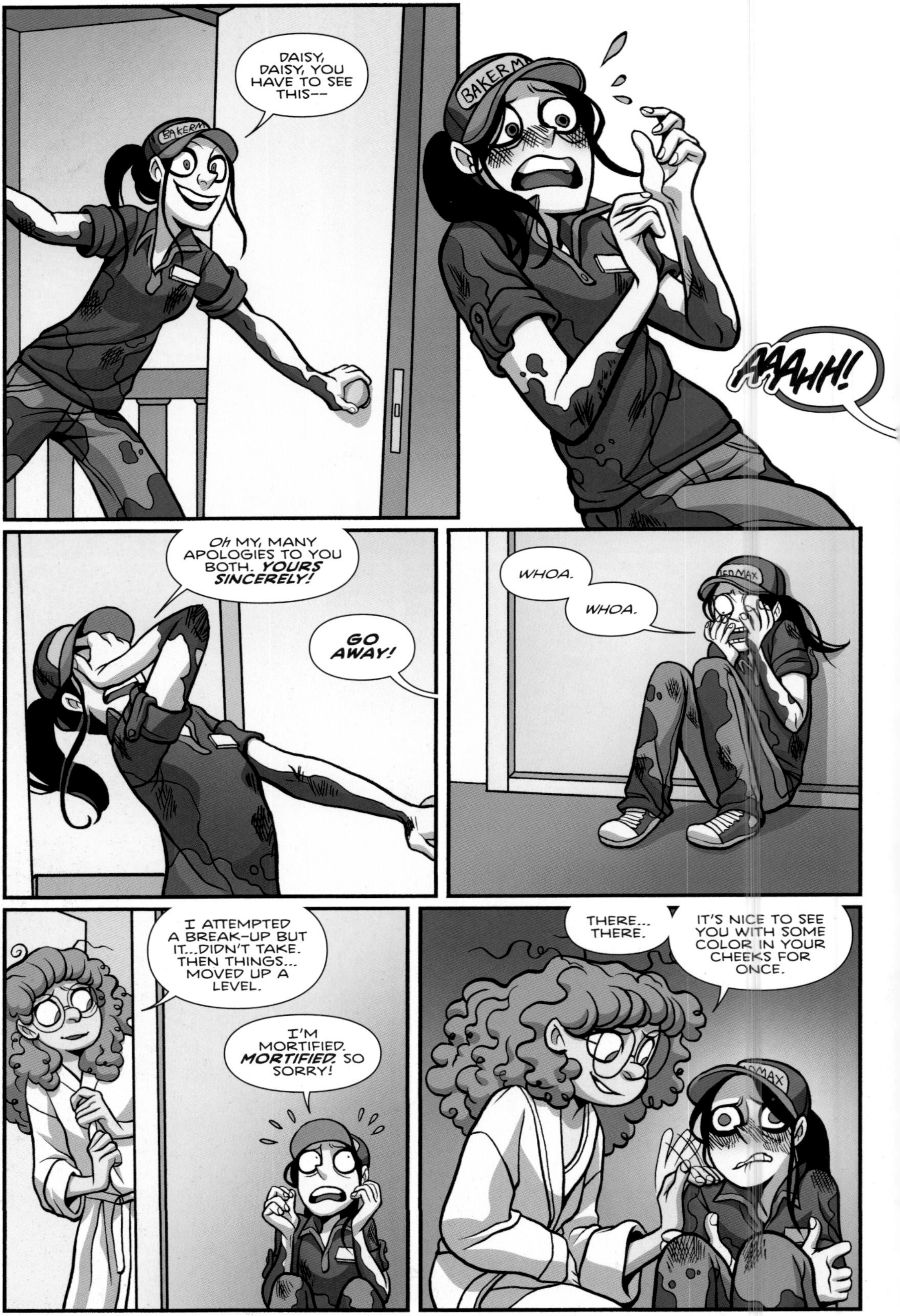
DAISY, DAISY, YOU HAVE TO SEE THIS--
BAKERM
AAAHH!
Oh MY, MANY APOLOGIES TO YOU BOTH. ***YOURS SINCERELY!***
GO AWAY!
WHOA.
WHOA.
I ATTEMPTED A BREAK-UP BUT IT...DIDN'T TAKE. THEN THINGS... MOVED UP A LEVEL.
I'M MORTIFIED. ***MORTIFIED.*** SO SORRY!
THERE... THERE.
IT'S NICE TO SEE YOU WITH SOME COLOR IN YOUR CHEEKS FOR ONCE.

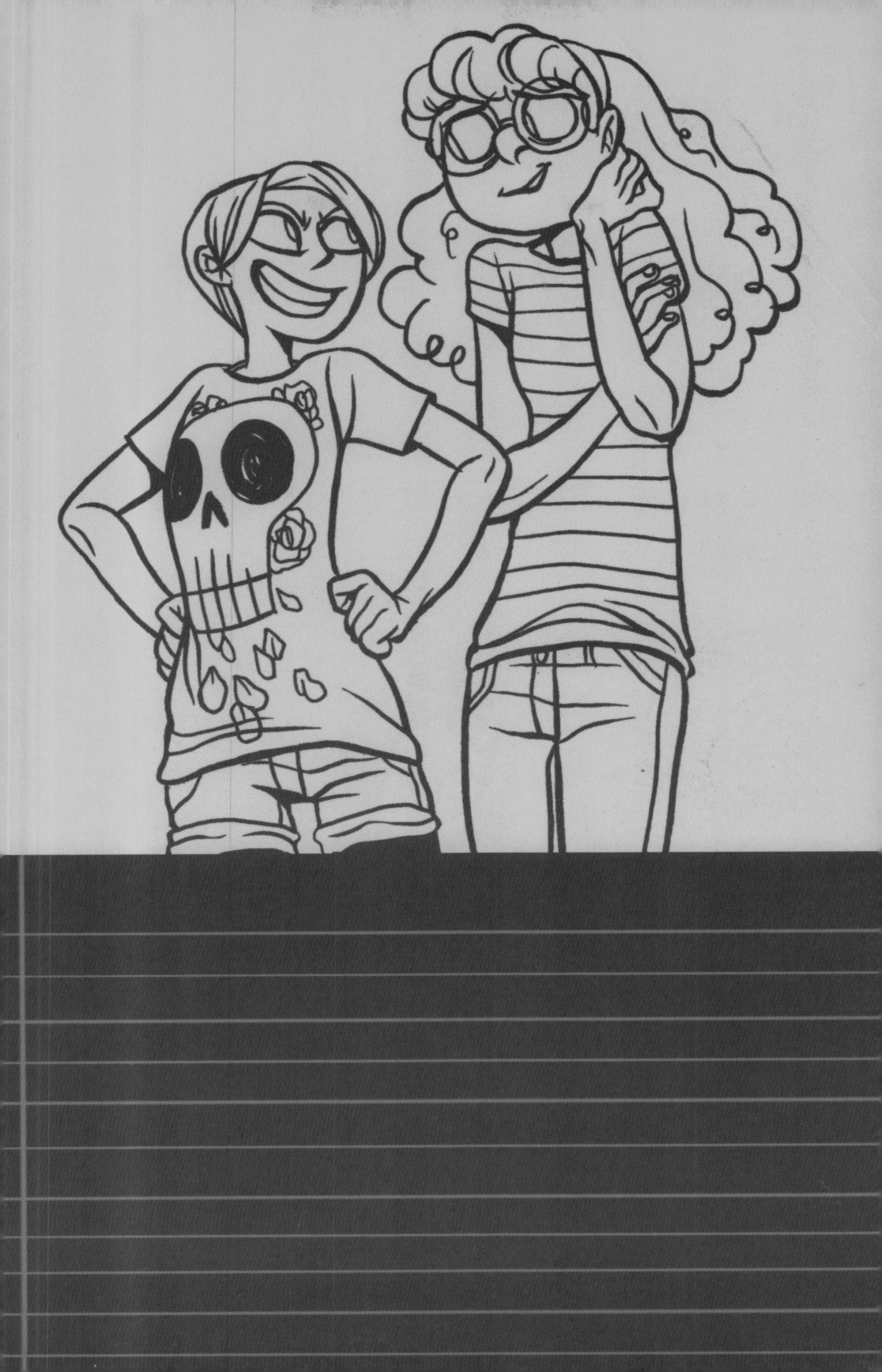

CHAPTER TWENTY THREE

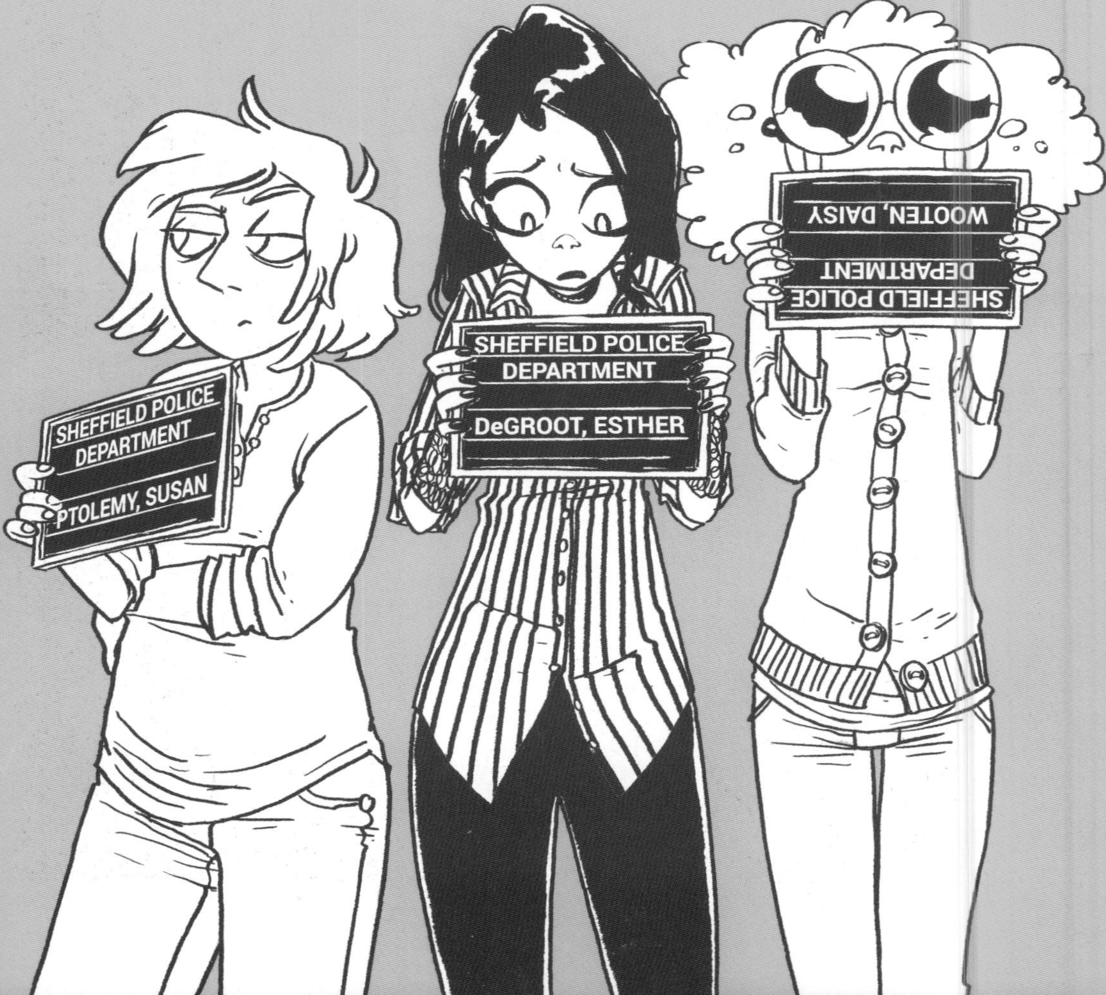
SHEFFIELD POLICE DEPARTMENT
PTOLEMY, SUSAN
SHEFFIELD POLICE DEPARTMENT
DeGROOT, ESTHER
SHEFFIELD POLICE DEPARTMENT
WOOTEN, DAISY

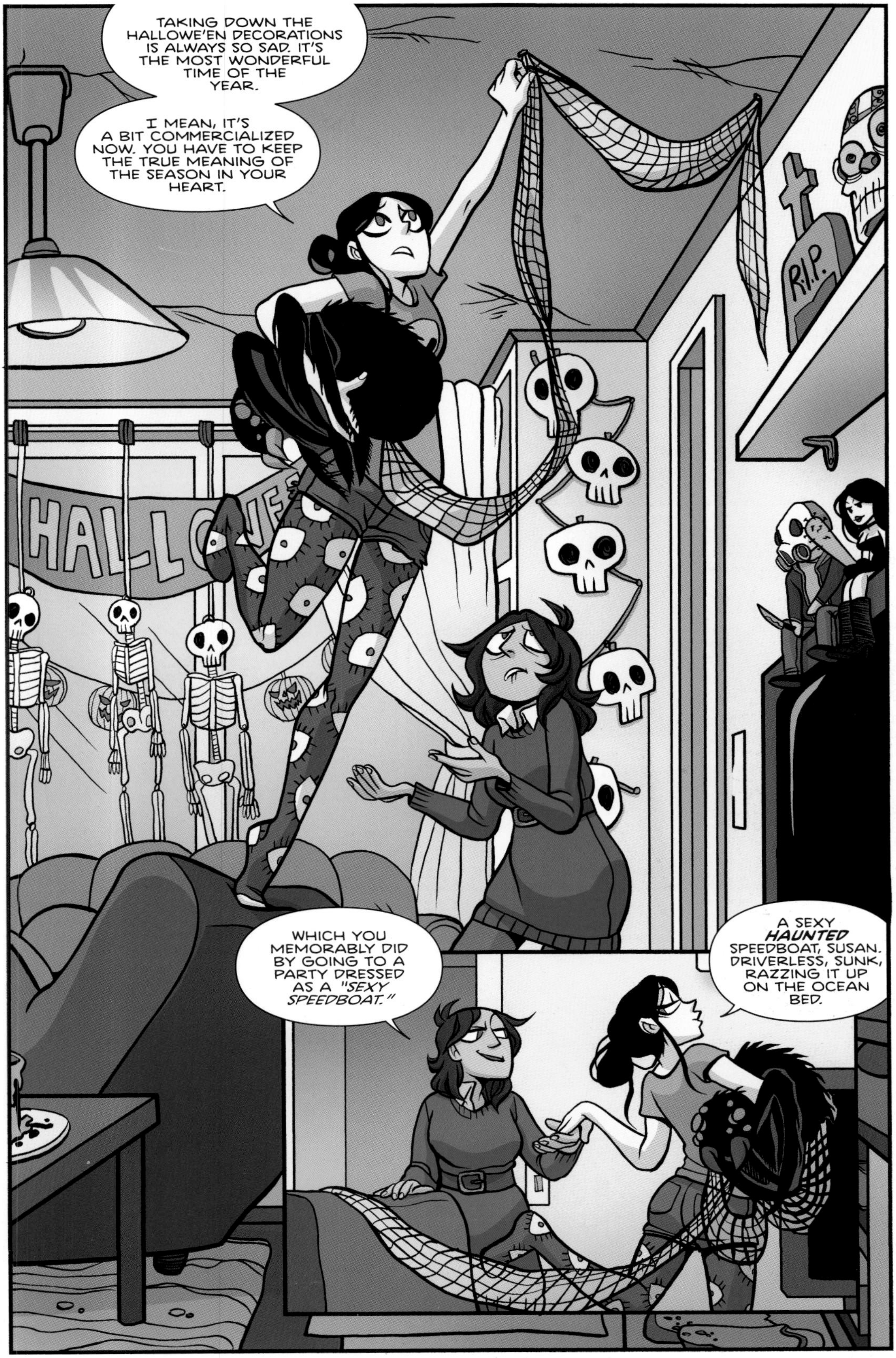
TAKING DOWN THE HALLOWE'EN DECORATIONS IS ALWAYS SO SAD. IT'S THE MOST WONDERFUL TIME OF THE YEAR.
I MEAN, IT'S A BIT COMMERCIALIZED NOW. YOU HAVE TO KEEP THE TRUE MEANING OF THE SEASON IN YOUR HEART.
R.I.P.
HALLO
WHICH YOU MEMORABLY DID BY GOING TO A PARTY DRESSED AS A *"SEXY SPEEDBOAT."*
A SEXY ***HAUNTED*** SPEEDBOAT, SUSAN. DRIVERLESS, SUNK, RAZZING IT UP ON THE OCEAN BED.

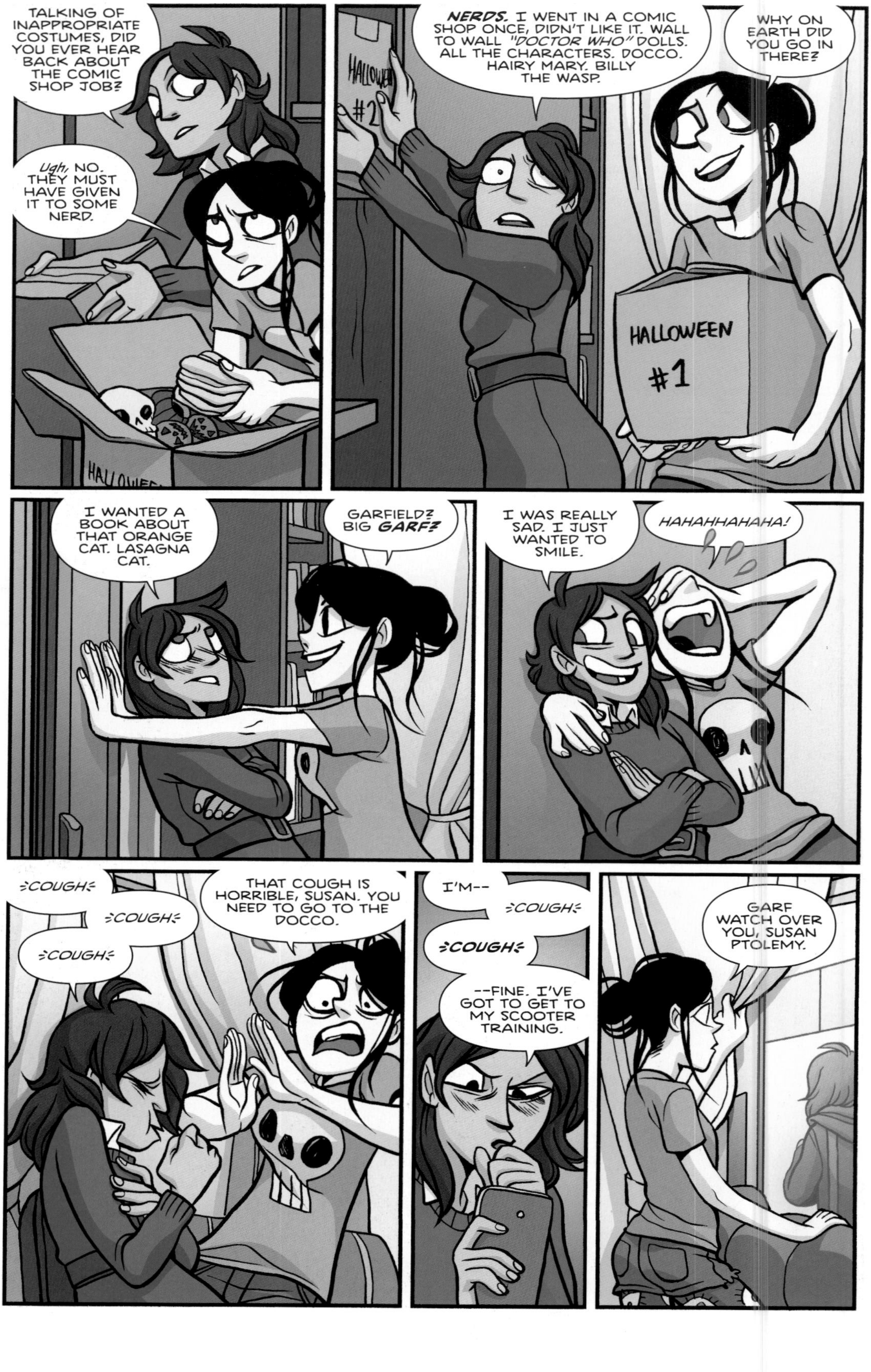
TALKING OF INAPPROPRIATE COSTUMES, DID YOU EVER HEAR BACK ABOUT THE COMIC SHOP JOB?
Ugh, NO. THEY MUST HAVE GIVEN IT TO SOME NERD.
HALLOWEEN
NERDS. I WENT IN A COMIC SHOP ONCE, DIDN'T LIKE IT. WALL TO WALL "DOCTOR WHO" DOLLS. ALL THE CHARACTERS. DOCCO. HAIRY MARY. BILLY THE WASP.
HALLOWEEN #2
WHY ON EARTH DID YOU GO IN THERE?
HALLOWEEN #1
I WANTED A BOOK ABOUT THAT ORANGE CAT. LASAGNA CAT.
GARFIELD? BIG GARF?
I WAS REALLY SAD. I JUST WANTED TO SMILE.
HAHAHHAHAHA!
COUGH
COUGH
COUGH
THAT COUGH IS HORRIBLE, SUSAN. YOU NEED TO GO TO THE DOCCO.
I'M--
COUGH
COUGH
--FINE. I'VE GOT TO GET TO MY SCOOTER TRAINING.
GARF WATCH OVER YOU, SUSAN PTOLEMY.

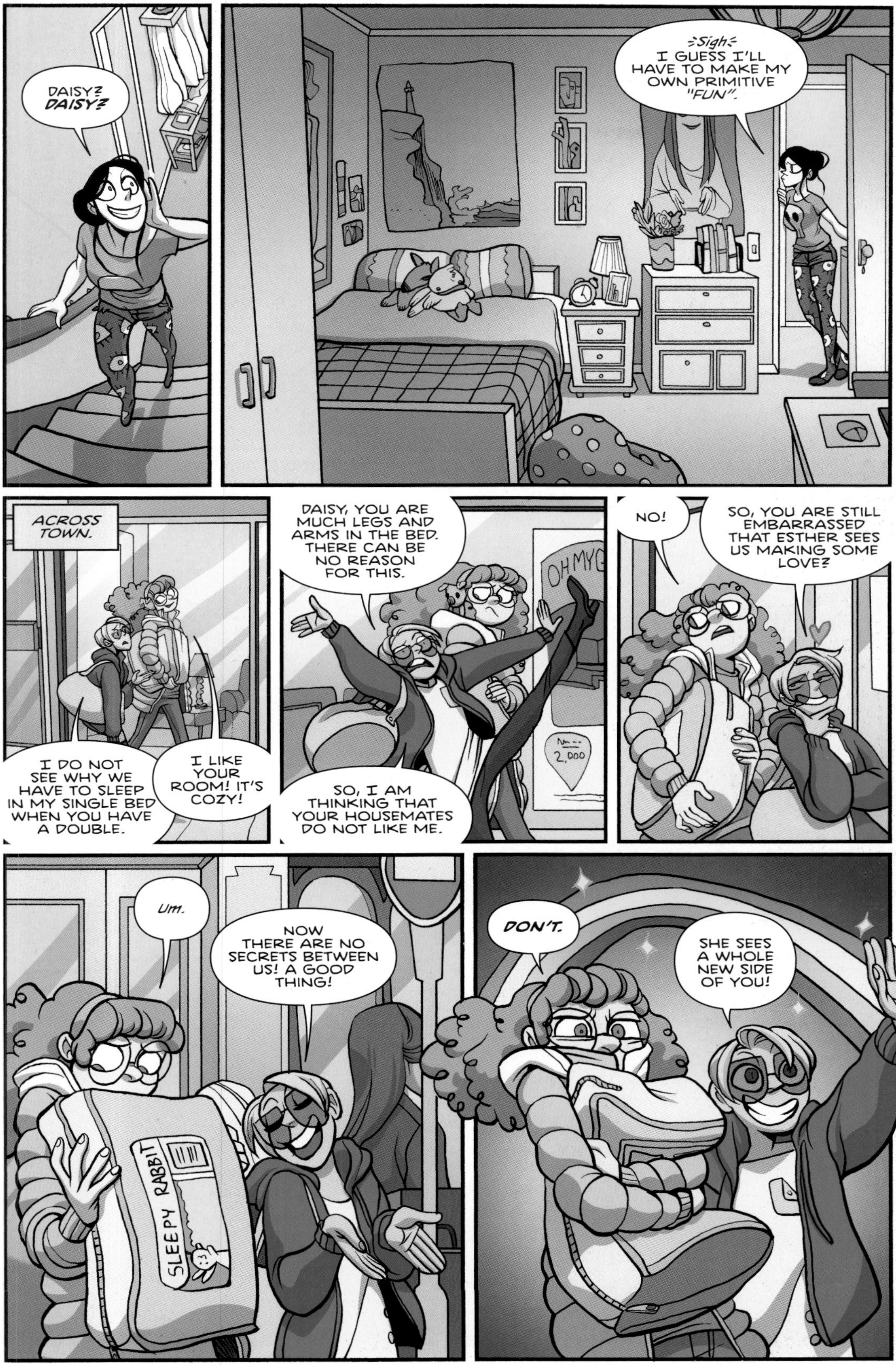
DAISY?
DAISY?
Sigh
I GUESS I'LL HAVE TO MAKE MY OWN PRIMITIVE "FUN".
ACROSS TOWN.
I DO NOT SEE WHY WE HAVE TO SLEEP IN MY SINGLE BED WHEN YOU HAVE A DOUBLE.
I LIKE YOUR ROOM! IT'S COZY!
DAISY, YOU ARE MUCH LEGS AND ARMS IN THE BED. THERE CAN BE NO REASON FOR THIS.
SO, I AM THINKING THAT YOUR HOUSEMATES DO NOT LIKE ME.
NO!
SO, YOU ARE STILL EMBARRASSED THAT ESTHER SEES US MAKING SOME LOVE?
Um.
NOW THERE ARE NO SECRETS BETWEEN US! A GOOD THING!
SLEEPY RABBIT
DON'T.
SHE SEES A WHOLE NEW SIDE OF YOU!

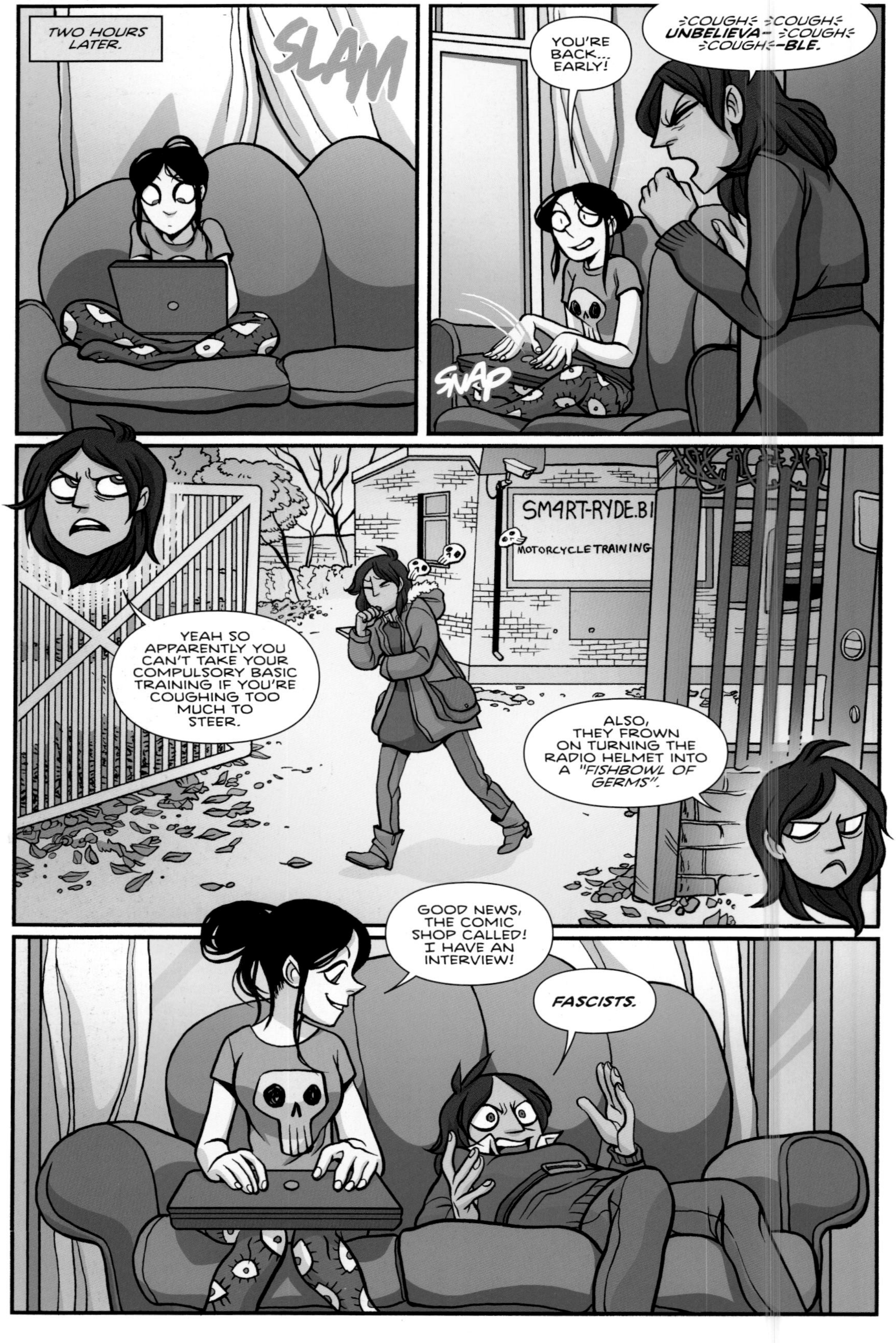
TWO HOURS LATER.
SLAM
YOU'RE BACK... EARLY!
SNAP
≈COUGH≈ ≈COUGH≈ UNBELIEVA- ≈COUGH≈ ≈COUGH≈ -BLE.
SM4RT-RYDE.BI
MOTORCYCLE TRAINING
YEAH SO APPARENTLY YOU CAN'T TAKE YOUR COMPULSORY BASIC TRAINING IF YOU'RE COUGHING TOO MUCH TO STEER.
ALSO, THEY FROWN ON TURNING THE RADIO HELMET INTO A "FISHBOWL OF GERMS".
GOOD NEWS, THE COMIC SHOP CALLED! I HAVE AN INTERVIEW!
FASCISTS.

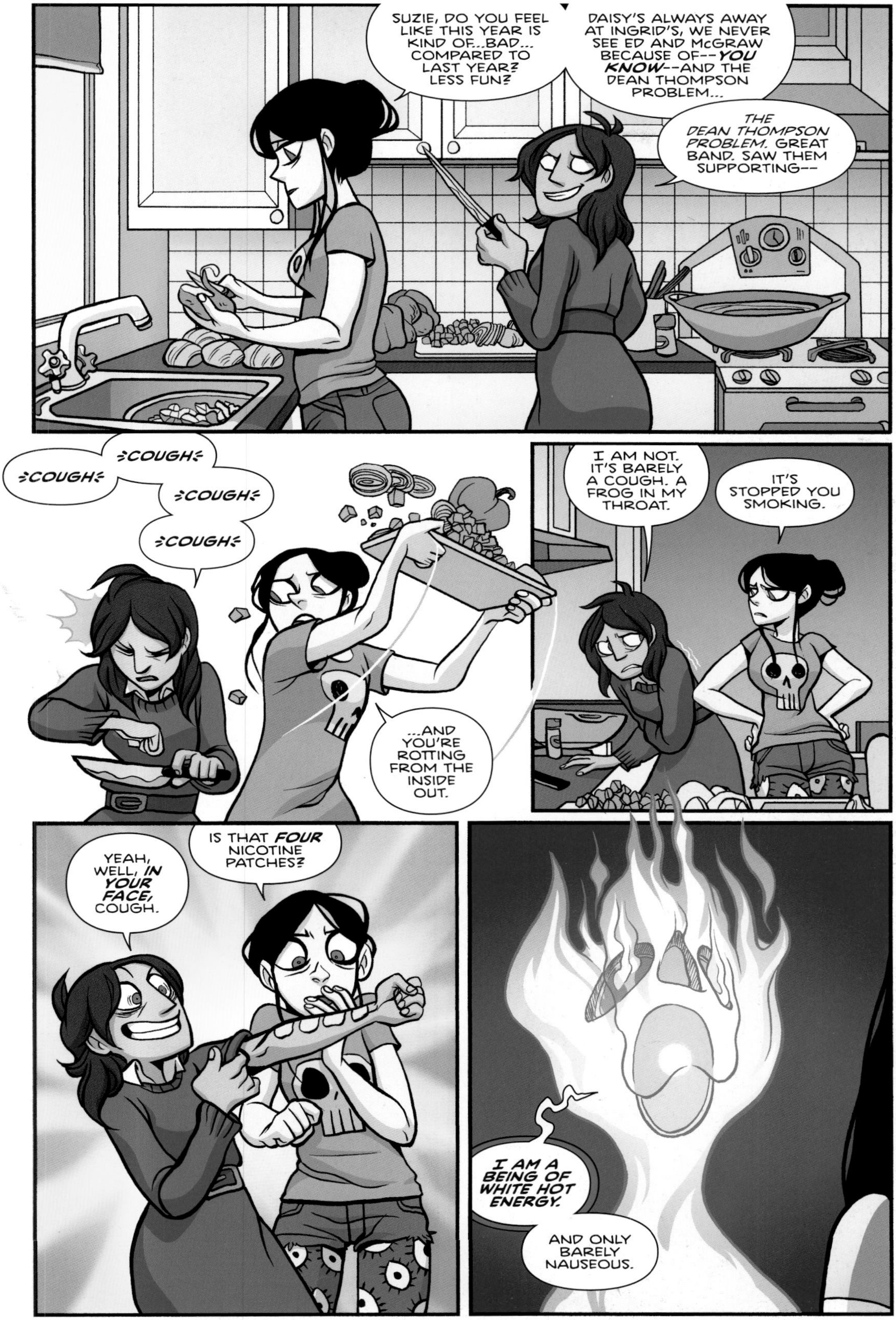
SUZIE, DO YOU FEEL LIKE THIS YEAR IS KIND OF...BAD... COMPARED TO LAST YEAR? LESS FUN?
DAISY'S ALWAYS AWAY AT INGRID'S, WE NEVER SEE ED AND McGRAW BECAUSE OF--YOU KNOW--AND THE DEAN THOMPSON PROBLEM...
THE DEAN THOMPSON PROBLEM. GREAT BAND. SAW THEM SUPPORTING--
COUGH
COUGH
COUGH
COUGH
...AND YOU'RE ROTTING FROM THE INSIDE OUT.
I AM NOT. IT'S BARELY A COUGH. A FROG IN MY THROAT.
IT'S STOPPED YOU SMOKING.
YEAH, WELL, IN YOUR FACE, COUGH.
IS THAT FOUR NICOTINE PATCHES?
I AM A BEING OF WHITE HOT ENERGY.
AND ONLY BARELY NAUSEOUS.

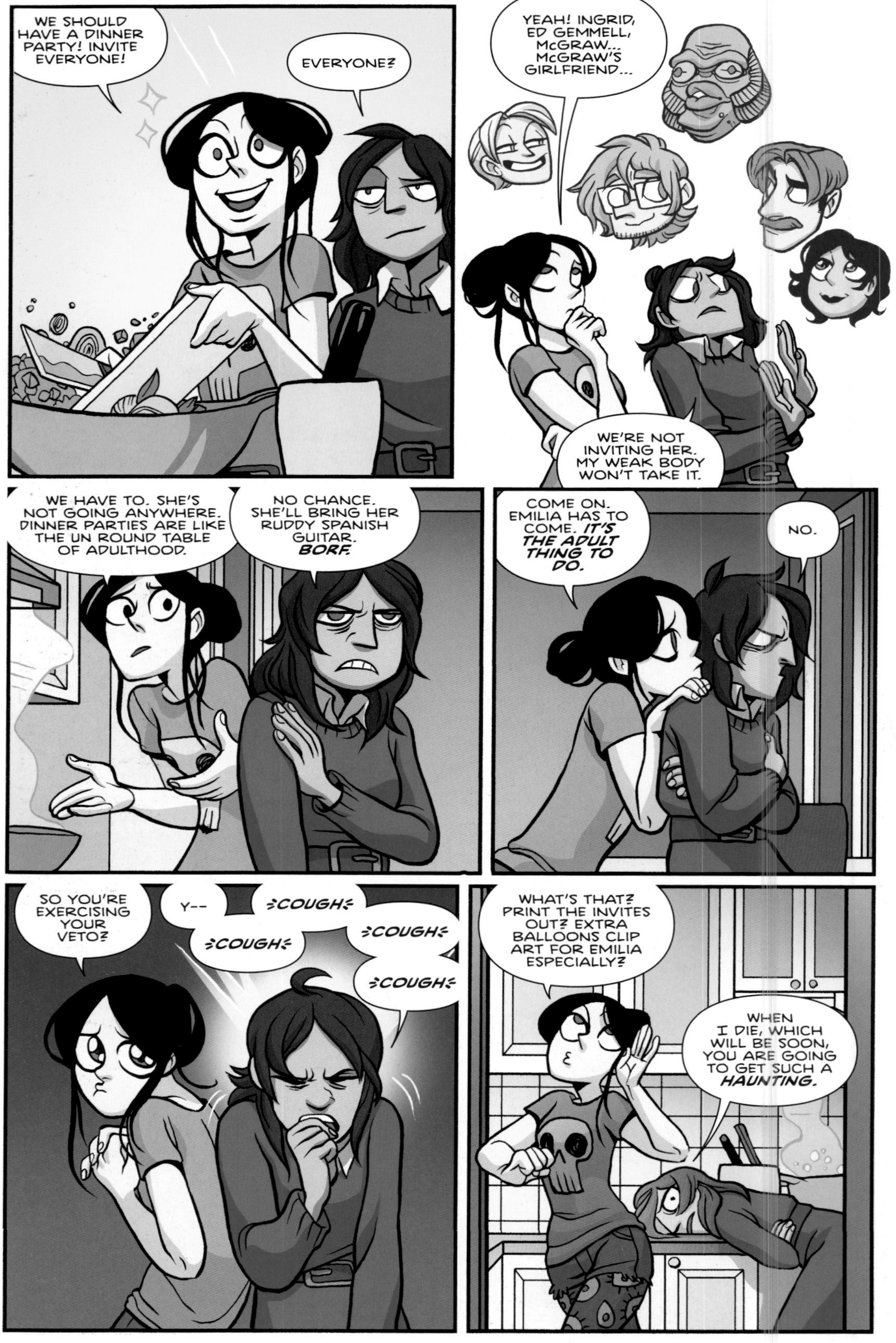

WE SHOULD HAVE A DINNER PARTY! INVITE EVERYONE!
EVERYONE?
YEAH! INGRID, ED GEMMELL, McGRAW... McGRAW'S GIRLFRIEND...
WE'RE NOT INVITING HER. MY WEAK BODY WON'T TAKE IT.
WE HAVE TO. SHE'S NOT GOING ANYWHERE. DINNER PARTIES ARE LIKE THE UN ROUND TABLE OF ADULTHOOD.
NO CHANCE. SHE'LL BRING HER RUDDY SPANISH GUITAR. *BORF.*
COME ON. EMILIA HAS TO COME. *IT'S THE ADULT THING TO DO.*
NO.
SO YOU'RE EXERCISING YOUR VETO?
Y--
COUGH
COUGH
COUGH
COUGH
WHAT'S THAT? PRINT THE INVITES OUT? EXTRA BALLOONS CLIP ART FOR EMILIA ESPECIALLY?
WHEN I DIE, WHICH WILL BE SOON, YOU ARE GOING TO GET SUCH A *HAUNTING.*

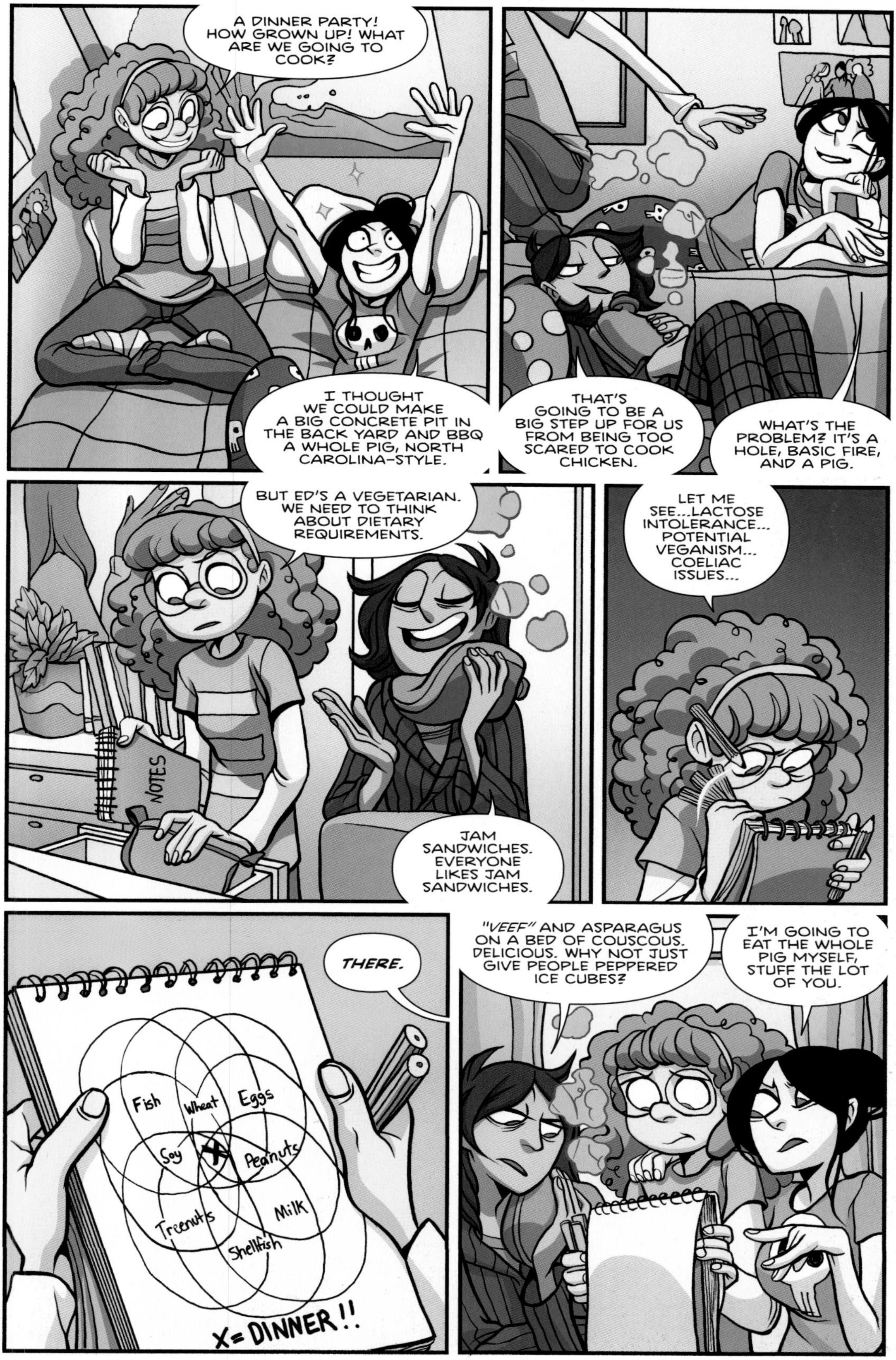
A DINNER PARTY! HOW GROWN UP! WHAT ARE WE GOING TO COOK?
I THOUGHT WE COULD MAKE A BIG CONCRETE PIT IN THE BACK YARD AND BBQ A WHOLE PIG, NORTH CAROLINA-STYLE.
THAT'S GOING TO BE A BIG STEP UP FOR US FROM BEING TOO SCARED TO COOK CHICKEN.
WHAT'S THE PROBLEM? IT'S A HOLE, BASIC FIRE, AND A PIG.
BUT ED'S A VEGETARIAN. WE NEED TO THINK ABOUT DIETARY REQUIREMENTS.
NOTES
JAM SANDWICHES. EVERYONE LIKES JAM SANDWICHES.
LET ME SEE...LACTOSE INTOLERANCE... POTENTIAL VEGANISM... COELIAC ISSUES...
THERE.
Fish
Wheat
Eggs
Soy
X
Peanuts
Treenuts
Milk
Shellfish
X = DINNER!!
"VEEF" AND ASPARAGUS ON A BED OF COUSCOUS. DELICIOUS. WHY NOT JUST GIVE PEOPLE PEPPERED ICE CUBES?
I'M GOING TO EAT THE WHOLE PIG MYSELF, STUFF THE LOT OF YOU.

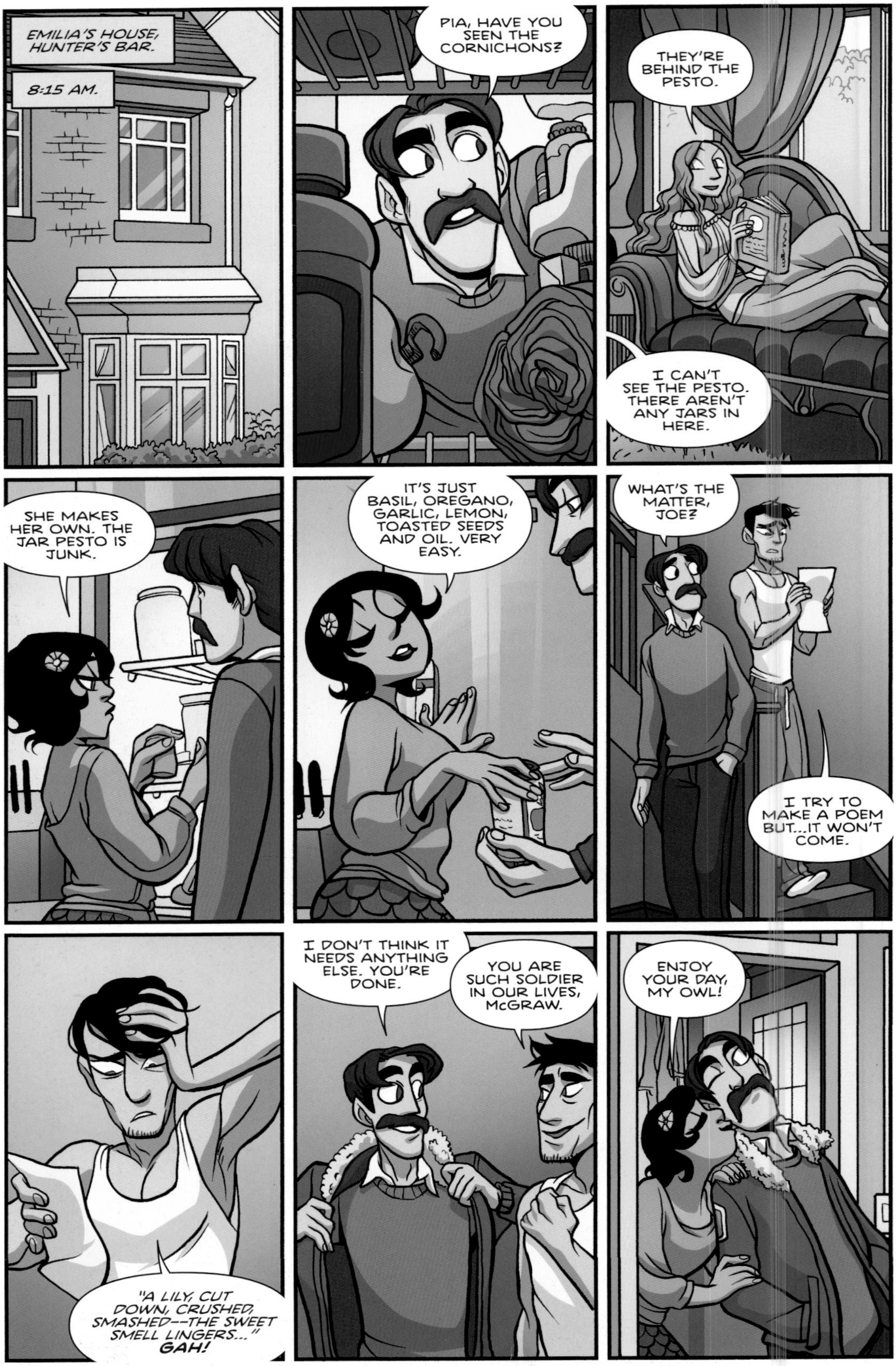
EMILIA'S HOUSE, HUNTER'S BAR.
8:15 AM.
PIA, HAVE YOU SEEN THE CORNICHONS?
THEY'RE BEHIND THE PESTO.
I CAN'T SEE THE PESTO. THERE AREN'T ANY JARS IN HERE.
SHE MAKES HER OWN. THE JAR PESTO IS JUNK.
IT'S JUST BASIL, OREGANO, GARLIC, LEMON, TOASTED SEEDS AND OIL. VERY EASY.
WHAT'S THE MATTER, JOE?
I TRY TO MAKE A POEM BUT...IT WON'T COME.
"A LILY, CUT DOWN, CRUSHED, SMASHED--THE SWEET SMELL LINGERS..." GAH!
I DON'T THINK IT NEEDS ANYTHING ELSE. YOU'RE DONE.
YOU ARE SUCH SOLDIER IN OUR LIVES, McGRAW.
ENJOY YOUR DAY, MY OWL!

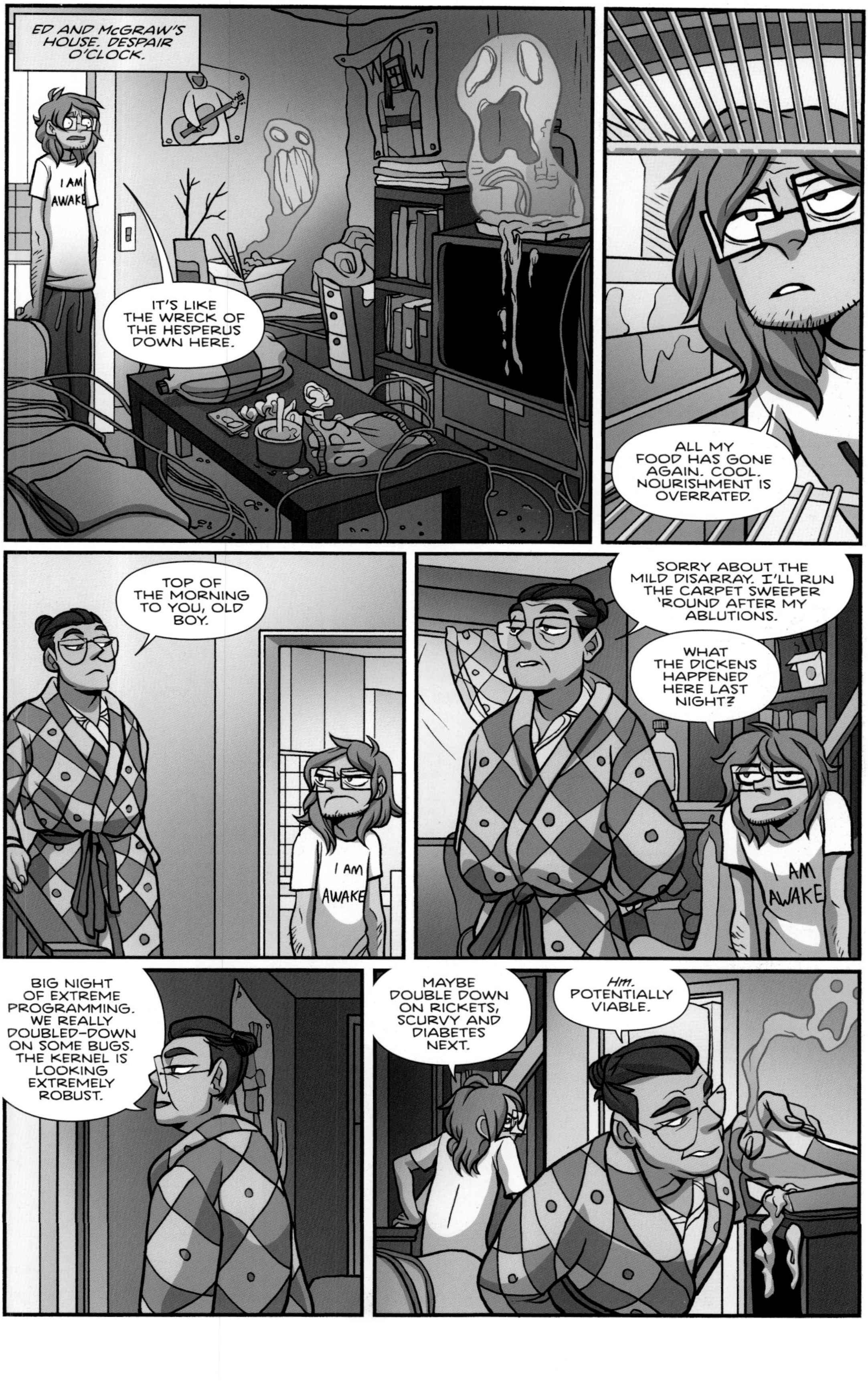
ED AND McGRAW'S HOUSE. DESPAIR O'CLOCK.
I AM AWAKE
IT'S LIKE THE WRECK OF THE HESPERUS DOWN HERE.
ALL MY FOOD HAS GONE AGAIN. COOL. NOURISHMENT IS OVERRATED.
TOP OF THE MORNING TO YOU, OLD BOY.
I AM AWAKE
SORRY ABOUT THE MILD DISARRAY. I'LL RUN THE CARPET SWEEPER 'ROUND AFTER MY ABLUTIONS.
WHAT THE DICKENS HAPPENED HERE LAST NIGHT?
I AM AWAKE
BIG NIGHT OF EXTREME PROGRAMMING. WE REALLY DOUBLED-DOWN ON SOME BUGS. THE KERNEL IS LOOKING EXTREMELY ROBUST.
MAYBE DOUBLE DOWN ON RICKETS, SCURVY AND DIABETES NEXT.
Hm. POTENTIALLY VIABLE.

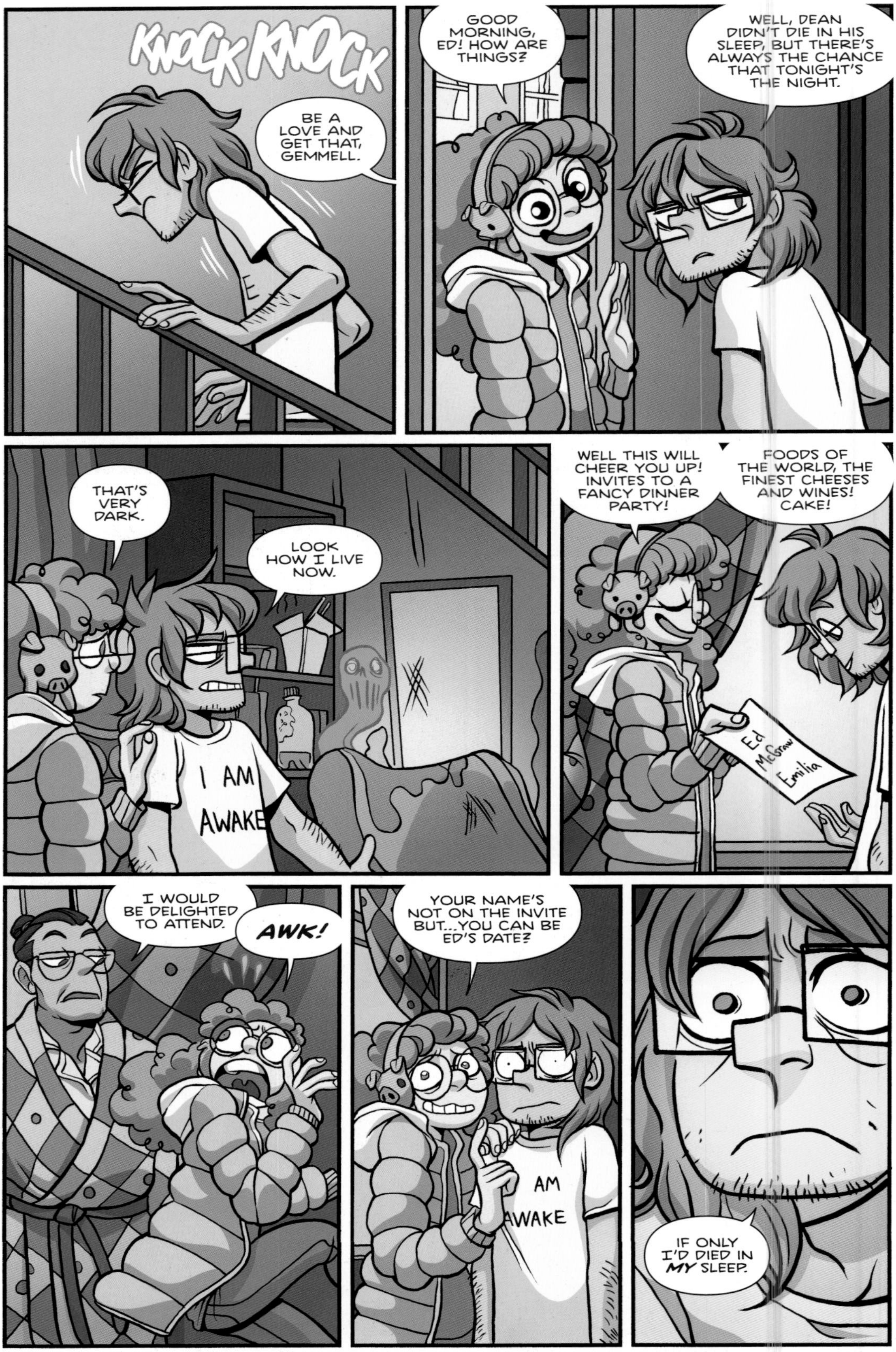
KNOCK KNOCK
BE A LOVE AND GET THAT, GEMMELL.
GOOD MORNING, ED! HOW ARE THINGS?
WELL, DEAN DIDN'T DIE IN HIS SLEEP, BUT THERE'S ALWAYS THE CHANCE THAT TONIGHT'S THE NIGHT.
THAT'S VERY DARK.
LOOK HOW I LIVE NOW.
I AM AWAKE
WELL THIS WILL CHEER YOU UP! INVITES TO A FANCY DINNER PARTY!
FOODS OF THE WORLD, THE FINEST CHEESES AND WINES! CAKE!
Ed McGraw Emilia
I WOULD BE DELIGHTED TO ATTEND.
AWK!
YOUR NAME'S NOT ON THE INVITE BUT... YOU CAN BE ED'S DATE?
AM AWAKE
IF ONLY I'D DIED IN MY SLEEP.

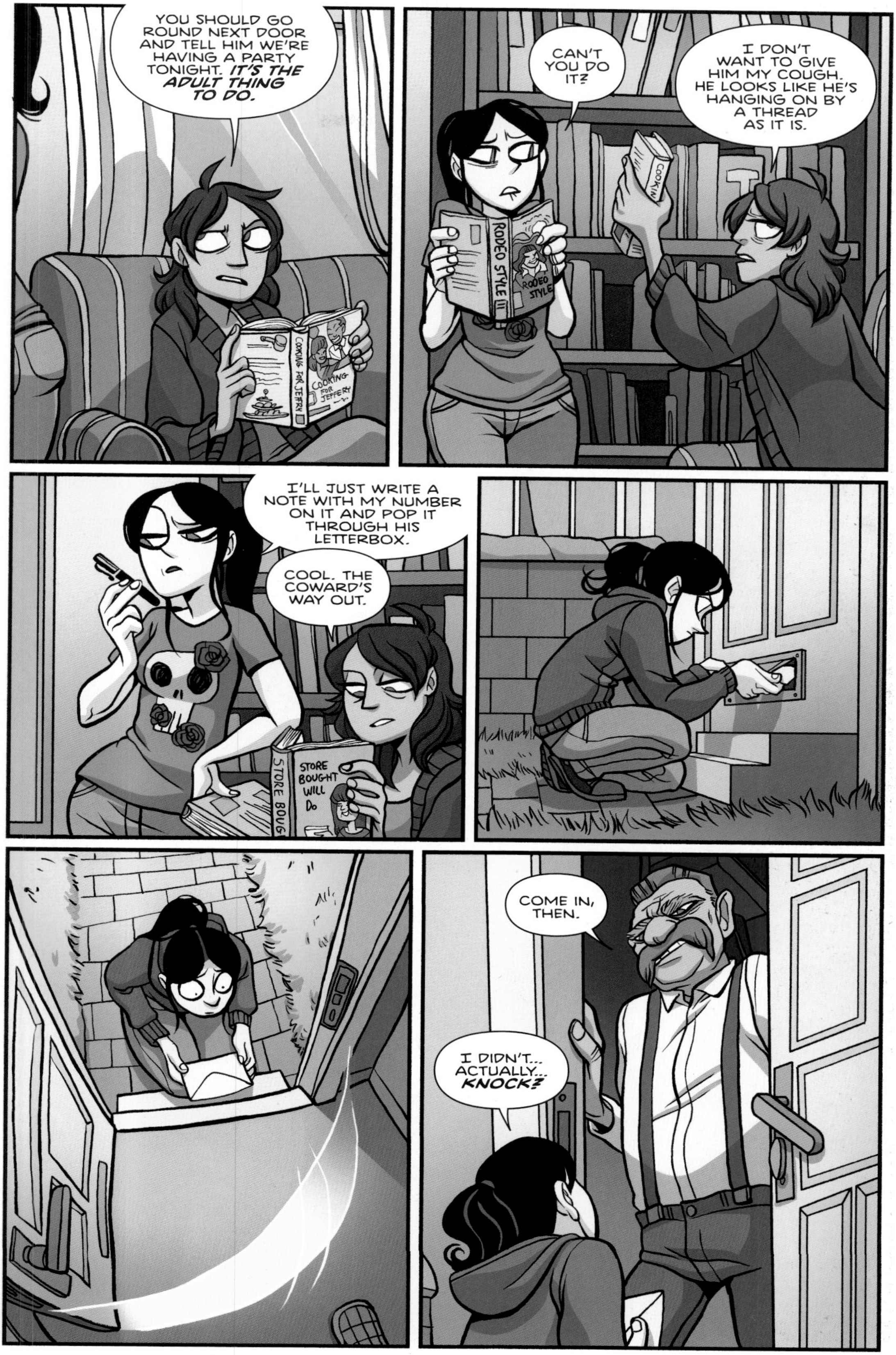
YOU SHOULD GO ROUND NEXT DOOR AND TELL HIM WE'RE HAVING A PARTY TONIGHT. *IT'S THE ADULT THING TO DO.*
COOKING FOR JEFFRY
CAN'T YOU DO IT?
I DON'T WANT TO GIVE HIM MY COUGH. HE LOOKS LIKE HE'S HANGING ON BY A THREAD AS IT IS.
RODEO STYLE
I'LL JUST WRITE A NOTE WITH MY NUMBER ON IT AND POP IT THROUGH HIS LETTERBOX.
COOL. THE COWARD'S WAY OUT.
STORE BOUGHT WILL DO
COME IN, THEN.
I DIDN'T... ACTUALLY... *KNOCK?*

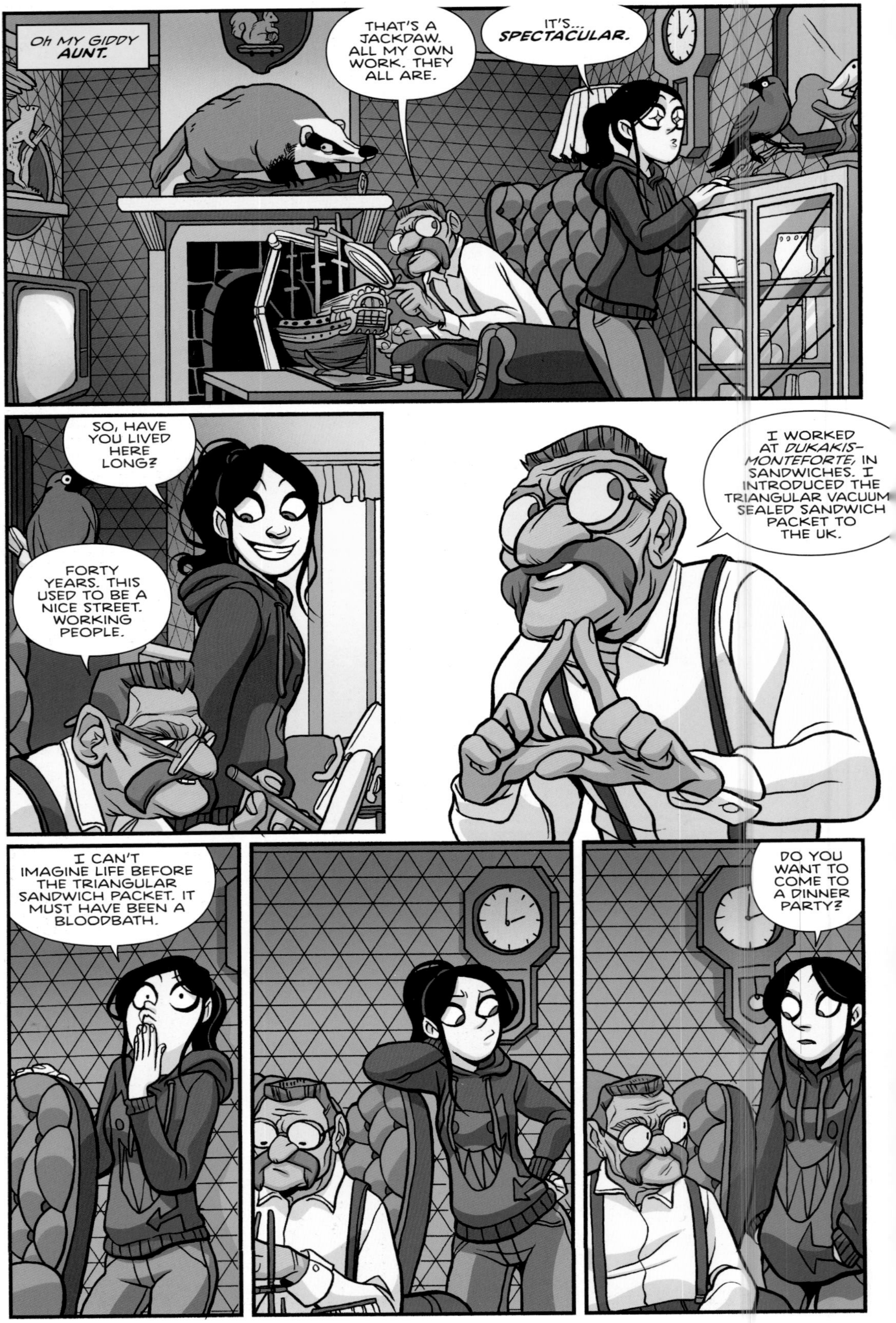
Oh MY GIDDY AUNT.
THAT'S A JACKDAW. ALL MY OWN WORK. THEY ALL ARE.
IT'S... SPECTACULAR.
SO, HAVE YOU LIVED HERE LONG?
FORTY YEARS. THIS USED TO BE A NICE STREET. WORKING PEOPLE.
I WORKED AT DUKAKIS-MONTEFORTE, IN SANDWICHES. I INTRODUCED THE TRIANGULAR VACUUM SEALED SANDWICH PACKET TO THE UK.
I CAN'T IMAGINE LIFE BEFORE THE TRIANGULAR SANDWICH PACKET. IT MUST HAVE BEEN A BLOODBATH.
DO YOU WANT TO COME TO A DINNER PARTY?

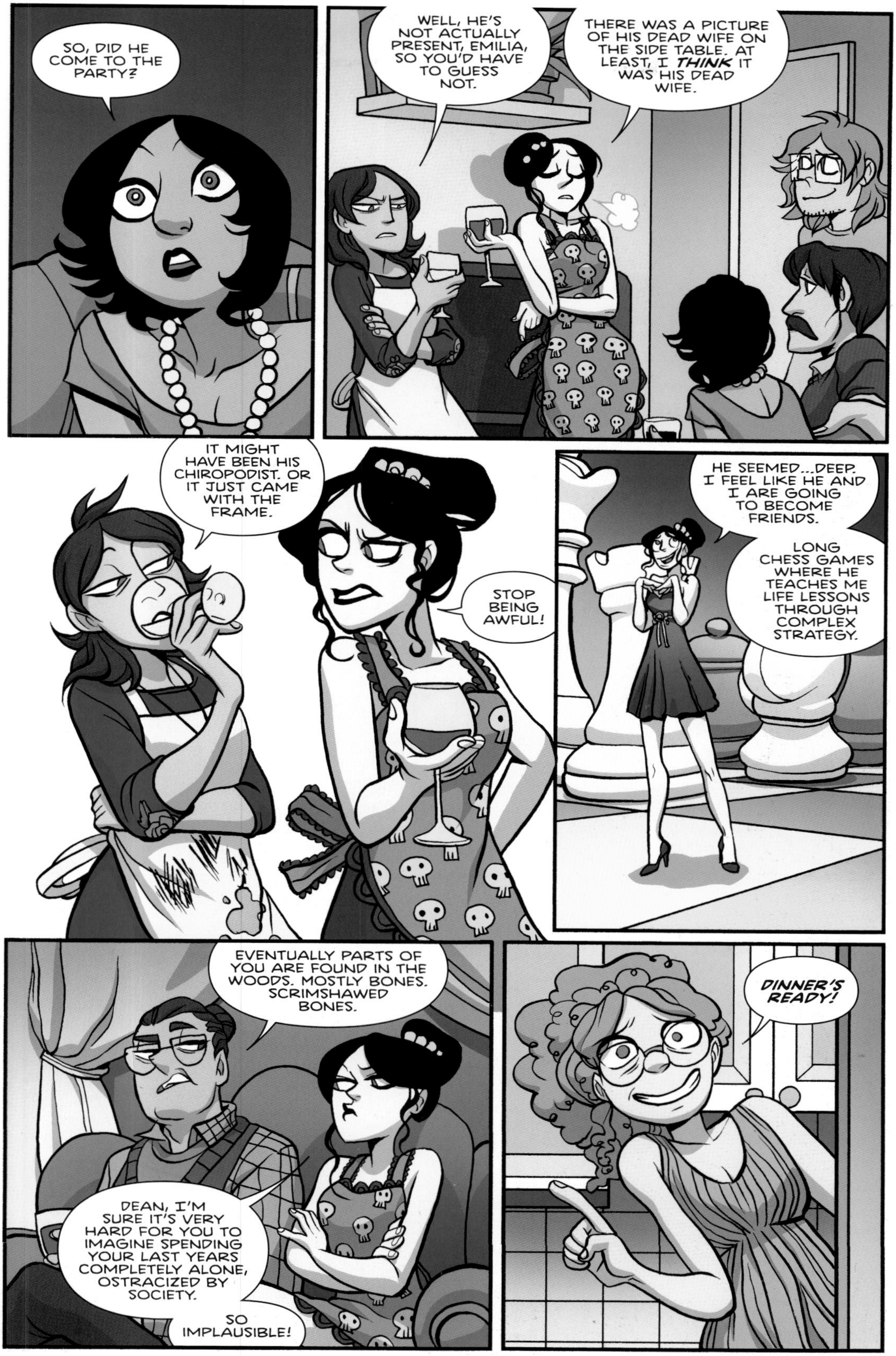

SO, DID HE COME TO THE PARTY?
WELL, HE'S NOT ACTUALLY PRESENT, EMILIA, SO YOU'D HAVE TO GUESS NOT.
THERE WAS A PICTURE OF HIS DEAD WIFE ON THE SIDE TABLE. AT LEAST, I *THINK* IT WAS HIS DEAD WIFE.
IT MIGHT HAVE BEEN HIS CHIROPODIST. OR IT JUST CAME WITH THE FRAME.
STOP BEING AWFUL!
HE SEEMED...DEEP. I FEEL LIKE HE AND I ARE GOING TO BECOME FRIENDS.
LONG CHESS GAMES WHERE HE TEACHES ME LIFE LESSONS THROUGH COMPLEX STRATEGY.
EVENTUALLY PARTS OF YOU ARE FOUND IN THE WOODS. MOSTLY BONES. SCRIMSHAWED BONES.
DEAN, I'M SURE IT'S VERY HARD FOR YOU TO IMAGINE SPENDING YOUR LAST YEARS COMPLETELY ALONE, OSTRACIZED BY SOCIETY.
SO IMPLAUSIBLE!
DINNER'S READY!

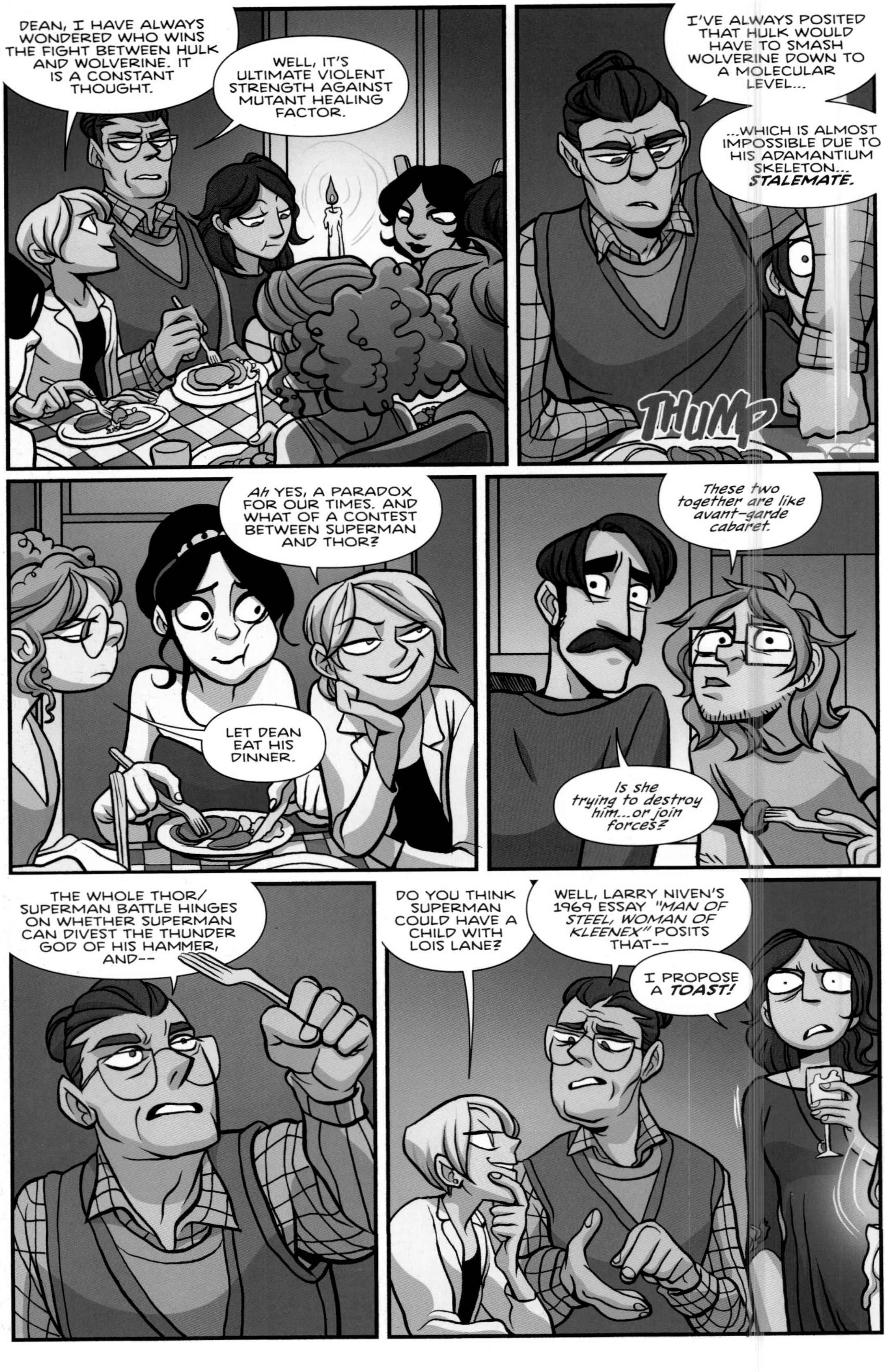
DEAN, I HAVE ALWAYS WONDERED WHO WINS THE FIGHT BETWEEN HULK AND WOLVERINE. IT IS A CONSTANT THOUGHT.
WELL, IT'S ULTIMATE VIOLENT STRENGTH AGAINST MUTANT HEALING FACTOR.
I'VE ALWAYS POSITED THAT HULK WOULD HAVE TO SMASH WOLVERINE DOWN TO A MOLECULAR LEVEL...
...WHICH IS ALMOST IMPOSSIBLE DUE TO HIS ADAMANTIUM SKELETON... STALEMATE.
THUMP
Ah YES, A PARADOX FOR OUR TIMES. AND WHAT OF A CONTEST BETWEEN SUPERMAN AND THOR?
LET DEAN EAT HIS DINNER.
These two together are like avant-garde cabaret.
Is she trying to destroy him...or join forces?
THE WHOLE THOR/ SUPERMAN BATTLE HINGES ON WHETHER SUPERMAN CAN DIVEST THE THUNDER GOD OF HIS HAMMER, AND--
DO YOU THINK SUPERMAN COULD HAVE A CHILD WITH LOIS LANE?
WELL, LARRY NIVEN'S 1969 ESSAY "MAN OF STEEL, WOMAN OF KLEENEX" POSITS THAT--
I PROPOSE A TOAST!

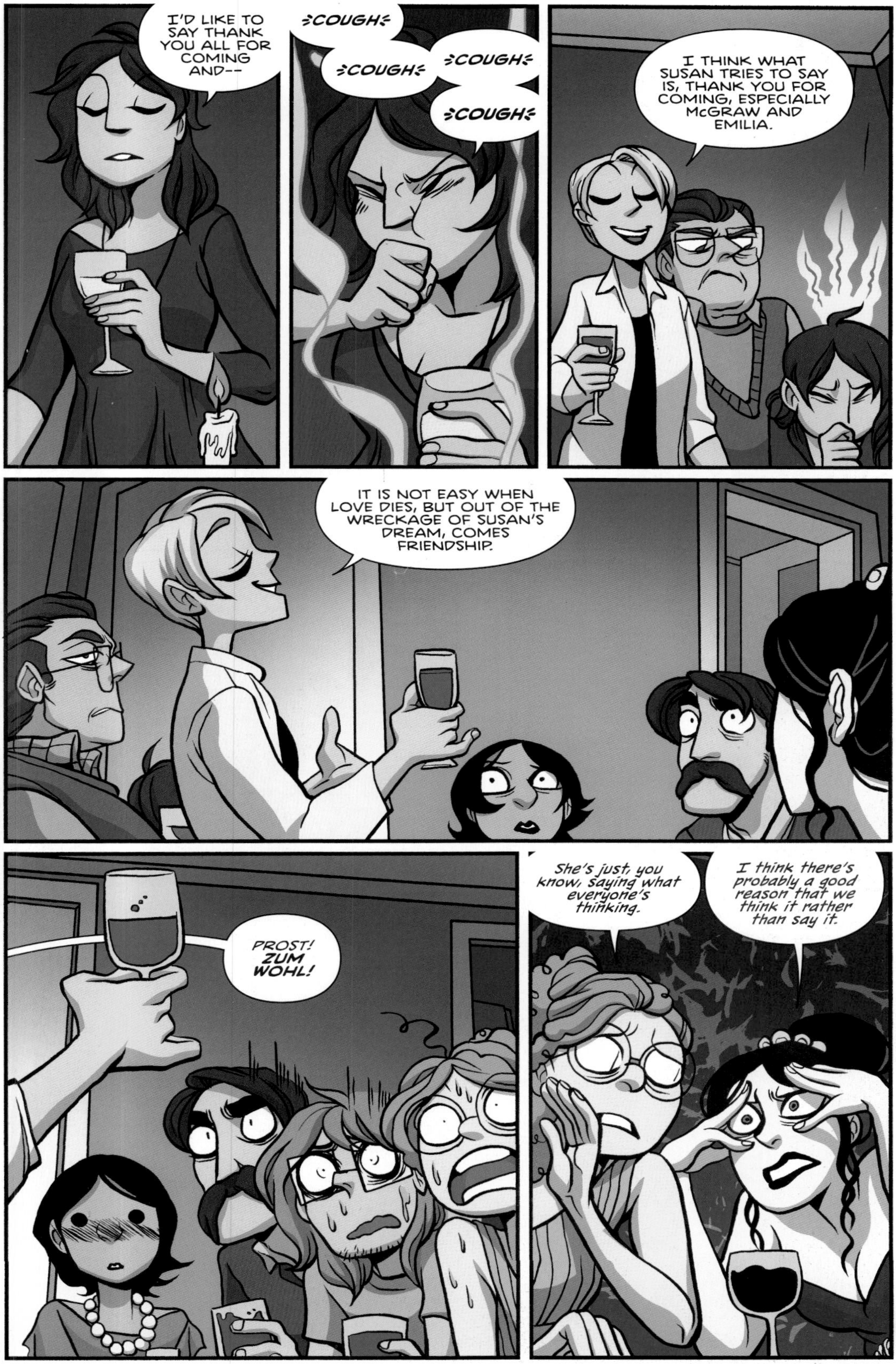
I'D LIKE TO SAY THANK YOU ALL FOR COMING AND--
COUGH
COUGH
COUGH
COUGH
I THINK WHAT SUSAN TRIES TO SAY IS, THANK YOU FOR COMING, ESPECIALLY McGRAW AND EMILIA.
IT IS NOT EASY WHEN LOVE DIES, BUT OUT OF THE WRECKAGE OF SUSAN'S DREAM, COMES FRIENDSHIP.
PROST! ZUM WOHL!
She's just, you know, saying what everyone's thinking.
I think there's probably a good reason that we think it rather than say it.

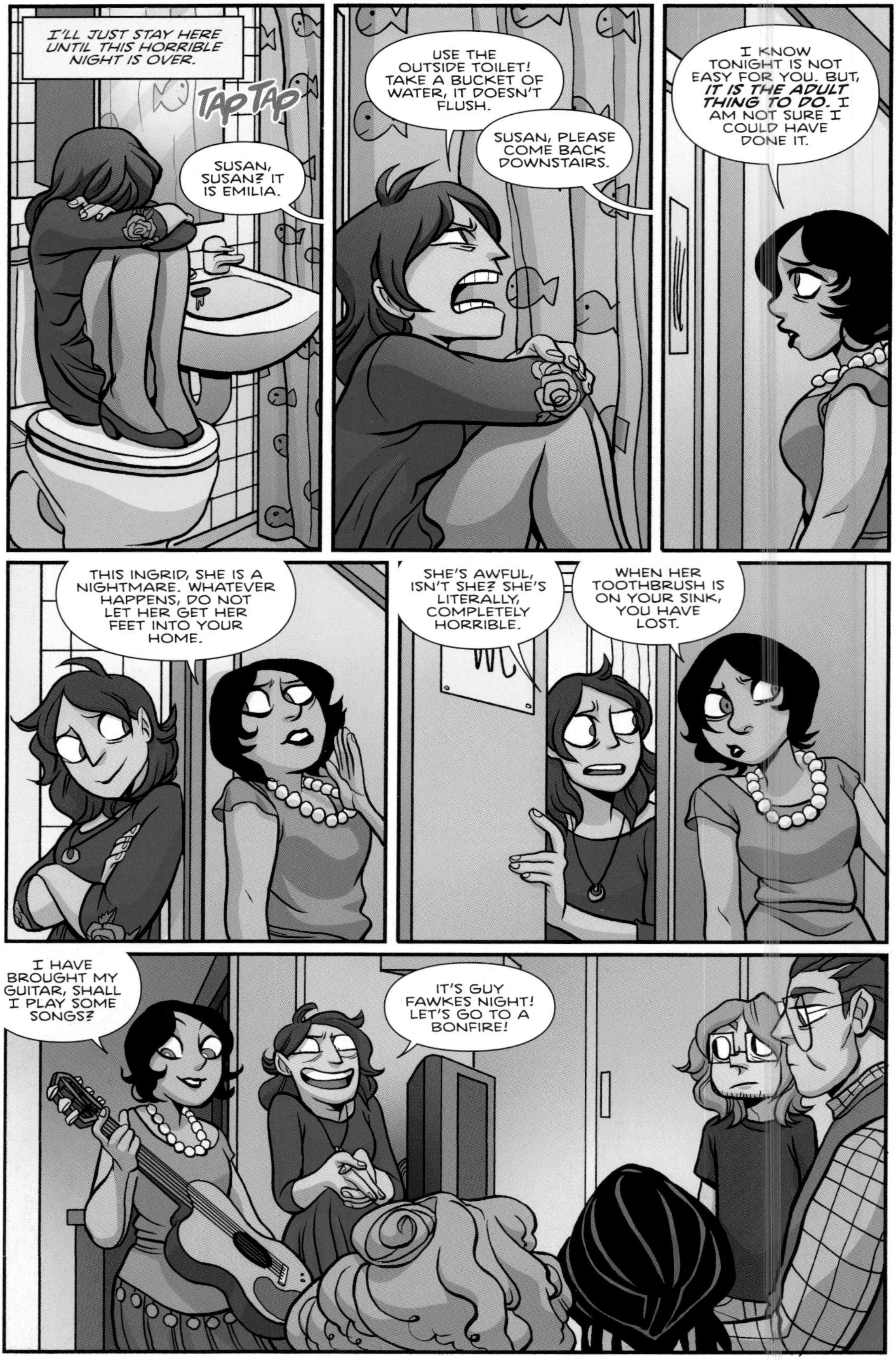

I'LL JUST STAY HERE UNTIL THIS HORRIBLE NIGHT IS OVER.
TAP TAP
SUSAN, SUSAN? IT IS EMILIA.
USE THE OUTSIDE TOILET! TAKE A BUCKET OF WATER, IT DOESN'T FLUSH.
SUSAN, PLEASE COME BACK DOWNSTAIRS.
I KNOW TONIGHT IS NOT EASY FOR YOU. BUT, IT IS THE ADULT THING TO DO. I AM NOT SURE I COULD HAVE DONE IT.
THIS INGRID, SHE IS A NIGHTMARE. WHATEVER HAPPENS, DO NOT LET HER GET HER FEET INTO YOUR HOME.
SHE'S AWFUL, ISN'T SHE? SHE'S LITERALLY, COMPLETELY HORRIBLE.
WHEN HER TOOTHBRUSH IS ON YOUR SINK, YOU HAVE LOST.
I HAVE BROUGHT MY GUITAR, SHALL I PLAY SOME SONGS?
IT'S GUY FAWKES NIGHT! LET'S GO TO A BONFIRE!

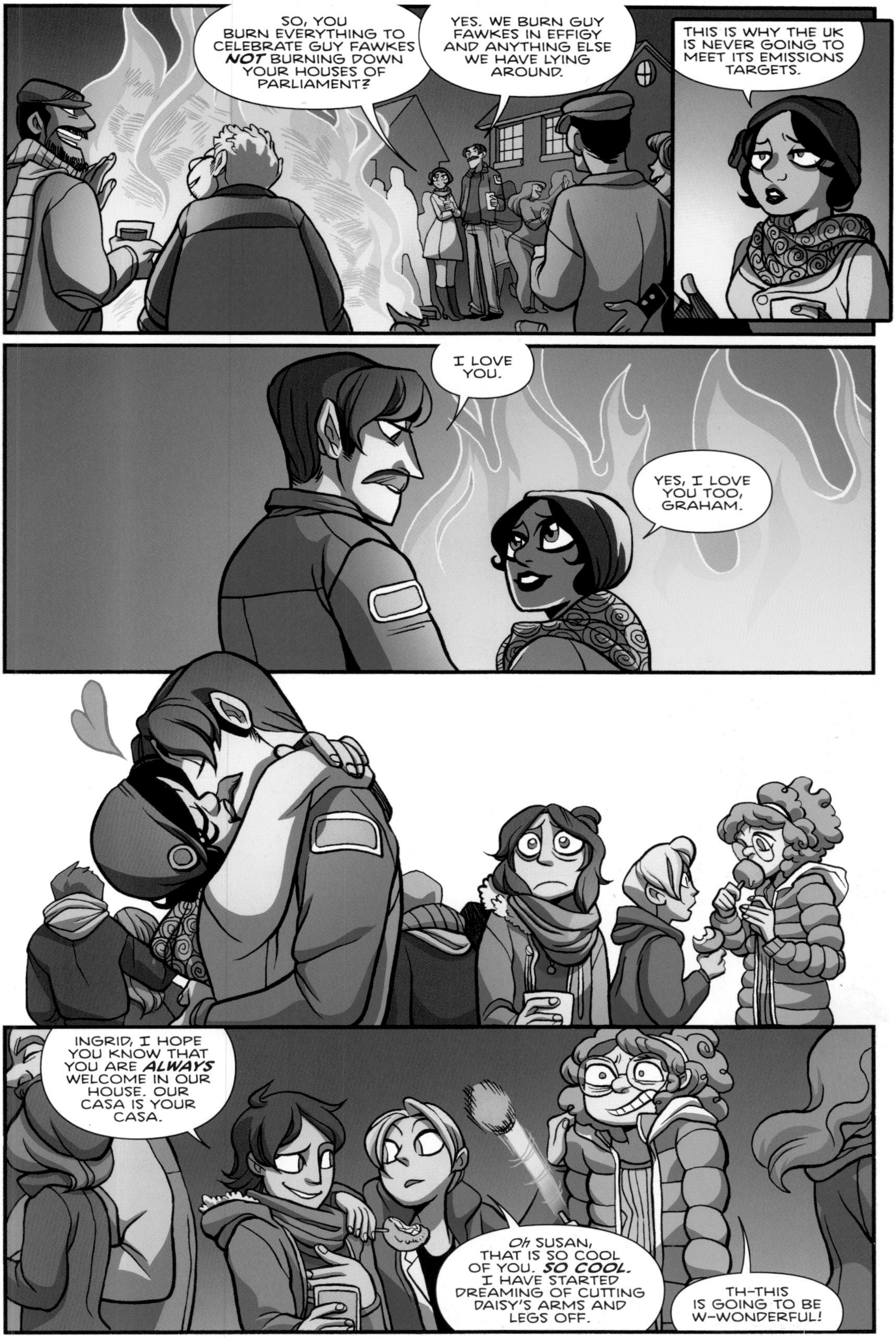
SO, YOU BURN EVERYTHING TO CELEBRATE GUY FAWKES *NOT* BURNING DOWN YOUR HOUSES OF PARLIAMENT?
YES. WE BURN GUY FAWKES IN EFFIGY AND ANYTHING ELSE WE HAVE LYING AROUND.
THIS IS WHY THE UK IS NEVER GOING TO MEET ITS EMISSIONS TARGETS.
I LOVE YOU.
YES, I LOVE YOU TOO, GRAHAM.
INGRID, I HOPE YOU KNOW THAT YOU ARE *ALWAYS* WELCOME IN OUR HOUSE. OUR CASA IS YOUR CASA.
Oh SUSAN, THAT IS SO COOL OF YOU. *SO COOL.* I HAVE STARTED DREAMING OF CUTTING DAISY'S ARMS AND LEGS OFF.
TH-THIS IS GOING TO BE W-WONDERFUL!

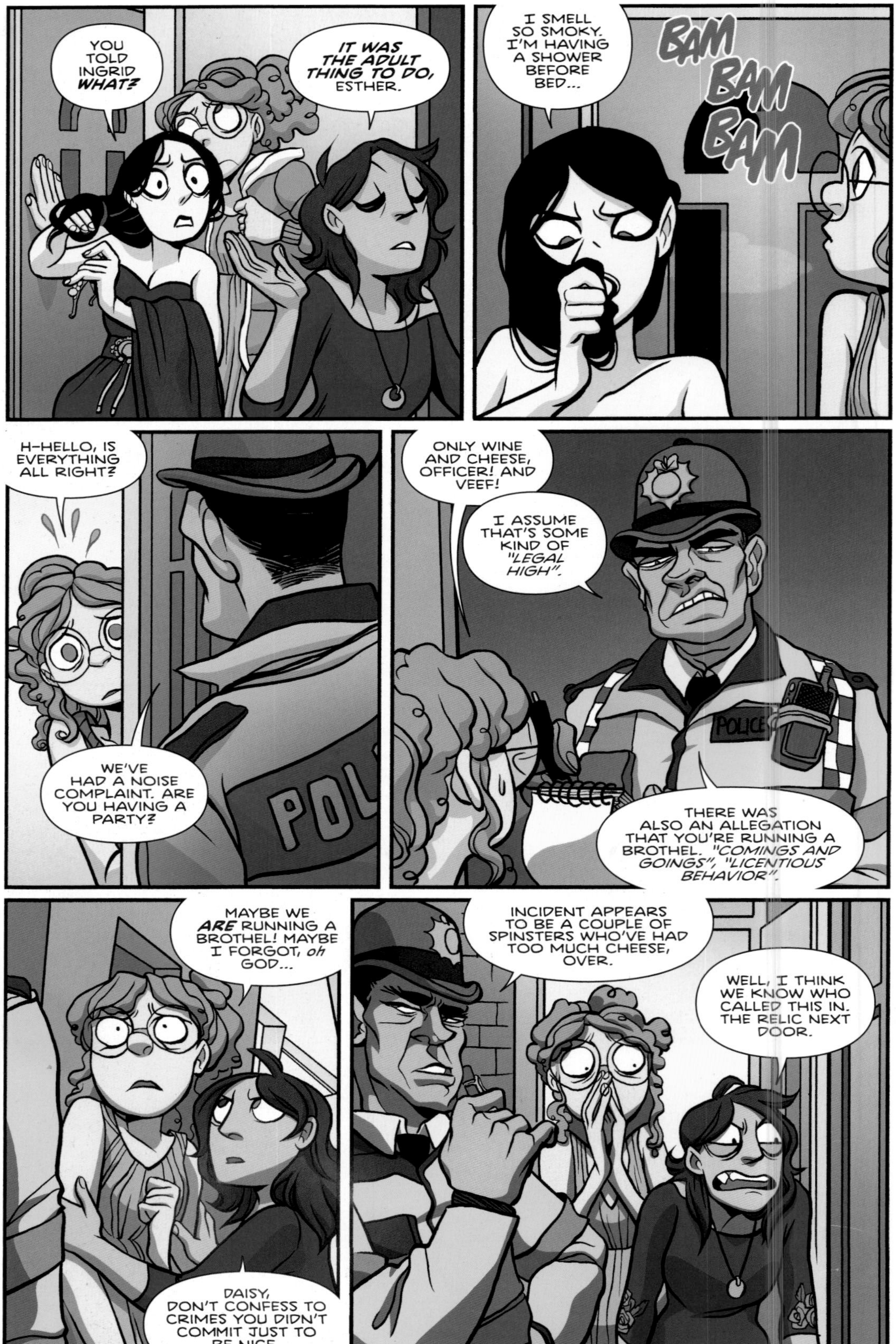
YOU TOLD INGRID *WHAT?*
IT WAS THE ADULT THING TO DO, ESTHER.
I SMELL SO SMOKY. I'M HAVING A SHOWER BEFORE BED...
BAM BAM BAM
H-HELLO, IS EVERYTHING ALL RIGHT?
WE'VE HAD A NOISE COMPLAINT. ARE YOU HAVING A PARTY?
POL
ONLY WINE AND CHEESE, OFFICER! AND VEEF!
I ASSUME THAT'S SOME KIND OF *"LEGAL HIGH"*.
POLICE
THERE WAS ALSO AN ALLEGATION THAT YOU'RE RUNNING A BROTHEL. *"COMINGS AND GOINGS", "LICENTIOUS BEHAVIOR".*
MAYBE WE *ARE* RUNNING A BROTHEL! MAYBE I FORGOT, *oh* GOD...
DAISY, DON'T CONFESS TO CRIMES YOU DIDN'T COMMIT JUST TO BE NICE.
INCIDENT APPEARS TO BE A COUPLE OF SPINSTERS WHO'VE HAD TOO MUCH CHEESE, OVER.
WELL, I THINK WE KNOW WHO CALLED THIS IN. THE RELIC NEXT DOOR.

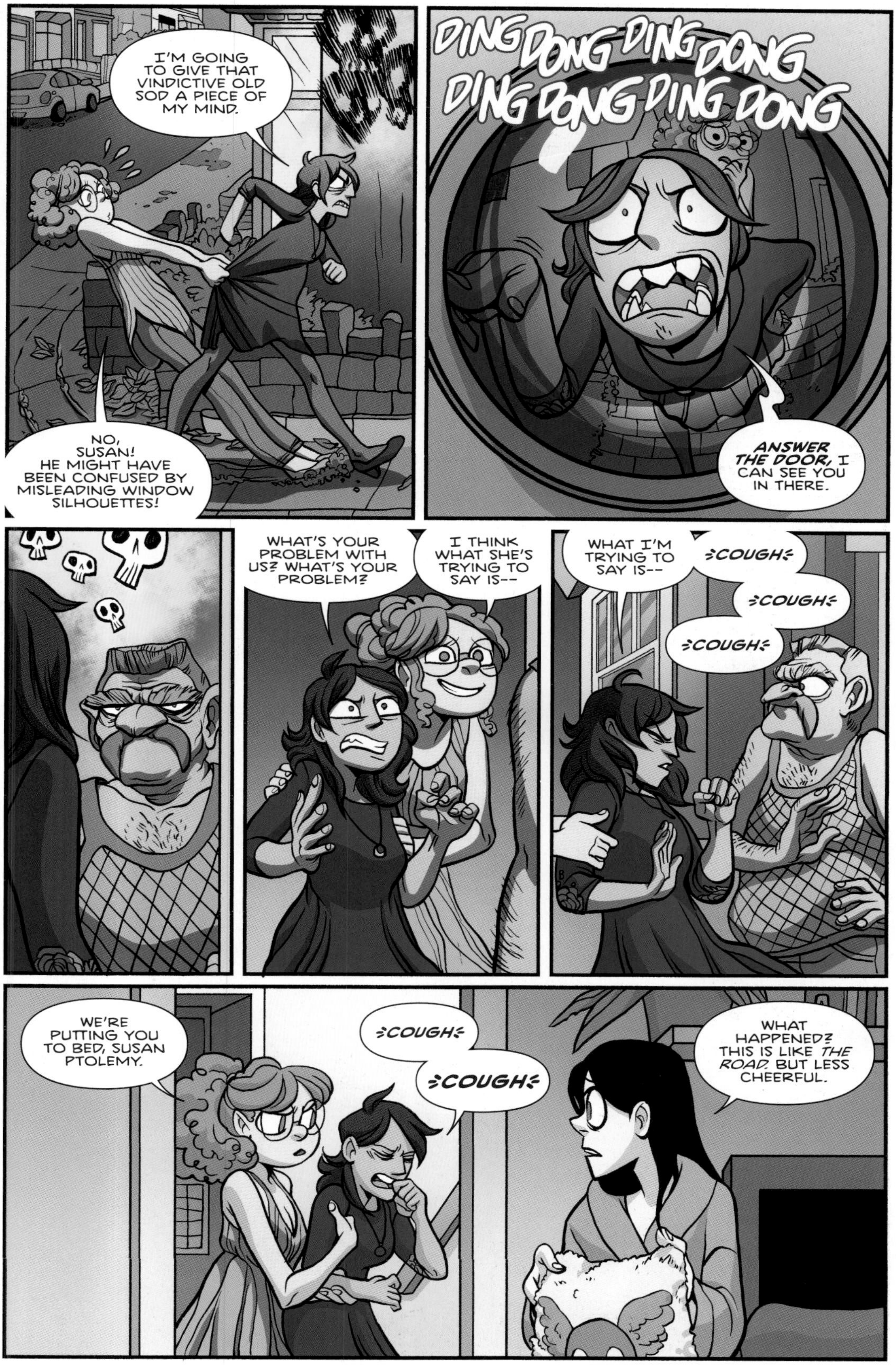
I'M GOING TO GIVE THAT VINDICTIVE OLD SOD A PIECE OF MY MIND.
NO, SUSAN! HE MIGHT HAVE BEEN CONFUSED BY MISLEADING WINDOW SILHOUETTES!
DING DONG DING DONG
DING DONG DING DONG
ANSWER THE DOOR, I CAN SEE YOU IN THERE.
WHAT'S YOUR PROBLEM WITH US? WHAT'S YOUR PROBLEM?
I THINK WHAT SHE'S TRYING TO SAY IS--
WHAT I'M TRYING TO SAY IS--
COUGH
COUGH
COUGH
WE'RE PUTTING YOU TO BED, SUSAN PTOLEMY.
COUGH
COUGH
WHAT HAPPENED? THIS IS LIKE THE ROAD, BUT LESS CHEERFUL.

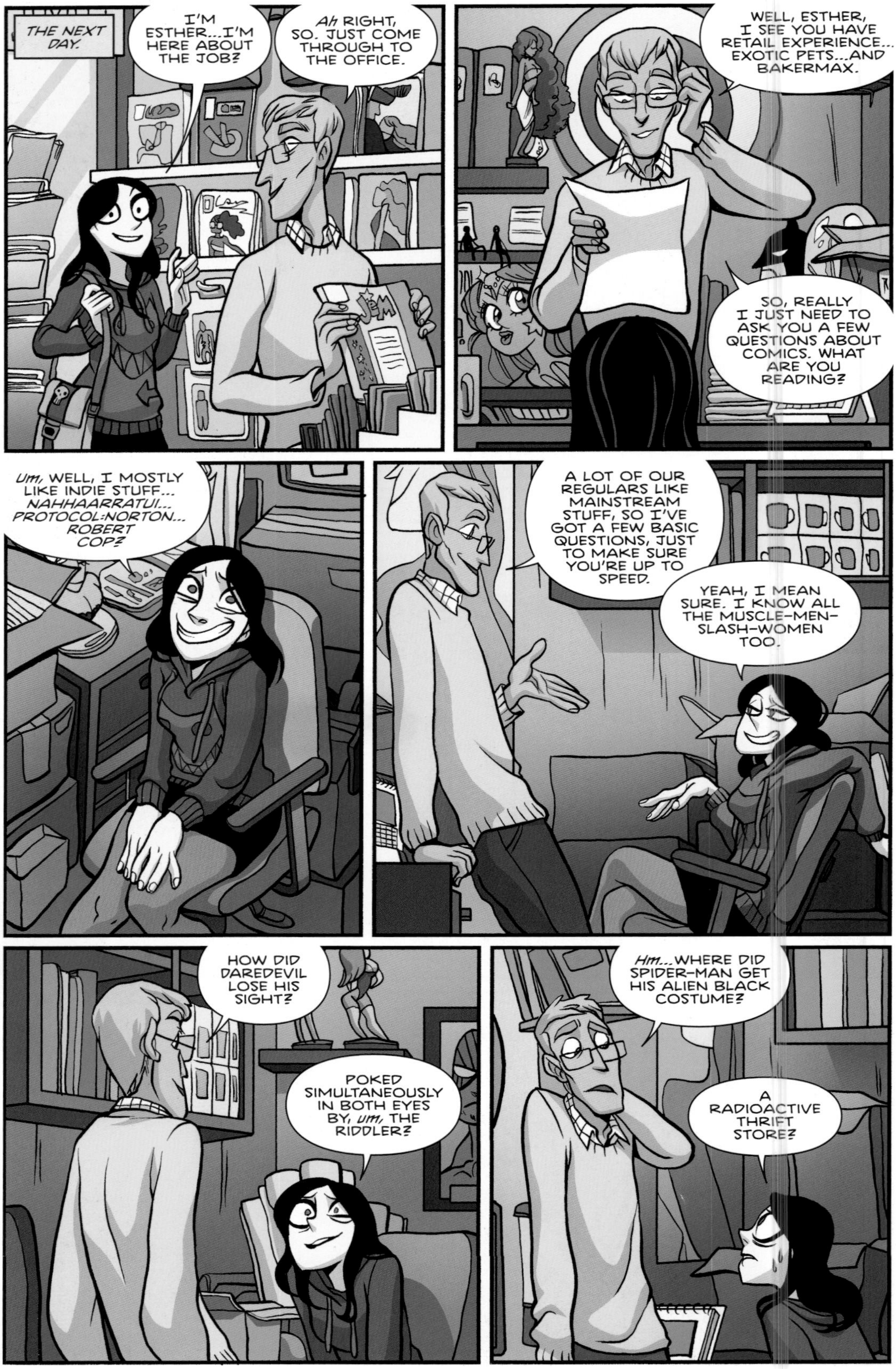
THE NEXT DAY.
I'M ESTHER...I'M HERE ABOUT THE JOB?
Ah RIGHT, SO. JUST COME THROUGH TO THE OFFICE.
WELL, ESTHER, I SEE YOU HAVE RETAIL EXPERIENCE... EXOTIC PETS...AND BAKERMAX.
SO, REALLY I JUST NEED TO ASK YOU A FEW QUESTIONS ABOUT COMICS. WHAT ARE YOU READING?
Um, WELL, I MOSTLY LIKE INDIE STUFF... NAHHAARRATUI... PROTOCOL:NORTON... ROBERT COP?
A LOT OF OUR REGULARS LIKE MAINSTREAM STUFF, SO I'VE GOT A FEW BASIC QUESTIONS, JUST TO MAKE SURE YOU'RE UP TO SPEED.
YEAH, I MEAN SURE. I KNOW ALL THE MUSCLE-MEN-SLASH-WOMEN TOO.
HOW DID DAREDEVIL LOSE HIS SIGHT?
POKED SIMULTANEOUSLY IN BOTH EYES BY, um, THE RIDDLER?
Hm...WHERE DID SPIDER-MAN GET HIS ALIEN BLACK COSTUME?
A RADIOACTIVE THRIFT STORE?

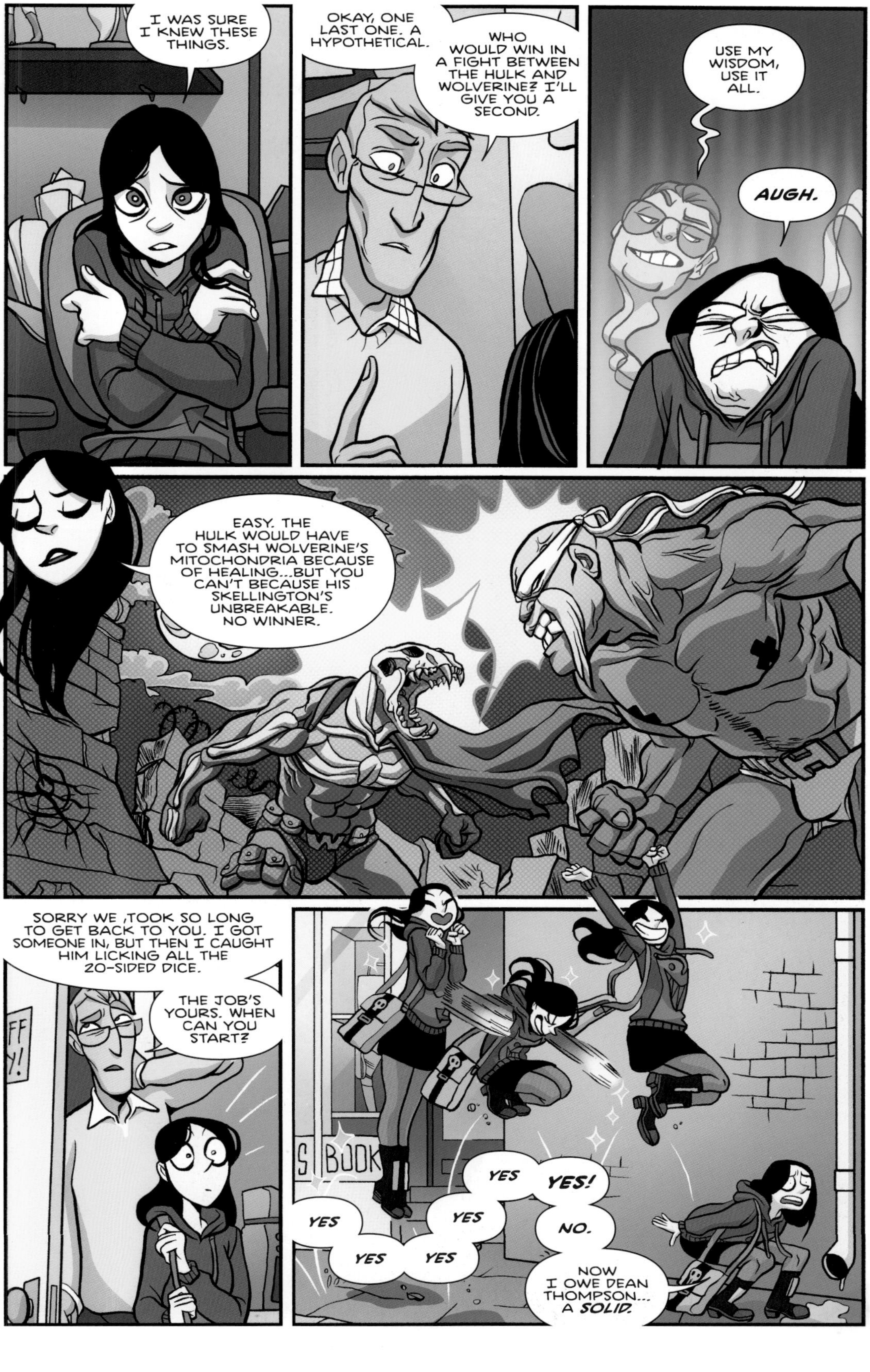
I WAS SURE I KNEW THESE THINGS.
OKAY, ONE LAST ONE. A HYPOTHETICAL.
WHO WOULD WIN IN A FIGHT BETWEEN THE HULK AND WOLVERINE? I'LL GIVE YOU A SECOND.
USE MY WISDOM, USE IT ALL.
AUGH.
EASY. THE HULK WOULD HAVE TO SMASH WOLVERINE'S MITOCHONDRIA BECAUSE OF HEALING...BUT YOU CAN'T BECAUSE HIS SKELLINGTON'S UNBREAKABLE. NO WINNER.
SORRY WE ,TOOK SO LONG TO GET BACK TO YOU. I GOT SOMEONE IN, BUT THEN I CAUGHT HIM LICKING ALL THE 20-SIDED DICE.
THE JOB'S YOURS. WHEN CAN YOU START?
YES
YES
YES
YES
YES
YES!
NO.
NOW I OWE DEAN THOMPSON... A *SOLID.*

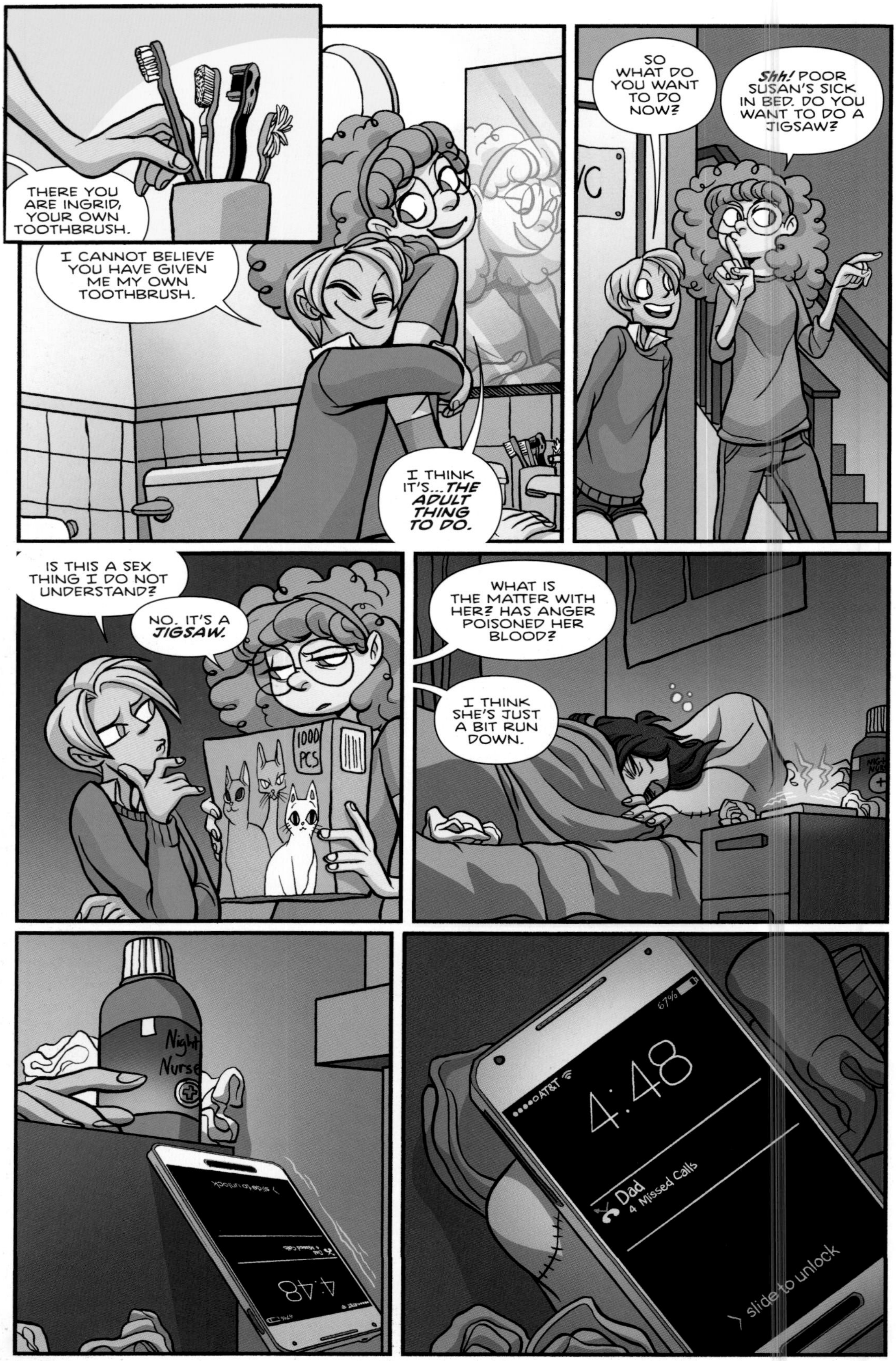
THERE YOU ARE INGRID, YOUR OWN TOOTHBRUSH.
I CANNOT BELIEVE YOU HAVE GIVEN ME MY OWN TOOTHBRUSH.
I THINK IT'S... THE ADULT THING TO DO.
SO WHAT DO YOU WANT TO DO NOW?
Shh! POOR SUSAN'S SICK IN BED. DO YOU WANT TO DO A JIGSAW?
IS THIS A SEX THING I DO NOT UNDERSTAND?
NO. IT'S A JIGSAW.
1000 PCS
WHAT IS THE MATTER WITH HER? HAS ANGER POISONED HER BLOOD?
I THINK SHE'S JUST A BIT RUN DOWN.
Night Nurse
AT&T
67%
4:48
Dad
4 Missed Calls
slide to unlock

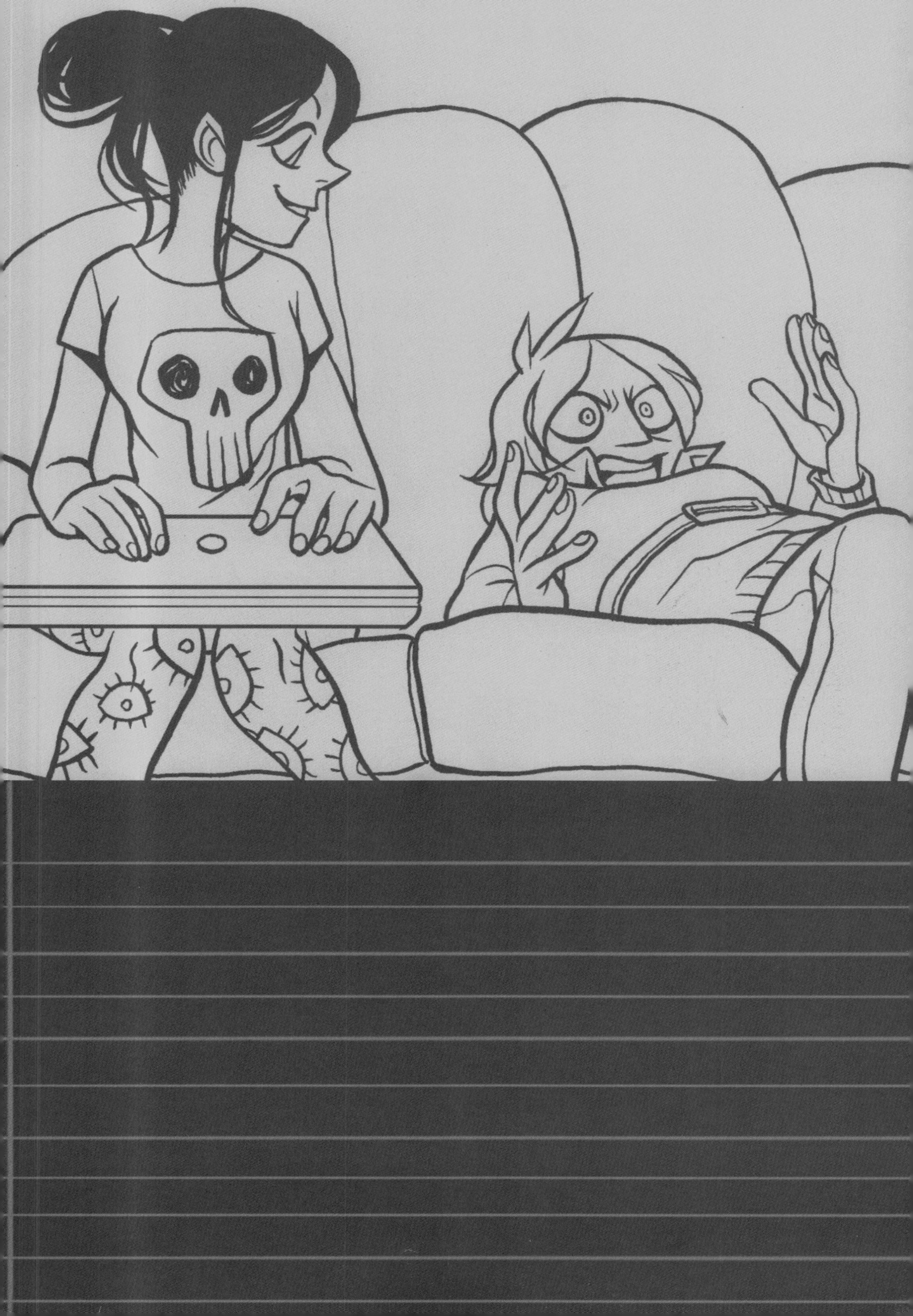

CHAPTER TWENTY FOUR

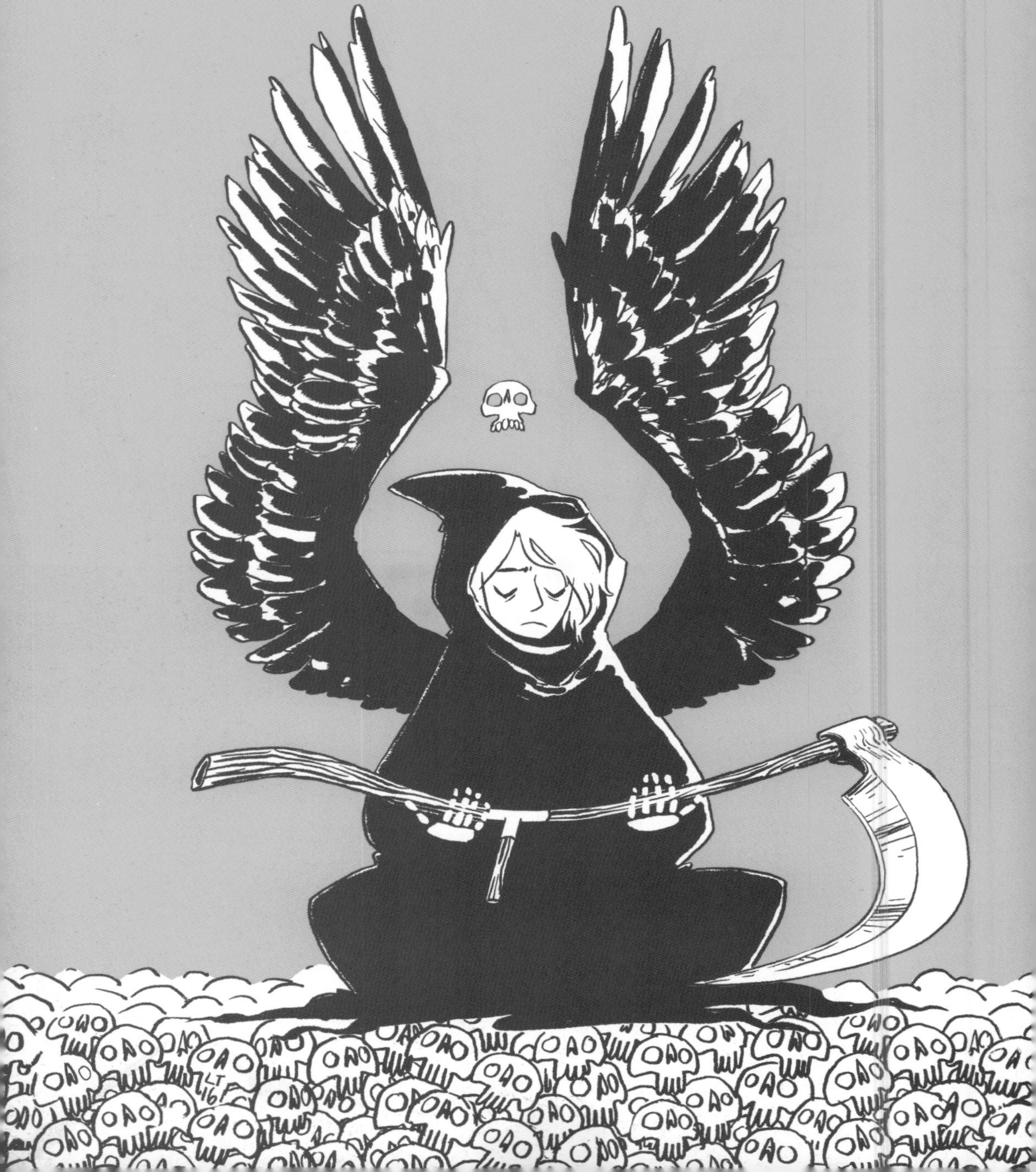

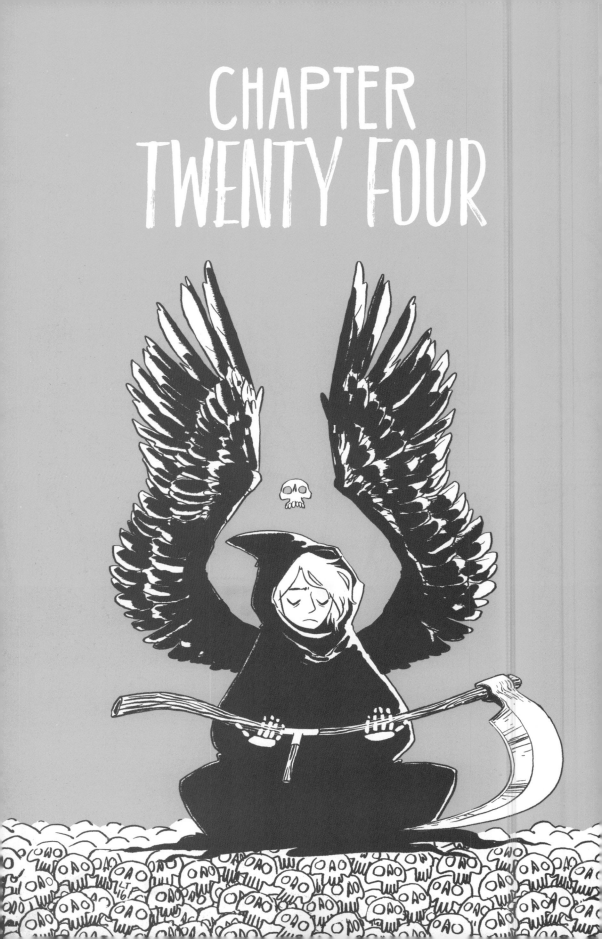

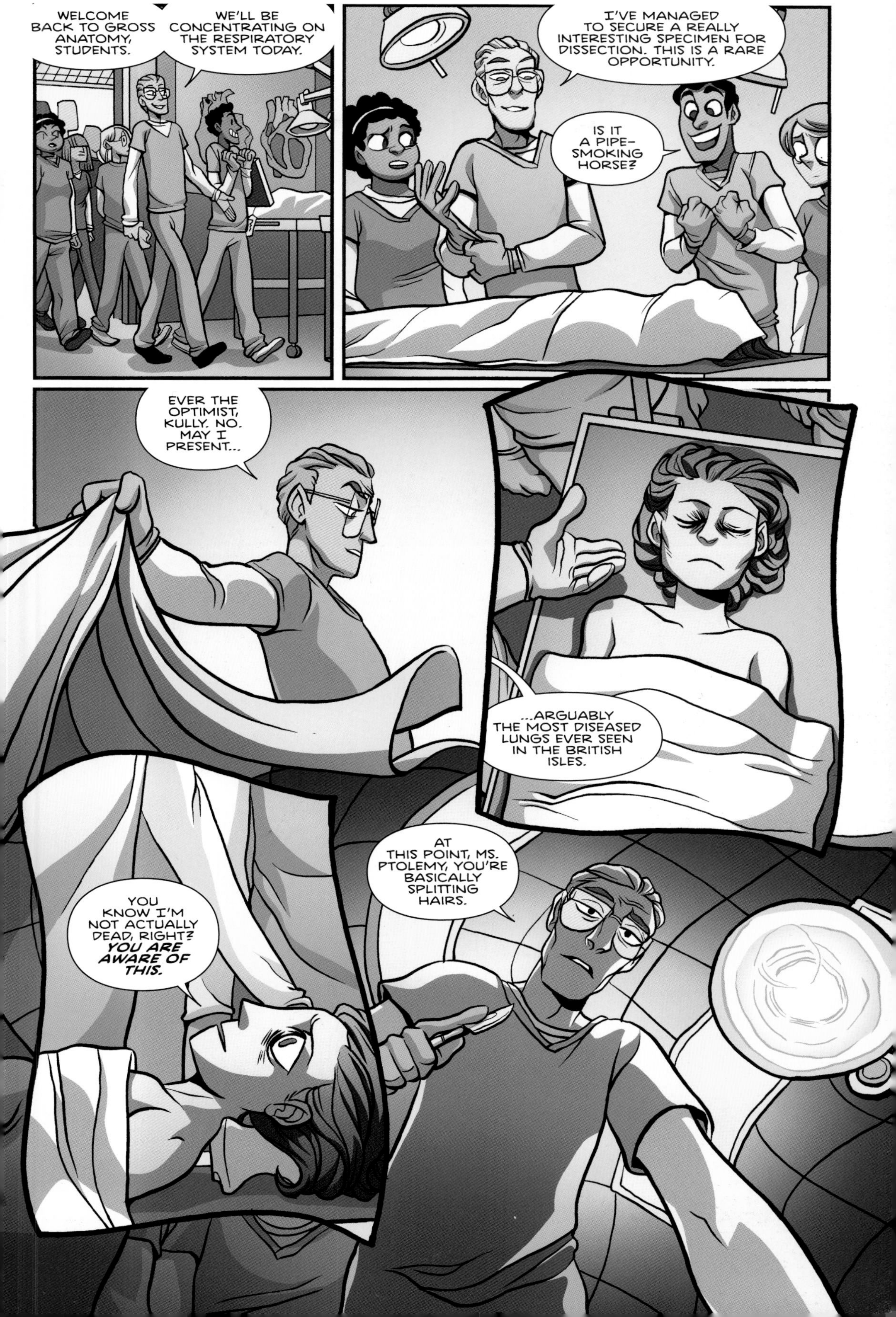
WELCOME BACK TO GROSS ANATOMY, STUDENTS.
WE'LL BE CONCENTRATING ON THE RESPIRATORY SYSTEM TODAY.
I'VE MANAGED TO SECURE A REALLY INTERESTING SPECIMEN FOR DISSECTION. THIS IS A RARE OPPORTUNITY.
IS IT A PIPE-SMOKING HORSE?
EVER THE OPTIMIST, KULLY. NO. MAY I PRESENT...
...ARGUABLY THE MOST DISEASED LUNGS EVER SEEN IN THE BRITISH ISLES.
YOU KNOW I'M NOT ACTUALLY DEAD, RIGHT? ***YOU ARE AWARE OF THIS.***
AT THIS POINT, MS. PTOLEMY, YOU'RE BASICALLY SPLITTING HAIRS.

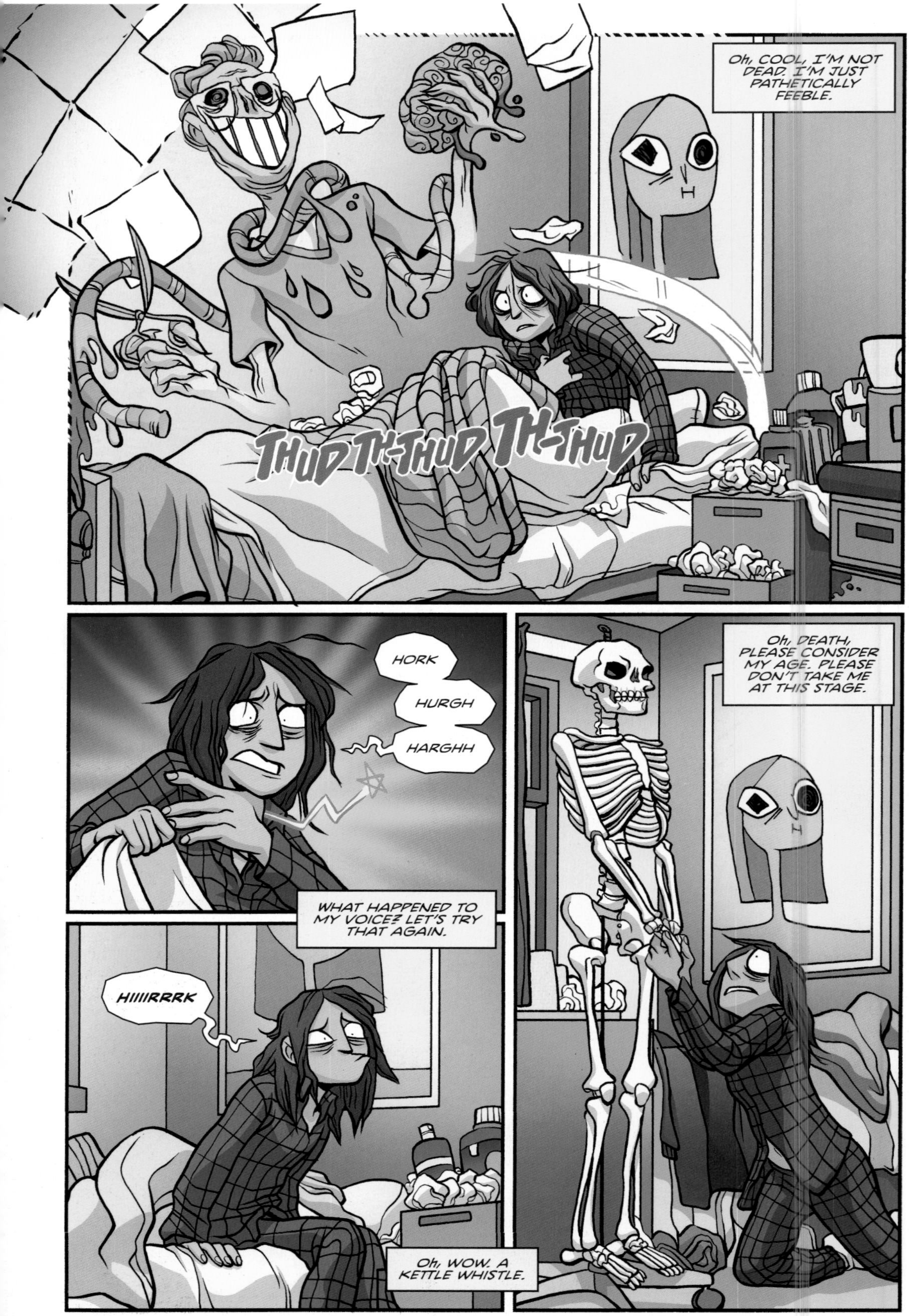
Oh, COOL, I'M NOT DEAD. I'M JUST PATHETICALLY FEEBLE.
THUD TH-THUD TH-THUD
HORK
HURGH
HARGHH
WHAT HAPPENED TO MY VOICE? LET'S TRY THAT AGAIN.
HIIIIRRRK
Oh, WOW. A KETTLE WHISTLE.
Oh, DEATH, PLEASE CONSIDER MY AGE. PLEASE DON'T TAKE ME AT THIS STAGE.

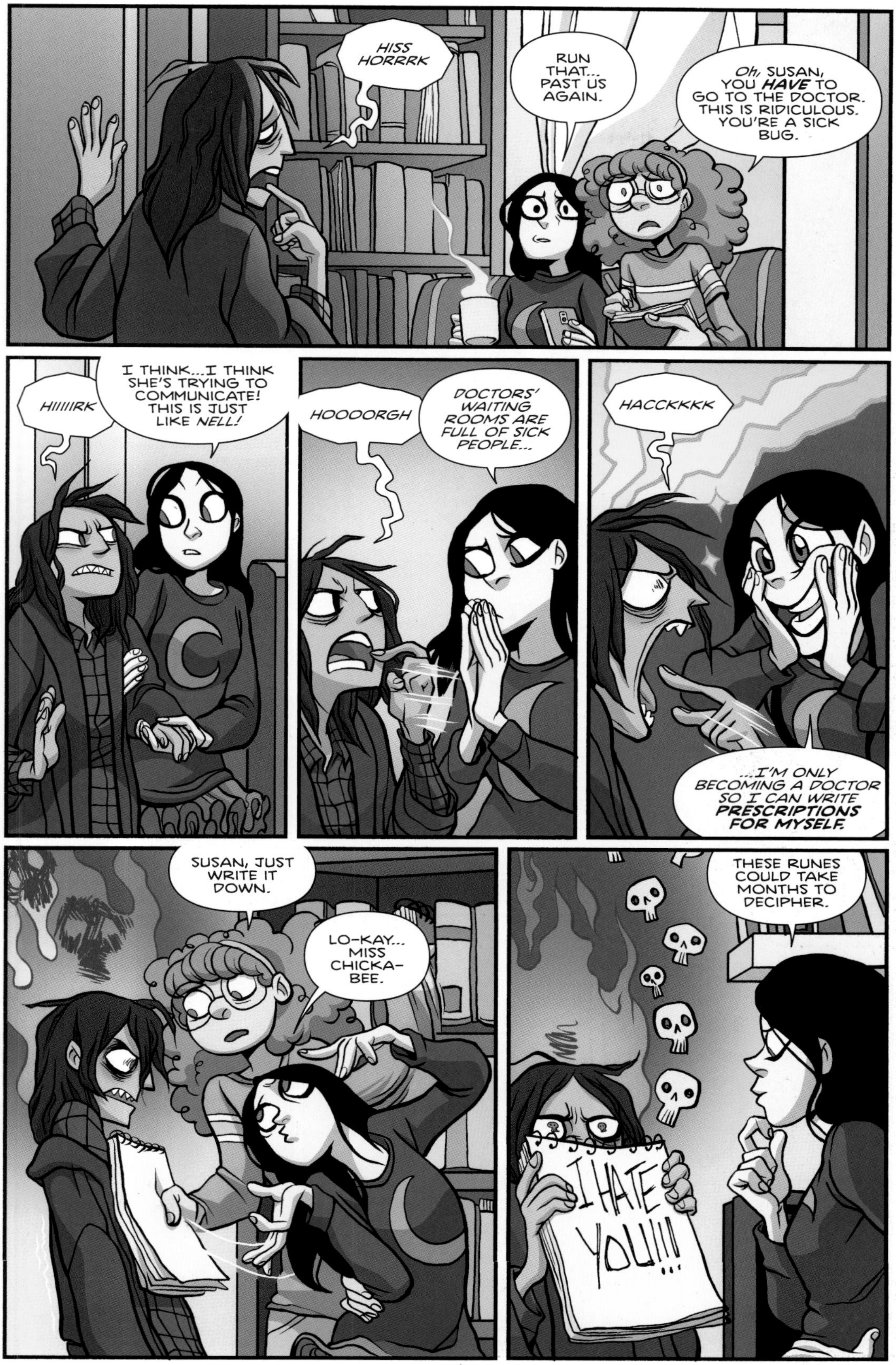

HISS HORRRK
RUN THAT... PAST US AGAIN.
Oh, SUSAN, YOU ***HAVE*** TO GO TO THE DOCTOR. THIS IS RIDICULOUS. YOU'RE A SICK BUG.
HIIIIIRK
I THINK...I THINK SHE'S TRYING TO COMMUNICATE! THIS IS JUST LIKE *NELL!*
HOOOORGH
DOCTORS' WAITING ROOMS ARE FULL OF SICK PEOPLE...
HACCKKKK
...I'M ONLY BECOMING A DOCTOR SO I CAN WRITE ***PRESCRIPTIONS FOR MYSELF.***
SUSAN, JUST WRITE IT DOWN.
LO-KAY... MISS CHICKA-BEE.
I HATE YOU!!!
THESE RUNES COULD TAKE MONTHS TO DECIPHER.

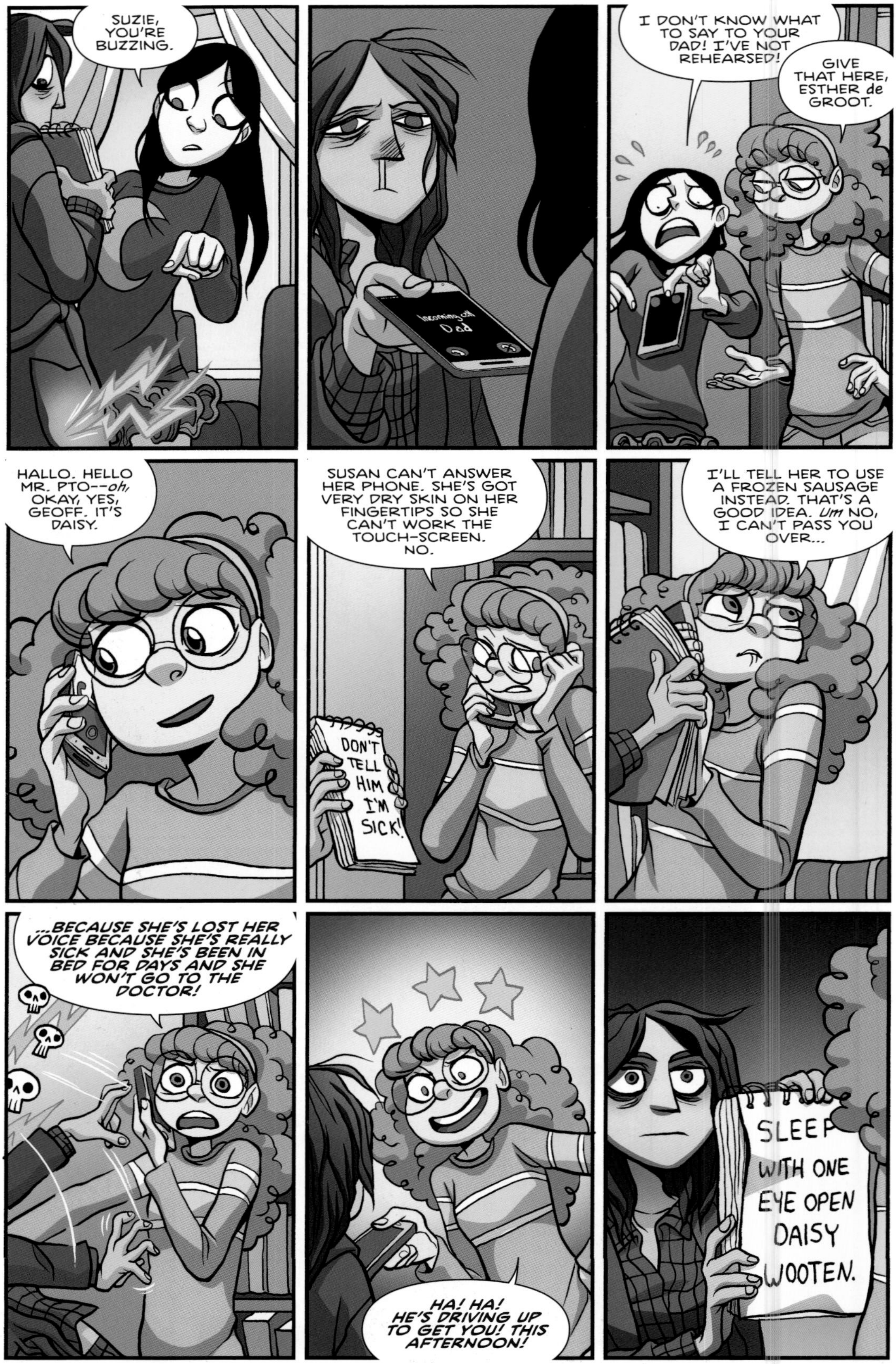
SUZIE, YOU'RE BUZZING.
Incoming call
Dad
I DON'T KNOW WHAT TO SAY TO YOUR DAD! I'VE NOT REHEARSED!
GIVE THAT HERE, ESTHER de GROOT.
HALLO. HELLO MR. PTO--*oh,* OKAY, YES, GEOFF. IT'S DAISY.
SUSAN CAN'T ANSWER HER PHONE. SHE'S GOT VERY DRY SKIN ON HER FINGERTIPS SO SHE CAN'T WORK THE TOUCH-SCREEN. NO.
DON'T TELL HIM I'M SICK!
I'LL TELL HER TO USE A FROZEN SAUSAGE INSTEAD. THAT'S A GOOD IDEA. *Um* NO, I CAN'T PASS YOU OVER...
...BECAUSE SHE'S LOST HER VOICE BECAUSE SHE'S REALLY SICK AND SHE'S BEEN IN BED FOR DAYS AND SHE WON'T GO TO THE DOCTOR!
HA! HA! HE'S DRIVING UP TO GET YOU! THIS AFTERNOON!
SLEEP WITH ONE EYE OPEN DAISY WOOTEN.

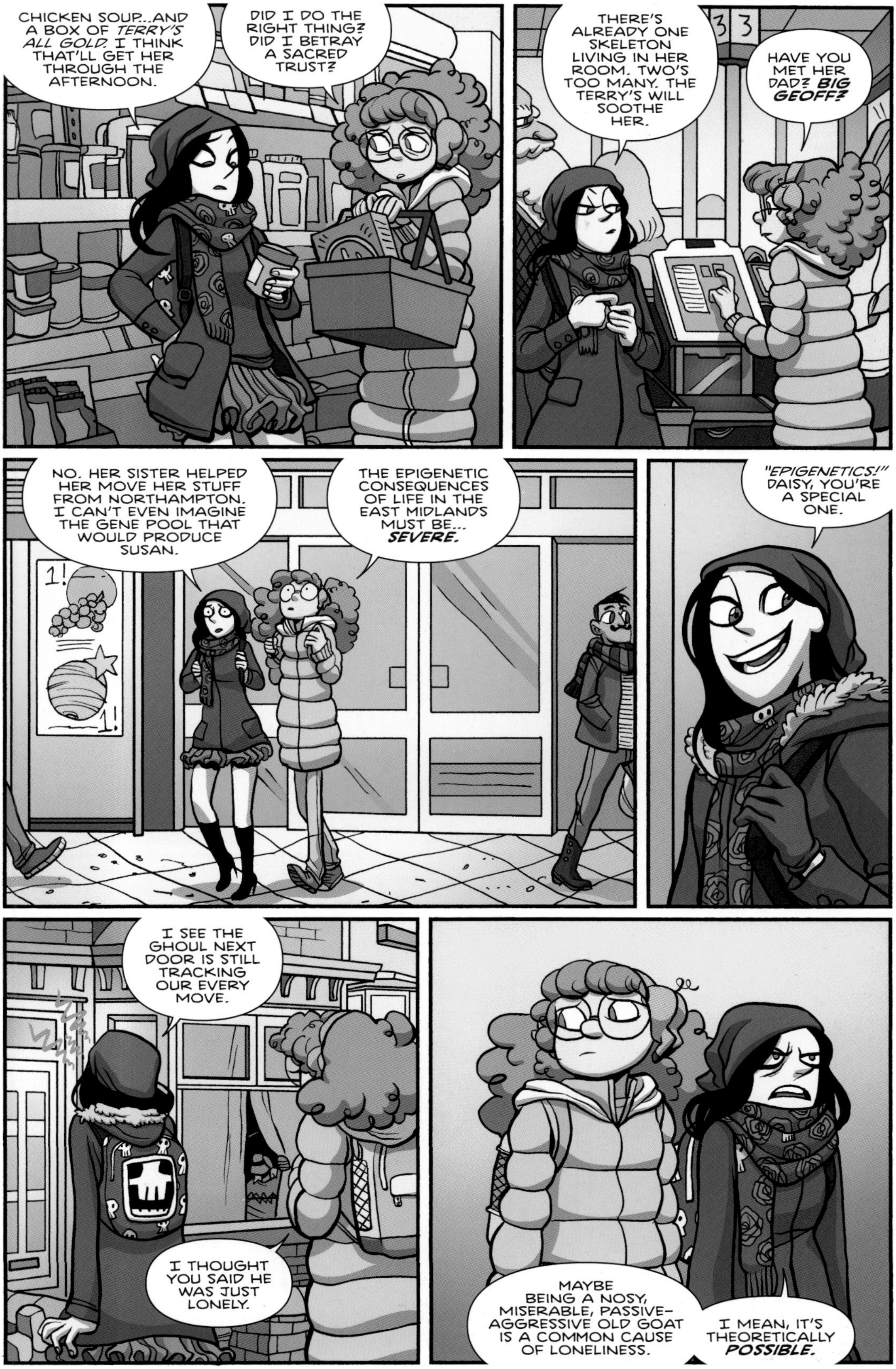
CHICKEN SOUP...AND A BOX OF TERRY'S ALL GOLD I THINK THAT'LL GET HER THROUGH THE AFTERNOON.
DID I DO THE RIGHT THING? DID I BETRAY A SACRED TRUST?
THERE'S ALREADY ONE SKELETON LIVING IN HER ROOM. TWO'S TOO MANY. THE TERRY'S WILL SOOTHE HER.
HAVE YOU MET HER DAD? BIG GEOFF?
NO. HER SISTER HELPED HER MOVE HER STUFF FROM NORTHAMPTON. I CAN'T EVEN IMAGINE THE GENE POOL THAT WOULD PRODUCE SUSAN.
THE EPIGENETIC CONSEQUENCES OF LIFE IN THE EAST MIDLANDS MUST BE... SEVERE.
"EPIGENETICS!" DAISY, YOU'RE A SPECIAL ONE.
I SEE THE GHOUL NEXT DOOR IS STILL TRACKING OUR EVERY MOVE.
I THOUGHT YOU SAID HE WAS JUST LONELY.
MAYBE BEING A NOSY, MISERABLE, PASSIVE-AGGRESSIVE OLD GOAT IS A COMMON CAUSE OF LONELINESS.
I MEAN, IT'S THEORETICALLY POSSIBLE.

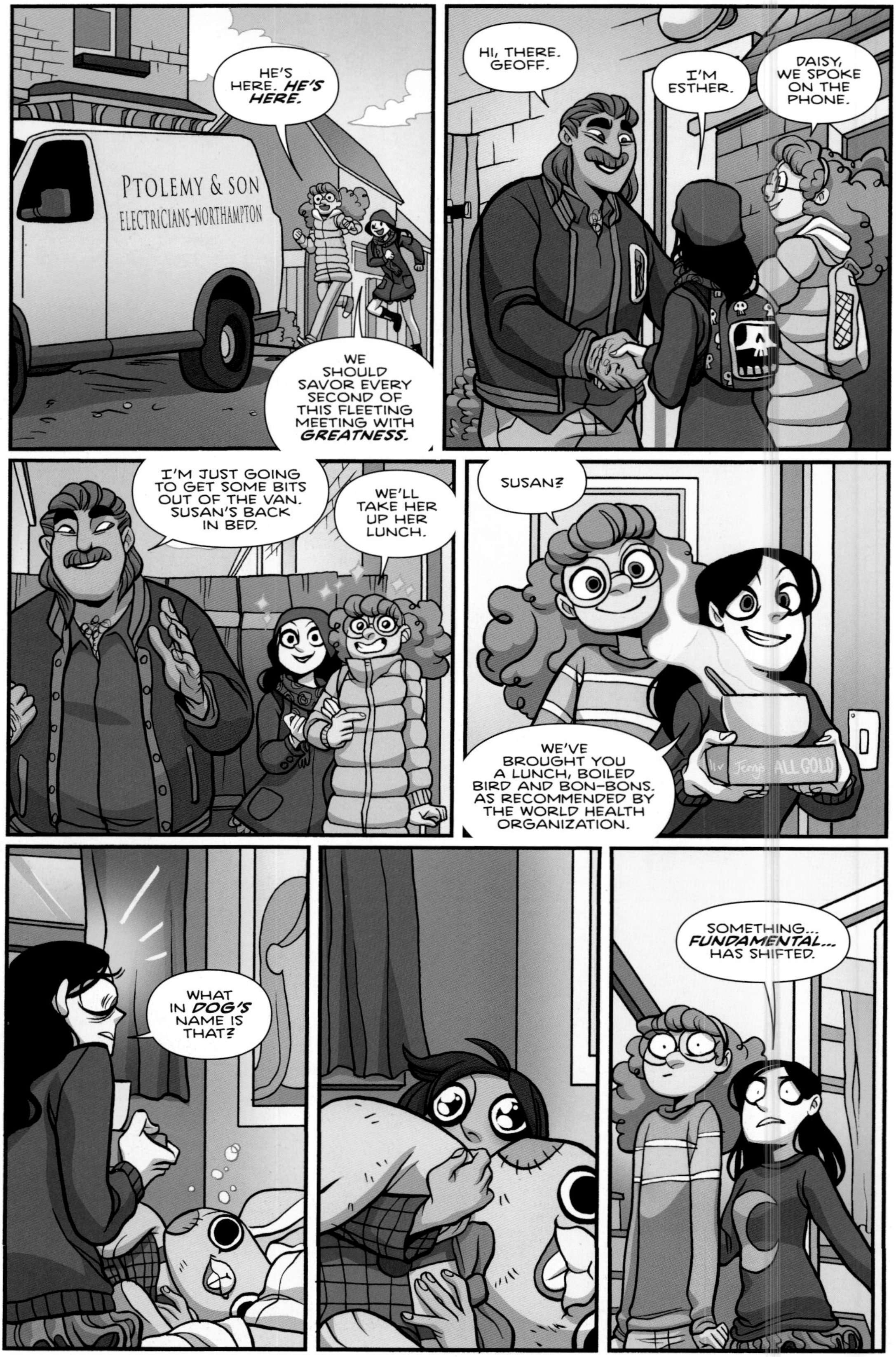
PTOLEMY & SON
ELECTRICIANS-NORTHAMPTON
HE'S HERE. *HE'S HERE.*
WE SHOULD SAVOR EVERY SECOND OF THIS FLEETING MEETING WITH *GREATNESS.*
HI, THERE. GEOFF.
I'M ESTHER.
DAISY, WE SPOKE ON THE PHONE.
I'M JUST GOING TO GET SOME BITS OUT OF THE VAN. SUSAN'S BACK IN BED.
WE'LL TAKE HER UP HER LUNCH.
SUSAN?
WE'VE BROUGHT YOU A LUNCH, BOILED BIRD AND BON-BONS. AS RECOMMENDED BY THE WORLD HEALTH ORGANIZATION.
ALL GOLD
WHAT IN *DOG'S* NAME IS THAT?
SOMETHING... *FUNDAMENTAL...* HAS SHIFTED.

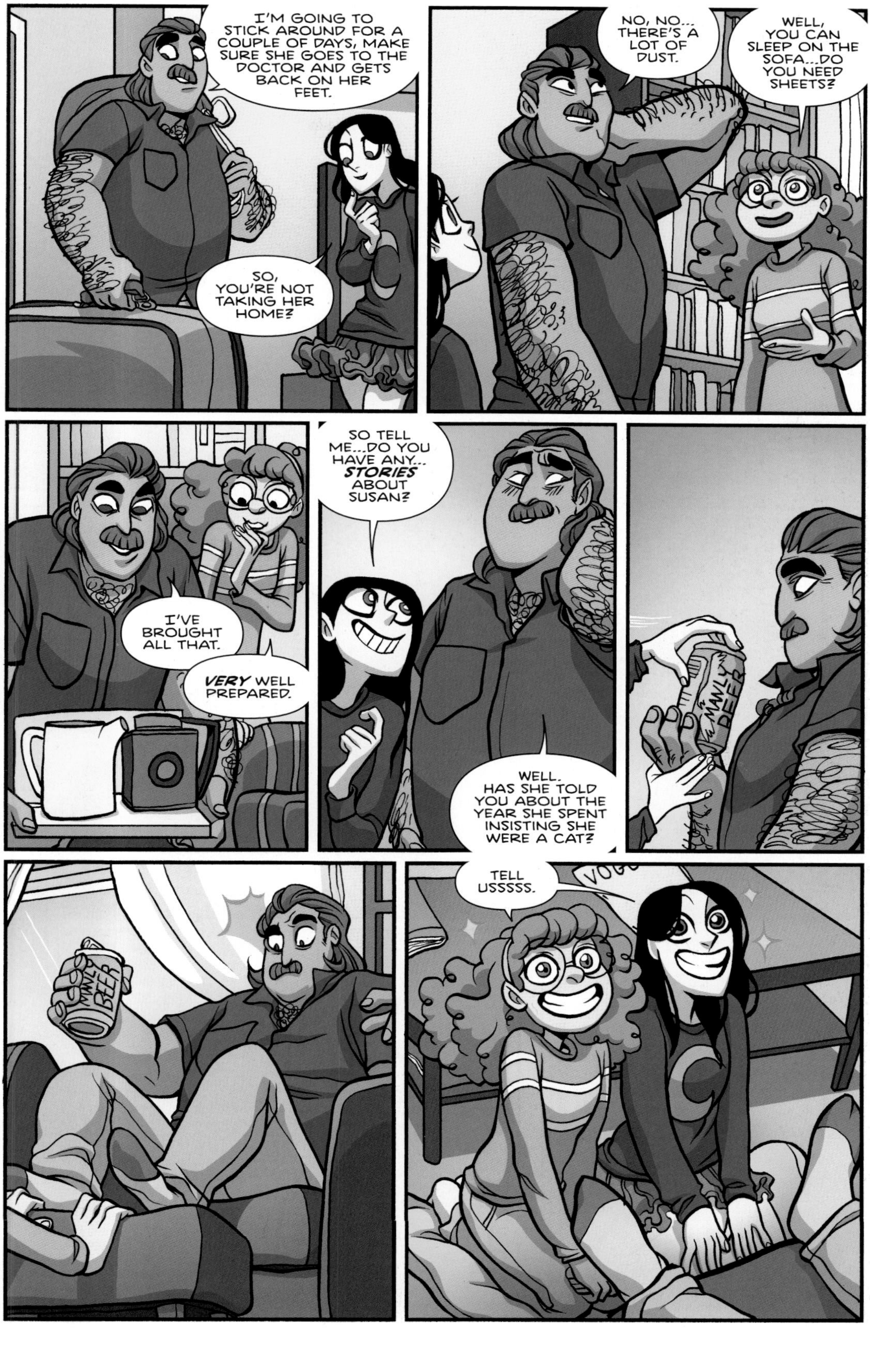
I'M GOING TO STICK AROUND FOR A COUPLE OF DAYS, MAKE SURE SHE GOES TO THE DOCTOR AND GETS BACK ON HER FEET.
SO, YOU'RE NOT TAKING HER HOME?
NO, NO... THERE'S A LOT OF DUST.
WELL, YOU CAN SLEEP ON THE SOFA...DO YOU NEED SHEETS?
I'VE BROUGHT ALL THAT.
VERY WELL PREPARED.
SO TELL ME...DO YOU HAVE ANY... ***STORIES*** ABOUT SUSAN?
WELL. HAS SHE TOLD YOU ABOUT THE YEAR SHE SPENT INSISTING SHE WERE A CAT?
MAWLY BEER
MAWLY BEER
TELL USSSSS.

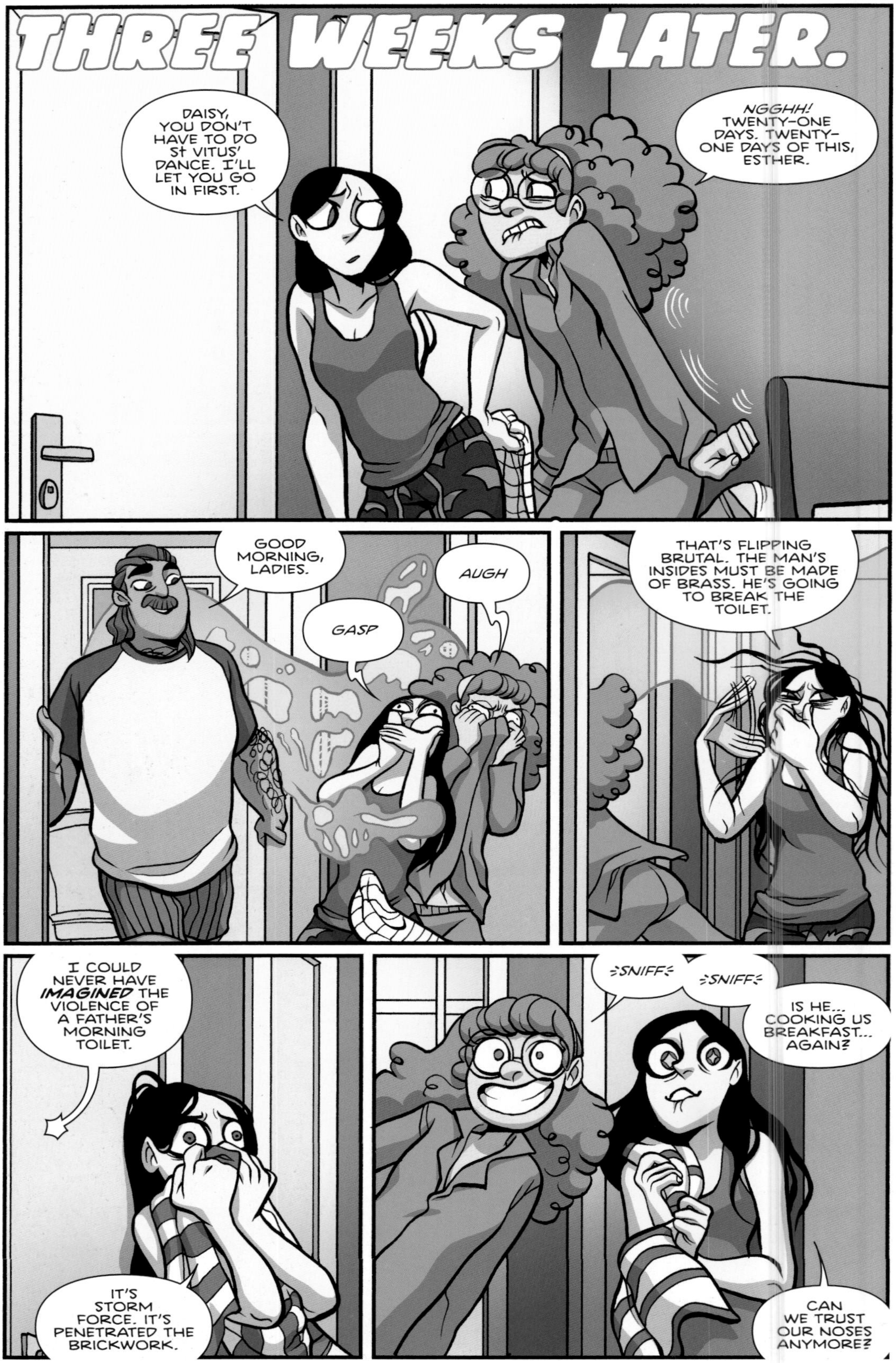
THREE WEEKS LATER.
DAISY, YOU DON'T HAVE TO DO St VITUS' DANCE. I'LL LET YOU GO IN FIRST.
NGGHH! TWENTY-ONE DAYS. TWENTY-ONE DAYS OF THIS, ESTHER.
GOOD MORNING, LADIES.
AUGH
GASP
THAT'S FLIPPING BRUTAL. THE MAN'S INSIDES MUST BE MADE OF BRASS. HE'S GOING TO BREAK THE TOILET.
I COULD NEVER HAVE IMAGINED THE VIOLENCE OF A FATHER'S MORNING TOILET.
IT'S STORM FORCE. IT'S PENETRATED THE BRICKWORK.
SNIFF
SNIFF
IS HE... COOKING US BREAKFAST... AGAIN?
CAN WE TRUST OUR NOSES ANYMORE?

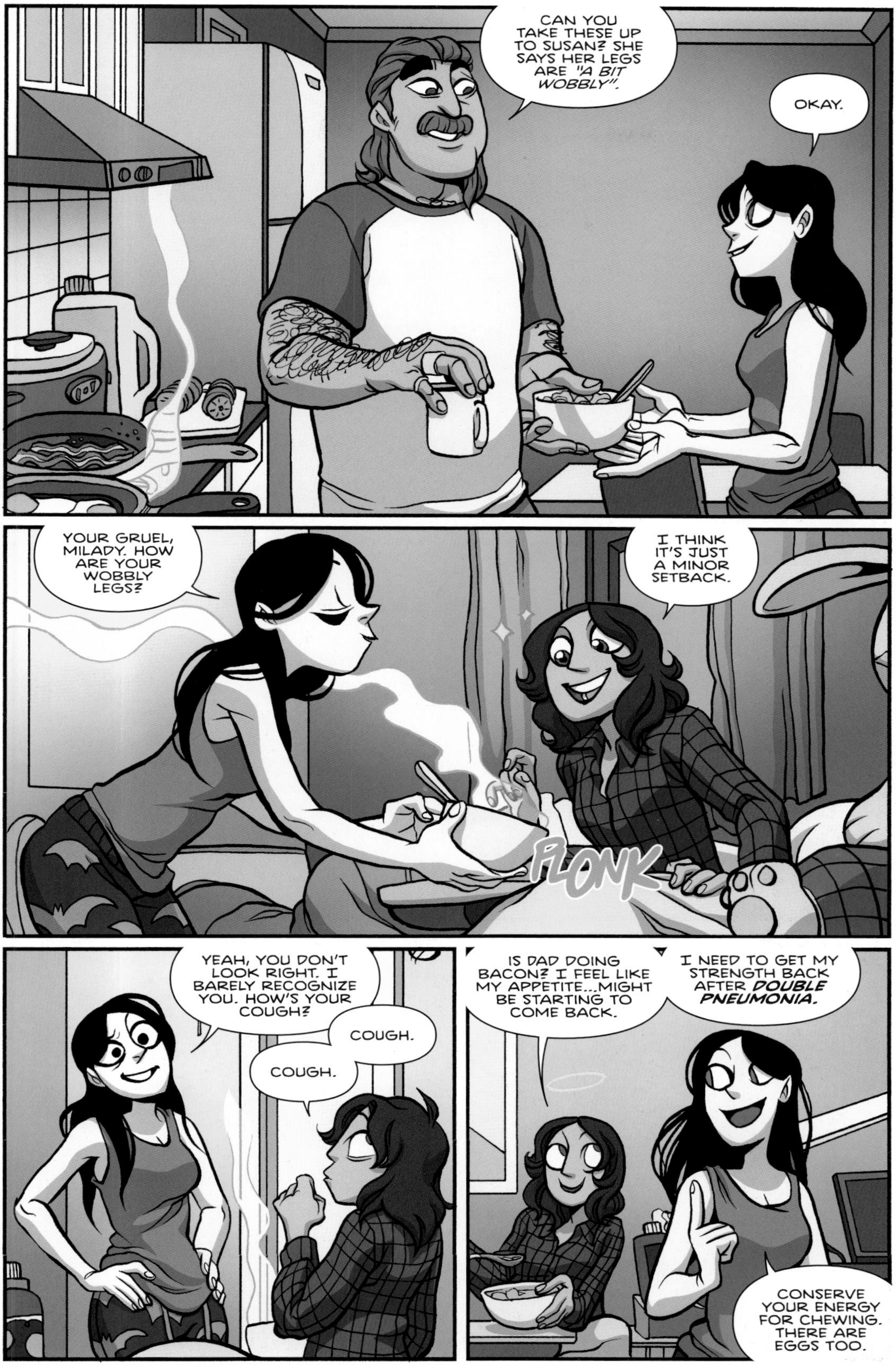
CAN YOU TAKE THESE UP TO SUSAN? SHE SAYS HER LEGS ARE "A BIT WOBBLY".
OKAY.
YOUR GRUEL, MILADY. HOW ARE YOUR WOBBLY LEGS?
I THINK IT'S JUST A MINOR SETBACK.
PLONK
YEAH, YOU DON'T LOOK RIGHT. I BARELY RECOGNIZE YOU. HOW'S YOUR COUGH?
COUGH.
COUGH.
IS DAD DOING BACON? I FEEL LIKE MY APPETITE...MIGHT BE STARTING TO COME BACK.
I NEED TO GET MY STRENGTH BACK AFTER DOUBLE PNEUMONIA.
CONSERVE YOUR ENERGY FOR CHEWING. THERE ARE EGGS TOO.

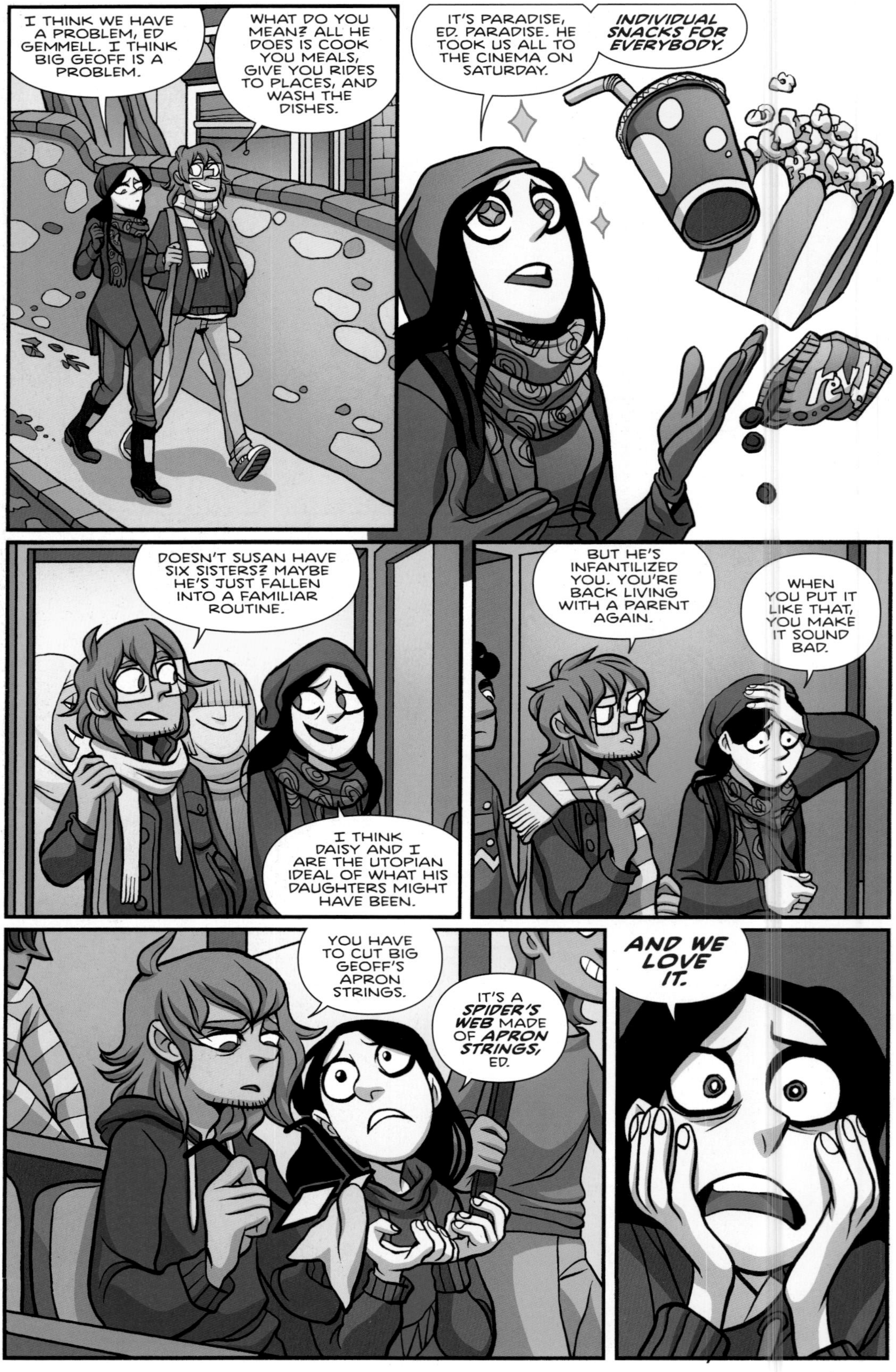
I THINK WE HAVE A PROBLEM, ED GEMMELL. I THINK BIG GEOFF IS A PROBLEM.
WHAT DO YOU MEAN? ALL HE DOES IS COOK YOU MEALS, GIVE YOU RIDES TO PLACES, AND WASH THE DISHES.
IT'S PARADISE, ED. PARADISE. HE TOOK US ALL TO THE CINEMA ON SATURDAY.
INDIVIDUAL SNACKS FOR EVERYBODY.
DOESN'T SUSAN HAVE SIX SISTERS? MAYBE HE'S JUST FALLEN INTO A FAMILIAR ROUTINE.
I THINK DAISY AND I ARE THE UTOPIAN IDEAL OF WHAT HIS DAUGHTERS MIGHT HAVE BEEN.
BUT HE'S INFANTILIZED YOU. YOU'RE BACK LIVING WITH A PARENT AGAIN.
WHEN YOU PUT IT LIKE THAT, YOU MAKE IT SOUND BAD.
YOU HAVE TO CUT BIG GEOFF'S APRON STRINGS.
IT'S A SPIDER'S WEB MADE OF APRON STRINGS, ED.
AND WE LOVE IT.

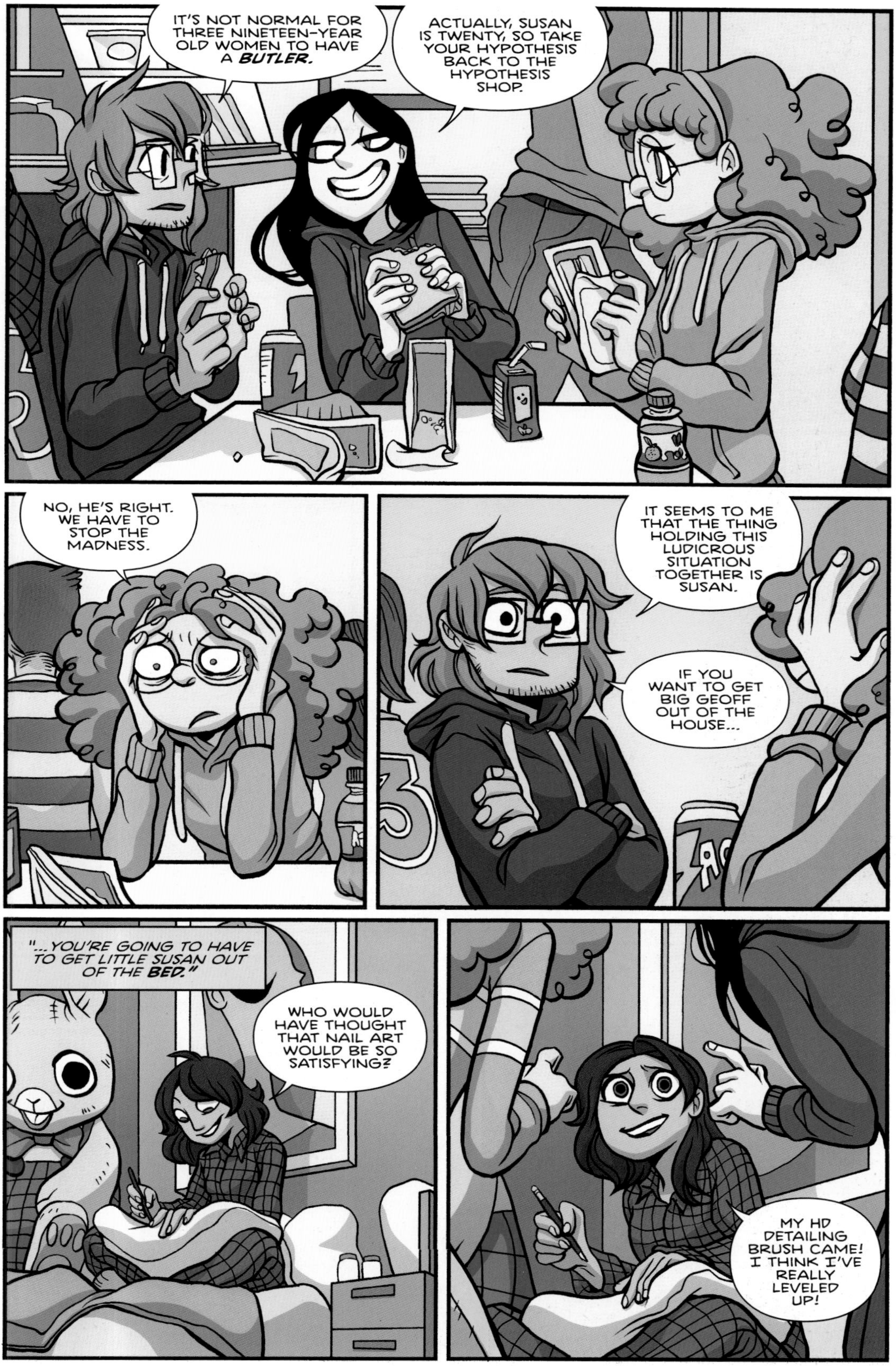
IT'S NOT NORMAL FOR THREE NINETEEN-YEAR OLD WOMEN TO HAVE A **BUTLER.**
ACTUALLY, SUSAN IS TWENTY, SO TAKE YOUR HYPOTHESIS BACK TO THE HYPOTHESIS SHOP.
NO, HE'S RIGHT. WE HAVE TO STOP THE MADNESS.
IT SEEMS TO ME THAT THE THING HOLDING THIS LUDICROUS SITUATION TOGETHER IS SUSAN.
IF YOU WANT TO GET BIG GEOFF OUT OF THE HOUSE...
"...YOU'RE GOING TO HAVE TO GET LITTLE SUSAN OUT OF THE **BED.**"
WHO WOULD HAVE THOUGHT THAT NAIL ART WOULD BE SO SATISFYING?
MY HD DETAILING BRUSH CAME! I THINK I'VE REALLY LEVELED UP!

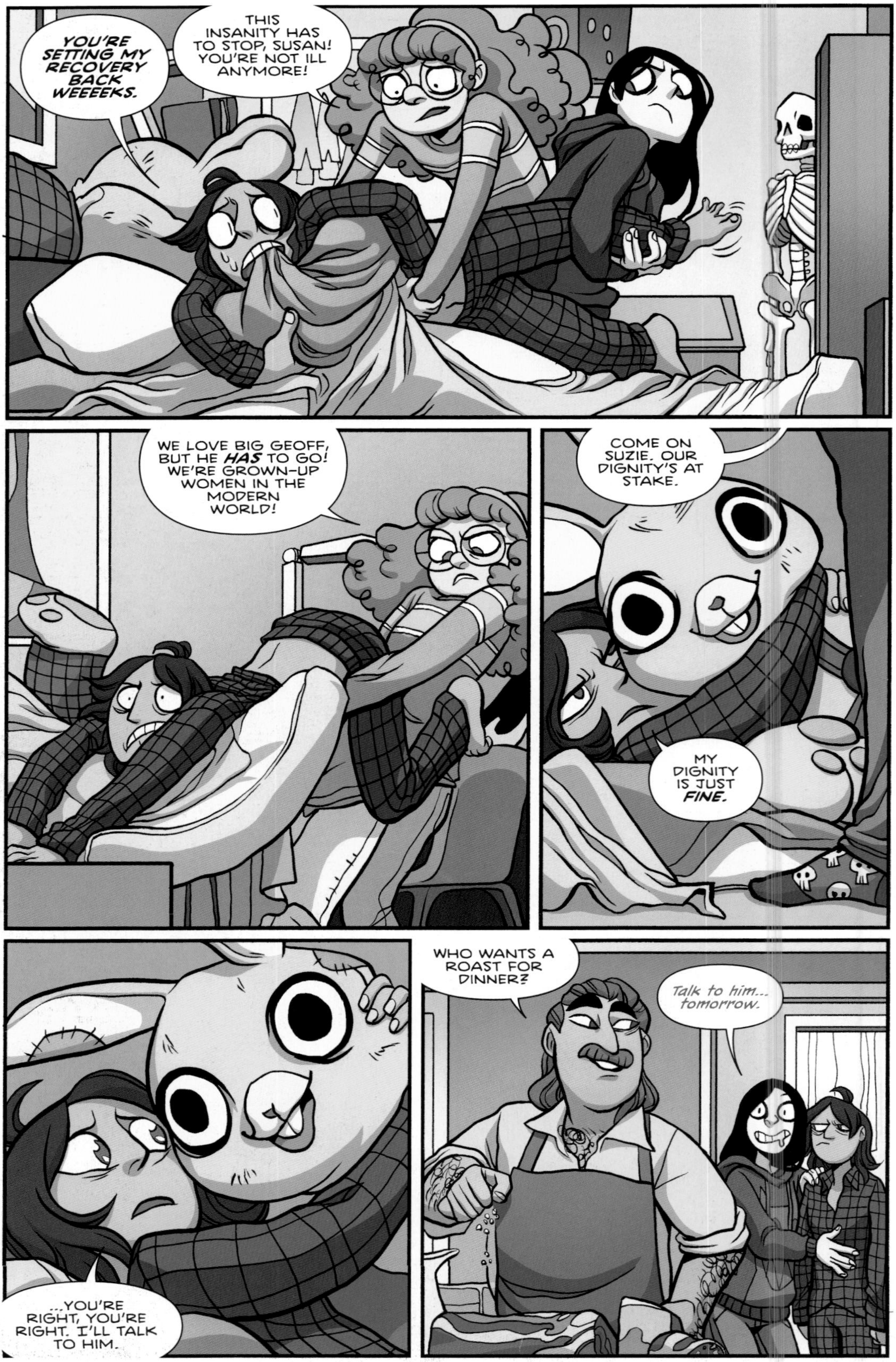

YOU'RE SETTING MY RECOVERY BACK WEEEEKS.
THIS INSANITY HAS TO STOP, SUSAN! YOU'RE NOT ILL ANYMORE!
WE LOVE BIG GEOFF, BUT HE HAS TO GO! WE'RE GROWN-UP WOMEN IN THE MODERN WORLD!
COME ON SUZIE. OUR DIGNITY'S AT STAKE.
MY DIGNITY IS JUST FINE.
...YOU'RE RIGHT, YOU'RE RIGHT. I'LL TALK TO HIM.
WHO WANTS A ROAST FOR DINNER?
Talk to him... tomorrow.

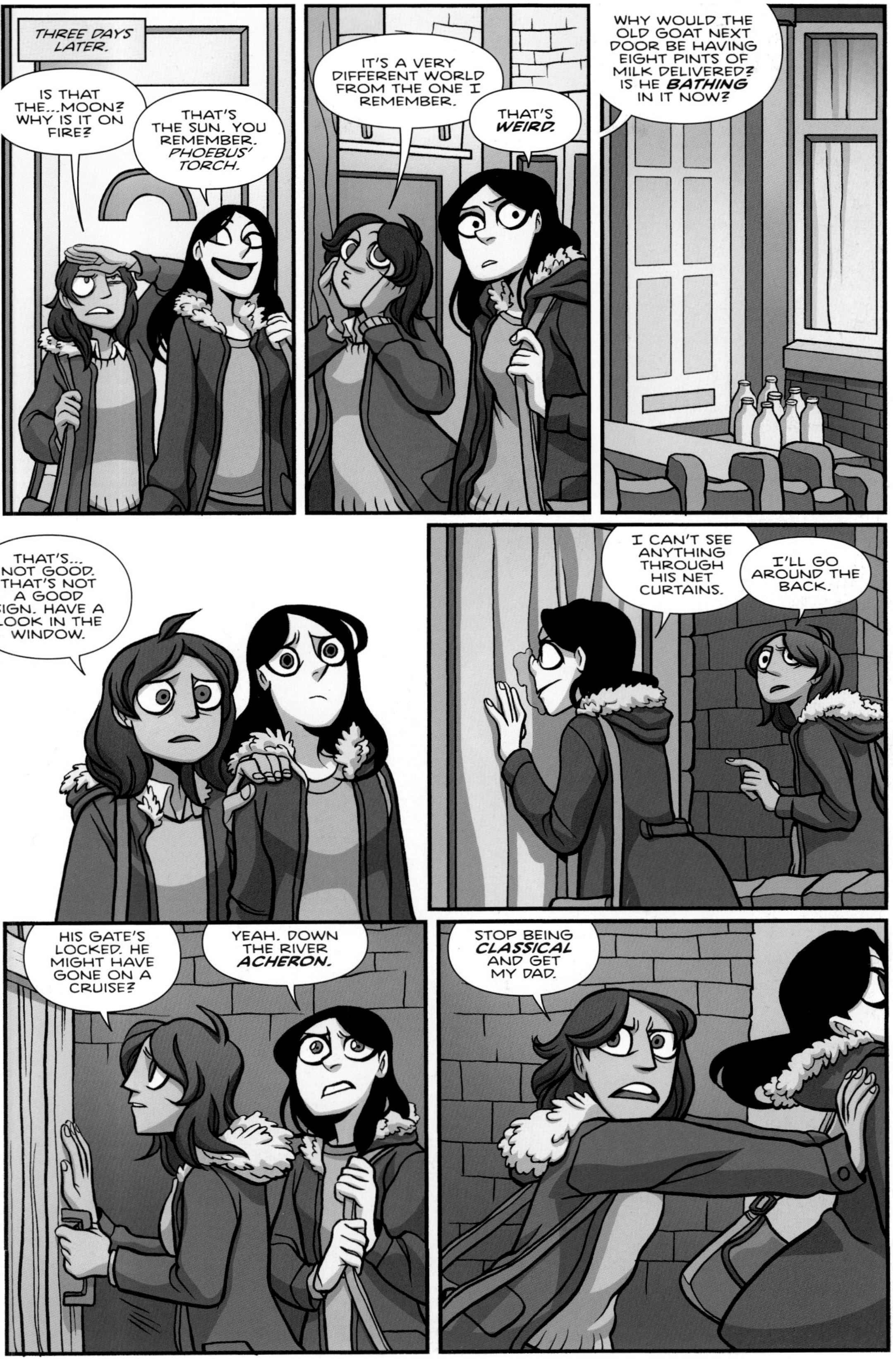
THREE DAYS LATER.
IS THAT THE...MOON? WHY IS IT ON FIRE?
THAT'S THE SUN. YOU REMEMBER. PHOEBUS' TORCH.
IT'S A VERY DIFFERENT WORLD FROM THE ONE I REMEMBER.
THAT'S WEIRD.
WHY WOULD THE OLD GOAT NEXT DOOR BE HAVING EIGHT PINTS OF MILK DELIVERED? IS HE BATHING IN IT NOW?
THAT'S... NOT GOOD. THAT'S NOT A GOOD SIGN. HAVE A LOOK IN THE WINDOW.
I CAN'T SEE ANYTHING THROUGH HIS NET CURTAINS.
I'LL GO AROUND THE BACK.
HIS GATE'S LOCKED. HE MIGHT HAVE GONE ON A CRUISE?
YEAH. DOWN THE RIVER ACHERON.
STOP BEING CLASSICAL AND GET MY DAD.

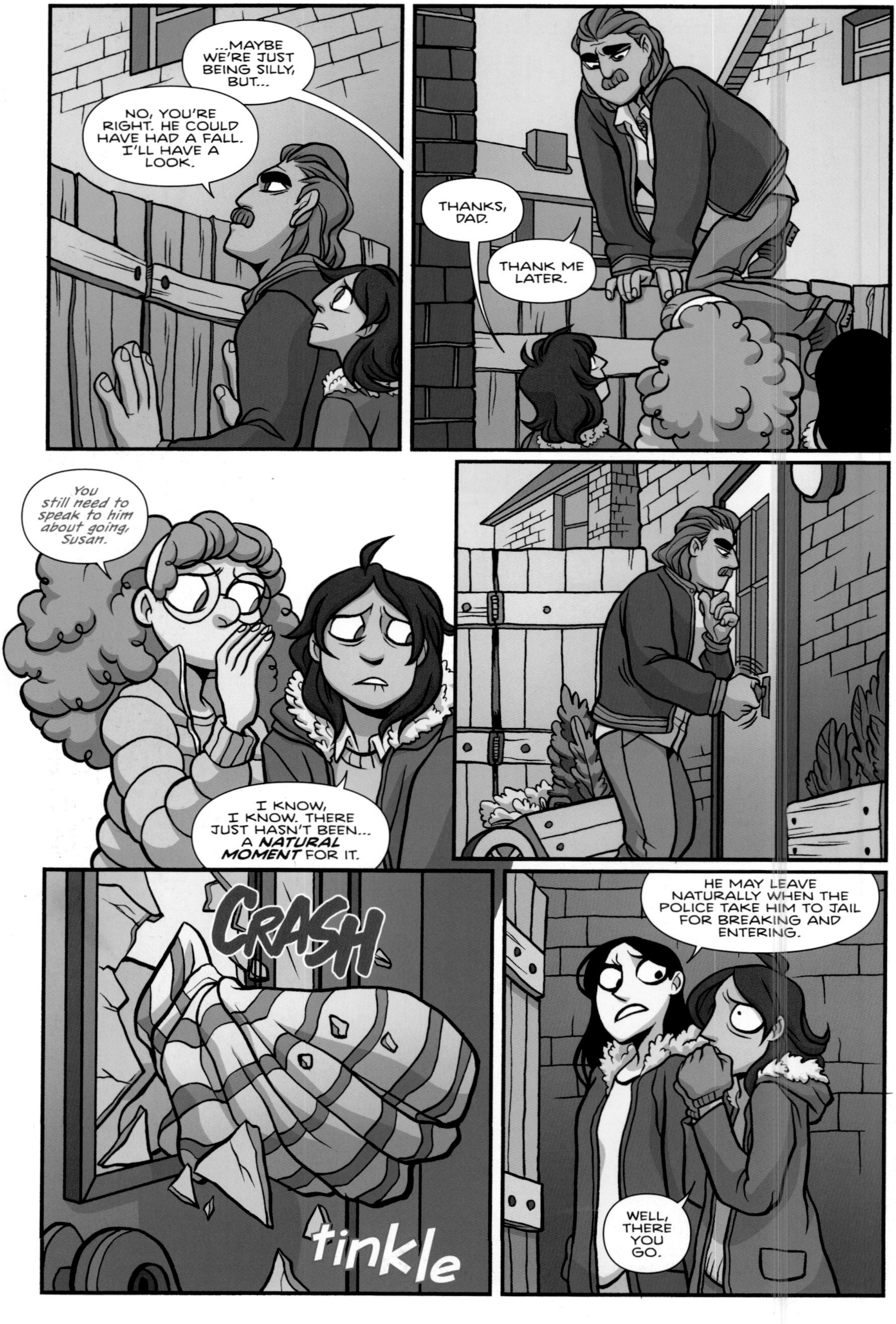
...MAYBE WE'RE JUST BEING SILLY, BUT...
NO, YOU'RE RIGHT. HE COULD HAVE HAD A FALL. I'LL HAVE A LOOK.
THANKS, DAD.
THANK ME LATER.
You still need to speak to him about going, Susan.
I KNOW, I KNOW. THERE JUST HASN'T BEEN... A NATURAL MOMENT FOR IT.
CRASH
tinkle
HE MAY LEAVE NATURALLY WHEN THE POLICE TAKE HIM TO JAIL FOR BREAKING AND ENTERING.
WELL, THERE YOU GO.

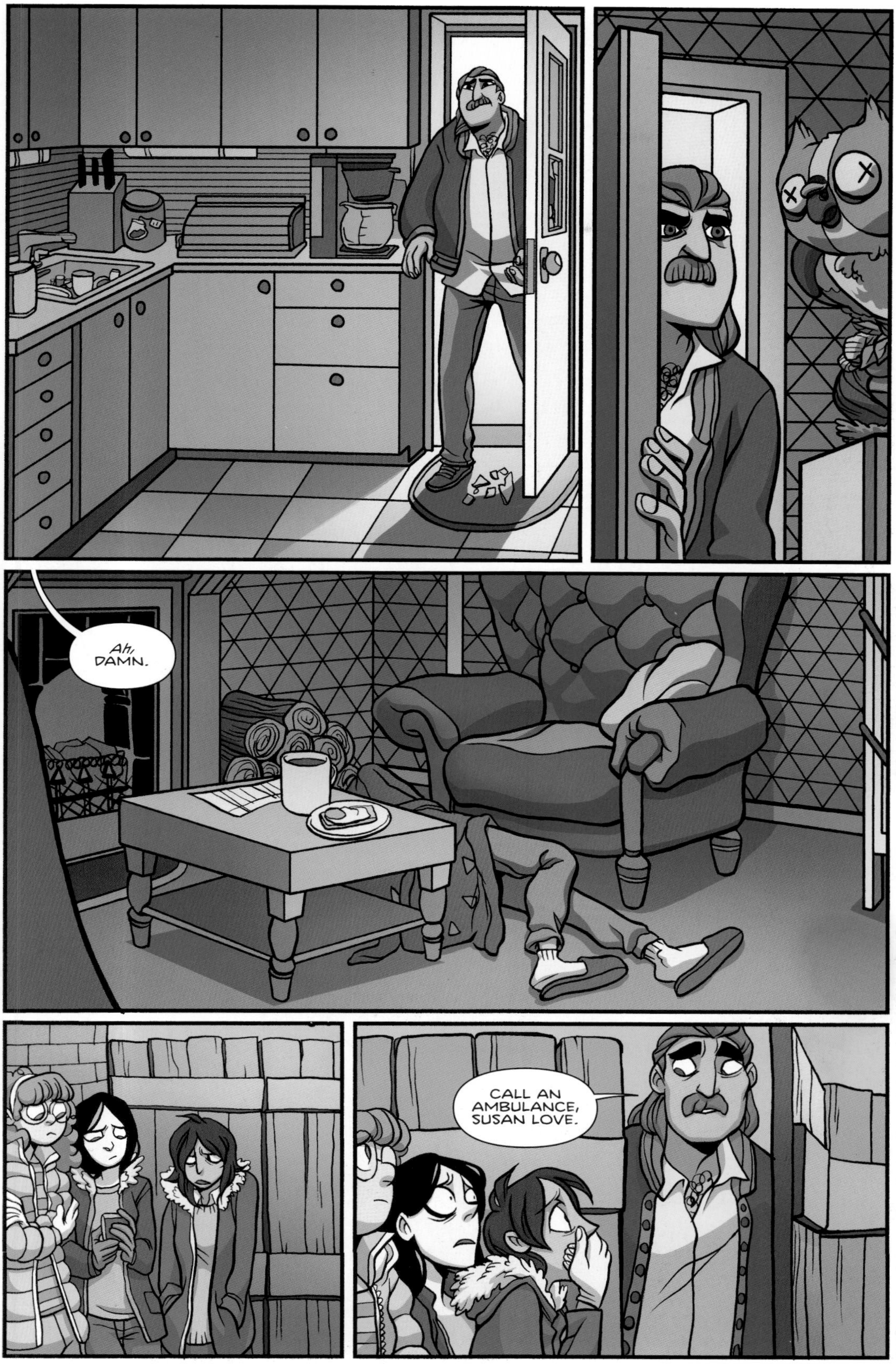
AH, DAMN.
CALL AN AMBULANCE, SUSAN LOVE.

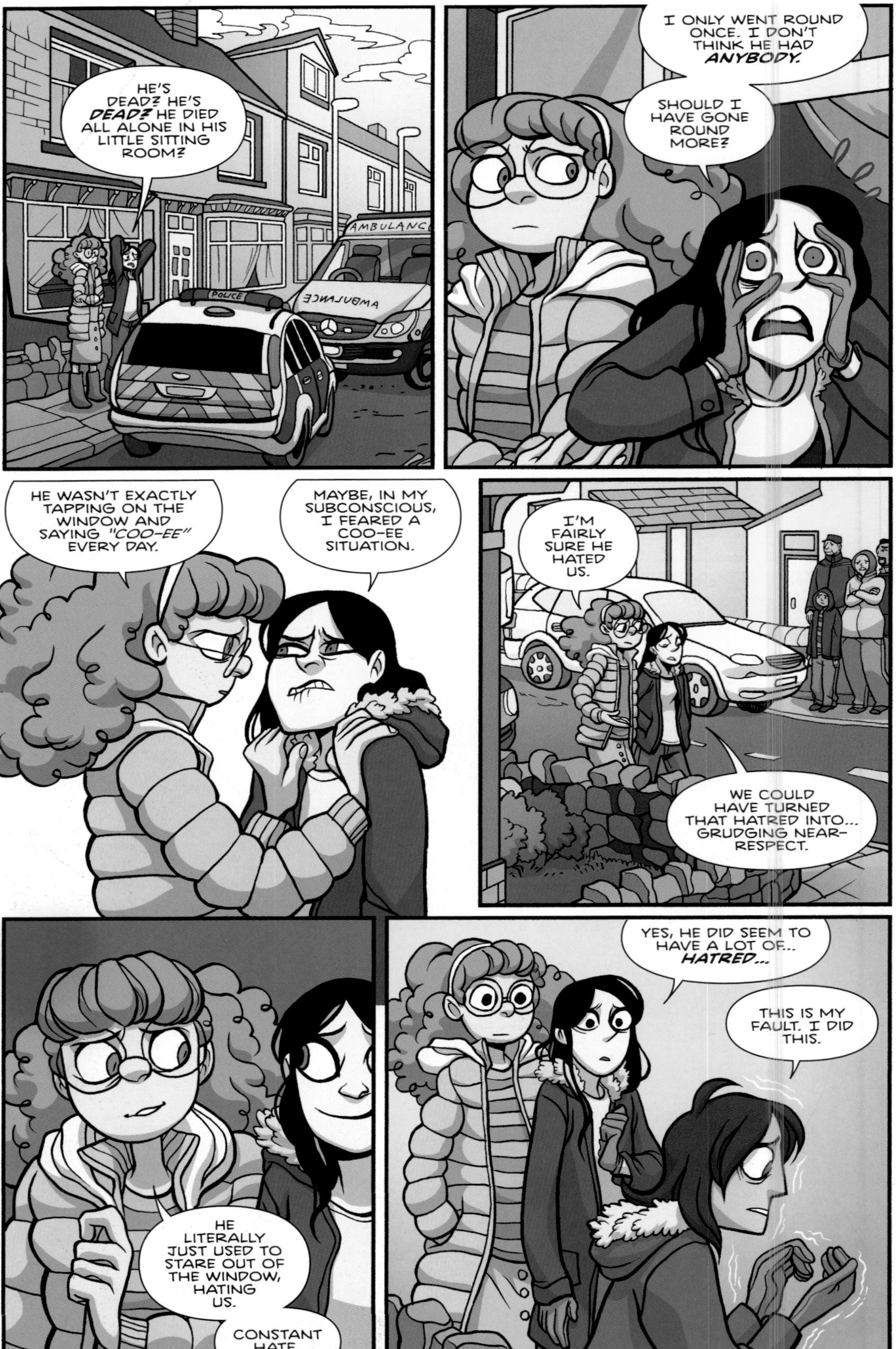
HE'S DEAD? HE'S DEAD? HE DIED ALL ALONE IN HIS LITTLE SITTING ROOM?
AMBULANCE
POLICE
I ONLY WENT ROUND ONCE. I DON'T THINK HE HAD ANYBODY.
SHOULD I HAVE GONE ROUND MORE?
HE WASN'T EXACTLY TAPPING ON THE WINDOW AND SAYING "COO-EE" EVERY DAY.
MAYBE, IN MY SUBCONSCIOUS, I FEARED A COO-EE SITUATION.
I'M FAIRLY SURE HE HATED US.
WE COULD HAVE TURNED THAT HATRED INTO... GRUDGING NEAR-RESPECT.
HE LITERALLY JUST USED TO STARE OUT OF THE WINDOW, HATING US.
CONSTANT HATE.
YES, HE DID SEEM TO HAVE A LOT OF... HATRED...
THIS IS MY FAULT. I DID THIS.

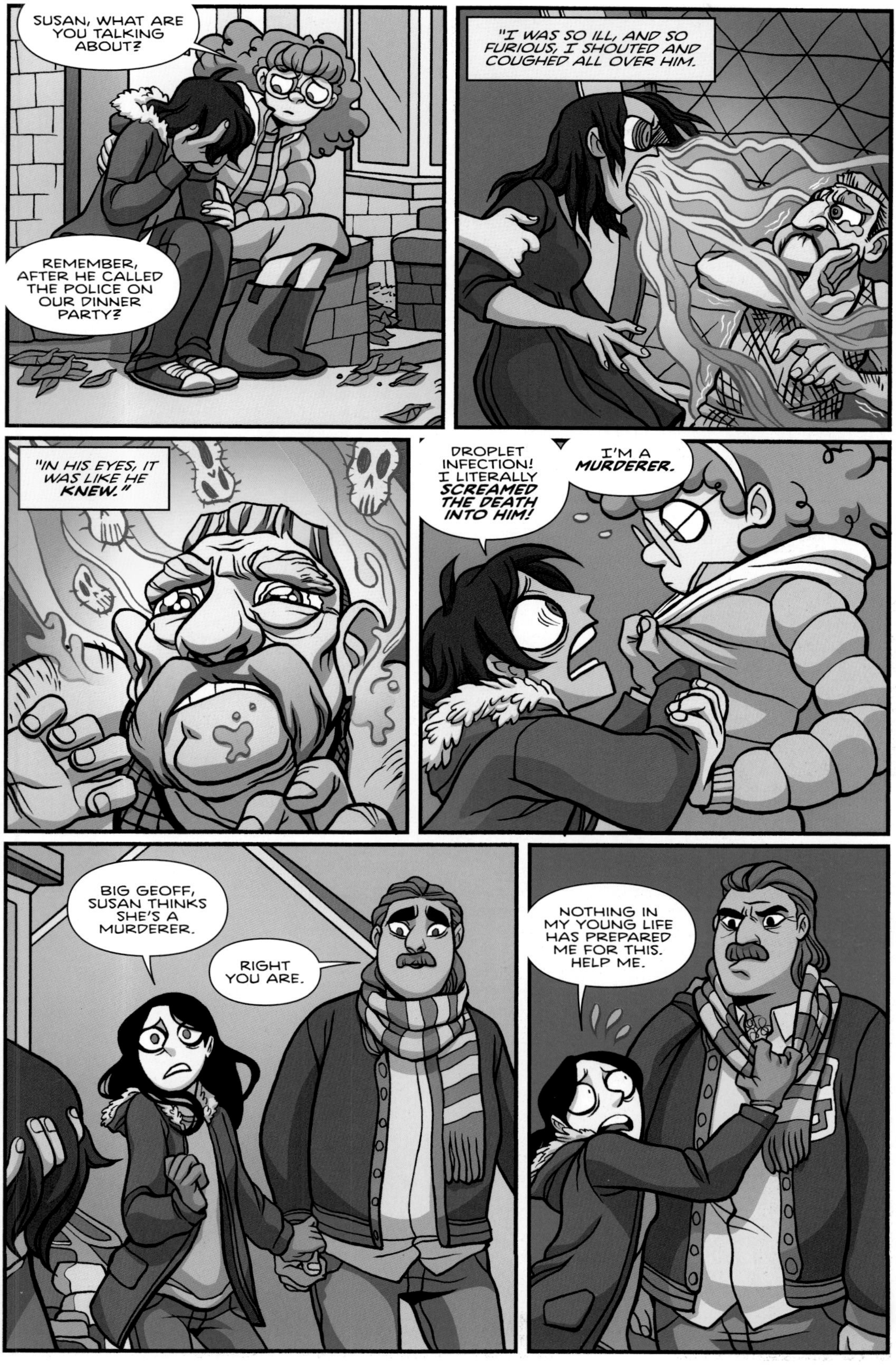
SUSAN, WHAT ARE YOU TALKING ABOUT?
REMEMBER, AFTER HE CALLED THE POLICE ON OUR DINNER PARTY?
"I WAS SO ILL, AND SO FURIOUS, I SHOUTED AND COUGHED ALL OVER HIM.
"IN HIS EYES, IT WAS LIKE HE KNEW."
DROPLET INFECTION! I LITERALLY SCREAMED THE DEATH INTO HIM!
I'M A MURDERER.
BIG GEOFF, SUSAN THINKS SHE'S A MURDERER.
RIGHT YOU ARE.
NOTHING IN MY YOUNG LIFE HAS PREPARED ME FOR THIS. HELP ME.

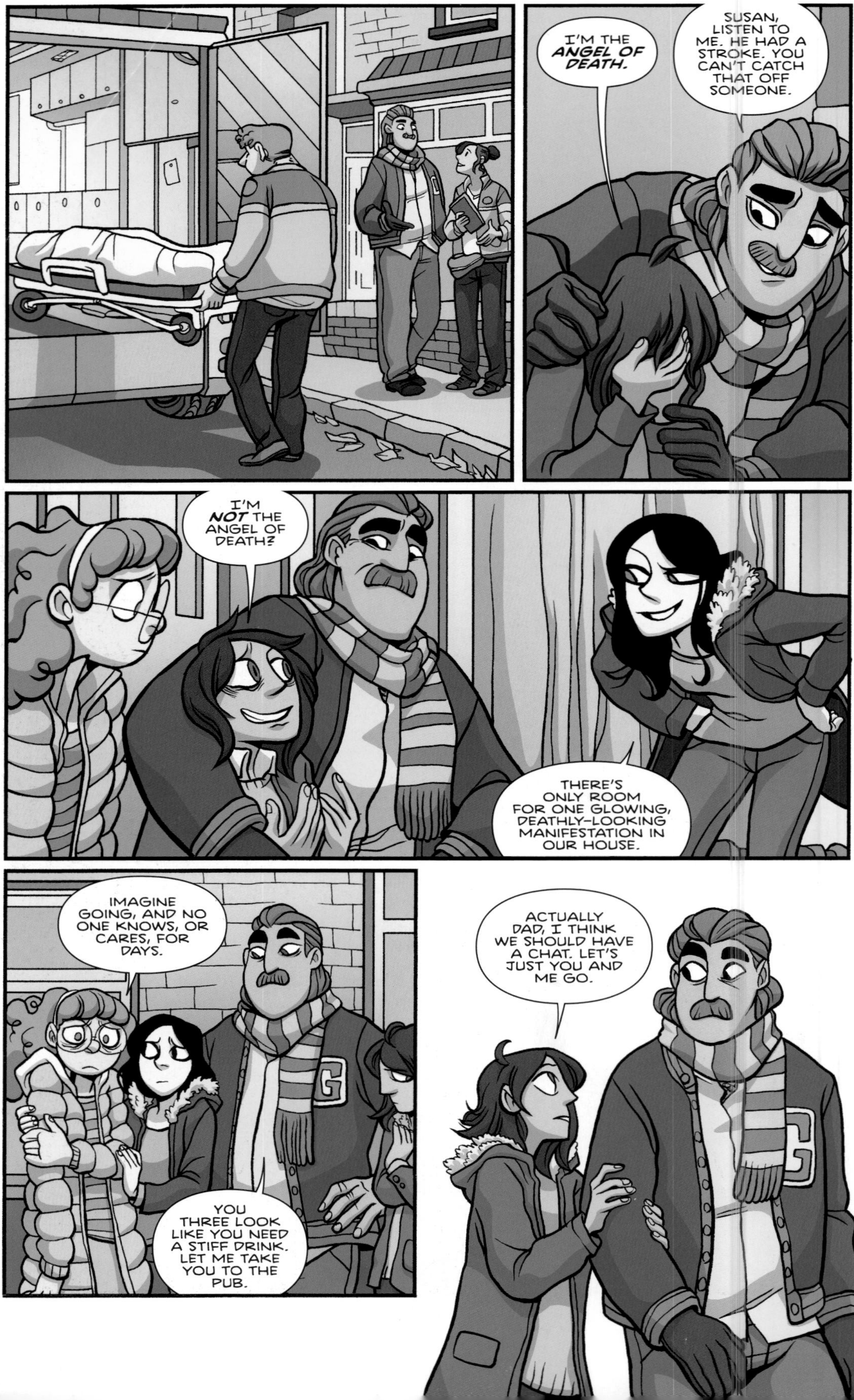
I'M THE *ANGEL OF DEATH.*
SUSAN, LISTEN TO ME. HE HAD A STROKE. YOU CAN'T CATCH THAT OFF SOMEONE.
I'M *NOT* THE ANGEL OF DEATH?
THERE'S ONLY ROOM FOR ONE GLOWING, DEATHLY-LOOKING MANIFESTATION IN OUR HOUSE.
IMAGINE GOING, AND NO ONE KNOWS, OR CARES, FOR DAYS.
YOU THREE LOOK LIKE YOU NEED A STIFF DRINK. LET ME TAKE YOU TO THE PUB.
ACTUALLY DAD, I THINK WE SHOULD HAVE A CHAT. LET'S JUST YOU AND ME GO.

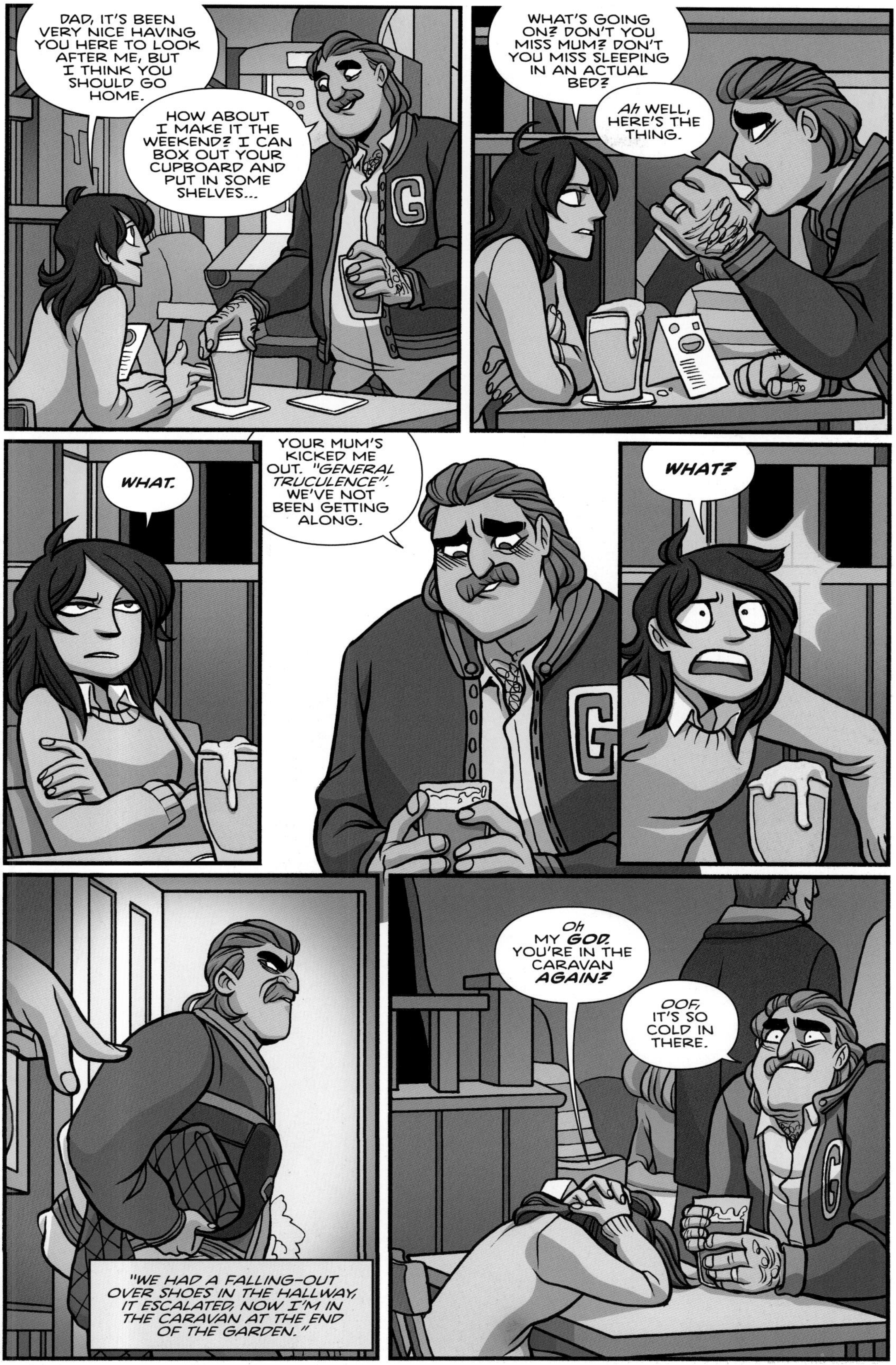
DAD, IT'S BEEN VERY NICE HAVING YOU HERE TO LOOK AFTER ME, BUT I THINK YOU SHOULD GO HOME.
HOW ABOUT I MAKE IT THE WEEKEND? I CAN BOX OUT YOUR CUPBOARD AND PUT IN SOME SHELVES...
WHAT'S GOING ON? DON'T YOU MISS MUM? DON'T YOU MISS SLEEPING IN AN ACTUAL BED?
Ah WELL, HERE'S THE THING.
WHAT.
YOUR MUM'S KICKED ME OUT. *"GENERAL TRUCULENCE".* WE'VE NOT BEEN GETTING ALONG.
WHAT?
"WE HAD A FALLING-OUT OVER SHOES IN THE HALLWAY, IT ESCALATED, NOW I'M IN THE CARAVAN AT THE END OF THE GARDEN."
Oh MY ***GOD,*** YOU'RE IN THE CARAVAN ***AGAIN?***
OOF, IT'S SO COLD IN THERE.

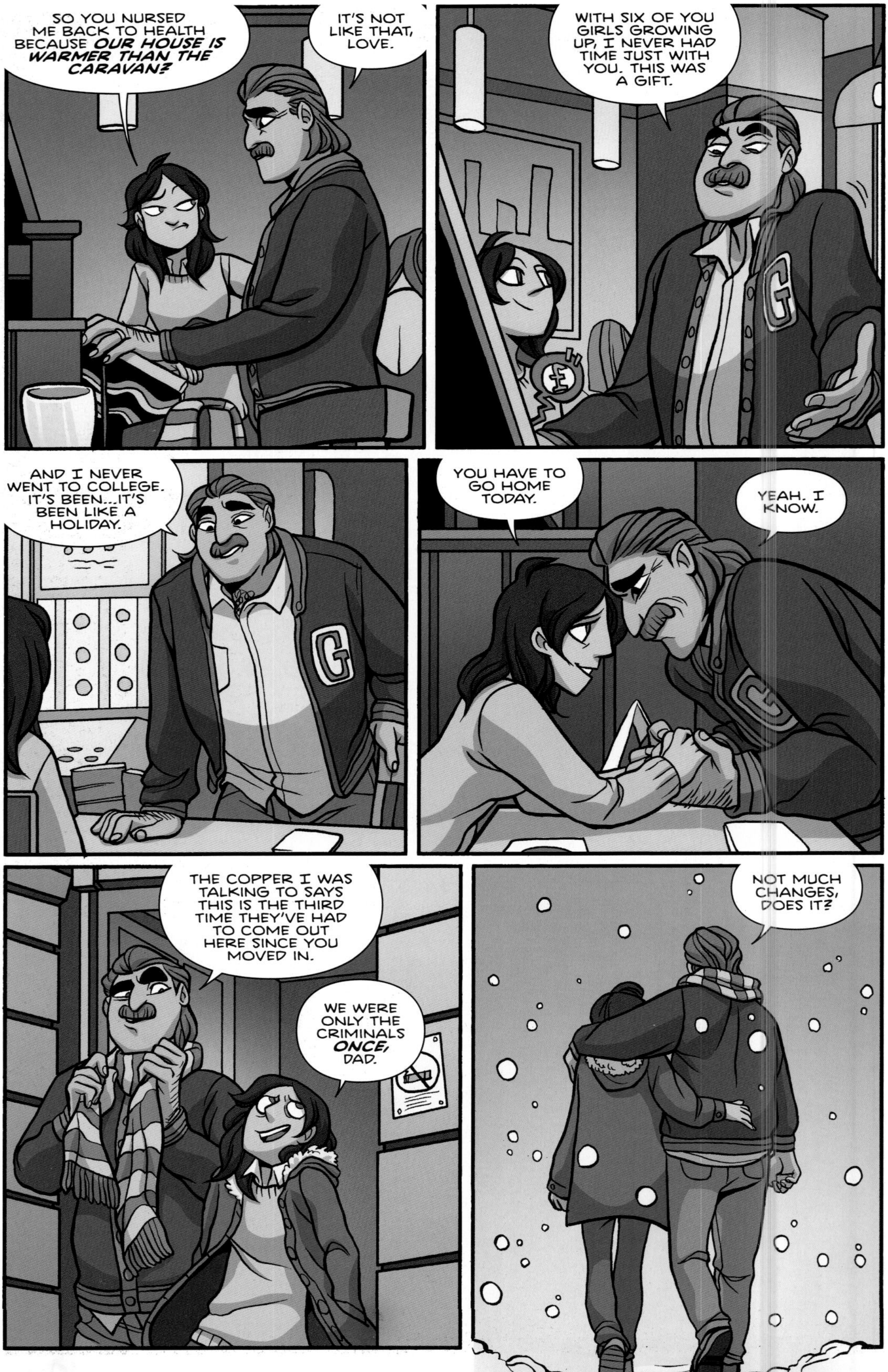
SO YOU NURSED ME BACK TO HEALTH BECAUSE *OUR HOUSE IS WARMER THAN THE CARAVAN?*
IT'S NOT LIKE THAT, LOVE.
WITH SIX OF YOU GIRLS GROWING UP, I NEVER HAD TIME JUST WITH YOU. THIS WAS A GIFT.
AND I NEVER WENT TO COLLEGE. IT'S BEEN... IT'S BEEN LIKE A HOLIDAY.
YOU HAVE TO GO HOME TODAY.
YEAH. I KNOW.
THE COPPER I WAS TALKING TO SAYS THIS IS THE THIRD TIME THEY'VE HAD TO COME OUT HERE SINCE YOU MOVED IN.
WE WERE ONLY THE CRIMINALS *ONCE,* DAD.
NOT MUCH CHANGES, DOES IT?

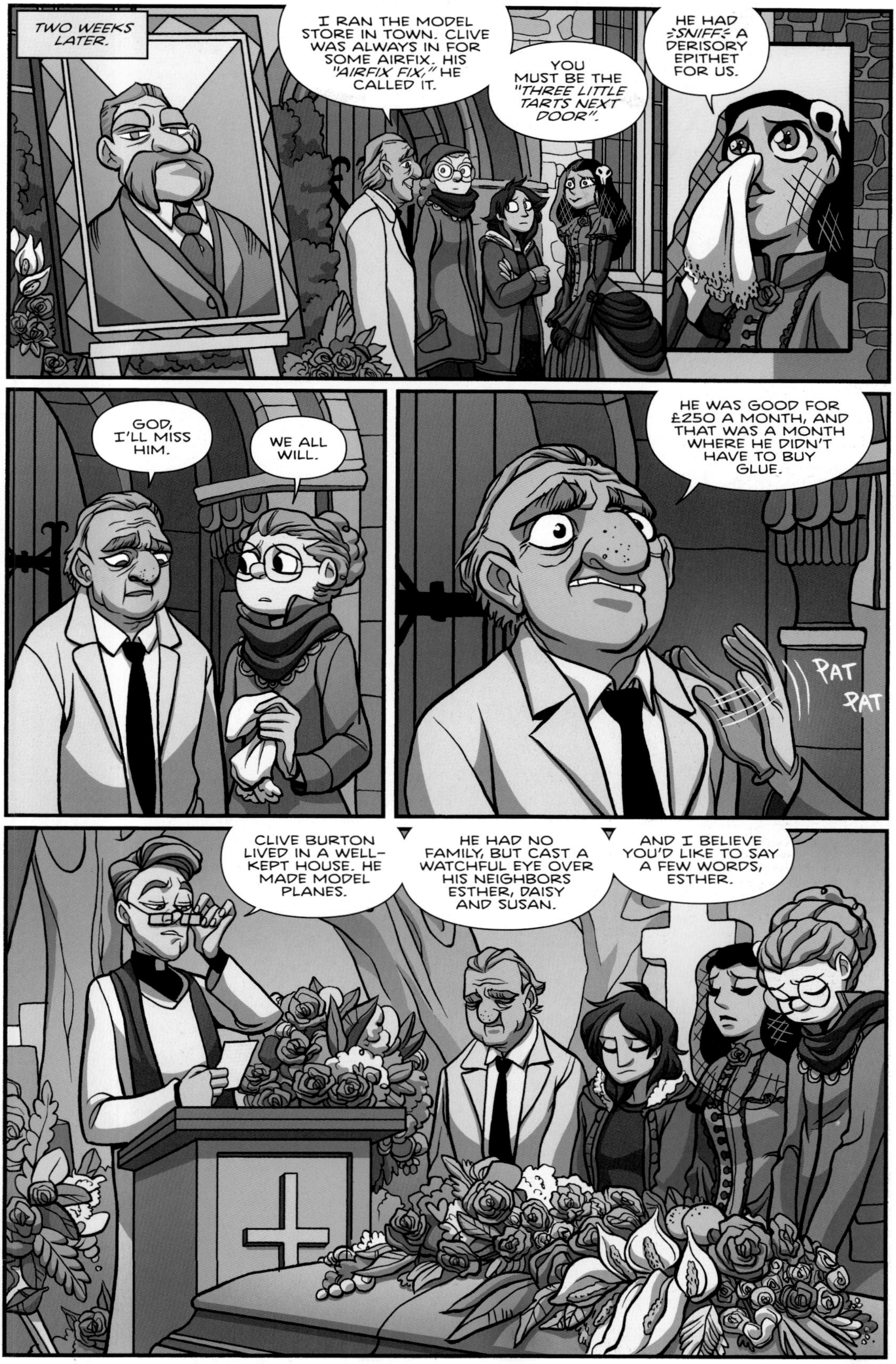
TWO WEEKS LATER.
I RAN THE MODEL STORE IN TOWN. CLIVE WAS ALWAYS IN FOR SOME AIRFIX. HIS "AIRFIX FIX," HE CALLED IT.
YOU MUST BE THE "THREE LITTLE TARTS NEXT DOOR".
HE HAD *SNIFF* A DERISORY EPITHET FOR US.
GOD, I'LL MISS HIM.
WE ALL WILL.
HE WAS GOOD FOR £250 A MONTH, AND THAT WAS A MONTH WHERE HE DIDN'T HAVE TO BUY GLUE.
PAT
PAT
CLIVE BURTON LIVED IN A WELL-KEPT HOUSE. HE MADE MODEL PLANES.
HE HAD NO FAMILY, BUT CAST A WATCHFUL EYE OVER HIS NEIGHBORS ESTHER, DAISY AND SUSAN.
AND I BELIEVE YOU'D LIKE TO SAY A FEW WORDS, ESTHER.

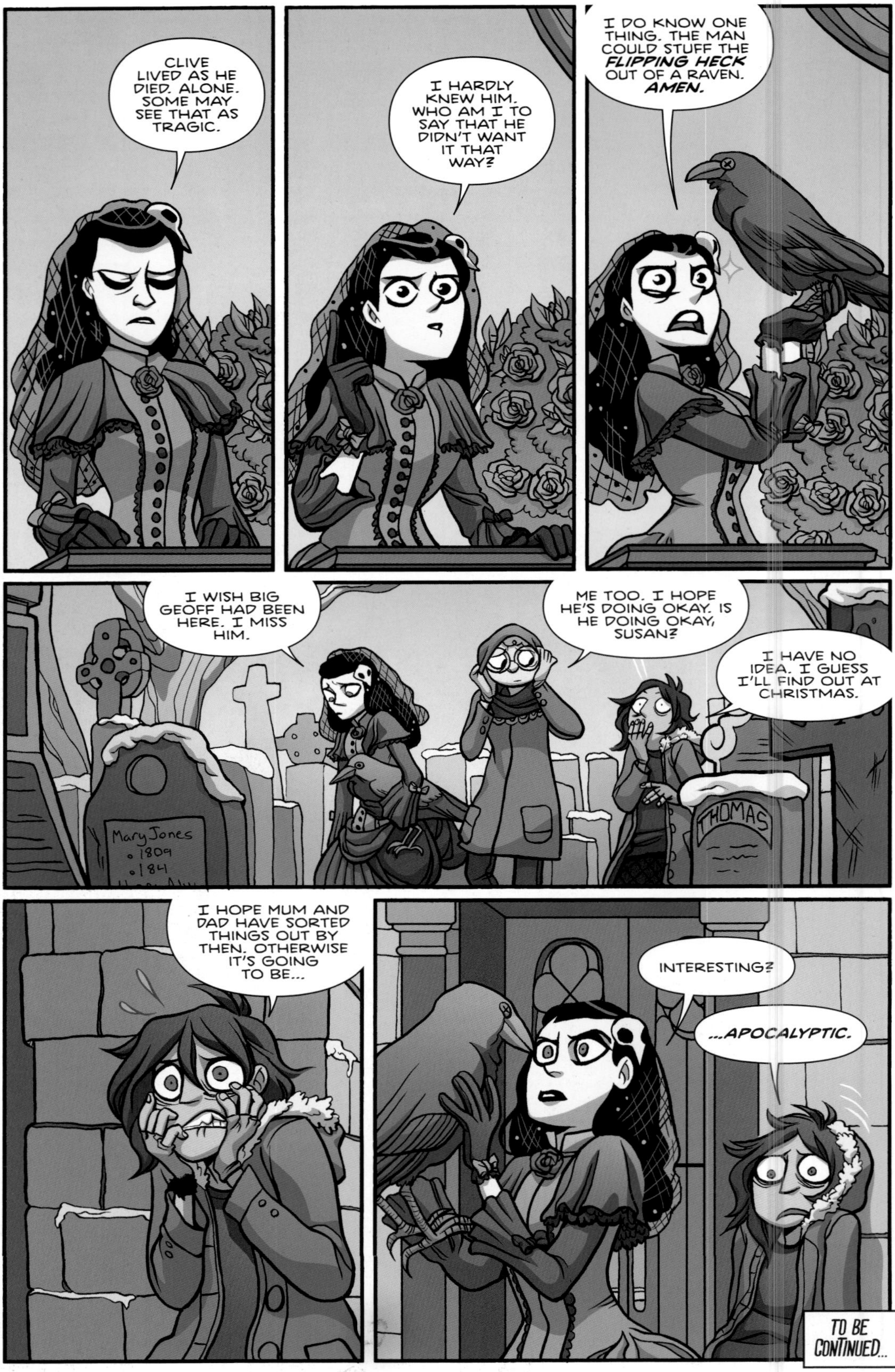

CLIVE LIVED AS HE DIED. ALONE. SOME MAY SEE THAT AS TRAGIC.
I HARDLY KNEW HIM. WHO AM I TO SAY THAT HE DIDN'T WANT IT THAT WAY?
I DO KNOW ONE THING. THE MAN COULD STUFF THE *FLIPPING HECK* OUT OF A RAVEN. ***AMEN.***
I WISH BIG GEOFF HAD BEEN HERE. I MISS HIM.
ME TOO. I HOPE HE'S DOING OKAY. IS HE DOING OKAY, SUSAN?
I HAVE NO IDEA. I GUESS I'LL FIND OUT AT CHRISTMAS.
Mary Jones
1809
184
THOMAS
I HOPE MUM AND DAD HAVE SORTED THINGS OUT BY THEN. OTHERWISE IT'S GOING TO BE...
INTERESTING?
...APOCALYPTIC.
TO BE CONTINUED...

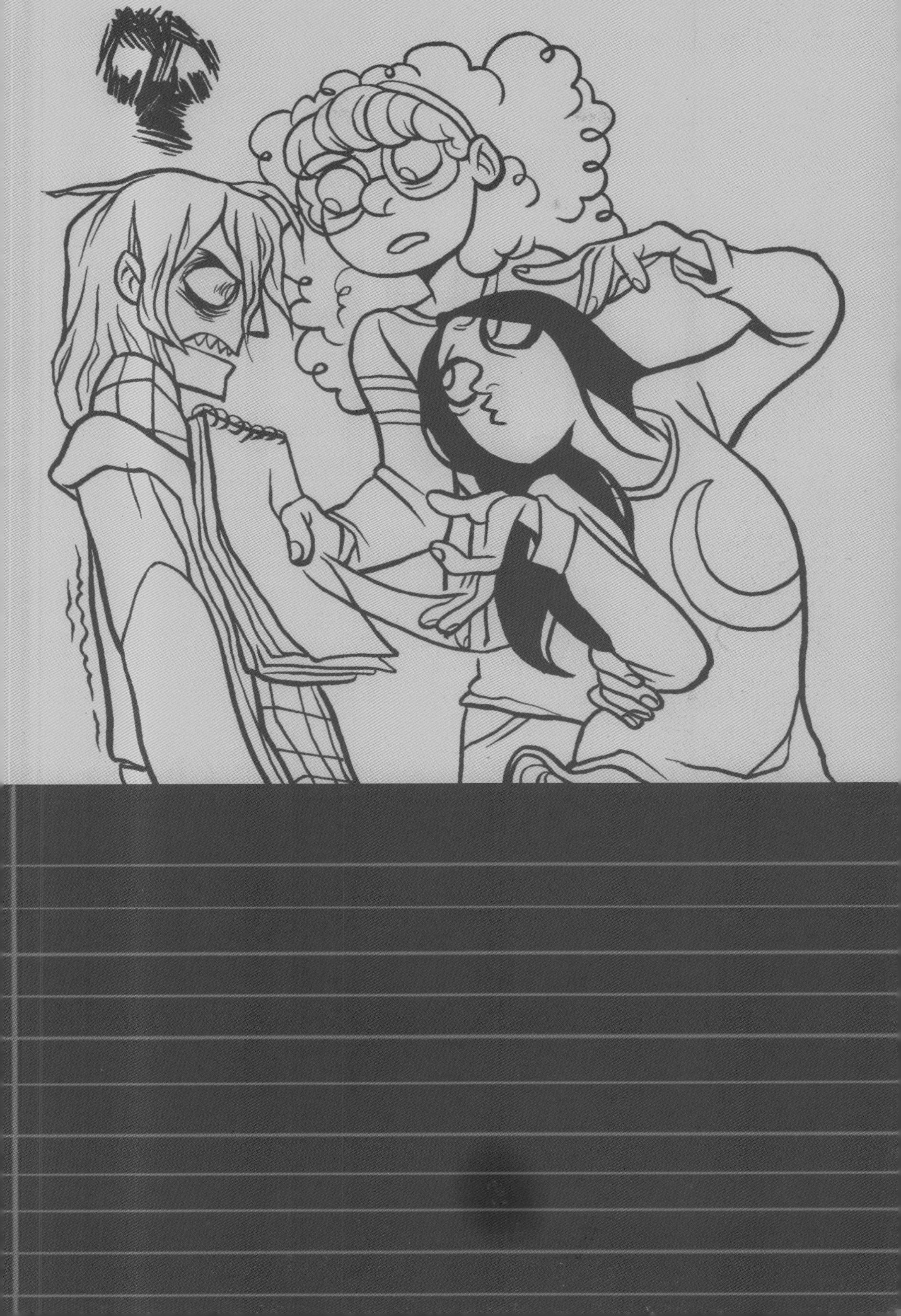

COVER

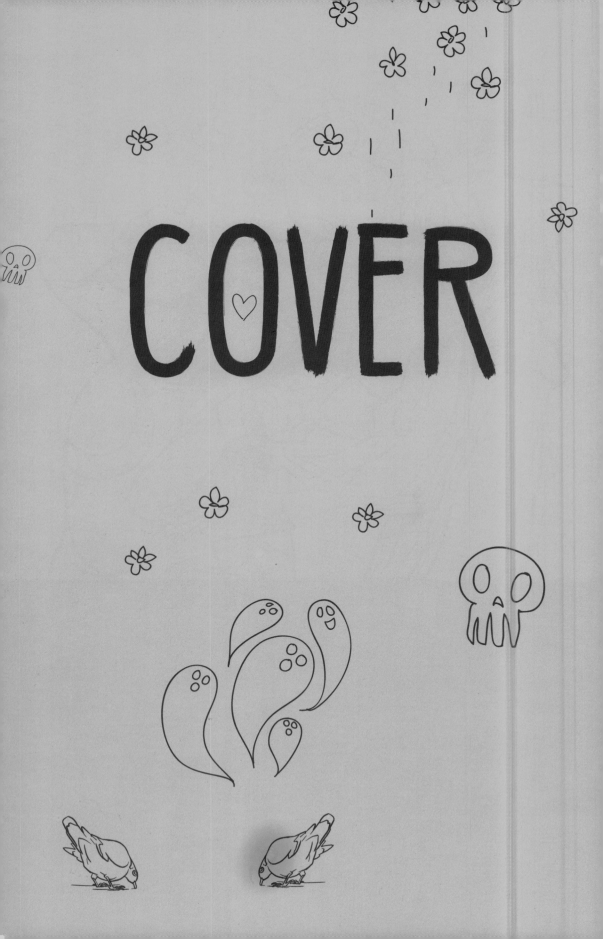

GALLERY

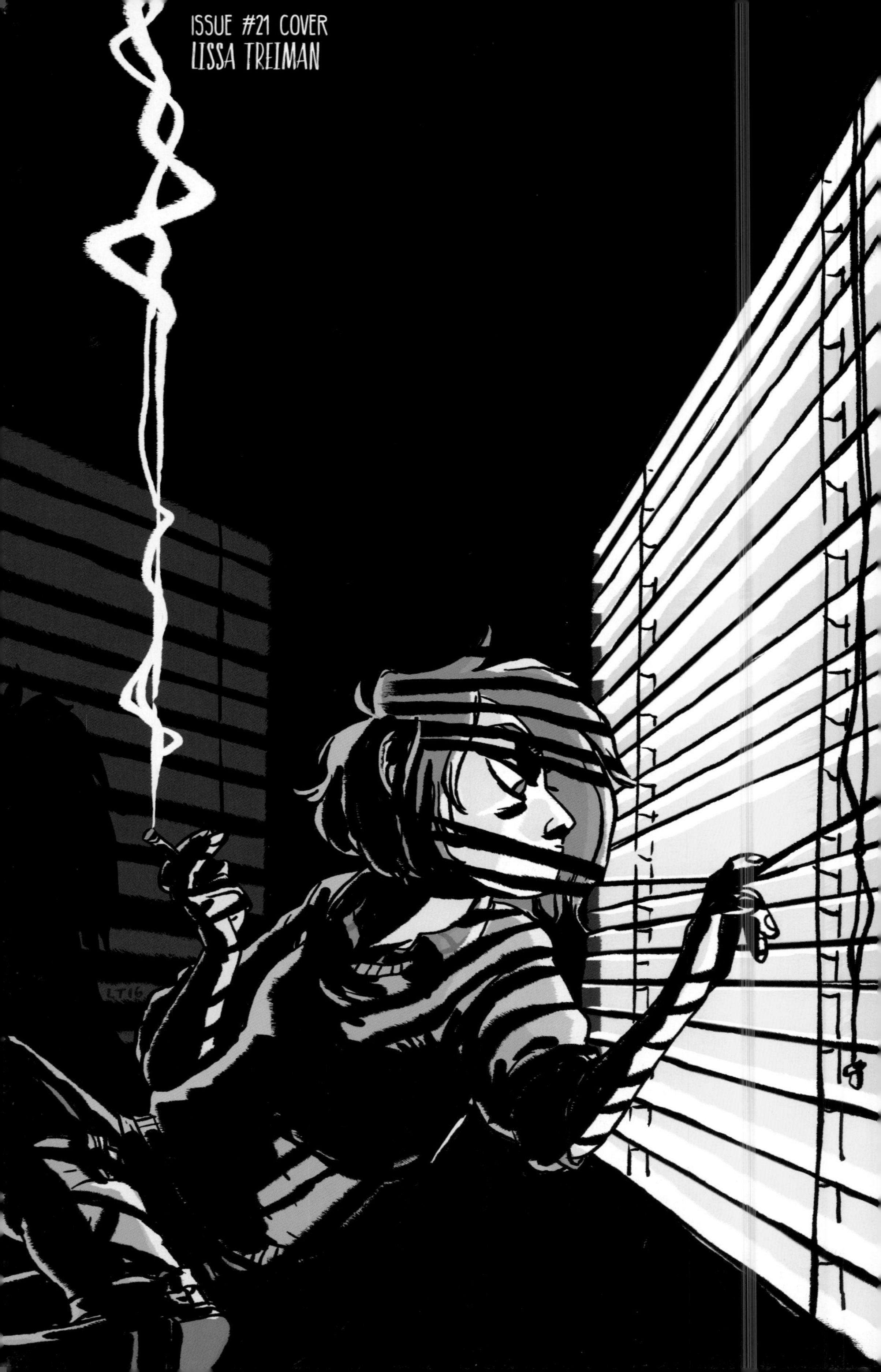

ISSUE #21 COVER
LISSA TREIMAN

ISSUE #22 COVER
LISSA TREIMAN

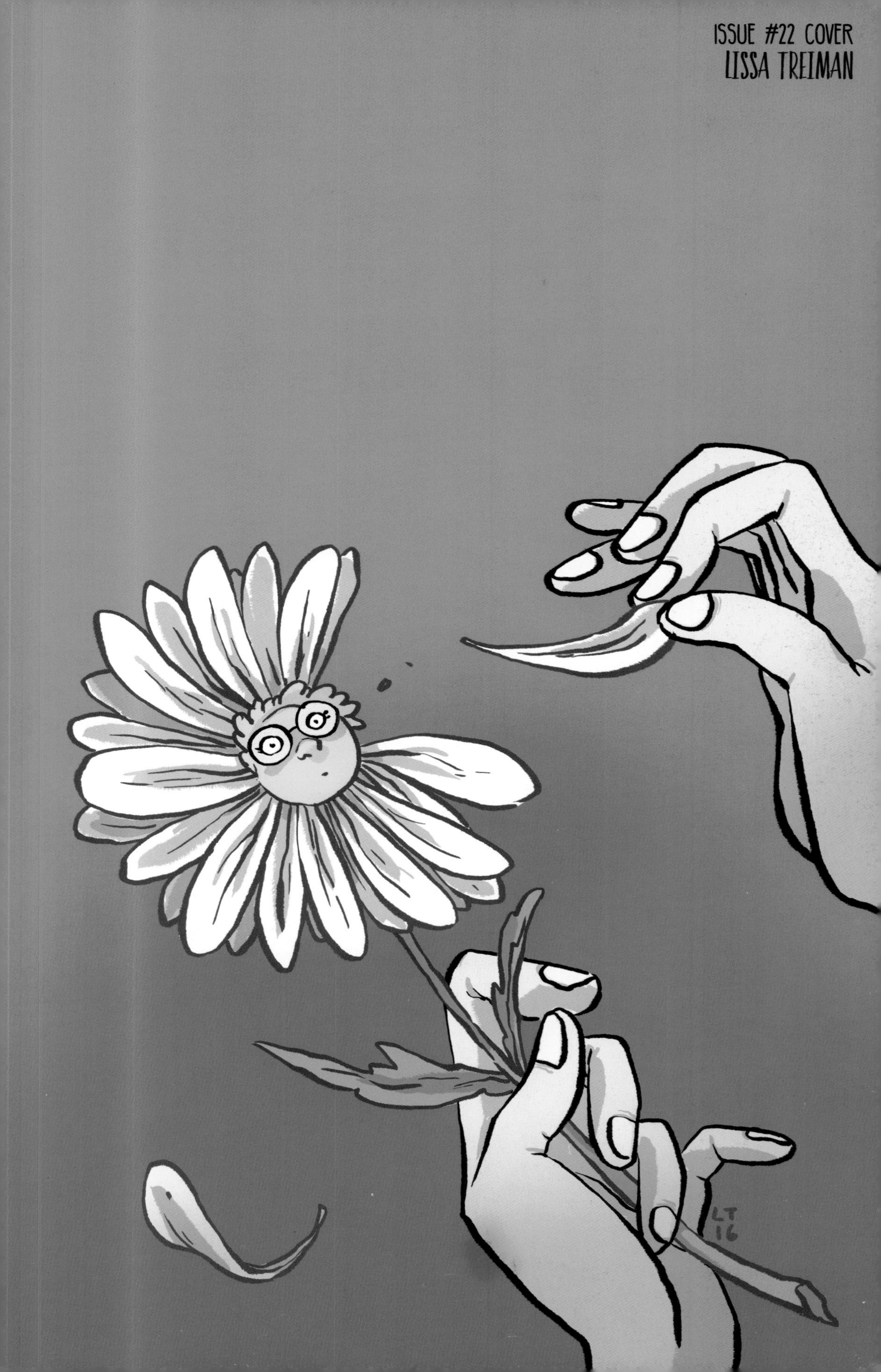
LT
16

ISSUE #23 COVER
LISSA TREIMAN

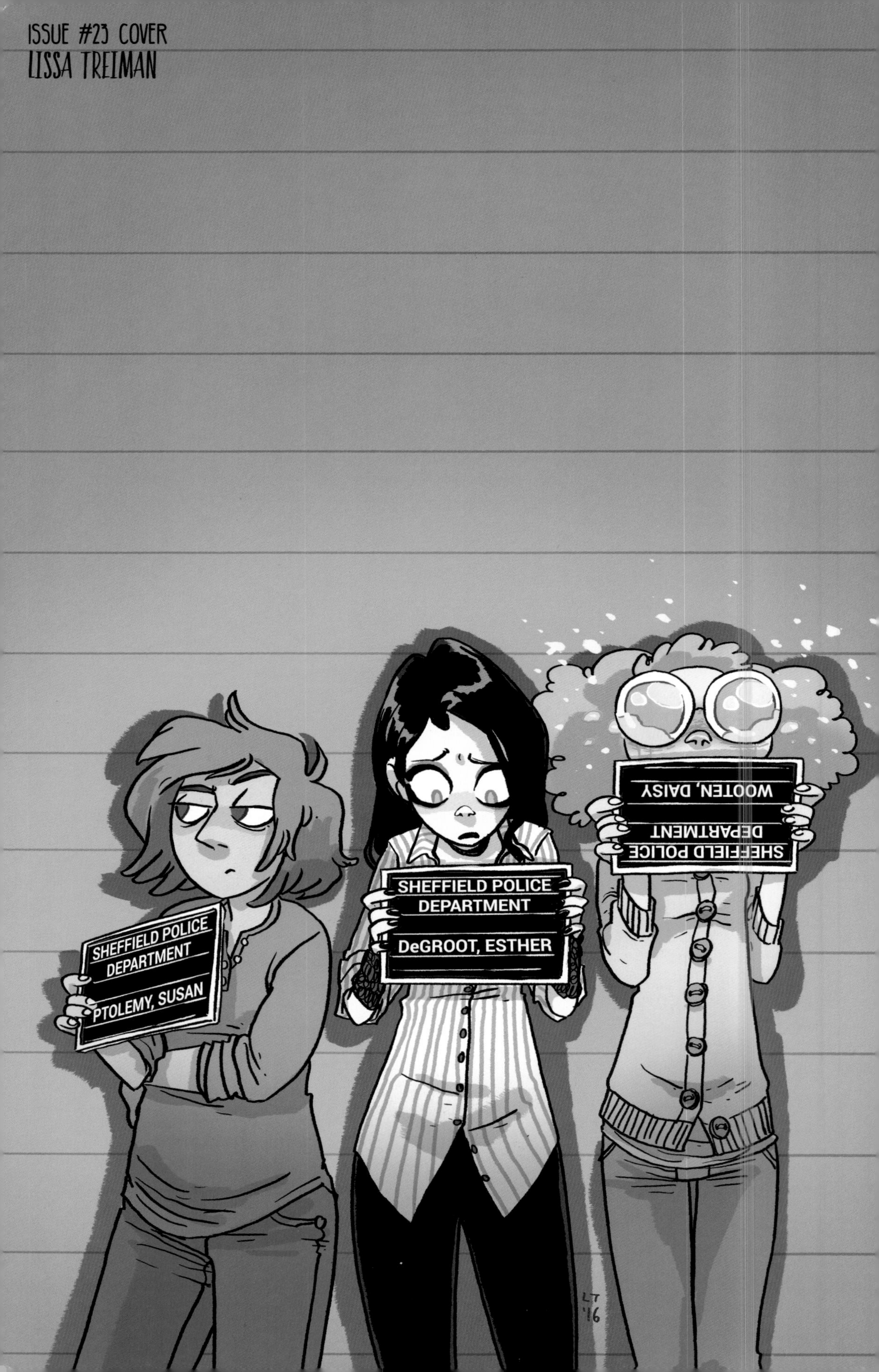
SHEFFIELD POLICE DEPARTMENT
PTOLEMY, SUSAN
SHEFFIELD POLICE DEPARTMENT
DeGROOT, ESTHER
SHEFFIELD POLICE DEPARTMENT
WOOTEN, DAISY
LT '16

ISSUE #24 COVER
LISSA TREIMAN

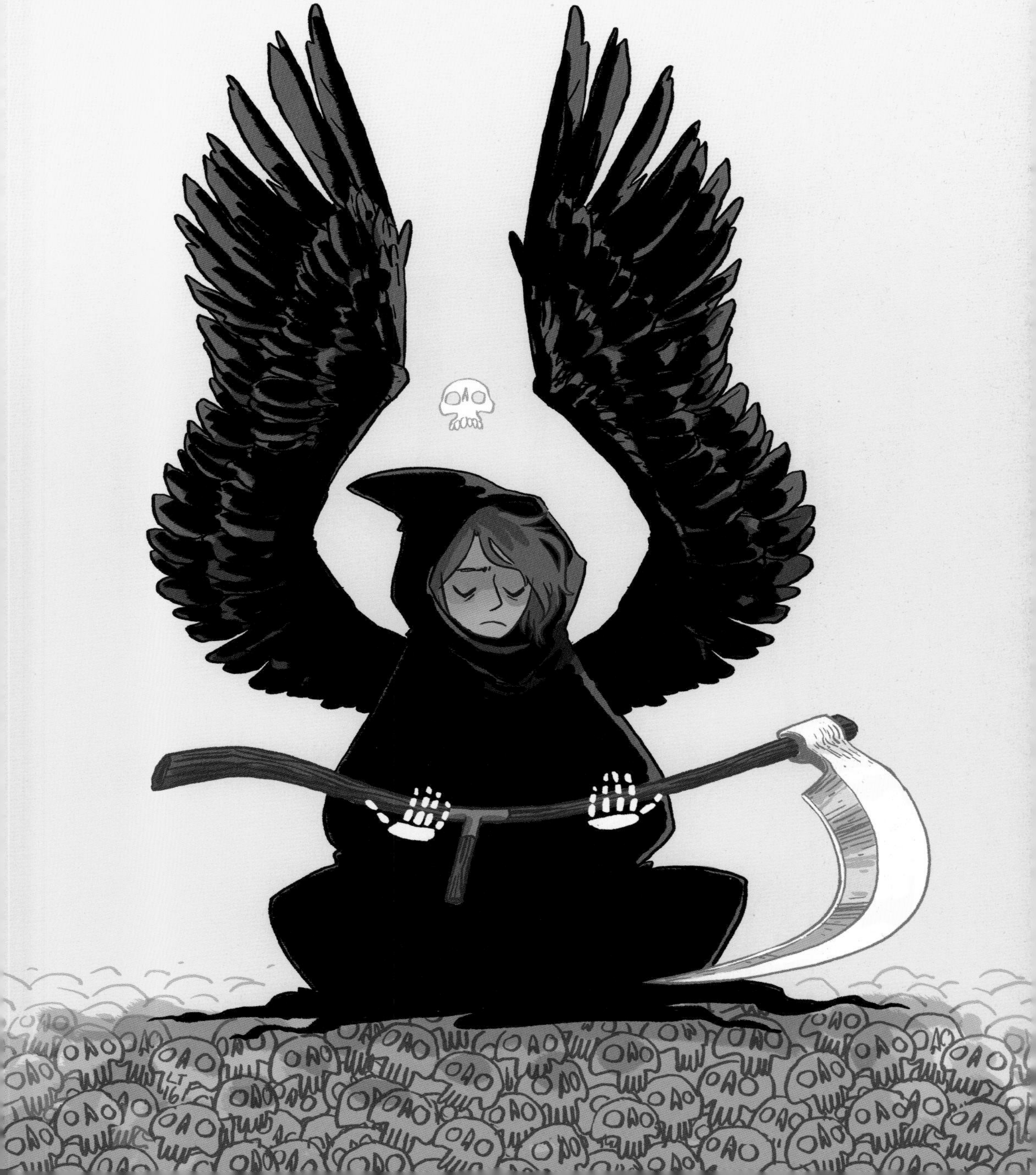

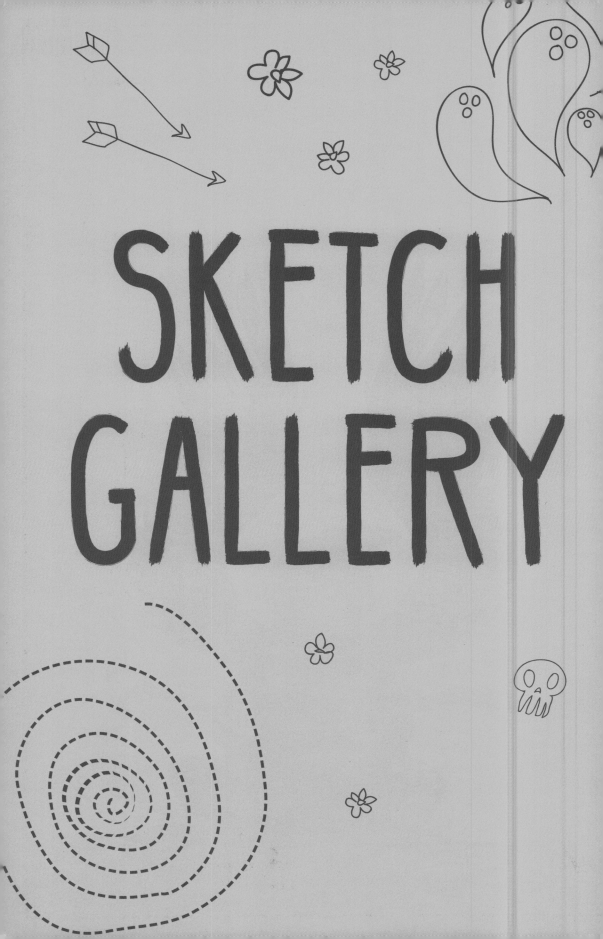

SKETCH GALLERY

CHARACTER DESIGNS BY JOHN ALLISON

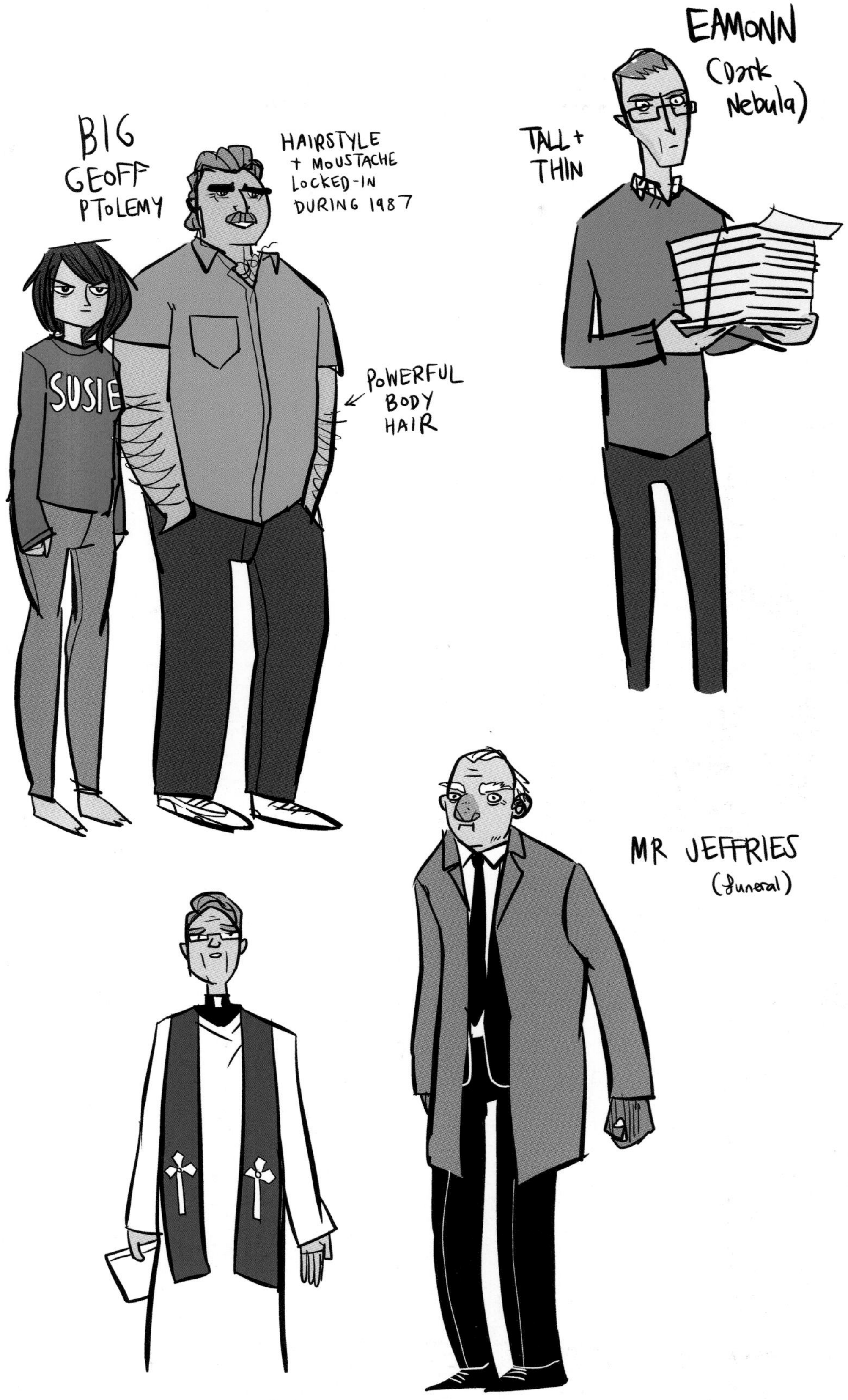
BIG GEOFF PTOLEMY
HAIRSTYLE + MOUSTACHE LOCKED-IN DURING 1987
SUSIE
POWERFUL BODY HAIR
EAMONN (Dark Nebula)
TALL + THIN
MR JEFFRIES (funeral)

CHARACTER DESIGNS BY MAX SARIN

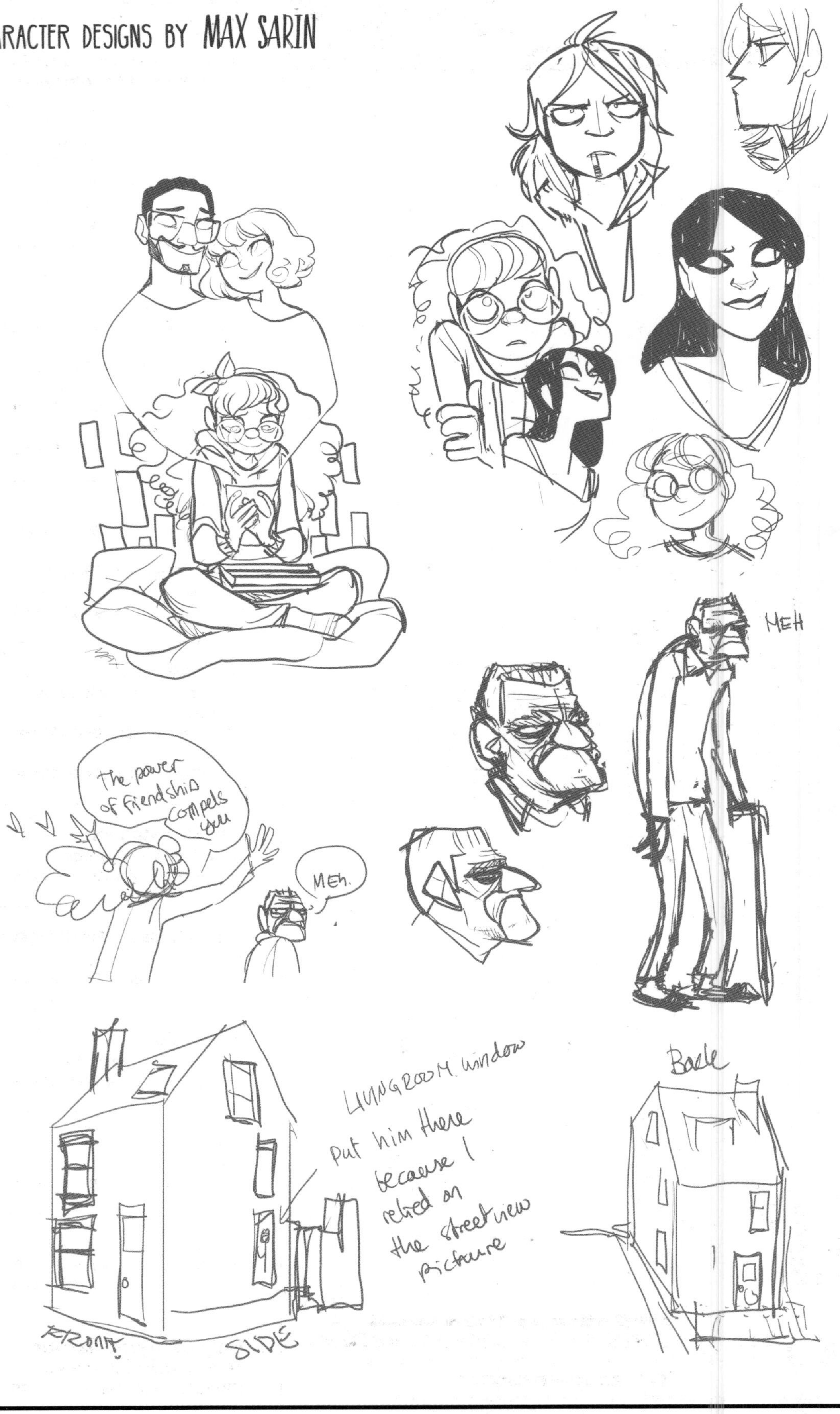

The power of friendship compels you
Meh.
MEH
LIVINGROOM window
put him there because I relied on the street view picture
FRONT
SIDE
Back

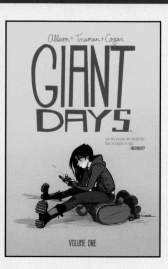

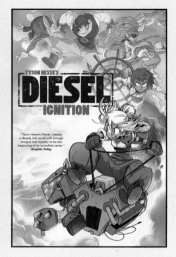

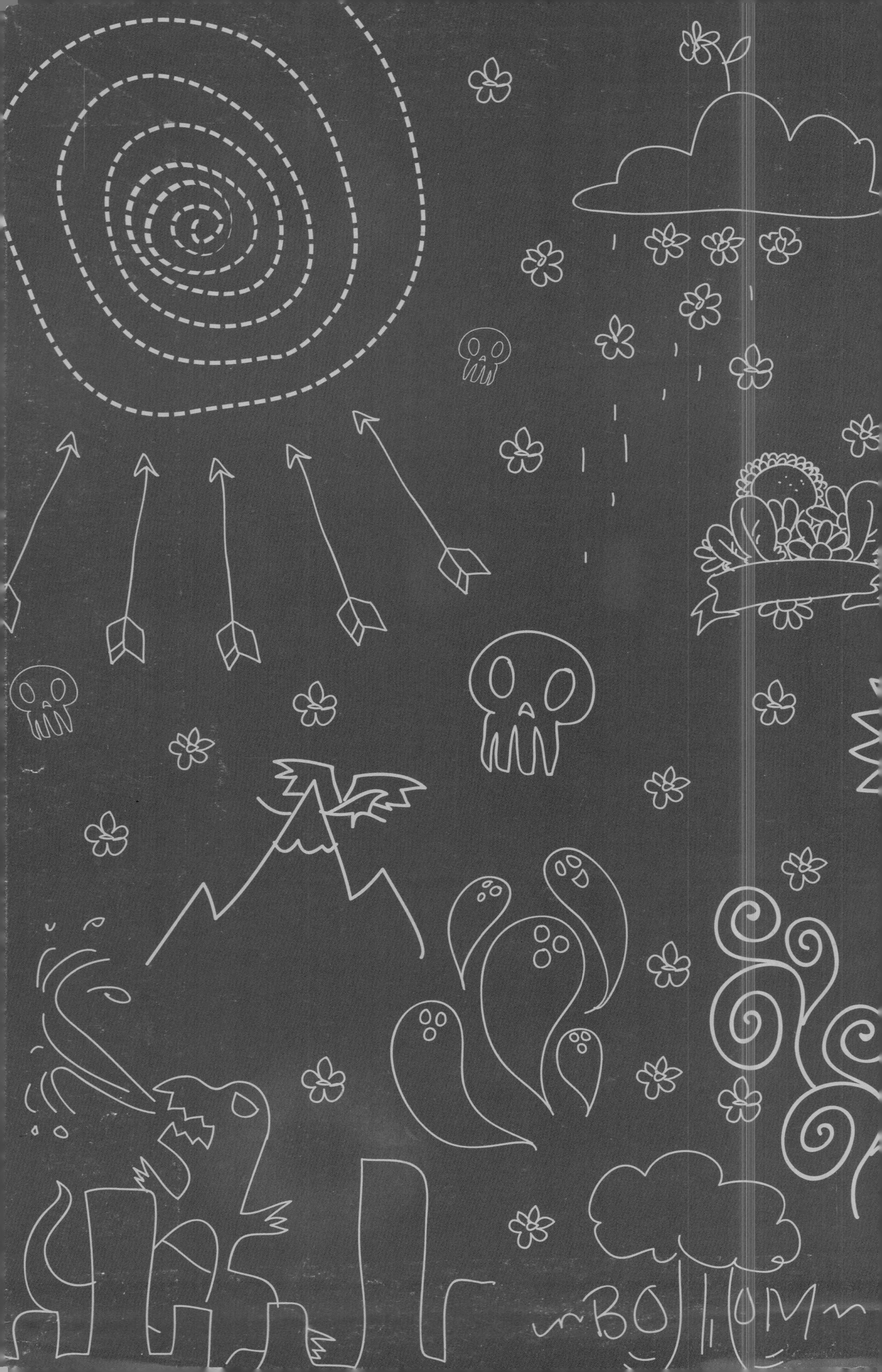
BOOM